THE BLOOD-DIMMED
TIDE IS LOOSED

THE BLOOD-DIMMED TIDE IS LOOSED

JOHN C. GALLAGHER

iUniverse, Inc.
Bloomington

THE BLOOD-DIMMED TIDE IS LOOSED

Copyright © 2012 by John C. Gallagher.

All rights reserved. No part of this book may be used or reproduced by any means, graphic, electronic, or mechanical, including photocopying, recording, taping or by any information storage retrieval system without the written permission of the publisher except in the case of brief quotations embodied in critical articles and reviews.

This is a work of fiction. All of the characters, names, incidents, organizations, and dialogue in this novel are either the products of the author's imagination or are used fictitiously.

iUniverse books may be ordered through booksellers or by contacting:

iUniverse
1663 Liberty Drive
Bloomington, IN 47403
www.iuniverse.com
1-800-Authors (1-800-288-4677)

Because of the dynamic nature of the Internet, any web addresses or links contained in this book may have changed since publication and may no longer be valid. The views expressed in this work are solely those of the author and do not necessarily reflect the views of the publisher, and the publisher hereby disclaims any responsibility for them.

Any people depicted in stock imagery provided by Thinkstock are models, and such images are being used for illustrative purposes only.
Certain stock imagery © Thinkstock.

ISBN: 978-1-4697-9559-1 (sc)
ISBN: 978-1-4697-9560-7 (hc)
ISBN: 978-1-4697-9561-4 (ebk)

Library of Congress Control Number: 2012904500

Printed in the United States of America

iUniverse rev. date: 04/17/2012

Things fall apart; the centre cannot hold;
Mere anarchy is loosed upon the world,
The blood-dimmed tide is loosed . . .
The Second Coming
William Butler Yeats

CHAPTER ONE

Most of us can remember when and where we first heard about something terrible. In this case I had laid out a set of blueprints on the kitchen table after dinner and was wondering why the architect had, uncharacteristically, omitted a safety feature in the specifications we had given her. Maybe she had passed the job on to an underling. If there was this mistake were there others? I was musing about what advice to give to the boss, who happened to be my Uncle Hugh, when the phone rang.

It was Hugh. His usual telephone greeting is the verbal equivalent of a slap on the back, but this evening his voice was flat and scarcely audible. "Mick . . . . It's your Uncle Hugh. It's Catherine . . . Catherine and Richard . . . They're . . . They've been killed."

Catherine was the youngest daughter of Uncle Hugh and Aunt Phyllis. A week ago we had sent her and her handsome husband off on their honeymoon. In the numbness that protects us from the full impact of tragedy I listened to myself stumbling over words meant to be consoling when no consolation was possible. As far as was known, Catherine and her husband had been murdered in Talcayan, a tiny country between Chile and Argentina. Probably it was the work of brigands. "Their bodies are being brought back tomorrow," Hugh said.

- 1 -

"Could you tell your mother?" Neither of us spoke for a moment and I heard a click on the other end of the line.

Mom had been writing letters at the dining room table and now she was watching me from the doorway. She stood silent for a minute after I told her what had happened and then walked over to the phone and punched in a number. I could follow the conversation fairly well without hearing Uncle Hugh's side of it: condolences, remarks that could be taken as questions if the other wanted to talk. Was it too late this evening for Michael and I to come over, or should we wait until morning? Oh, Phyllis was resting. Probably the best thing for her.

Putting down the receiver she said, as much to herself as to me: "Poor Phyllis and Hugh . . . I don't know what . . ." She had lost the calm composure of her telephone conversation, murmured that she would be ready to go to Hugh and Phyllis's about eight tomorrow morning, and went upstairs.

My cousin Catherine was one of the kindest, gentlest people I knew. If we had any concern about her it was how she would fare in a world that doesn't always protect the kind and gentle. Her parents were relieved and delighted when she became engaged to Richard Tipping, who returned her abundant affection and gave her the same sense of security that she had grown used to over her twenty one years of life. At their wedding a week earlier it was easy to imagine them growing old together, loved, contented and surrounded by family and friends.

But they would not grow old.

It was early September. Autumn comes early in Edmonton, Alberta. It was dark and the cold drizzle kept most people inside, but I needed to walk. As usual on the occasion of a disaster, somewhere just below the surface I was arguing with God. Why was it Catherine who was killed? That question seemed to imply that it would be better if someone else had been killed, and that made no sense either. So the argument came around to the fact that regarding what really matters we don't have a clue. As an army padre once told me, that's the price we pay for not knowing everything, or as he put it, for being finite minds. So far I haven't been able to get beyond that, and I don't expect I ever will.

My thoughts drifted back to Catherine when she was about six years old and she and her two older sisters were in the kitchen when I got home from my summer round of mowing lawns. "We're making cookies," Catherine announced, brandishing the fork she was using to flatten the dough before the pan went into the oven, "and I'm the squisher." On most Saturdays my three female cousins would quit the acquiescent atmosphere of their home for the more regimented order of Mom's kitchen. They would come "to help Aunt Margaret", and within minutes would be busy following instructions. By the time they sat around the table consuming the fruits of their labor they felt they had earned their reward. Apparently they enjoyed the sense of accomplishment that came with completing a task up to their aunt's exacting standards, and had come to recognize "you three young ruffians" as an expression of affection.

That was in a faraway world where ugly, horrible things did not happen.

The next morning Mom and I crossed the North Saskatchewan River over the Quesnel Bridge, drove up Whitemud Drive and pulled off into Riverbend, the neighborhood where many of Edmonton's captains of industry have built their mansions. Uncle Hugh's idea of really living is waiting for sunrise in a duck blind, the more uncomfortable the better. On our periodic fishing expeditions, when the wind and the cold rain more or less guaranteed that no one else would have malignant designs on the perch and pickerel of Northern Alberta, he would shame me out of a warm bed to accompany him on to the lake because "they've got to be biting in weather like this." Huddled under an imperfectly water-proof sou'wester I would pray that the fish would mind their own bloody business and ignore the worms and other delicacies we threw into the water to entice them to their doom. A couple of tugs on his line would keep Hugh out on the lake all evening and half the night. So it wasn't a taste for luxury and ease that had attracted him to this neighborhood. He probably thought it would please Aunt Phyllis.

It was Uncle Hugh who met us at the door. He looked at the cup and saucer in his hand as though wondering how they got there, then set them on a small table before reaching out to greet us. Of medium height, slim, wiry, with bushy eyebrows and a full head of steel gray hair, he usually exudes energy and loud enthusiasm, but as he shuffled ahead of us down the hallway in a shapeless grey cardigan, grey slacks and scuffed slippers he looked like an old man; and I detested the thought.

Although the house had been practically a second home to me, that morning the quiet made it feel strange. Even after the children had grown up, until the previous week two of the three daughters had still lived there, and neither they nor their father spoke in hushed tones. It was not uncommon while on the first floor to hear a shout from somewhere overhead inquiring about who was at the door or whether anyone had seen someone's ski boots. That morning the house might have been a tomb.

Aunt Phyllis was sitting on a sofa when we entered the living room and she rose unsteadily to greet us. Seeing her and my mother together I was struck, not for the first time, at the genius for friendship that could draw together two such different people. Phyllis was blond, gentle, rather frail, still preserving the delicate features that had made her one of the local beauties when she had married (below her station her parents thought) thirty years earlier. She was the perfect society wife, wonderfully adept at making people feel good. My mother was dark, strong featured, outspoken and as a patient advocate at Misericordia Hospital she spent much of her time saying things to professionals that they would prefer not to hear. As they hugged, Aunt Phyllis hardly trusted herself to speak, whispering thanks and twisting the tiny handkerchief with which she dabbed at her eyes.

Within minutes Mom had drawn Aunt Phyllis into the kitchen to "show me where everything is" so they could prepare something for the people who would be dropping by during the day. "Ellen has to attend a staff meeting this morning," Hugh said after the women had left the room. "Her boss wouldn't want to have to think for himself even for one morning. I have to get to the office for an hour or so to sort out what needs to be done there. Joanne is coming in at about eleven. Would you mind picking her up? Toby and Gwen won't get in until this evening and they'll be renting a car at the airport." Normally Hugh's instructions were precise and crisp, but this morning he paused between sentences as though searching for the next thought.

An hour later I was on my way to Edmonton International. Joanne was the oldest of Hugh's and Phyllis's children. In late adolescence she

THE BLOOD-DIMMED TIDE IS LOOSED

seemed to have adopted a philosophy of life from the musical, *Aunty Mame*: life is a banquet, and most poor shmucks are on a diet. She had made the mistake of marrying someone too much like herself, and it was not clear that they had found out how to live life to the fullest between parties. But Joanne was kind and likable, and apart from causing worry to her parents her foibles hurt mostly herself.

Others in the baggage claim area were looking around for familiar faces, but I was almost beside Joanne and had said her name before she looked up. We hugged, mumbling half-sentences. My questions drew only brief answers from her and we retrieved her bags and walked to the parking lot mostly in silence. As we pulled on to the road out of the airport she kept her head turned towards the passenger side window and after a minute muttered, "It's just so damned unfair." I had already gone through that argument with myself, but I couldn't think of anything to say that would help poor Joanne.

My memory of the next several days is of walking in a daze through the prescribed rituals, complicated by there being not one but two families weighed down with grief: the wake, shaking hands, listening to and mumbling trite expressions, sitting mainly in silence, occasionally trying to say something vaguely normal, the funeral Mass, the graveside farewell, the reception afterwards in the parish hall; Aunt Phyllis trying to bear up and subsiding now and then into sobs; Uncle Hugh, held together I suspected by an anger just below the surface; Catherine's two sisters trying to help their mother and turning for support to my mother, their Aunt Margaret.

People talk about Catholic rituals bringing consolation to those who grieve. When your world is turned upside down and makes no sense, the rituals give you something to do and some assurance that it is the proper thing to do. The words at the funeral don't always console me, however, especially when I wonder whether the deceased was really prepared for death. In this case the words should have been comforting. Catherine had not only been nice and eager to please. She was a solidly good person. I don't have any trouble with the truths of the Catholic faith when they are stated in the abstract, but when the priest at a funeral talks about the certain hope of resurrection I sometimes wonder how certain I am. In the case of Catherine, anything

- 5 -

but a glorious resurrection would look like a miscarriage of justice. Maybe when I become a better Christian I'll experience that peace that the world cannot give.

As the reception after the burial was winding down Uncle Hugh came over, put his hand on my shoulder and thanked me, as he had been thanking everyone, for helping the family get through these days. Would I be free for a meeting in his office at 9:30 tomorrow morning? Since he was my boss, the only likely reason for my not being free would be if he needed me elsewhere. He wanted to talk to a few people about whether there was any point in trying to get further information about what had happened to Catherine and Richard.

At 9 A.M. the next morning Mom and I pulled out of our driveway and headed down 170th Street again to Whitemud Drive. The sun was shining and the aspens and cottonwoods were starting to show hints of the gold and tan and russet that would later spread across the broad valley of the North Saskatchewan River. Whenever I have been away, my homecoming is not complete until I have renewed my acquaintance with the valley's endless paths through woods and parks, under bridges, alongside golf courses, here hushed and surrounded by evergreens, there breaking out into vantage points from which to view the downtown skyline. My devotion to the valley and its ravines can be judged from the fact that at the age of fourteen I, along with a free spirit we called Gismo, could take credit for a city ordinance banning paint-ball activities in Mill Creek between the river and Whyte Avenue.

On this morning we stayed on the Whitemud Expressway for several miles beyond Quesnel Bridge and pulled off at the Southland Mall. Typically, instead of leasing several floors of a downtown office building my uncle had rented space on the ground floor of a shopping concourse. For half the money and with free parking he had all the space the company head offices required and it was less than a minute's drive from an expressway. Apparently he didn't feel the need for walnut paneling and a phalanx of secretaries to impress his business associates.

At 9:25 A.M. there were five of us gathered around the table in Hugh's office: Hugh's two daughters, Mom and myself, along with Henry

Tipping, Catherine's father-in-law. Judge Tipping was a tall, grey haired man with a suitably courtly manner. Normally before a meeting there would be some chatter but this morning we hardly spoke beyond initial greetings. I got up to get some coffee at a sideboard, not because I needed more caffeine but because it was awkward sitting around in silence. No one took me up on my offer to bring them something.

I thought about how differently Hugh's four children had responded to being raised by a father who could be overpowering but was often indulgent, and by an easy-going, affectionate mother. Joanne was the spoiled one. She was elegant, her chestnut hair perfectly coiffed, no sign this morning of the misery she had shown the last few days.

Then there had been Catherine, the youngest, the pleaser. She had been nice to everyone; and nearly everyone, without trying, had been nice to her.

Joanne and Catherine were pretty. Ellen was beautiful. If Catherine was like her mother, Ellen took after her father. She suffered fools no more gladly than he did, was capable of the same harsh humor but usually she kept it under stricter control. Not only was Ellen intelligent, but her mind seemed to be always at work. At twenty seven years of age she was assistant administrator of a large hospital. Every year as a matter of course she seemed either to get a promotion or leave one organization to get a better job at another.

Toby, or Tobias, their brother, would not be at the meeting. He was staying with his mother because Hugh didn't want her to be alone even for one morning. Ellen's good judgment was needed at the meeting. Joanne could be spared from the meeting, but her relationship with her mother remained strained. Toby at age twenty six was an Assistant Professor of Mathematics at the University of Waterloo. Had he attended the meeting he would probably speak up once or twice to show that he was paying attention, and his remarks would indubitably be correct and intelligent but have only tenuous relevance to the matter at hand. Perhaps Toby had retreated into academe, where he easily excelled, in order to escape competition with his father. He seemed to sense that he was a disappointment to Hugh, and that may have been why Aunt Phyllis had an especially soft spot in her heart for her only son.

CHAPTER TWO

At almost exactly nine o'clock Hugh entered the office accompanied by Colonel Will McGrath. Will was my mother's brother, a widower, retired from the military, currently keeping himself busy with a greenhouse operation in Brampton, Ontario. He looked the part of the military officer, closely trimmed hair and mustache, two hundred pounds distributed over a six foot two frame. What remained of his hair was mostly grey with enough coloring to show that he had originally been a redhead. He was an imposing figure, no doubt an intimidating figure to some.

Uncle Will dropped by once or twice a year to visit Mom but he was not close to the Hugh Hannigan family, and no one would have remarked had he not come to the funeral. I looked over at my mother to catch her reaction to her brother's inclusion in the meeting, but she was wearing her most inscrutable expression. Probably Will's presence was her doing. It made sense. He had spent his last few years in the armed services as a military attaché at several Canadian embassies in Latin America and he spoke Spanish.

Uncle Hugh entered the room quietly and sat down. He began by thanking Judge Tipping for his presence and his strength during this terrible time. He spoke slowly, almost without expression, as though the iron control that he had imposed on his emotions had drained him

- 8 -

of energy. In a manner completely out of character, he looked around as though having to ponder what came next, before continuing. "Colonel McGrath has been helping us get through to the authorities, as you may know, and I'm very grateful for his help. Will, if you would just fill us in on what you've found out."

The colonel's presentation was concise and to the point. "Talcayan is this sliver of land tucked in between Chile and Argentina. As you know, Catherine and Richard were on a tour through the Andes from Rio Quarto in Argentina to Valparaiso on the Pacific coast. It's a beautiful part of the world. At San Martin apparently they told the bus driver they were going to take a side trip and they'd catch up with the tour in Mendoza. The bus got to Mendoza, and there was no Catherine or Richard. The driver called his people in Rio Quarto to see if they had any word, which they had not. The driver was told to proceed with the tour as scheduled, and the office would see to reporting the couple as missing. That was Friday. For some reason there was a delay, and word that they were missing didn't reach here 'til Monday, a day after local authorities reported that their bodies had been found near the village of Cantal in Talcayan."

Will explained that Canada has no embassy or consulate in Talcayan. What little diplomatic business Canada has with that country is handled by the embassy in Santiago. The personnel there had been unable to learn anything about the case, and advised that the political situation in Talcayan was so chaotic that the police might not be in a position to investigate this crime. Even if they could, they might have no great desire to do so. Our people in Santiago would continue to make inquiries and keep us informed. Will had suggested that they send someone into Talcayan to investigate. They responded that their agent would lack diplomatic standing and would be in no position to pressure local officials to cooperate. Will's reading of the situation was that the embassy would like us just to drop the case. "Whether we should do any more," Will concluded, "is, I gather, the point of this meeting."

There were several questions. Did Will think that the situation was really so bad that the police would not or could not investigate? Yes, he thought that at least on this point our officials in Santiago were well informed. If we couldn't get action from the local police, did Canada have any leverage with the national government to get them to act? Will shrugged. The question presumed that there was a government in control. The fact was, the president was hanging on to his position only because the army was too divided to agree on who would lead a junta. The soldiers had not been paid for months and half of them had drifted back to their home regions to find work. In the present situation whatever political power existed was exercised by local authorities, mainly mayors of cities and leaders of armed gangs that called themselves armies. For the national government to send agents to investigate the murder of a couple of tourists was for the time being out of the question. Tourism was not a major industry, so they didn't worry about scaring off visitors.

Could the U.S. embassy in Talcayan be prevailed upon at least to look at the situation and see if there was anything further to be learned? The U.S. embassy had warned the few American nationals in the country that it could no longer guarantee their safety, and if they stayed they did so at their own risk. If information became available, Will would be informed.

Why would Catherine and Richard have crossed over into Talcayan? It seemed like a strange place to spend part of their honeymoon. Here Uncle Hugh broke in. Several weeks ago he had talked to Catherine and Phyllis about rumors of the discovery of silver and cobalt in southern Talcayan. He knew little about this obscure land, and he would have to learn a lot more before deciding whether Hannigan Industries should invest there. If Catherine and Richard looked at a map and discovered that they were just a few miles from that country they may have thought it would be interesting to report when they returned that they had actually seen the place. They wouldn't have known about the chaotic situation there.

Was there any other avenue that might provide information? Will replied, "I've been in touch with the police officer in the village of Cantal, where the bodies were found. He told me that all of the available information was in the initial report which was sent to the family. That report is less than a half page long. It tells us only that the bodies were found, identified, judged to be victims of foul play and returned to next of kin in Canada."

The colonel then ticked off further steps he proposed to take. He would contact several Latin American diplomats whom he knew. There were two Catholic missions in Talcayan run by American priests. A U.N. agency was just wrapping up a project to provide safe drinking water in the eastern part of the country. Someone from one of these groups might at least provide a lead about local sources of information. Will was in the process of contacting all the other people on the tour bus to see if Catherine and Richard had told anyone about their plans. "But don't expect too much," he concluded. "We might get a few scraps of information, but I doubt that anyone will tell us what really happened."

At this point in a normal meeting Uncle Hugh would sum up what seemed to be the practical alternatives. When he did nothing to move the discussion forward I suggested that we couldn't do much until we knew whether these other inquiries gave us some answers. If they didn't, then we had two choices, either drop the issue or send someone to Talcayan to investigate. Maybe someone, police or private citizen, would know something about what had happened. Whatever we learned could be turned over to any officials who still seemed to have some authority. If we could provide them with facts maybe it would spur them into action. We might not learn much, but we might learn something, and we would at least have done what we could to bring closure to the matter.

When pressed for details I answered that we had to be vague until we learned more about the situation. At this point Hugh, with an "as if I didn't know" expression, asked who I had in mind for this expedition. I replied that my work as Director of Security gave me a little bit of experience relevant to the problem, and I could take a few days off work. It shouldn't take too long. It would be mainly asking questions in one small area of the country.

"Those . . . those animals who did it," Hugh said, "It's monstrous to think that there's nobody to bring them to justice. If you go you might find out something. You might not. And you can be as careful as you like, but it may not be that safe nosing around in a strange country. We'll have to think about it."

Uncle Will broke in. "Do you speak Spanish, Mick?" I did not. "Well then, lad, it'll be a bit awkward if you have to bring a translator along.

It would be a lot simpler for me to take a few days off and go down there and take a look around."

Hugh objected with some force. The Hannigans had no right to ask this of him. He had already done more than could be expected of him. Will brushed the objection aside. "Don't worry about that, Hugh. It's no great sacrifice. My workers will thank you for getting me out of their hair for a few days." I had reservations about trying to manage without the language and I suggested that both Uncle Will and I go. Hugh just repeated: "We'll have to think about it."

Mom, who had been silent up to that point, broke in: "I've noticed that the two volunteers are both ex-soldiers. Do you find any significance in this, Hugh?"

He smiled a little grimly. "My guess is that these military types are easily bored, . . . but you have a point, Margaret. There's no denying that there could be some danger. How much danger we have no way of knowing. There's no reason why it has to be soldiers, or ex-soldiers, who take the risk; but they do know better than the rest of us how to smell danger and avoid it, and they know better how to deal with it if it happens. If you have misgivings though, Margaret, they will certainly not be ignored."

When Mom did not pursue the point the meeting broke up. As we emerged into the hallway Ellen asked me whether I would like to take a short walk, and we sauntered out on to the sidewalk.

"Ellen," I said, "It seems pointless to ask how you're doing when there's no way you could be all right."

She answered after a few seconds. "At first I was just numb. Then I guess I went into the Irish Catholic thing. You know . . . death is damnable, but there's not a bloody thing you can do about it, so you just stick out your jaw and get through it. I guess that's what our ancestors learned from centuries of fighting losing battles. Anyway, it worked until the wake, but then I saw the body and I thought, 'My God, they've done that to my little sister.' That's when I just about fell apart."

Ellen fought back tears and stood with her hand on my shoulder as though steadying herself. "You know that Mom and I will do anything we can," I said. "It's just so frustrating, not being able to help."

"That's why I wanted to talk to you," Ellen replied. "You probably volunteered to go to that place, Talcayan or whatever it is, just because you're desperate to do something for us. But you should know, you don't owe our family anything. You've given back more than you've taken. You've always been . . . this terrific big brother for us."

I explained that if I was their big brother, I thought of the three of them as sisters. If it turned out that it would help matters if I went to Talcayan I would be doing it to satisfy myself as much as to satisfy anyone else. Besides, it was not as though we were accompanying Wyatt Earp to the OK Corral. I knew how operate quietly and not ruffle any feathers. "I know my limitations," I said. "For some reason your father has an inflated estimation of my ability, but I don't. I know when to act and when to let go."

"Sure, when you get down there, you'll just make a few discreet inquiries. Mick, it's not a matter of recognizing one's limitations. I agree with Dad. The rest of us are great at smart talk, but if we're going into battle, it's you I want out there in front. What I worry about is you wanting to do too much."

Our extended family is close and we really care for each other but we're not much given to fulsome praise, so this encomium from Ellen left me a bit embarrassed. Probably because she sensed this, she added: "Well, when you're down there maybe you'll find a pretty señorita to comfort you in your old age. It's coming up fast you know."

It was a good to see that Ellen could still slide into the bantering that was a normal part of our conversations, and I replied that I would keep an eye out for a handsome caballero with a preference for mature women. In a minute we were back in the foyer where Mom was waiting.

"Aunt Margaret, this compulsion to go off to somewhere in the Andes half way round the world," Ellen asked, "Would you say your son is just slightly demented?"

Mom was used to this sort of remark from her favorite niece. "It's a day to day thing. It's best to humor him."

"Yeah, I know. We must be patient. Well, I've got to get back. Nothing gets done at Edmonton General unless the assistant ogre is around to terrorize the help."

When we got back to the house Mom suggested that she could prepare an early lunch and I could then go back and get in a long afternoon's work As we sat down at the kitchen table I asked her what her real thoughts were about my going to Talcayan. She explained that Hugh would probably not send me if she objected. "But it's not my decision to make. It's yours. If you think the risk is not that great and you think it's worth it, then go ahead."

We began our meal in silence for a minute or two, and then my mother continued. "You know, Michael, I've always had a hard time thinking of either you or your father doing the actual work of soldiering, though I'm sure you did it well. But it seems to me both of you thought too much to be really good soldiers. I could never understand how you could be so thoughtful and also be ready to do the terrible things a soldier sometimes has to do. I know it bothered your father. He came to terms with it by recognizing that sometimes the innocent have to be protected against evil men and sometimes that can't be done without killing. But he didn't consider himself to be one of the innocent. He said once that when you are in uniform the enemy sees you as fair game, not as someone who is innocent, and they're right. I don't think your father could ever have killed just to preserve his own life. For the last couple of years he used to say that as an officer his first concern was to avoid fighting whenever there was a chance of resolving a situation in some other way. He hoped that at some future time killing would no longer be the way an army won a war. He once said to me—suppose two people in a bar attack each other with knives. If no one intervenes one or both of them will probably be killed or seriously injured. If the police arrive and are more powerful than the two fighters, no one needs to get hurt. Can't that method apply to war?"

"Michael," she continued, "I would have liked to have had a houseful of kids. You had to stand in for all the children I didn't have. You've done it well."

Touched as I was by the affirmation from the two women who meant most to me, they still sounded too much like they were telling me what they wanted me to know, just in case I didn't come back from Talcayan. But it was not a time to have one's head messed up with imaginings. Uncle Will and I would keep our eyes open and stay out of trouble.

As he had predicted, Colonel McGrath's search for more information produced only sparse results. Several of those who had been on the tour with Catherine and Richard had remembered the handsome couple, were shocked and grieved by the news of their deaths but knew nothing about their intentions or plans before they left on the side-trip to Talcayan. One positive result of Will's inquiries was the identification of two people who might be sympathetic to our concerns: the bishop of the second largest city in Talcayan and the mayor of another city. An American missionary had suggested their names because they were among the few who were doing anything effective about the mess the country was in. Both of them had been skeptical about whether the murders could be solved but were willing to meet with whoever we sent.

It was decided that Uncle Will and I should travel to Talcayan. Even before this decision was made I had purchased a Spanish-English dictionary and a book entitled *Practical Spanish* and began to study for a couple of hours each evening. Once the decision was made for us to go I enrolled in a language school that promised wonderfully quick results. The secret, I suspect, was that after paying the exorbitant tuition one couldn't afford to slack off.

Any project involving either Hugh Hannigan or Will McGrath would not fail from lack of planning. Will studied everything he could find about Talcayan. The task was not overwhelming. The print media had not discovered any public thirst for information about that obscure land. Professors had found ways of securing tenure and promotion without publishing learned treatises on the economics, history, literature or religious situation of the country. Will's main sources were people who had some acquaintance with the place, some he knew from his years spent in Canadian embassies and others he heard about who were willing to give him a few minutes. When he wasn't studying about our destination he was arranging for visas, airline tickets, vehicle rentals, etc.

About a week after we got the go-ahead for our venture into South America Colonel McGrath called. "Something has come up," he began. "It sounds as though someone wants to warn us off the case. I don't take it too seriously, but you should know about it. That police officer

- 15 -

in Cantal—he's the guy said the half-page he sent to Hugh was all the information we were going to get. I wondered whether police could get away with something like that, so I did a little digging. It turns out, a few years ago a bunch of countries in the western hemisphere, including Canada and Talcayan, signed on to a protocol to protect nationals of one country who are traveling in another. It states that if there is a crime or a suspected crime against a foreign national, the police in the host country must treat it as they would a crime against one of their own citizens. Also, the police in the host country are required to convey to the next-of-kin of the persons who are harmed, or to authorities in their home country, whatever has been discovered about the case as well as the investigative measures that have been taken.

"Armed with this information, I got back to the guy in Cantal. When he repeated that we already had all the information we were going to get, I quoted the protocol. He sputtered for a while, then asked me to repeat my name and give my address, which I did. When I insisted that he give me the information required by law he said that he would consult with his superiors and get back to me. Well, days passed and he didn't call back. When I called him again he referred me to an officer in the nearby city of Valdez, some guy named Alonzo Langer.

"I called the office in Valdez and was put through to Capitan Langer. When I stated my case he started to grill me. He wanted my name again, my address, telephone number, passport number, etc. This time all I gave was my name. When I asked him why this other information was needed he said it was so they could make sure that I was who I claimed to be and had a right to the information. I suggested that he send the information to whatever South American embassy or consulate in Canada was handling affairs for the Government of Talcayan. I would present my credentials to that office and they could decide whether I had a right to the information. That set Captain Langer back for a few seconds, but then he explained that he couldn't trust the personnel in foreign offices and he would have to do the investigating himself. I told Captain Langer that I would be making inquiries elsewhere. I was about to hang up when he broke in. Was my address such and such?—and he gave my address. No doubt he had gotten it from the officer in Cantal.

THE BLOOD-DIMMED TIDE IS LOOSED

"To sum things up, we can be pretty sure now that there was a cover up, and it doesn't stop at Cantal. Maybe the police, some of them at least, are tied up with some crooked organization. And that thing about my address, I presume it was a warning . . . 'we know where you live', that sort of thing."

I asked Will whether we should be worried. In his opinion, it was a bluff. No one from Valdez was going to show up in his back yard with a suitcase full of dynamite. On the other hand, we should pay attention to the fact that this Langer character would threaten violence. It was hardly a reason to abandon our projected trip, but it did mean that we should be cautious and try to get in and out of the country without Langer and company being any the wiser.

Before I go much farther with this story I should explain a few things about my family. My father, Gerard Hannigan, was a captain in the Canadian Armed Forces on what was euphemistically called a peace-keeping assignment in Cyprus when the jeep in which he was riding struck a land mine and he and the driver were killed. I was less than two years old at the time, so my only images of my father come from photographs. My mother never remarried and she's not the kind of person whom you ask to explain why. She was only twenty four years old when she became a widow. Maybe she never met someone who could take the place of Gerard Hannigan, or maybe prospective suitors sensed that she was not your cup of tea if you were looking for a subservient mate. In any case, I grew up as the only child of a single parent. When I started school Mom began to volunteer for several organizations, settling eventually on visiting the sick at Misericordia Hospital. By that time the number of religious sisters available to work in health care had declined drastically. The last sister to be the administrator of Misericordia hired my mother as a part-time patient advocate. That sister had an eye for talent. She may also have had a chip on her shoulder towards the medical profession.

My Uncle Hugh had been a surrogate father to me, taught me many of the skills of boyhood and occasionally set me straight when I had done something particularly stupid. Hugh Hannigan had an endless repertoire of stories, usually funny and often not at all complimentary. If he had a fault it was that his gift for the apt phrase could be withering when turned on someone who had incurred his anger or disgust. With me, however, he had been unfailingly patient.

I joined the Canadian Armed forces after high school. It was not, as far as I can recall, an effort to follow in my father's footsteps. It was more a process of elimination. I was a good student, but Uncle Hugh's children were reminders that some people are considerably more intelligent than I am. I was a better-than-average middleweight boxer, but as my coach often reminded me, some day I was bound to meet an opponent just as quick as I was and who punched with a lot more power. I was a not-bad hockey player, but although I was similar to Wayne Gretzky in height and weight, the resemblance ended there. I was not "going anywhere" in any direction, so without much agonizing I became a soldier. Six years later I had reached the rank of sergeant and at the age of twenty four I returned to civilian life.

CHAPTER THREE

To provide Colonel McGrath and me with a plausible cover for our visit to Talcayan, Uncle Hugh decided to combine our visit with an exploration of possible reserves of silver and cobalt in the southern part of the country. The company's chief geologist, Dieter Helfrich, and his assistant were to accompany Uncle Will and myself, and all four of us would spend the first several days of our stay in southern Talcayan near a town called Amparo. Dieter would not need to bring much equipment. An earlier, more enlightened regime in Talcayan had decreed that reports of all geological surveys and explorations were to be filed with the government. Those filed by commercial interests were kept confidential unless the companies responsible for the work failed to take action within ten years; but the government itself had done some surveying, and its findings were in the public domain, so Dieter could combine this with a site inspection and his own brand of intuition and perhaps get some idea about whether further investigation was justified. Will and I would spend the first several days looking at the security situation, business climate, infrastructure and other factors that would determine whether further investment might be justified.

So two weeks before our departure I met with Dieter Helfrich. Hugh's policy was to hire the best available and he was a good judge of talent. Dieter, with full qualifications in mining engineering and geology, was living in Austria with his wife and seven children and a considerable debt when he read an advertisement that Hannigan Industries had placed in a number of European newspapers. Although uprooting his family and leaving his homeland behind were not pleasant prospects, the salary Hugh dangled in front of him solved his financial problems, so the Helfrichs traded the scenery around Salzburg for residence in Canada's most northerly large city. When they pined for the Austrian Alps the Helfrichs consoled themselves with visits to Jasper National Park in the Rocky Mountains, a four hour drive to the west.

I read somewhere that people who are thought of as pessimists often are in fact optimists, because their dissatisfaction arises from overly high expectations. Dieter allowed no such high hopes to contaminate his pessimism. Not wanting to go to bed with my mind full of Dieter's reasons why the project would end in disaster, I chose a morning hour to meet with him to work out details of our trip. His first words when I sat down were, "So I will have two ex-soldiers to protect me from those crazy rebels in South America."

I explained that Will and I were not going there to protect him and that he would be in more danger if he were on Whyte Avenue when the bars closed on Friday night than he would be in the Amparo district. Will and I were there just to look at security and other factors relating to a possible future project. "Besides," I said, "At the first hint of trouble we all get to hell out of there. There'll be an airplane at a nearby field to fly us out."

"Well, I hope not get to hell. Out of hell I prefer." Dieter loved to misinterpret English idioms, his way of demonstrating the deficiencies of the language. I spent a half hour or so writing down all the things that he would want for his time in Talcayan. He was definite about what would be needed and I knew better than to question his judgment. I left him happily grumping about the whole project. "Maybe I'll just close my eyes and I'll intuit where the silver is?" He knew very well that there would be plenty of useful information to occupy him during the few days he would be in the country, but he wasn't going to waste a golden opportunity to complain.

I enjoy air travel, or at least I did a few years ago. When I see people arriving from and embarking for exotic places, especially when I'm one of those embarking, I'm like a child on Christmas Eve. Colonel McGrath on the other hand was all business at Edmonton International, checking extra baggage, looking at schedules, calculating how much time we would have to change planes. I suppose a colonel is more accustomed than a sergeant to seeing that everything runs according to plan. Will appeared to relish being back in harness, embarking on an assignment that had about it at least a suggestion of adventure. As we waited, Dieter reminded us with grim satisfaction of all the things that could be missed in a routine maintenance check of an airplane. His assistant, Bradley Klein, a pale young man who had apparently built up an immunity to Dieter's Apocalyptic worldview, was his usual taciturn self.

We had hardly settled into our seats for the first leg of our flight when Will began a review of our marching orders. "As you know, Mick, your Uncle Hugh has put you in charge." When I voiced my puzzlement about this arrangement Will answered that it was his own idea, not Hugh's. "First, in the unlikely event that something untoward happens, it'll be easier for your family to accept if it wasn't someone else who put you in harm's way. Second, this is officially a trip to look into mineral deposits and you're a company official. I'm not. Third, you are admirably suited to be in charge."

I questioned the third qualification. "Nonsense," he replied. "I've talked to Herb Jansen. He claims that you were one of the best combat soldiers he ever trained; expert marksman, extremely quick reflexes, resourceful. In any case, if you need advice I shall be happy to provide it." I did not doubt that last statement.

"It may help you understand the situation, Mick," he continued, "if I tell you something about Talcayan." I had been expecting a lecture along those lines. A man can't immerse himself in an obscure subject for nearly six weeks without wanting to unload the details on somebody. I settled back, happy to learn about the land for which we were bound.

"The Spanish and Portuguese, good Catholics all, conquered Central and South America for God and country. As they saw it, either God or

- 21 -

country must have been interested mainly in gold and farm land that already belonged to the native people."

To hold up my end of the conversation I mumbled something to the effect that probably explorers in those days didn't recruit their crews from convents and monasteries. A lot of Christians contradict their beliefs by the way they act.

"And you call these people Christians?"

I opined that they may not be very good Christians, but you don't have to be a good Christian to be a Christian. "Maybe so," he said. "But I suggest you think about the Toronto Maple Leafs."

"Do I have to?"

"Humor me. Suppose Toronto makes the playoffs next spring and is playing, let's say, the Boston Bruins. Toronto fans will root like maniacs for a Toronto victory, and the Boston fans will be no less maniacal on behalf of the Bruins. Now what motivates your Maple Leaf fan? Do the Maple Leafs stand for some grand principle? Do they struggle to preserve a precious way of life against the evil Boston Bruins? No. Their fans cheer for the Leafs because it's their team. Now a lot of so-called Catholics are more fans than believers. It's their Church, so they cheer for it. If it were really their beliefs that made them Catholics would they be so slovenly about the way they practice, or don't practice, their religion?"

I answered honestly that I didn't know, and Uncle Will, apparently satisfied that this issue was settled, returned to the main topic.

"The present territory of Talcayan was part of the huge colony of New Spain. For a while it was under the viceroy of Peru, but later it became part of the viceroyalty of Rio de la Plata. In a way it was lucky for the native people that the land had no gold and was drier than most of that part of the world. The greediest Spaniards gobbled up the best land, and the Spanish families that grabbed the territory that is now Talcayan were only moderately greedy. They established seven huge estancias—what they call haciendas in other parts of Latin America. The territory was only sparsely populated before the Spanish arrived. A few native people fished in the rivers. Some cultivated small fields, and many of them irrigated their plots with river water. You can imagine how much work that was with the technology they had. Some were hunters, the main game animals being the guanaco, a smaller version of the llama, and the agouti, which is a sort of rabbit but bigger. Wild life was not plentiful and only a few nomadic bands supported themselves in that way."

Colonel McGrath's account continued. When the Spanish families settled in Talcayan they didn't take over the holdings of the farmers or fishermen. They did divide up the unclaimed land among themselves and run cattle on it. This took away the livelihood of the hunters, but apparently the latter were noted mainly for being hungry much of the time, and most of them went to work for the Spanish ranchers in exchange for food, a cottage and a bit of money. In time the native farmers began to profit from commerce with the Spaniards, getting better strains of grain to grow, planting fruit trees imported from Europe, selling some of their produce to the Europeans. Nobody got rich but most of them didn't go hungry. Once in a while there would be friction between the indigenous people and the Spaniards but it rarely rose to the level of violence.

The Spanish authorities paid little heed to this part of their empire. It yielded but scant revenue. They were not anxious even to provide police or troops to defend Spanish interests in the area, especially as there didn't seem to be much trouble there in any case. The main town, San Isidro, had the only garrison with troops and police. Elsewhere, whatever need there was for policing was usually taken care of by the seven families, the heads of which met regularly to attend to whatever joint interests they had and to iron out disputes. Each estancia had a number of workers who could be counted on to defend their herds against rustlers if need arose, which it seldom did. If someone in a town attacked another in a drunken rage, the by-standers usually took care of it. They might be fifty or a hundred miles away from San Isidro so calling in the police was not an option. The one area of government in which the inhabitants of that area were fully conscious of Spanish rule was the judiciary. A judge in San Isidro heard cases for that part of the territory, and several other judges toured the more remote districts. This was the situation through the centuries while this area was under the viceroy of Peru, and it didn't change much when in 1776 it became part of the viceroyalty of Rio de la Plata.

- 23 -

As is well known, the revolutions that spread through Latin America and won independence in the early 19th century were for the most part not uprisings of the indigenous people against the Europeans. The revolutions were led by the Creoles, Spanish who had settled in the new world. In the region controlled by the seven families the people didn't get excited about the revolution. The Spanish from Spain had no strong motive to hold on to a territory that had no gold and but small profit from agriculture. The landowners, businessmen and professionals in the territory had never been much bothered by the authorities from Spain, and they suspected that any change of regime was as likely to be for the worse as for the better. The indigenous people didn't see much to choose between being governed by Spaniards in Spain or by Spaniards in South America. There were no battles on the soil controlled by the seven families, and the inhabitants of the region gave tepid support to whatever army happened to be closest.

Eventually a triumphant revolutionary force marched into the territory. The inhabitants, while not hostile, seemed to be ungrateful and unenthusiastic about the benefits of liberation. Nor did the revolutionary army find much booty. The locals had hidden the few valuables they had, and presented to the revolutionaries an appearance even more destitute than was their real situation. A platoon loyal to Spain was trapped in the garrison in San Isidro. Enrique Perera, one of the estancia owners, averted bloodshed by arranging its safe conduct to the nearest accessible seaport.

After the colonies won their independence the territory of the seven estancias came under the rule of Argentina. The authorities in Buenos Aires wanted to bring all of the territories of the large, new country under the control of a strong central government. A delegation from Buenos Aires met with Perera, who was nominated by the other landowners to act on their behalf. He greeted the Argentine representatives with as much pomp as was consistent with the impoverished image he sought to project. He assured them that the residents for whom he spoke were strong supporters of centralized government. The landowners were poor and could not afford to provide proper policing and build roads, and they were delighted that a strong national government would now

THE BLOOD-DIMMED TIDE IS LOOSED

take over those responsibilities. Also, there would be need for several regiments to keep the armies of Chile at bay.

The next delegation to meet with Perera represented a federalist movement that was fighting for greater autonomy of the various regions. Perera assured them that the people for whom he spoke had always favored a decentralized government. The landowners were very poor and could not afford to build roads or even to pay a proper police force. They looked forward to being annexed by a more prosperous region that would take care of these matters; and of course it would be necessary to train and support an army to ward off the Chileans.

In the end few taxes were imposed, only a few miles of proper roads built and no national police or soldiers were stationed anywhere in the territory. After some years of benevolent neglect the landowners took advantage of the threat of war between Chile and Argentina and declared the independence of the nation of Talcayan. They did so with as little fanfare as possible, lest they alarm their neighbors. They asked Enrique Perera to be their first president. He explained that his great contribution to the country had been to discourage others from doing anything, but being president would require other skills. This protestation convinced the landowners that he possessed exactly the qualities needed to lead them into the future, and eventually he agreed to do so.

Talcayan, it was clear, had lacked the true revolutionary spirit.

A more-or-less benevolent oligarchy ruled until the 1920's. Then the people who had provided whatever governance there had been up to that time made the mistake of centralizing the police force under the command of an adventurer who didn't go along with the country's semi-anarchist tradition. He decided that Talcayan had failed to reap the full benefits of the revolution and he undertook to correct this error. He professed to be a Marxist and gave eloquent speeches about wresting power from the oppressors. He succeeded in taking some power away from the landowners, and from that point on Talcayan was able to share with much of the rest of Latin America the benefits of military juntas, followed by economic collapse and popular discontent, followed by a strong man, followed by another junta. There was now a need for a larger army, without which the ruling group could not expect

- 25 -

to hold on to power. Armies required financing and that meant taxes. Then it became necessary to hire inspectors to look into tax fraud, for which the citizens of Talcayan showed a modest talent. Recently those in power had adapted a form of globalization that consisted mainly of diverting international aid into their private bank accounts, and this in turn guaranteed that there would usually be another generation of aspiring despots waiting in the wings to seize power and get their fair share of the booty.

At present, Will concluded, the president of Talcayan is a man called Sergio Gracida. He came to power several years ago with the usual promise to end corruption. He differed from his predecessors in that he seemed intent on actually fulfilling his promises. He reduced the army drastically, and that left him vulnerable to a number of other gentlemen who had prudently expanded their private armies, if "army" is the right term to denote a group of undisciplined and poorly trained bullies. Normally this would have been the moment for another military junta, but because the government had not been able to pay them for the last eight months, many of the soldiers had wandered off to find other means of livelihood. The several leaders with private armed followers were too suspicious of each other to form a single group capable of overawing the opposition. Gracida would stay "in power", if it could be called that, until such time as somebody or some group felt strong enough to replace him.

Colonel McGrath occasionally indulged his Irish birthright to improve on stories when the original characters had failed to exploit the dramatic possibilities of the situation, but he did his homework and you could depend on him to get the essentials right. So this was the situation in the land that we were approaching above the clouds at over 500 miles per hour.

CHAPTER FOUR

We landed in Valparaiso late at night, cramped and weary, caught some sleep in a hotel near the city center and set off about noon the next day by train across the Andes through San Felipe to Mendoza. It was a chance, Will explained, to enjoy some magnificent scenery. Magnificent yes but, depending on my mood, I don't always enjoy being reminded that I'm a tiny speck in the universe. Will had been to Mendoza before, but for Dieter, Bradley and me it was a revelation to arrive in a sizable and beautiful city of which we had been unaware until several weeks earlier. From the train station we went directly to a rental agency where Will had arranged for us to pick up a Toyota Corolla along with an almost new Land Rover to explore off-road areas. We were on the road as the sun came up the next morning. The route we took, south east from Mendoza, was not the most direct, but it would take us to the entry point where Señor Robles, the mayor of Amparo, had arranged for us to pass smoothly through customs and immigration.

We had flown from autumn to spring. The vineyards were coming to life after winter pruning and the orchards on the hillsides were in bloom. I had expected something like the semi-arid country of the American southwest, but the countryside was green and lush. The sky was clear, the air fresh and still cool. Gradually the land became flatter and drier,

- 27 -

open ranch land with only scattered trees and bushes. We turned west on a gravel road that a sign identified as Camino del Campo. It was just as well that traffic was sparse, because each passing vehicle threw up clouds of dust. Every couple of kilometers we would spot a human habitation or a small herd of cattle, usually some distance from the road.

After about forty minutes travelling west we sighted a low building ahead of us in the distance. As we drew close a marker informed us that we were leaving the Republic of Argentina and entering the Republic of Talcayan. Judging from its customs and immigration quarters at this isolated border crossing, Argentina did not place a high priority on commerce with its tiny neighbor. The offices of Talcayan were slightly more impressive. Instead of a bungalow of weathered wood there was a neat, two-story, brick structure surrounded by well-tended gardens. We pulled up beside two cars and a dented pick-up truck parked at the side. A slim, uniformed official came out briskly to meet us. After a cursory examination of our two vehicles and their contents he led us into the office, looked at our documents and handed Will some forms. When he had filled them out Will looked around as though he were expecting something or someone, shrugged and brought the papers to the official. After a brief exchange he backed away from the counter and turned to the rest of us.

"I've paid the 1,000 pesos that the form says is the fee. He's asking for 2,500 more. I was told that officials might try to charge extra. It's a bribe to our way of thinking, but they probably think of it like we think about tipping a waiter. It's the way things are done. Hugh doesn't want us to start paying bribes. If we start doing that they'll expect us to keep it up."

At that moment an impressive figure in a police uniform emerged from the washroom, wiping his hands with a paper towel. Think of a National Football League lineman about five years into retirement and you have the physical type. With his brown skin, black hair and drooping mustache, he would have fit Hollywood's image of a Mexican bandit except for his size. He held out a huge hand. "I am Aldomar," he said in Spanish in a tone suggesting that in well-informed circles the single name was sufficient identification. "Mayor Robles has asked me to help you."

Will and the giant approached the official and for several minutes Aldomar did most of the talking in rapid, idiomatic Spanish, and Will had to give me the gist of the conversation as it progressed. Aldomar was explaining that these good men from Canada were on their way to search for silver and cobalt in the Amparo region. Mayor Robles was anxious that Hannigan Industries should bring good jobs to his people. If officials force Mr. Hannigan to pay bribes he will not establish mines, and there will be no new jobs, and Señor Robles will be very disappointed. He, Aldomar, was infinitely patient and kind hearted, but the mayor had other associates who were of a different mind. "They are men of action," he confided to the official. "They are not like you and me. They do not negotiate."

Then as if to demonstrate his own mastery of the fine art of negotiation, he turned away and remarked to Will that this was all very bad. How could he go back and tell Mayor Robles that he, Aldomar, had failed to get the Canadian businessmen through customs and immigration in a satisfactory way? "Señor Robles will blame me," he moaned. "He will say that I have not been sufficiently forceful."

The animated conversation at the counter resumed. Judging by his gestures, the official was explaining that the lot of a customs agent was not a happy one. Aldomar spoke more slowly, so I could catch some of what he was saying. His theme was that he too knew what it was like to have a heartless boss, but "What can you do?" It was becoming obvious that what Aldomar thought he could do was to stand, sad-faced, at the counter until such time as the official had stamped and initialed the necessary documents. Bowing to the inevitable, the official stamped and initialed and we were on our way.

Outside the customs office Aldomar explained that the country was going through a period of upheaval, but if we kept our three vehicles as close together as the dust allowed and did not exceed the speed limit no-one would bother us. In order to force myself to converse in Spanish and perhaps pick up some useful information in the process, I joined Aldomar as he led the way in his pick-up truck.

We continued westward and were soon surrounded by hills which gradually became higher and steeper. From the higher spots on the road we could see the peaks of the Andes. The hills here apparently did not get enough rain to support the vineyards and orchards we had seen earlier. The country was far from barren, however. There were trees of various kinds, with here and there a stand of ceibos that would later be aflame with crimson flowers. After a little more than an hour we turned south and descended into a broad valley where everything was a deeper green. At the bottom of the valley was a swift flowing river about thirty yards wide that Aldomar identified as the Rio del Rey. The "Rey" had referred to Christ the King, but the more enlightened regime that came to power in the 1920s had seen fit to discard this reminder of the religion of the colonizers. We crossed a gracefully designed bridge that Aldomar pointed out as one of the architectural attractions of the territory. It was called *El Puente Ingles* in honor of the English who had financed its construction.

Once across the bridge the road turned west and roughly followed the river upstream. Along both sides of the river there were plots of land, some of only a couple of acres, others considerably larger. Each plot contained a cottage, fruit trees, a garden, perhaps a shed for a cow or some sheep. Aldomar explained that the lots were irrigated during the dry season. Some of the more prosperous owners had water piped on to their land. Others would bring the water from the river to their lots in barrels hauled on donkey carts. While there was little indication of affluence, there were no abandoned buildings, broken fences and rusting machinery that one associates with rural poverty.

After several miles we reached the town of Amparo. Again, the impression was of limited resources but by no means of squalor. It was laid out, as most of the towns in Talcayan proved to be, around a central square on which stood a town hall, market, police station, church, school, medical clinic and several eating places. We pulled up to the town hall, a two-story brick structure with columns across the front and an arched doorway. We had left Mendoza at about 6 A.M. and it was now almost noon. Aldomar's terrible Señor Robles turned out to be a little, round man, middle-aged, balding, with thick glasses. He came towards us bowing and smiling. Sensing that Señor Robles would want to know the pecking order of his guests, Will introduced me as the head of the delegation. The mayor gave me a slightly deeper bow than he gave to the others and asked, in a Spanish that I could understand, whether Aldomar had taken good care of us. I replied that his care for us had been impeccable. Our host then hurried us off for a much appreciated meal at a restaurant across the square from city hall.

The North American practice of the working lunch seemed to have penetrated to Amparo, because Mayor Robles lost little time in getting down to business. He placed great hope in our visit and the possibility of better jobs for his people. They were poor, the population was growing and there was not enough land to support an increase in the number of farmers. We tried to dampen his expectations without disappointing him unnecessarily. On this visit we would make only a first investigation, to see if an extensive assay might be warranted. If the latter indicated enough ore to justify investment, we would also have to consider security and the political situation. We could not invest if the government proved to be unstable or if it was unable to guarantee that our equipment and supplies would be safe.

Señor Robles hastened to assure us that the unrest in the other parts of the country did not extend to the Amparo district. South of the Rio del Rey law and order prevailed and crime rates were low. We pointed out that we could not entirely bypass the national government. We would be paying taxes, importing and exporting goods, and our holdings would be subject to seizure by a national government that was so minded. The mayor regretted that the country was in a bad state, but during the last half century no government had confiscated foreign-owned property and he was confident that we could do business profitably. The main thing, he insisted, was that here, where the mines would be located, security was solid.

It was Saturday. After the meal we four Edmontonians defied the local custom and headed directly to work. Dieter departed to make contact with a local translator, a retired teacher of English whom Will had engaged as part of his elaborate preparations before we left Canada. Dieter, his assistant and their translator would start on the documents that Señor Robles had obtained from the national records in San Isidro. I took Aldomar with me in the Land Rover to explore the territory where silver and cobalt had been found. Will opted to see what he could learn by hanging around town.

That evening Will and I were guests of Señor and Señora Robles. The latter, stylishly dressed and made-up, clearly attached importance to her status as wife of the mayor of Amparo and *de facto* authority for the whole territory south of Rio del Rey. She was a gracious hostess and neither Will nor I objected to being treated as guests in the grand manner. After supper the colonel and I retired to the guest suite in the Robles home and compared notes. Will and Dieter were responsible for filing reports to Hugh Hannigan, and I gave Will what I thought Hugh would want to know about our first day. Aldomar and I had visited the site of several abandoned mines, which seemed to be the most likely place to begin further investigation. These were located in rugged country, but building a road into the general area should not be prohibitively expensive. If bulk of the ore turned out to be farther west, in the mountains, then my amateur observations would be useless and it would be necessary to bring in engineers to study the situation. The colonel reported that Señor Robles seemed to have overstated his ability to ensure security. In Will's wanderings he had learned that a gang from San Martin, a village north of the river, regularly sent agents into the territory to gather "taxes" which were really payments to keep the gang from raiding the ranches and the lots along the river.

Perhaps Dieter and Bradley, housed in a nearby hotel, would have something more encouraging to report.

The next morning Will, Dieter and I attended Mass. The church was the only stone structure on the square and its steeple towered over the town. The interior was more cluttered and colorful than most North American Catholic churches have been since the 1960s. The numerous pictures had probably been painted by local artists. The whole effect was conducive to prayer so long as one remembered that one was not there as an art critic. The church was almost full. The priest, gray haired and austere in appearance, spoke slowly enough that I was able to follow most of what he said.

We had met Dieter outside of the church and chatted for a moment. On the way in Will whispered to me: "Your friend seems to be relatively cheerful. Do you suppose he has discovered something encouraging?" I

THE BLOOD-DIMMED TIDE IS LOOSED

thought that maybe the fact that it was Sunday explained his improved spirits. Dieter was convinced that this earth is a vale of tears, but maybe on Sundays he turned his mind to higher things—a sort of twenty-four hour respite from pondering the world's headlong rush to disaster; or maybe he was just relieved that the crazy rebels had not yet attacked us.

It turned out that Will's guess about the source of Dieter's good mood was correct. Whatever his thoughts about the generality of human affairs, there was one earthly blessing in which Dieter allowed himself to rejoice, and that was any positive indication of the existence of valuable mineral deposits. As we learned after Mass, Dieter had discovered that a silver mine south of Amparo had operated from 1908 to 1926. It had been the property of the owner of a huge estancia and it had been a paying proposition. The so-called Marxist regime had freed the mine from its oppressive owner and had closed it two years later. Even if it was closed because the ore ran out, Dieter pointed out, it could be that with the limited means at their disposal they had failed to locate the mother lode.

An Australian company had prospected the area more recently. They had even gone so far as to conduct a study preparatory to building a road into an area well to the west of the places Aldomar and I had visited the day before. The Australians had filed a report with the national geological registry six years ago but they had made no further investments. Dieter would have loved to get a look at that report, but it would not become public for four more years, and then only if the authors took no further action. Dieter thought it likely that they had found something worth pursuing but the political situation and security concerns had caused them to shelve the project temporarily. True, the Australians had not bought up the mineral rights to the area, but at that time they had begun to invest heavily in Bolivia and their shareholders may have balked at another speculative investment. In any case, Dieter now knew what to look for the next day when he and his translator would tackle the documents stored locally and the newspaper reports from six years earlier when the explorations had taken place.

On Monday morning Will and I packed our gear, thanked our hosts for their hospitality, promised to stay in touch, and departed, ostensibly to look elsewhere in Talcayan for possible suppliers for a mining venture in the Amparo district. At 9 A.M. we crossed El Puente Ingles. A kilometer or two north of the bridge we pulled off the road on a trail leading to a clump of trees about a half kilometer from the road. We stopped and pulled from the trunk of the car a wooden crate that Will had picked up the previous afternoon. It had been flown in on a small airplane that landed in a field near Amparo. It contained a Rem 7313 rifle with scope, two Beretta 70 pistols and plenty of ammunition, objects that might have aroused undue interest if we had brought them through the customs office two days earlier.

I tested the firearms and adjusted the sights as needed. I was a little discouraged at how out-of-practice I was. I fired off a few rounds from the rifle to get back into the habit of holding steady, breathing properly, regulating pressure on the trigger, until I was able to place five bullets within about a six inch circle at fifty yards. It was not shooting at a high competitive level but it would have to do for now. Will was uneasy throughout the exercise, and as we placed the weapons back in the trunk he muttered that he hoped to blazes we would not have to use them. He was right. If it came to shooting it would mean that we had stirred up much more trouble than we had intended.

A few minutes after we had resumed our journey Will remarked: "You would have been a fine soldier, Mick, but you left the military. Mind you, I'm certainly not blaming you, but I'm curious as to why."

I explained that joining the armed services had not been something about which I agonized. I wanted to do something that I could do well. I could think quickly on my feet. My high school grades had been good but not great. I wanted something with lots of physical activity but where I would also be using my brain, and I thought army life would provide it. By the end of boot camp I realized that if I had been playing my cards more shrewdly I would have gone to university, enrolled in R.O.T.C., maybe enjoyed several years of intercollegiate hockey as a second or third line center, and entered the armed services with a commission. I applied for officer training but it didn't happen. I suspect that the reason was my moodiness. I would go for weeks avoiding company, not talking unless I had to. Occasionally someone observing my mood would tell me to cheer up. I should paste a grin on my face and be happy; and then there were those who thought they were being hilarious when they would call me "smiley".

My C.O. even told me to talk to the psychiatrist. The shrink was a good guy, no mumbo-jumbo, just common sense. After several sessions he told me that I was suffering from mild depression, which came as no surprise to me. He said it wasn't anywhere close to clinical depression, nor did I show signs of bi-polar disorder. So the thing to do was to figure out whether there were certain situations that brought on my moods. I decided that there were a couple of things. If I had to put forth a lot of effort to accomplish something I could stay at it enthusiastically for a time, but after a while without some progress I would start feeling down. Also, I did a lot better when there was physical activity and some challenge. At our fourth meeting the psychiatrist suggested that I needed a job where I could change the situation when I felt a mood coming on, and the army, with its emphasis on following orders, doesn't allow for that. I took his opinion seriously and returned to civilian life.

"Besides," I concluded, "My distinction in the army was marksmanship. I was very good with a pistol. In competitions on the rifle range I was never defeated. If I stayed, my main value to the army would be to hide in the bushes and shoot people who couldn't see me. That's not the kind of thing that people recall fondly at your wake."

I don't know whether my explanation made things any clearer to Uncle Will, but it helped me.

During the previous several days I had been so caught up in the prospects of mineral deposits south of the Rio del Rey that for the first time in many weeks the feelings occasioned by my cousin's murder had receded to the back of my consciousness. That morning as we headed north those black thoughts flooded back. Less than two hundred kilometers from where we had stopped, Catherine and her husband had spent their terrible last day.

We continued north, crossed El Camino del Campo, and within an hour came to a fork in the road. To the left lay the capital, San Isidro; to the right lay Avila, where we were to meet with Bishop Kendel, one of the two people who had agreed to talk to us. We reached Avila before noon. I had done my homework and knew that this was the second largest city in the country, with about 75,000 inhabitants. Its workshops and

- 35 -

factories produced clothing, leather goods, jewelry, furniture, sacks and rope made out of locally grown hemp. We joined the locals who were having a leisurely meal in the restaurants along the main street. Our appointment with the bishop was not until the next morning, so I took my Spanish grammar with me and reviewed my verb forms while I explored the city on foot.

At the meeting the next morning, the first thing I noticed about Bishop Kendel was that he looked like a smaller version of Andres Galaraga, the marvelous Venezuelan first baseman who played for many years in the National League. His could be the face of a saint or of a rogue, but whichever it was, those strong, native features proclaimed that the owner was someone of consequence. The bishop greeted us politely but with some caution. His secretary had advised us that His Excellency had a busy schedule, so Will launched without preliminaries into the reason for our visit. He explained the interest of Hannigan Industries in possible investment in the Amparo district. The bishop nodded approval and asked a couple of questions. Will then explained what had happened to Catherine and Richard and our desire to find out the circumstances of their death.

After a minute the bishop's expression darkened and he broke in. "And you find that our police and justice system are lacking?" Will was a bit taken aback by the challenging tone, and after a pause explained that Catherine's father had indeed been bothered by the lack of information. Again the bishop interrupted. "And you intend to bring some North American justice to Talcayan?" At this point Will paused for a moment and then stood up. "Excuse me, Your Excellency. I know your time is valuable. We are happy to have had this opportunity to inform you of our interest in coming to Talcayan. There is really no reason for us to detain you further." I stood up, we both bowed to Bishop Kendel and started towards the door.

"Wait. I beg you, be seated." The bishop's voice was less challenging but still wary. "What exactly do you want from me?"

We turned back but remained standing, and Will explained that our hope was that His Excellency would know of someone who lived near the village of Cantal, where the bodies were found, who would provide information or tell us where such information might be found.

What would we do with the information? If we found out anything that incriminated anyone, or anything that justified further investigation, we would turn it over to the police or to whatever authority would be able to pursue the case. Here the bishop shook his head. "This country, I am sorry to say, is in near chaos. You may not find anyone willing to investigate further. Then what will you do?"

"Then," said Will, "we will probably ask the Canadian government to make representations to the Talcayan authorities; and perhaps ask the Canadian foreign service to approach United Nations offices to see if anything can be done."

The bishop looked skeptical. "And you can do this? The Canadian government will do what you ask?"

"It won't listen to us. It may listen to Hugh Hannigan, the father of the murdered woman. He is a person of some importance in Canada and has contacts in the government."

The bishop paused for a moment and then explained that he knew no one who lived in Cantal. His nephew, Antonio Rossi, lived in the city of Valdez a few miles from Cantal. "He's a good man. He might be able to help you. He works with the newspaper there. If you wish I will call him and tell him you will see him soon."

Will said that this would be a great help to us. We thanked His Excellency, he wished us Godspeed and we were back on the street fifteen minutes after we had left it.

"I may have seemed hasty in there," Will said. "But if you let them walk all over you they lose respect for you and they won't take you seriously." Will had spent eight years attached to consulates and embassies in that part of the world. I had been there three days. I did not argue.

CHAPTER FIVE

We drove east and after about an hour on a gravel road we passed through the village of Cantal. Somewhere around here Catherine had been murdered, maybe down in that little ravine or over there by that clump of trees. The road wound down into the valley of the San Isidro River, the northern boundary of Talcayan, on the south bank of which lay the city of Valdez. By noon we were lunching in a sidewalk café across the street from the offices of the *Valdez Semana,* the local newspaper. We strolled around the square for a few minutes to give the newspaper personnel time to digest their noon meal. The woman at the front desk directed us to an office with the nameplate: Antonio Rossi, Assistant Editor.

The rugged build and face of the young man who greeted us suggested a welterweight boxer or a roustabout on an oil rig, an impression offset by his styled hair, crisp shirt and silk tie. He greeted us genially and explained that his uncle had called to tell him about our intended visit. Had we dined? Would we like coffee?

I asked him in careful Spanish about the fact that his name was Italian. He replied that his mother, the sister of Bishop Kendel, was half Calchaqui but there must have been a German or Austrian among her ancestors to account for her maiden name. Antonio's father had been a mixture of Spanish and Italian. In other words, he was a typical

- 38 -

citizen of Talcayan. You can find textbooks that tell you, he explained, that the Calchaqui are extinct. Probably the experts didn't see any more bands roaming around the country so they decided the people didn't exist any more. But no one told the Calchaqui women, so they kept on having babies. Except for His Excellency, Aldomar and several individuals attending Mass the previous Sunday, we hadn't seen anyone with strong Native American features. Antonio explained that there had never been a large population of aboriginals in this part of the continent. The present indigenous population mostly avoids the towns and cities, preferring to work on the ranches or cultivate the small lots along the rivers.

Getting down to business, we explained the two purposes of our visit. Antonio explained that the issue of the deaths of Catherine and Richard was very sensitive. He hoped we would not be offended, but he would need to check our story. He left and returned in a minute with a gray-haired woman who spoke English. Without information from us other than the names "Hugh Hannigan", "Hannigan Industries" and "Edmonton, Canada" she succeeded in getting Hugh on the phone after several minutes. She first had me tell Hugh what was going on, and then she asked him to verify the reasons we had given for visiting the country.

Antonio took the answers as sufficient proof that we were who we claimed to be, and he began to explain the local situation. The mayor of Valdez was a man named Miguel Flores. He controlled the city and attempted to control the surrounding countryside. The local police were completely under his thumb. His police chief was Capitan Langer. Flores and Langer were not fond of Antonio, because he had from time to time criticized them in print. Antonio had gathered incriminating information about the two and stored it where the police would probably not find it. He explained that we would not be meeting with his editor, Señor Gallego. The editor was a good man, but to survive he had to steer clear of trouble with Mayor Flores. Gallego knew that Antonio had incriminating information about the mayor and his police chief, but he neither looked at it nor asked about it. He would not want to be informed of our visit. If events took a bad turn he would need be able to swear that he had not been aware that there were two men from North America in Valdez inquiring about a police matter.

Antonio didn't know the police officer at Cantal but presumed that whoever he was he would be under the influence of Flores and Langer. If we were thinking of questioning that official we should know that word of it would probably get back quickly to Langer. Antonio thought it strange that he had not heard of the violent deaths of two tourists six weeks earlier. Murder in the commission of a robbery was rare in Talcayan. If there had been a cover-up, the question was why. It could be that the officer in Cantal was too lazy to investigate properly and he wanted the news of the murders suppressed. Possibly the officer was protecting the murderer; but he would find it hard to arrange for the bodies to be sent out of the country without word leaking out, unless he had the cooperation of someone higher up.

We wanted to find out whether the local police had done any investigating and whether there had been an examination of the bodies to determine the precise cause of death. If there had been a report, it should be at the office in Cantal. The problem would be to get hold of it.

We stood up to leave and thanked Antonio for his help and he replied that he shared our desire to get to the bottom of the mystery. When we asked about a decent but moderately priced hotel he shook his head. If we registered at a hotel we would have to surrender our passports. Before morning Capitan Langer would know that there were two Canadians in town. If he were implicated in a cover-up of the murders, the presence of Canadians would make him suspicious, especially because just a few days earlier Colonel McGrath had questioned him about the murders. Antonio suggested that we stay at his house. He and his wife lived alone in the home he had inherited from his father and there was plenty of room. We could also take our meals with him and his wife. We accepted the rooms but declined to put his wife to the trouble of feeding us.

Antonio's residence was a colorfully painted, two-story, frame building almost hidden behind a row of ombú trees. Antonio's wife looked and acted like someone who paid considerable attention to her appearance, but she was pleasant and apparently amenable to two strangers staying in their home for a day or two. Antonio had explained that he would tell her only that we were representatives of a Canadian mining concern looking for information about the political situation in Talcayan with a view to possible investment. If Flores and company learned of our presence and objected to it, Señora Rossi could honestly say that the only thing she knew about the two men to whom she had given shelter was that they were possible benefactors of the economy of Talcayan.

Rossi disappeared and returned shortly with his file on Flores and Langer in a cardboard box, which he handled it as though it were an explosive. He explained that his wife knew nothing about it and must, for her own good, learn nothing about it. Apparently Antonio was sufficiently anxious to find allies in his crusade against Flores that he was willing to trust a couple of strangers with information that, in the wrong hands, could seal his fate.

The material in the files was indeed explosive. Antonio didn't have documentary proof of the more serious crimes but his information, placed in the hands of a competent investigator, could lead to convictions for bribery, extortion, misuse of police power and possibly for murder. When we went out for our evening meal we took the file with us. The afternoon's reading had made me sufficiently conscious of the threatening milieu of Valdez that before getting in the car I took one of the Berettas from the trunk and put it in a shoulder holster.

After the evening meal Will dropped me off at the Rossi residence and returned to Antonio's office where the latter would show him a few newspaper files that might be of interest. I wanted to work off the rust that must have accumulated in my muscles during the last few days of inactivity, so I jogged along a circuitous route that took me finally to the newspaper offices, where Will and Antonio were winding up their work and Will had made his routine call to Hugh Hannigan to report our progress or lack thereof.

Unless we were to drop the investigation entirely we needed to visit the police officer in Cantal. The next morning we made the short drive to that village, which consisted mainly of frame buildings on either side of a dusty road with two or three short streets branching off to either side. The scattered houses were dusty, as were the automobiles parked in front of the houses. In the small police station the dust had blown in under the door and gathered on the unpainted wooden floor.

The sole occupant of the office, middle-aged, bald and paunchy, wore a wrinkled and not overly clean uniform of blue trousers and short-sleeved, blue shirt with a holster and gun on his hip. Will, adopting the demeanor of an old acquaintance dropping by for a chat, sauntered in and plopped down uninvited in the only unoccupied chair. I took up my position near the door. To complete the picture we should have been wearing black hats and I should have been cleaning my fingernails with a six-inch switch blade. The sign on the desk indicated that we were speaking to Officer Tomas Costa.

Will identified himself as the person with whom Officer Costa had spoken recently. We were agents of a mining company in Talcayan to check out reports of mineral deposits and had been instructed while in the area to visit the village where the boss's daughter and her husband had been killed more than six weeks earlier. We had read the brief letter that Officer Costa had sent to the father of the murdered woman and would like to know more of the details, and in fact to see the police report concerning their deaths.

Office Costa was clearly uncomfortable. He opted for an aggressive line and explained that police reports were confidential. Will then quoted the provisions of the protocol which had been brought to Officer Costa's attention in their earlier telephone conversation. "Are you saying" Will asked him, "that you have decided to refuse us access to this report even though required to do so by an agreement to which the government of your country is a party?"

Officer Costa stated that he was indeed refusing to show us the report. Will then asked him how it had happened that no news of the murders had been allowed into the local newspaper. Costa replied that newspapers have no right to all the information the police possessed. At this point Will dropped the casual manner and shifted in his chair to face Costa squarely. The way that this had been handled, he stated, suggested that there had been a cover-up. International law was clear that when tourists who are legally in a country are harmed, the authorities of that country must try to discover the facts of the case without delay. "Have you, Señor Costa, decided to deny to these families their legal rights?"

Costa sneered that he was not concerned about some agreement someone had made years ago. We would find that what applied here was the law of Talcayan. Will replied that the two of us only wanted to keep him from getting into trouble. But our boss was a powerful man, and he was very disturbed that his daughter and her husband were murdered while visiting this country. Our only business was to bring back information; but if we told our boss that authorities in Cantal refused to cooperate he would conclude that they were guilty. This time Señor Costa had to deal only with peaceful businessmen. Later he might have to deal with international authorities and foreign police officers. If Will had added that these foreigners were men of action and did not negotiate I'm not sure I could have kept a straight face.

Officer Costa was rattled. There was nothing he could do, he explained. The whole affair was outside of his jurisdiction. Will perked up. How was it outside of his jurisdiction? Costa blurted out that he had not even seen the bodies. He had merely filed the report. Who had told him to file the report? Here Costa looked down at his desk. Did the murders take place in the vicinity of Cantal? Costa shook his head. Then they must have taken place in the jurisdiction of Valdez. Only the officials in Valdez could have applied pressure on him to file the report. Costa said nothing. Was it Capitan Langer? Another shake of the head. Was it Señor Flores? Still another shake of the head. So it was some other police official in Valdez?

Costa burst out, "You can threaten me all you want with what someone thousands of kilometers away might do. I have to worry about people who are closer to home." Will assured him that we would do our best to make sure that he was not blamed for any information he gave us. "You are wasting your time here," Costa growled. "I have no more information for you."

In case Costa might report to Langer or Flores that two nosy Canadians were heading towards Valdez, we left Cantal in the opposite direction, circled and eventually got back on the road to Valdez without again passing by the police station. It would have been wiser to have packed our bags and taken them with us, but it was only gradually sinking in that at the moment there was nothing further we could do in this part of the country.

It looked like the murder had occurred within the jurisdiction of the Valdez police and they had decided that they might avoid being held accountable for an investigation if they could get Officer Costa to file the report. In that case, to get further information we would have to deal with the objectionable characters running Valdez. This was the kind of dangerous venture we had assured the folks in Edmonton we would avoid. By making our presence known to Officer Costa we were as much as revealing it to Captain Langer. They would not know, however, that we were staying in Valdez. Once out of that area we could forget about Señor Flores and his minions, make our way back to Amparo, help Dieter to wind up affairs there, return the Land Rover and the Toyota to the rental agency in Mendoza and fly home.

CHAPTER SIX

We had miscalculated.

Back at the Rossi residence no one answered the door bell. We used the key Antonio had lent to us and went up to our rooms. It took me about three minutes to throw my stuff into a bag. When I went to Will's room he had all of his clothes laid out on the bed and was folding them carefully. I left to pick up some edibles to munch on the way. When I returned fifteen minutes later there was a police car in front of the Rossi residence.

We had not expected any action from Langer, but it was hard to give a benign interpretation to the presence of the police. I had a few seconds of acute indecision before the front door opened and an officer stepped out, followed by Will in handcuffs with another officer behind him, and they got into the car. I couldn't tell whether any of them noticed me in the Toyota a half block away.

Nothing better occurred to me than to follow them. Maybe by the time we got to the police station I would have figured out what to do; but we didn't go to the station. The squad car turned on to the central street of Valdez and continued out of town and I followed several hundred yards behind. A couple of miles outside of town they turned off on a side road that wound upwards through a wooded area. I followed them, shortening the distance between us to make sure they saw me. After

- 45 -

about a mile over the bumpy trail apparently the officers decided to do something about me. They stopped. I stopped about one hundred fifty yards behind them. They began to back towards me. I backed up enough to keep the same distance between us. They stopped. I stopped.

I was idly imagining this being repeated until we had backed into Valdez, but then the passenger door of the police car opened and an officer started to walk towards me, pistol in hand. I backed up a few yards to give me some extra time, sprang the trunk, pulled the rifle out of the trunk, checked that it was loaded, stood behind the car door, aimed the rifle at the approaching policeman and called on him to stop. He was tall, perhaps in his late thirties, his dark hair cut rather short and with a white streak running roughly along where his hair was parted on the left side. Armed with a pistol and facing a rifle, he was not in a strong bargaining position. He stopped.

Within seconds the back door of the police car on the driver's side opened and Will got out followed by the driver. Since the latter was much shorter than Will and prudently stayed behind him, there was almost nothing of the driver visible. He and Will then began to walk towards me. Again I called on him to stop. He stopped and told me to throw down the rifle or he would shoot my friend. With Will's help I explained that I had no reason to throw down my rifle. If I did so, they would kill both of us. This left them with two choices. They could let Will go, in which case no one got hurt; or they could shoot Will, in which case I would shoot both of them.

The driver apparently thought there was another choice, because Will and he began to approach again. I trained the rifle at Will's right shoulder and waited. After six or seven steps Will stumbled, falling away to his left. The moment I saw the driver's right shoulder I fired. Police manuals may say that to stop an assailant you aim at his vital parts, but in this situation a shoulder appeared a tenth of a second before the torso, and that tenth of a second could be important.

I knew from the way the officer spun that I had hit him in the spot at which I had aimed. I trained the rifle on the other officer and he gave up without an argument. In a minute we had freed Will from the handcuffs, appropriated the officer's guns and located a first-aid kit in the police car. There was bleeding from front and back of my

THE BLOOD-DIMMED TIDE IS LOOSED

victim's shoulder where the bullet had gone clean through, but from the amount of blood my guess was that he was not in immediate danger. Will applied as good a pressure bandage as he could produce with the materials at hand. The other officer called the hospital in Valdez to have them prepare for an emergency arrival, and then I disabled their radio. Their documents indicated that the tall man who had first emerged from the car was Officer Julio Lara, the shorter one was Officer Pablo Cruz, both of the Valdez Police Department.

They drove ahead and we followed. A police car leading the Toyota at high speeds would raise less alarm than if the order were reversed. As we sped back towards the city Will explained that a few minutes after I left to pick up the snacks the front door bell had begun to ring insistently. Supposing that it was some sort of emergency, Will had gone to the door to inform the visitors that neither of the Rossis was at home. The two uniformed officers at the door pushed their way into the house without asking permission. Making no pretence of following recognizable police procedure, they instructed Will to put his hands behind his back and cuffed him. They debated whether to wait around for my return but Will convinced them that I had driven to Avila to visit a banker and might not be back until the following day. Will had not noticed me as they left the house and was not aware that I was in the picture until his captors spotted the Toyota following them after they pulled off the highway on to the side road.

Will had protested to the two that he was acting for a Canadian mining concern investigating investment opportunities in Talcayan, that they must have mistaken him for someone else if they thought that he was of interest to the police. They made no attempt to argue. They knew our names and they knew that we were Canadians. The closest they came to explaining why they were apprehending him was the remark that he would find out very soon that the local police could take care of their own business.

Officer Costa had presumably told the Valdez police that two foreigners had been inquiring about the Tipping murders. If elements within the Valdez police force were implicated in the murders or a cover-up they would certainly be concerned; but how had they known where we were staying? Either Rossi's office or his home may have

- 47 -

been bugged, or someone at the newspaper offices may have seen us when we were there and tipped off the police. Maybe Señora Rossi had talked to someone about the two Canadians staying at her place.

When we reached the city limits we left the trail of the police car and drove to the Rossi residence to pick up our luggage. There was no sign of activity as we approached. With pistol in hand and as quietly as possible I opened the front door and stole upstairs. The house was silent. Both of our bags were packed. I left the key on a table in my room, and with one bag under an arm I was able to carry both bags down the stairs and out to the car while keeping the gun in my free hand.

We had just pulled away from the curb and were discussing the best route to take out of the city when Will interjected: "We had better do something about Antonio. If they know we were staying at his place and they're convinced that we've been nosing around, then he's probably in trouble."

In case his telephone might be bugged we drove to the newspaper offices. Valdez is not a large city, and in several minutes we were at the *Valdez Semana* building. No police vehicles were visible. Will hurried into the building while I fidgeted and tried to imagine what I would do if the police arrived. No ingenious strategy sprang to mind.

Will returned after a few minutes shaking his head and remarked that Señor Rossi seemed to be playing a dangerous game. When Will had walked in on him, Antonio had put a finger to his lips, unscrewed the cover of his telephone, carefully removed a listening device with tweezers and put it in a small box which he put in a drawer. He explained that a couple of months ago he found the bug in his office telephone. He leaves it there for ordinary calls, but when he wants privacy he takes it out. He thinks it can pick up conversation in the office as well as on the phone. Sometimes, like the day before when we first spoke to him, he leaves the listening device in a drawer for the better part of a day while he takes care of sensitive business.

Rossi had explained that Flores and Langer might suspect him of being in cahoots with us, but he claimed that he was safe for the time being. If Antonio was to be believed, his father had known a number of shady characters and in fact on different occasions had acted as their lawyer in trials in Argentina. Antonio claimed that he himself had never had any business ties with any of these people, but he knew them. When he began to get threats from Langer, which presumably originated with Flores, he went to one of his father's old associates named Armando Longo and asked him to intervene. Longo agreed to inform Flores that Antonio Rossi was off limits as far as the Valdez police were concerned, and if Flores had evidence that Rossi was placing the mayor in danger he was to bring that evidence to Longo, who would decide whether further action was justified.

Rossi was convinced that he was safe as long as Langer or Flores lacked proof that he was acting in a hostile way towards them. If called upon to explain our presence in his home or office Antonio would simply tell the truth, that we were agents for a mining company learning about the business climate of the country prior to investing. His enemies couldn't prove that he was omitting any essential facts.

Antonio had asked Will to call him after a few minutes, by which time the bug would be back in his telephone. Will was to tell Antonio that something urgent had come up and Will and I had to leave suddenly, and we couldn't thank him enough for his hospitality and his assessment of the business climate in Talcayan. It would help Hannigan Industries considerably in deciding about developing the mineral resources south of the Rio del Rey.

While we located a pay telephone Will and I discussed alternative ways to get out of town quickly. On the other side of the river was Argentina. All we had to do was cross a bridge, but that bridge would probably be guarded by Langer's minions; and in any case the Argentine authorities might not look kindly on a couple of foreigners fleeing the police. So after Will had put in the call to Antonio we took the road that we knew, back through Cantal towards Avila.

We traveled more or less in silence until we began to feel that we were beyond the immediate reach of Señor Flores. Eventually Will relaxed, leaned back and remarked: "We really can't complain about lack of excitement, can we? By the way, I can now vouch not only for your marksmanship but also for your reflexes. There must have been a whole millisecond between when I started to stumble and when that bullet shot by. The poor bugger never had a chance."

- 49 -

"Well, I had an advantage. I was ready for what happened. He was not."

"Well now, how could you be ready if I myself didn't know what I was going to do until the last second? I was just praying for a miracle—that those two would come to their senses, and then I noticed that you were keeping the rifle trained on my right shoulder."

"You play bridge, don't you?" I asked. "Suppose you have a hand that makes only if the player on your right has three hearts to the king. That's the way you play it. There's no point in dithering. Right now I can think about the possibility that my aim isn't as sharp as it used to be, or that the sights of the rifle might have gotten jolted out of line, or that you wouldn't drop off to your left. Back there all I thought about was that I was going to put that bullet exactly in the man's shoulder and I was going to do it the instant you moved enough to give me a clear shot."

"You don't get nervous?"

"Yeah, if I don't know what to do I get nervous. If there are three possibilities and I wonder whether I have chosen the wrong one, I'll be nervous. When I know what I have to do I usually stay calm."

Will could tell the most improbable story without losing his imposing manner, but after a pause he began to chuckle, sounding enough like Sydney Greenstreet in *The Maltese Falcon* that I half expected him to add: "By Gad sir, you are a character." We drove in silence for a while and then Will continued: "Too bad the guy had to get to the hospital. I would have liked to sweat the two of them. We aren't even sure who sent them. They could be acting on their own but it's not likely. We know that Langer is somehow in on the cover-up in Cantal."

As far as we knew, Flores or Langer would not have enough confederates outside of the Valdez area to track us down once we left the city. On the other hand, for the immediate future the mayor seemed to be untouchable. If Dieter was finished with his work we could leave right away. Besides Bishop Kendel, a second person had been suggested to us as a source of information—Rodrigo Laval, mayor of the town of Marino. We would have a word with Señor Laval on our way back to Amparo.

Before reaching Avila we turned south on an alternate route that would take us through Marino. We found a shady spot at the side of the road, put together some sandwiches from the bag of groceries I had bought that morning, washed them down with lemonade, relaxed and enjoyed the scenery in companionable silence. Flores and his ilk were not going to spoil our last day or two before returning to late fall in Edmonton.

Back on the road Will waved towards the passing landscape. "It's nice country. For centuries people have lived here. No one got rich, but at least for about three centuries after the Europeans came no one starved. I'm sure you had the usual mixture of good and bad people, but they didn't have to worry about private armies and getting pushed around by bullies. Then one day a smart guy decides that he's going to be the liberator of his people and this is what you get."

He added after a minute, "Do you think that all this evil is the result of accident? Maybe the old timers were on to something when they talked about Satan."

I had no opinion on that topic, so we went on to swapping army stories, and I thought Will might enjoy hearing about Diz.

When I first met Diz I supposed that he had picked up the name because he was a bit flaky, but I found out that his last name was Dean, so probably the nickname was in honor of the great St. Louis Cardinal right hander. Diz used to read books, and not just novels but heavy stuff: history and economics and philosophy. The guys in camp liked him well enough but they didn't spend too much time with him, probably afraid that some of that learning might rub off on them.

Diz mistook my politeness for interest, so I found myself listening to him expound his ideas at some length. He had begun university on a scholarship. It was the only way he could afford it because his mother was a single parent supporting three kids. He got really interested in some university subjects, not so interested in others. His second year English professor was a man of great fluency and used expressions like "soi-disant", "revanchist" and "weltanschauung". Dr. Mills would say things like "If I dare say so, Mark Twain was a forerunner of contemporaries like Ginsberg . . ." At this point the professor would look around at the students, from whose mien he could discern that he might indeed dare, and in fact he could be several degrees more daring without provoking any alarming reaction. Professor Mills got on Diz's wrong side early on by stating that a certain poem on the curriculum "scarcely rises to the level of doggerel verse that one finds in *The Cremation of Sam McGee.*" It was precisely this work of Robert Service that had originally convinced Diz that poetry need not be a complete waste of time.

So he and several of his buddies decided that Dr. Mills was the instantiation of a pain in the butt. They expressed their attitude by sprinkling their written assignments with spurious quotes. Ponderous witticisms with an archaic sound might be ascribed to Samuel Johnson, for example; jocose remarks of more modern tone would be distributed among the likes of O. Henry, Will Rogers and Mort Sahl. Diz claimed that he became quite expert at inventing peevish quotations to be ascribed to H.L. Mencken, and one of his friends could come up with paradoxes as Chestertonian as anything in G.K.C.'s *Orthodoxy* or the Father Brown stories. They found that working together inspired them to greater creativity in the production of term papers; so a few days before an assignment was due and they had laid out the general lines of their papers, Diz and three or four of his pals would lay in a supply of Molsen's Golden Ale or some equivalent spur to creativity and work into the night filling their essays with spurious quotations.

Diz attributed his academic demise to sheer bad luck. "What kind of chuckle-headed teaching assistant" he complained, "wastes a beautiful Sunday afternoon in the library establishing that the book *The Diaries of Samuel Pepys*, annotated with Introduction by D.L. Fish-Harlingen, M.A. (Oxon.), London, Rutledge and Keegan Paul, 1937, does not exist?" Not only did Diz get a zero for the major paper in which he had included the offending reference, but the odium occasioned by his creativity led to a mediocre grade in a course which he would normally have aced. This, combined with a low grade in physics, which Diz claimed he merited fair and square through lack of either study or aptitude, dropped his average below the level required to keep his scholarship.

So Diz joined the army as the easiest way to escape his mother's vocal disapproval of his wasted opportunities. It worked out all right, he claimed. He was able to send back some money each month to help with the rent and clothes for his siblings, and he himself, once basic training was over, had plenty of time to read whatever he wanted.

CHAPTER SEVEN

The sun was low on the horizon as we drove into Marino. It was about the size of Valdez, but where the latter city gave the appearance of a modern, bustling place that would like to attract business and industry, Marino seemed to be happy, or at least complacent, about being old, provincial and picturesque. It was arranged, like Amparo, around a square that contained the only architectural pretensions in the city, the rest consisting mainly of cottages on lots averaging perhaps a half-acre in size, most of them with small gardens. We dropped by the city hall, got an appointment with the mayor for the next morning and then booked into a slightly shabby hotel.

After showering off the dust of the trip the colonel found a pay phone and sent a message to Amparo for Dieter explaining what had happened to us. We had claimed to be investigating possible minerals resources, and if by chance Flores or someone else in Valdez heard about two others from Canada doing the same thing, then Dieter and Bradley might come under suspicion and should therefore not delay their departure.

The next morning we dropped by the city hall. Mayor Laval, stocky, middle aged, looked like Vince Lombardi in his glory days as coach of the Green Bay Packers. He greeted us pleasantly, if a little quizzically.

- 53 -

When we had explained our purpose his eyes opened wide. "Ah, I remember now. The Maryknoll priest sent you." He pressed a button on his desk and asked his secretary to see if Dolores was busy. If she was not, would she have a few minutes to attend a meeting in his office?

We had scarcely sat down when there was a knock at the door and a young woman strode in. Mayor Laval said, "This is my daughter Dolores. I have always thought that she should have been an opera singer, but she decided that being a lawyer is a surer way of making a living. I have two assistants. Arturo, an old friend of mine, takes care of routine matters. I call on Dolores when some problem requires special attention. Me, I mainly sit back and take the credit when something good happens."

Dolores smiled briefly and nodded in acknowledgement of our presence.

During my six month apprenticeship with the chief of security for Falconbridge Mines I spent a good deal of time working with one of his assistants named Maurice Beauchamp, who had remarkable powers of observation. We would walk into a restaurant, he would spend a minute looking over the crowd, then sit down at a table facing the wall. I would ask him: "The middle-aged woman in the red coat—who is sitting opposite to her?" He would then describe the other person in such detail as to delight any police officer questioning a witness. The first time he did it I remarked that this ability was astonishing, quite beyond my comprehension. He replied that this was because I had lazy eyes. I looked and didn't see, and what little I saw I forgot; but he insisted that I could learn to observe and to remember what I had observed. What good is a safety officer who inspects a construction sight, for example, and doesn't notice the things he should or forgets what he has seen?

To sharpen my skills we would in our spare time play a game he called "Sherlock". We would walk into a horticultural show, for example, and Maurice would give me two minutes to identify an exhibitor, an avid student of horticulture, an aesthete who was there just to look at nice things, and someone who was dragged there by a spouse. I learned fairly quickly to look for tell-tale signs that would identify a plausible candidate for each category. What was more difficult was remembering the details to be recited back to Maurice twenty minutes later in the coffee shop. So he taught me to invent stories or spurious identities to help me remember. A gentleman with a German accent would become a former member of the Baader-Meinhof gang, his pale complexion proving that he had spent the last twenty years in prison, his black briefcase no doubt containing the plans to the uranium mine in Chalk River that he was planning to blow up.

Since leaving the mentorship of Monsieur Beauchamp I had not kept up the practice, but for some reason it came to mind when Señorita Laval had taken a chair opposite me and fastened her eyes on something that caught her interest outside the window to my left. I could imagine Maurice's quick take on the señorita. "High cheek bones; with a little eye liner she'd look exotic enough to inhabit a Hollywood version of a harem. Not gorgeous enough to beat out Yvonne De Carlo as the sultan's favorite, but a good candidate for the jealous number two. A little miffed right now, I'd guess. Probably busy and doesn't like being interrupted. No make up, but she knows how a professional woman is supposed to dress. Didn't buy that pant suit in Marino. Not a hundred percent Caucasian. Walked in like she owned the place, probably because she has the confidence of Daddy. She'll be outspoken. The hair band—either she's having a bad hair day or it's the only way she can manage that unruly black mane. Hasn't spent a lot of time making herself attractive. Possibly a feminist who on principle refuses to please men. Doesn't walk like someone who spends a lot of time in high heels and gowns. Not a socialite then. The lean look of an athlete—maybe a tennis player or swimmer to judge from her shoulders. Or maybe she does hard physical work. If she put herself in the hands of a beautician he'd thin those eyebrows. She looks directly at you like she's measuring you. Probably a lawyer's trick to impress clients and overawe witnesses."

The point of the exercise for Maurice was not to draw reliable conclusions but simply to notice things and remember them.

Meanwhile, Mayor Laval was asking us about ourselves. He then explained that his father, living in France in 1940 and married to a Jewess, had fled with her to Argentina just before the Nazi occupation. In Argentina they had found enough sympathy for the Nazis to make them uncomfortable and had proceeded westward to Marino. They originally intended to return to France but they never did. Rodrigo was born in Talcayan. "I am half Jewish," he said, "and half French from Brittany, which may mean that I have more Celtic than Frankish blood in my veins."

Rodrigo's parents had believed in education and sent their son to L'École Polytechnique in Paris, where he studied engineering. He returned to Marino, married a local girl, worked for the city and eventually became mayor. His two sons had emigrated to Argentina to find better jobs. Dolores and his two younger daughters lived at home.

Dolores' self-introduction was brief. After she had practiced law for several years with a firm in Buenos Aires she had concluded that she would be happier working for her father than defending some of the clients who were served by the firm.

The preliminaries attended to, Señor Laval explained that the Maryknoll priest had given him a general idea of our concerns, but we had better explain it to him all over again. Will assumed his military briefing mode and gave a succinct account of what had brought us to Talcayan and what we had encountered in Amparo, Avila, Valdez and Cantal. Before leaving the country we were making this last stop to gather information about the political situation and business climate that would influence Hannigan Industries' decision regarding the mineral resources south of El Rio del Rey. We would also be interested in learning anything that might help us to uncover the truth about the deaths of Catherine and Richard Tipping, but we realized it might not be possible to solve that mystery.

At this point Señorita Laval broke in. Would the mines be safe? Quite often one hears about disasters. Will indicated that I was the person in charge of safety. With Will translating where needed, I assured her that Hannigan Industries had an excellent safety record, and there had not been a loss of life or serious injury in any of the mines in the years during which I had my present job, and the safety record of the company had been excellent in the years before that.

Señorita Laval pressed on. What is the likelihood that Hannigan Industries would establish a mine in Talcayan? I replied that we had only very incomplete knowledge at this time. We probably knew enough to justify bringing in a team to explore and drill test holes to find out what kind of ore was present. Dolores asked whether I could say, from what I knew, whether there was a realistic chance of Hannigan establishing a mine, or was the talk of mining quite secondary to our concern with the crime that had been committed. Will broke in and replied that Hannigan Industries was already interested in possibilities in Talcayan before the murders, but the fact that we came looking for information about the murder meant that the company began investigations earlier than would otherwise have been the case. "However," and here Will paused for a moment, "Hannigan Industries never opens a mine in a place where it is not welcome."

Señor Laval assured us that we were indeed welcome, and with the subtlest of hand gestures signaled his daughter to back off. "So you want information about the political situation?" Being assured again that such was the case, he pulled out a pipe and busied himself with filling it while he organized his thoughts. Then he looked out the window for a few seconds before beginning.

"I understand you already know about Señor Gracida, our president?" Will nodded, yes.

"Gracida is not a bad man; but he is in a weak position. He has come under the thumb of others. His weakness has led to even more lawlessness than usual. Even some of the ruffians who run our cities are getting concerned. His days in power are numbered.

"To understand our situation, you have to start with Señor Rendon. He has been the mayor of San Isidro for eight years. San Isidro, you realize, is our biggest city, the capital city, perhaps 125,000 people. Rendon is clever and he is ruthless. Like most of the mayors of cities, he is the main authority for much of the adjacent countryside. Like several of the mayors he has a police force that operates like his private army, and he has enriched himself at the expense of the taxpayers and of foreign aid from the United Nations and other granting agencies. However, he has considerable support within San Isidro. The people will tolerate a criminal as mayor if he steals only a moderate amount and keeps other criminals from operating openly in his territory. I suppose you can look at the money he grabs for himself as the price the city pays for security."

Will asked how someone like Señor Rendon becomes the mayor. Are there elections? Mayor Laval paused again before answering.

"Every four years in each city we have an election for city council. The newly elected council then elects a mayor, who may or may not be a member of the council. They usually recognize the wisdom of choosing the person who has the most armed followers. . . . You know, in much of Europe during the Middle Ages a lord or a count would live in a castle and control the surrounding countryside. What he did for his subjects was protect them from marauders. In exchange, his subjects paid a tax or worked so many days a year in his fields. If you were lucky your protector would be fair. If he became weak then someone stronger would come along, lay siege to the castle and if successful, take control of the countryside. When our structures break down we settle for living under one strong tyrant rather than be the victims of every brigand who happens to pass by."

"If Rendon is so powerful," Will asked, "Why doesn't he become president himself?"

The mayor frowned. "The other mayors are afraid of Rendon. If he ever became president he would want to consolidate his power. He could do that by bringing charges against any mayor who tried to oppose him, and he would probably get convictions. So the other mayors don't want Señor Rendon to become president. However, no one is likely to assume that office if he objects. He holds sway in San Isidro, but he cannot take on the rest of the country. You see, we have our own version of the balance of powers.

"As for the national government, we elect a senate every four years. The newly elected senate then elects a president. It can be complicated. Suppose, for the sake of simplicity, that our mayors are in a good mood and none of them actually threatens physical harm to the senators. The latter agree that the president must be someone who can get along with the mayors. If you get one of those stubborn presidents who will not listen, then you are in for a lot of trouble. So the senators consult before they vote, and the person they vote for usually has the support of the mayors of San Isidro and of at least a couple of other cities. Preferably too the new president is willing to make enough concessions that most of the people with private armies will not be motivated to oppose him militarily."

Señor Laval paused for further questions or comments, and when none were forthcoming he continued. "Yes, now. That's Rendon. The two most important cities after San Isidro are Avila and Magdalena. Combined they have about 145,000 citizens, more than San Isidro. Carlos Guzman has been the mayor of Magdalena for over fifteen years. His father was mayor before him. There is a kind of law, I think. The more corrupt the mayor, the more violent he has to be to stay in power. Guzman had been quite violent. Augusto Calderon in Avila was elected three years ago. Bishop Kendel and a few others tried to change things, and Calderon came to power promising to bring honesty and efficiency to the administration and to prosecute criminals without fear or favor. As far as I can see, he has not done so."

"Why?" Will asked. "Why has he not done so?"

"I don't know the situation in Avila very well," the mayor replied. "Dolores, you know more about it."

Señorita Laval seemed to have been day-dreaming, and it took her a few seconds to collect her thoughts. "Yes? You're asking about Señor Calderon? He wants to be a hero. Three years ago the way to be a hero was to lead the movement started by Bishop Kendel to bring about reform. Calderon does not have his own army. Once in power he found that he had to compromise, to buy the cooperation of people with power—the chief of police, the factory owners, those who had political ambitions of their own. Pretty soon he found out that whatever power he had at the beginning had been bartered away. He has not been cruel. Maybe he hasn't had the power to be cruel; but he seems to be unable to deliver on the promises he made three years ago."

The mayor took up the narrative. "Next, there is Valdez. Miguel Flores is simply a criminal who has seized control of a city. Rendon and Guzman at least try to do something good for their citizens, even though they cheat them. Flores is a brute. In a healthy society he would be in jail.

"Then there is Señor Robles. Amparo is only a town, really, but it is the major town south of Rio del Rey. Robles is called the mayor but he is actually elected by all of the property owners in the area and he has authority over everything south of the river. He has been accused of using his influence as mayor to help his friends, but that is the kind of criticism almost any politician is likely to receive from his opponents. Mayor Robles has not enriched himself from his office and he certainly works hard for his people. As far as national affairs go, Señor Robles has one principle. Leave us alone. He is not much interested in what goes on north of El Rio del Rey. I like him but I do not count on him to play a part on the national scene."

"How about Marino, Mayor Laval?" Will asked, "How does it fit into the national scene?"

Laval began tentatively. You had to know the history. About twenty five years ago an especially savage individual named Branco managed to get himself elected mayor of Marino. He stole from the treasury, extorted money from anyone who wanted favors, even got into disputes with other mayors. After about two years some citizens got together to do something about it. Their leader was the owner of one of the largest estancias in the area, Señor Gomez, who rode into town with twenty of his herdsmen carrying rifles. They were joined by a large part of the citizenry of Marino and paraded into this square that you see in front of you. Branco had built a new city hall, really a sort of fort. It's that building you can see across the square—it's a hotel now. He and a number of his followers lived on the second and third stories of that building. Gomez and his men set up a barricade in front of it, being careful to keep something solid between themselves and the building. He set up another barricade to cover the rear entrance and stationed some of his armed men behind the barricades.

Then several wagons drove into the square with food and drinks. A band began to play and they celebrated a fiesta. That night everyone went home except for the men who remained on duty behind the barricades. The next day was Sunday. Both of the churches in the town sent their congregations down to the square to take part in a procession. Again there was food, music and lots of noise well into the afternoon. That night again the armed men took up their positions. The next day was the Feast of All Saints, and that was an excuse for another fiesta. By this time not only was the whole city excited, but people came in from the countryside because they had heard about what was going on. What was happening was that the people were already celebrating their victory over Branco even though not a shot had been fired.

The next day was the Day of All Souls. The bishop came from Avila, and in the morning they celebrated Mass in the square with the largest crowd that had ever assembled in the town. Over a loudspeaker the bishop talked about the need to pray for the souls of all of those who have died during the past year. He then read out a list of those from Marino who had died, and the list contained the names of several whose deaths, it was suspected, had come at the hands of Branco's gang. But instead of stirring up the crowd against the mayor, the bishop thanked God that the forces of evil were being overcome even as he spoke. There is no need for fighting and for guns, he said. If there is anyone who has been living a life of violence and now wishes to live in peace, let him put aside his weapons and join us here in prayer and celebration.

When the Mass was over many of the people stayed and prayed the rosary while they processed around the square. Whether it was because of the prayer or because Branco and friends were running low on food, a white flag appeared at the door of city hall. A delegation wished to find out whether the bishop's word held . . . that anyone who put aside his weapons would be welcomed. Señor Gomez replied that this was so. Señor Branco however and his two lieutenants must surrender themselves and stand trial. After a few minutes about fifteen men came through the front door with their hands raised to show that they were not carrying guns. Mayor Branco and his two lieutenants were not among them. A squad of armed men then entered the building and arrested the three. Branco's gang had been cast out, Laval chuckled, by prayer but with very little fasting.

Before he left, Señor Gomez exacted from the city fathers the commitment that they would not try to exercise control over the countryside. Ever since then, that commitment had been honored. Five years ago the old mayor was ready to retire and some leaders in the city asked Rodrigo Laval to let his name stand for election. The newly elected council chose him as mayor, and he was reelected a year ago.

The final chapter in Laval's history lesson concerned Professor Pablo Javier. He was born in San Isidro but for some years taught political science at a university in Buenos Aires. He had been brought back to Talcayan as an advisor by Gracida in his first fervor for reform. Before long Javier had realized that Gracida would never do what he had promised to do. Javier no longer had a teaching position, so he joined a group of businessmen in Talcayan who had formed a sort of national Chamber of Commerce to coordinate their efforts at economic development. Javier had been the director of this organization for a couple of years and was successful at getting funds from outside agencies to aid economic development, and according to reports all of those funds had been used for the purposes for which they were given. It was the hope of Laval and like-minded people that Professor Javier would become the next president of Talcayan. It was far from a sure thing, however, because he was as likely as Rendon to move against the dishonest mayors. But the doctor had some popular support, and in the confusion and near despair of the times perhaps individuals would be sufficiently alarmed to curb their greed and allow the election of someone who might halt the downward spiral of the country into chaos.

The mayor had one last point. They had been fortunate to get rid of Branco twenty five years ago without bloodshed, but violence has been the curse of Latin America at least since the end of colonial times. Señor Laval stated that he was not a pacifist. He believed that at times it is one's duty to use violence against evil men as a last resort to protect the innocent. "If you can find me a war," he said, "where the generals bring a saint along with them to point out what they can or cannot do, I'll join. But on this continent the fruit of war has been to replace one bad government with another. This process is not going to stop if we continue to try to solve our problems by killing."

These last words were spoken with a seriousness that left us silent for a while. Will gestured to me—did I have any questions? I wondered about the gang from San Martin that had been raiding the Amparo district. Dolores answered this time without waiting for her father's encouragement. Rafael Fraga was a bandit who had established his base in San Martin. He had a gang of perhaps forty followers, enough to allow him to terrorize the district but not so many as to require too wide a sharing of his ill-gotten gains. They preyed on any victims they could find. They extorted money from those who could not defend themselves. They hired themselves out to do people's dirty work for them. They were so brazen that they had imported an army tank and

- 62 -

several other military vehicles, and the citizens of the territory were terrified of them. Thus far Fraga had directed his depredations only towards the area south of El Rio del Rey, and the mayors north of the river were happy to ignore him.

Our meeting over, Dolores Laval accompanied us to our automobile. She made a couple of starts to say something and finally blurted it out in fluent if slightly accented English. "Forgive me for being so aggressive in my questions. It would be most unfortunate if I have said something that discourages your company from providing good jobs for our people. I am sure that Papa will do what he can to help, and if there is anything I can do, I hope you will ask me."

Will assured her that Hannigan did not base decisions on the tone of people's voices. This time Dolores actually smiled, if a little grimly, as we shook hands. As I started the car Will growled. "At least the blasted woman didn't say that she would feel terrible if the jobs were lost, as though it's her feelings we should worry about."

CHAPTER EIGHT

When we arrived in Amparo Señor Robles was waiting for us and he was beside himself. My first thought was that something had happened to Dieter and Bradley. "No, no," Robles replied. "Thank God they got off all right yesterday. It's that damned fool Fraga. He's moved in and he's trying to take over. He's heard about the possibility of mines being opened and he says that whoever develops those mines will have to deal with him. The fool thinks that a foreign investor is going to do business with scum like him."

Fraga and some of his men had arrived at noon the day before, after Dieter and Bradley had departed. Apparently Fraga had been planning for some time to move his headquarters to Amparo. If other brigands could be mayors, he must be as well. Robles had appealed to the three estancia owners in the district, but they all refused to act. Fraga had heavy weapons, including a Leopard I tank. The ranchers would not ask their herdsmen to take up arms against such a force. Besides, they had been paying off the bully for years, and maybe nothing much would change simply because he was moving across the river.

Fraga had returned to San Martin but he had left some of his men in Amparo to prepare suitable accommodations for the leader. For Señor Robles it was not only a challenge to his authority but a blow to

- 64 -

his hopes for economic development of the region. Trying to calm him down, I pointed out that Colonel McGrath had some experience in these matters. We extracted from the mayor the promise to do nothing for a day or two, while Will assessed the situation. At this point Aldomar brightened perceptibly.

When Robles and Aldomar had departed Will remarked that I had been rather free with offering his expertise. I apologized for having spoken quickly, but all that had been offered was a look at the situation. After some thought we were able to come up with several ways in which someone like Fraga could be stopped, but the local people would probably not do it on their own. We had determined to leave as quickly as possible and that was certainly what Hugh Hannigan expected of us; but it was infuriating that an outlaw could come in and act as the *de facto* authority for this part of the country and thereby, incidentally, destroy its economic prospects.

Our ruminations led us back to El Puente Ingles to look at the lay of the land. By the time we got back to Amparo we had tentatively decided on several things. That night I had a long conversation with Uncle Hugh. When I had explained the situation to him his first response was, "What kind of savages are they down there?" Normally this kind of response would have exploded out of him, but then it was spoken with a sort of sad resignation. I replied that probably they had a mix of good and bad in Talcayan much like what you would find anywhere. The problem was that the usual controls over the worst elements in society had broken down.

Hugh listed a few reasons why what we proposed was risky at best, but then shifted gears and remarked that this seemed to be one of those situations in which to withdraw could look like an act of cowardice. That response was not what one might expect from a captain of industry, but Uncle Hugh hadn't gotten to where he was by being cautious. At the age of thirty he had borrowed enough money to purchase the small mining company for which he worked, took the company public and used the funds from the sale of shares to expand the enterprise. A few years later the stock market went through an "adjustment" and the price of the shares dropped. My uncle mortgaged his home, raised as much money as the banks would lend him and bought up all the shares

- 65 -

he could afford. Within a couple of years the stock rebounded, he was able to sell some of his shares at a higher price, pay off his debts and retain majority ownership of a medium-sized and very profitable company. A zealous overseer of the Toronto Stock Exchange, viewing Hugh's sudden rise in fortune, had him investigated for some sort of malfeasance—insider trading or stock manipulation or something like that. The case against him collapsed when a number of former stockholders testified that when the shares had begun to drop in price they had received letters from Hugh assuring them that the company was sound and begging them not to sell.

So thanks to Uncle Hugh's adventurous spirit I had permission to stay in Talcayan for another two weeks and make several purchases that had not been in the original estimates for our trip. The next day Señor Robles announced that the time had finally come to do something about the dangerous section of road as it curved to the west after crossing El Puente Ingles. All of the road-building equipment that the mayor could commandeer began moving and leveling the earth, clearing bushes and in general changing the course of the road to give drivers a better view of on-coming traffic as they made the turn towards Amparo.

The next step was to secure the cooperation of the owners of the three large estancias south of the Rio del Rey. Señor Robles mused that although they had turned down his previous appeal for help, his wife might have more success. This struck the colonel and me as curious, but we were soon to witness the redoubtable señora in action.

Several days after Fraga's challenge to Mayor Robles, the mayor and his wife hosted a dinner for Señor and Señora Sangallo, proprietors of the estancia farthest from Amparo. It was an occasion for Roberto Sangallo to meet Will and myself. He was a middle-aged man of medium height with the easy manner of someone who is not anxious to make a good impression, or perhaps of someone who knows that he makes a good enough impression without going out of his way to do so. His face was tanned as one would expect of a rancher, but for this occasion his clothing would not have been out of place at an embassy reception. His wife was a vivacious brunette who looked too young to have raised five adult children.

Will was introduced as a highly respected former colonel in the Canadian army and a diplomat who had served in Canadian embassies throughout the world, including Buenos Aires and Lima. Will performed with aplomb sufficient for two or three highly respected soldiers and diplomats, listened intently to the ladies, made jokes, asked intelligent questions, laughed appreciatively at the right moments. I began to suspect that a military attaché gets more practice attending soirees than advising on military strategy.

I was introduced as the Director of Security of a major mining concern in Canada, a recognized expert in the field. Incidentally, Señor Robles added, Señor Hannigan was the best marksman in the Canadian army during his time in that force. So there was one fact about me that Mayor Robles didn't have to embellish. Roberto Sangallo looked at me quizzically and wondered whether marksmanship was a qualification for being Director of Security. I assured him that my job consisted mainly of making sure that proper safety measures were followed in all the operations of the company. I could be quite confident that my job would not require gunfire. As someone only beginning to learn Spanish I was able to get by with a few badly spoken phrases. Without that excuse my unfamiliarity with diplomatic niceties would, I am sure, have lowered the tone of the event considerably.

For the occasion Señora Robles had commandeered the services of an excellent chef. The meal began with antipasto, proceeded through four more courses to a light dolce, the courses accompanied by, in turn, a white wine, a red wine and an Asti Spumante, finishing with sambuca, or Grand Marnier for anyone who wanted to break from the Italian motif. Conversation naturally turned to why Will and I were in the country. The elephant in the room was of course the presence of Fraga's goons at the center of town. By the third glass of wine however the polite reticence of the guests was sufficiently overcome to allow the subject to come up. "This scoundrel Fraga," Mayor Robles began, "has been a thorn in the side of southern Talcayan now for many years. He has stolen, he has practiced extortion, he is a coward who has operated in secret. However, now he has made a mistake. He has come out into the open, and he has done it at a moment when we on our side have an advantage that will allow us to remove Rafael Fraga and his gang from this territory."

"I refer," Robles continued. "to Colonel McGrath and Señor Hannigan. Fraga is not only the enemy of all of the citizens of Talcayan south of El Rio del Rey. He has also made himself the enemy of Hannigan Industries. I have been conferring with Colonel McGrath, and he assures me that Fraga can be driven out of this part of the country, and removed from San Martin."

The mayor paused for a moment to let that sink in, then continued. "This criminal can be defeated, and defeated probably without gunfire. If there is gunfire, the good colonel assures me, it will be our men firing on Fraga's gang from cover. We have available the means of neutralizing his armor. The colonel's plan must be kept secret, and of course you will speak of this to no one, but I have seen the plan, and I am convinced that it will work. But for this plan to work the people of this territory must become active. I am not asking that anyone in the Amparo district run a great risk. We require, however, a number of men who are willing to cooperate. The danger will be no greater than if you venture out on the highway at night to drive to San Isidro and back. This is a God-given opportunity. We must act now."

Señor Sangallo asked Will why he was willing to undertake this operation. For some reason Will answered that I was really the person whom Hannigan Industries had put in charge of the trip to Talcayan and I could answer that question. He was probably retaliating for my having been so free about offering his services. In halting Spanish and with help from Will I explained that normally we would have walked away from a threatening situation like this. However, Mayor Robles had convinced us of the importance of the mining operation to the citizens around Amparo, and we found it intolerable that a felon like Fraga could prey on the people with apparent immunity and ruin their chances for greater prosperity.

Señor Sangallo replied that certainly it was the responsibility of the citizens of Talcayan to throw out this would-be tyrant, but how could we be sure that we could succeed without a slaughter of innocent people? Here Robles intervened rather excitedly to reassure him that it was possible. "I tell you," he said, "It is the providence of God that has

THE BLOOD-DIMMED TIDE IS LOOSED

sent us these two men. It would be a shame not to make use of their talents."

Sangallo replied that Robles' assurance meant much to him. He was hesitant however to send his men into battle. They had grown used to the idea that Fraga was unassailable and it might be hard to convince them that he could easily be defeated. That was more or less where the conversation ended. Señora Robles steered us away from the topic, asking the Sangallos about one of the women of the estancia who had been to Amparo recently with a sick child, and from there the conversation turned to how fortunate they were to have two competent doctors and a splendid clinic in the town. Soon after that, the party broke up.

The next evening the mayor and his wife repeated the exercise with Señor and Señora Calvino, an older couple. Señora Robles, still bejeweled and gowned for a formal occasion, was all deference. The cuisine changed from Italian to French. God played a lesser role the second night and money came to the forefront. Think of what it would be worth to have a flourishing industry in the neighborhood. Señor Calvino's prosperous estancia would become even more lucrative if there were a larger local population able to purchase his products and Fraga couldn't extort his illicit share. The owner nodded, was suitably appreciative of the need to act, and as cautious as Señor Sangallo had been.

The next night it was the turn of the owner of the third estancia to be wined and dined. Señor Chavarria was a widower, and brought his daughter and her husband, Felipe Diaz, who ran the day-to-day operations of the estancia. For this event Señora Robles had dressed simply and without jewels. She gently put Señora Diaz at ease and had her happily reminiscing about her school days when Señora Robles had been her teacher. The food and wine were authentic Argentine. Mayor Robles hinted that he did not intend to run for the office of mayor when his present term ran out. He wanted to be able to hand over a trouble-free city and region to his successor. At this point Felipe Diaz showed an increased interest in the conversation, and at the end of the night the mayor had something closer to a firm commitment from

- 69 -

Chavarria than he had been able to get from his guests on the previous two nights.

Meanwhile it was important that the Fraga camp in San Martin be reconnoitered, a task complicated by the fact that the outlaw had set up a road block on the one access road to the village, and his men were checking the identities of all travelers. San Martin was nestled at the edge of the mountains. To reach it from Amparo one drove north from El Puente Ingles and after about twenty kilometers turned westward on a winding mountain road. The roadblock was about a kilometer from the highway.

The morning after our dinner with the Chavarria family a driver took Aldomar and me to a point about a half kilometer from where the road to San Martin left the highway. Aldomar had some knowledge of the terrain, and once he sensed that something was afoot he had been chaffing at the bit for action. The driver was to pick us up somewhere along this stretch of road at four P.M., by which time we should have accomplished our mission.

From the point where the driver dropped us off it was about five miles to San Martin "as the crow flies". Your average crow undertaking the journey, however, would not have to climb up and down hills, splash through marshes and push through shrubs and reeds while being reassured by a companion that the mosquitoes currently snacking on his blood are probably not the kind that spread malaria. On the positive side, Aldomar was a pleasant companion. It apparently did his heart good to think about fighting Fraga. He told stories, explained the local flora and fauna, gave his opinions about life in general and life in Talcayan in particular. Some of it I understood. I wasn't sure whether Aldomar cared about being understood. Perhaps he just needed to talk, but he was patient when I would ask him to repeat something more slowly.

After a couple of sweaty hours we were still some ways from our destination. We found a clear spot fairly high up, where the wind kept the bugs from congregating, and sat down to make a lunch of the food and drink that Aldomar had brought. Having done justice to several cold beef sandwiches we headed north and quickly arrived at the road to San Martin. By that time it had warmed up and I took off my jacket and put it in my backpack along with my shoulder holster and Beretta.

The graveled road ran along a stream flowing out of the mountains. The only traffic we encountered was a man driving a donkey with a cartload of hay. There were patches of shrubs with bright red blossoms, and every now and then we would catch the scent of the wild flowers blooming between the road and the forest. The air was fresh, the surroundings bucolic, and the two of us could have been farm hands trudging home for our midday meal.

It's difficult to say where the village of San Martin begins. After a mile of uninhabited forest we began to pass small frame bungalows set off by themselves here and there. Farther on the cottages were closer together, though each still had around it enough space for a garden and the occasional fruit tree. We reached an open space that the planners must have intended to become a central square, although thus far there were only six or seven structures around the periphery. A couple of side streets ran away from this open space, ending a couple of hundred yards to the south. At the end of one of them was the saw mill that constituted the main industry of the village.

We occupied a bench in the square while we caught our breath. From where we sat we could see an ugly wall farther to the west, mostly cinder block along with bricks of varied colors in a random order, as though the builders had run out of material and used whatever rubble happened to be lying around. On the hard-packed ground in front of us a dozen or so boys were playing soccer. I was deliciously tired, closed my eyes and dozed off. When I awoke the soccer game had ended and several of the boys were wandering in our direction. They stopped to look at us, then gathered courage and approached. Aldomar entered into a lively conversation with them which I couldn't follow, but he had an attentive audience, and from the way that the lads looked at me I suspect that Aldomar was making of me a more interesting character than was warranted by the facts.

He pointed to one of the smaller boys who had been crouched on the ground tying his shoe but was now moving away, apparently crying. After a brief exchange with the tallest of the lads, Aldomar called the younger boy over and seemed to be trying to jolly him into a better mood, without much success. Then Aldomar turned to me and, reverting to the simpler Spanish he had been using earlier, explained that the boy's name was Roberto, the sole of one of his shoes had become detached from the upper during the game and because it was the only pair he had his mother would scold him. The problem could easily be remedied if there were shoes for sale in the village, but the only store was a grocery. "Wait here a couple of minutes," Aldomar said, "I'm going to take Roberto for a walk."

Aldomar started across the square with the boy in tow, heading towards the grocery store. I caught up with them and explained I had more expense money than I needed for my stay in Talcayan and I would like to pay for whatever would be helpful to Roberto. Aldomar paused for a few seconds, then brightened and said that if we both chipped in we could get Roberto and his mother a little extra. Within several minutes, following the boy's instructions, Aldomar had filled several paper bags with basic groceries and a bag of candy. Roberto eyed a box where some sandals were piled together and asked whether he could get a pair. From his diffident manner one might have thought that he was asking for some major favor; perhaps he was. He sorted through them until he found what he wanted and added them to our purchases.

We then accompanied Roberto to his home. His mother met us at the door, a thin, tired looking woman whose first reaction to the arrival of her son in the presence of two strangers was fear that he was in some trouble. Aldomar reassured her with a story about how Roberto had ruined his shoe running an errand for us, and so we felt responsible, and wondered whether this little offering would help. The mother looked puzzled, and I suspect she would have refused our offerings except for politeness, and no doubt her family could use the groceries.

CHAPTER NINE

A dirt road ran west from the center of the village for several hundred yards and ended at a steep, rocky incline. When Fraga and his gang had moved into the area they had built two relatively large houses at the end of that road. As the gang's numbers grew Fraga convinced several owners along the road to accept his offer for their homes rather than incur his displeasure, and his followers, some of them with families, now resided in these dwellings. When he acquired the Leopard tank he built an enclosure to house it along with several other military vehicles. It was a wall of this enclosure that we had seen from the bench where we rested on our arrival.

We were not going to learn much from gazing at the ten-foot-high wall other than that the enclosed space was more-or-less square, from eighty to a hundred feet on each side. I suggested that if we could get to a ledge on the mountainside several hundred feet above the enclosure we could see what lay inside those walls. Aldomar replied that it would be easy enough to get up there—just walk up through the woods. For several hundred yards you could follow a logging road, then just veer to the right. The problem was that Fraga might not like us doing that, and he probably had men patrolling the area.

"Would Fraga's men recognize you?" I asked Aldomar.

"Quite possibly. I've had dealings with some of them."

- 73 -

"Where does the logging road go?"

"It runs up a ways, more than a kilometer, but then the slope becomes too steep for a road."

"Okay. You stay here. I'm going hiking. I'll meet you at the church in a half hour or so." I gave Aldomar my gun, reasoning that if I ran into any of Fraga's men on the trail they might have trouble believing that a tourist would be carrying a Beretta. A skeptical Aldomar accompanied me a couple of hundred yards to the foot of the logging road. I took the remains of the lunch he had brought. What could more disarming than a hiker munching a crusty sandwich and washing it down with cold tea?

"Suppose I spot someone who looks unfriendly. Is there another way out of the woods?"

Aldomar thought for a minute. "There's only this one road. As you can see, there's not much undergrowth. You can move easily through the forest, but you can come down only on this side of the mountain."

I set off uphill at a leisurely pace. Here the trees were mainly evergreen and larger than the ones through which we had hiked that morning. The road led in a direction slightly away from the ledge I had seen, so after a few minutes I angled off to the right and began to pick my way through the forest towards a spot from which I might get a look into the enclosure. Up to that point the day had been strenuous but enjoyable.

Within minutes of leaving the road I sensed movement behind me. Turning, I saw two uniformed men emerge from the trees a hundred yards away. One, who was looking in my direction, was holding an assault rifle with both hands, pointing it straight ahead. The other was pulling on a leash, on the other end of which was a largish dog.

I got that sinking feeling that I had just done something really asinine. In the face of real armed men, and of a real dog for that matter, the ruse of passing myself off as a tourist stood out as a shining example of stupidity. I had not heard of the Fraga bunch actually executing anyone, but they just might make an exception in my case. The more likely immediate prospect was that these men would take me to headquarters for their leader to decide how best to make use of someone who had obligingly blundered into his hands. Fraga might use me to teach a lesson to potential intruders, and that opened up all sorts of gruesome possibilities. The thought of Colonel McGrath having to bargain for my safety or plan some sort of rescue, all because I had left my brains at home, was almost as scary as the prospect of being at the mercy of the outlaw.

Were it simply a matter of the two men I stood, a good chance of getting away. The trees provided plenty of cover. I had enough stamina and speed afoot to outdistance an average pursuer. But that dog changed the odds. The fact that I didn't have much idea of the terrain into which I would be fleeing worried me even more; and there was also the small matter that the two men could probably call upon others to help if I chose to turn this into a manhunt. So I was left with the desperate expedient of following my original plan.

Assuming as casual a pose as my nerves allowed I waited for the two men to cover the ground between us. The dog, a German Shepherd, seemed eager to make my closer acquaintance. Our combat training had shown us that an unarmed man is far from defenseless against even a large dog, but the counter-measures one might take did not contemplate the beast being backed up by a man with a rifle. Snarling dogs remind me of bullies, trying to scare you enough that you will flee from them rather than attack. My Hannigan cousins years ago had owned a St. Bernard who answered to the name of Roscoe, when he bothered to answer to anything; and Roscoe cheerfully dispensed with preliminaries before galloping into battle any time his canine supremacy was challenged. He apparently saw no need to announce his intentions ahead of time before engaging the enemy. This German Shepherd however belonged to a different school of thought, threatening me with horrible consequences if given the opportunity.

The man with the rifle began speaking to me rapidly, and when I was able to get in a word I explained that I was a foreigner with a limited grasp of Spanish, so would he please speak slowly. This threw him off his game for a moment, but he asked my name, slowly. When I had answered, he asked for my identification. I gestured towards my backpack with an inquiring look, and when he nodded assent I slowly withdrew my passport and gave it to him. He looked it over with an expression that suggested that it was giving off a foul odor, then handed it back and asked me what I was doing here in the woods. I answered that I was going for a walk, that in my few days in Talcayan I was taking advantage of the beautiful mountain trails. He informed me that I was in trouble because I had trespassed on territory where I had no right to be. I replied that I had been assured that these were public lands. He snarled something that I couldn't understand, directed me to put my hands behind my back and snapped a pair of handcuffs on me.

My best defense seemed to be to give my questioner the impression that his superiors might be interested in me, so I asked him to take me to his commanding officer. He told me I was in no position to tell him what to do. I couldn't argue with that. He continued questioning me and I continued to reply that I would speak only to his commanding officer. Eventually he decided he was getting nowhere, poked me in the ribs with the muzzle of his rifle and directed me to walk in front of him. We rejoined the road up which I had strolled only a few minutes earlier, and we headed downwards.

Reaching the foot of the logging road, we had taken only a few steps in the direction of the village when some distance away I discerned a figure ambling toward us. As it came closer I recognized that it was Aldomar. I had been trying to figure out what to say when my captors took me to Señor Fraga, and had given no thought to what to do if we should meet my guide. I made perhaps my only sound tactical decision of the day. I kept my mouth shut.

As he came within hailing distance the giant waved towards my two captors with a worried look and asked in a loud voice whether they knew whom they had arrested. The two remained silent until they were only a few feet away from him. He made a little bow, greeted the two of them respectfully, and repeated his question. The man with the rifle replied that I was a Canadian whom they had caught trespassing on the mountain. Aldomar waved this answer aside. Did they realize who this Canadian was? Aldomar launched into a succinct explanation that I was an officer of a major company and I was in Talcayan to investigate the feasibility of opening some mines that would greatly enrich the country. Mayors Robles and Guzman had entrusted me to Aldomar, to accompany and protect me while I examined the terrain before returning to Canada to advise the president of the mining company. The two mayors would be furious should I come to harm.

Aldomar apparently adhered to the principle that in a pinch one should stay as close to the truth as is practical. The only outright untruth in his account was the inclusion of Mayor Guzman among my protectors, an important addition in view of the fact that Fraga's his minions could not be expected to defer to Mayor Robles, whom their leader had defied.

My captors took Aldomar's story seriously, but they couldn't be expected to surrender their prisoner without an argument. They asked Aldomar how he and I had gotten by the road block. Throwing up his hands, Aldomar urged the two men to tell Señor Fraga immediately to dismantle this affront to all the citizens of the district. If it remained in existence, one of these nights the local ranchers would surely take matters into their own hands and the results would be bloody. Aldomar explained that some of his own men had wanted to clear out the road block, but Mayor Robles had counseled patience and had instructed Aldomar and myself to avoid trouble by taking a cross-country route around that obstruction.

The questioner changed the subject. Why were we snooping around in this area? This man—he poked me again with the end of his rifle—pretends that he was just out for a walk. This is not a tourist area. Aldomar hesitated for a second, and then explained that the situation seemed to require that he divulge something that should be kept secret. Hannigan Industries knew there was valuable ore south of the Rio del Rey. However, their geologists suspected that there were more valuable deposits farther north, near San Martin. Señor Hannigan had been sent to look at the area to see if it contained any of the kind of rocks that might indicate the presence of silver or other valuable ore.

Aldomar spoke as one anxious that my captors not bring disaster on themselves by causing me harm. He promised that if I were released immediately he would say nothing of the incident to either Mayor Guzman or Mayor Robles, and that he was confident that I would find it in my interest to do the same. As he made his points he looked at his watch several times, indicating that of course his way was the only way out of this impasse but my captors would be well advised not to drag their feet about it. Without further argument they relieved me of the handcuffs and waved to Aldomar to take me away, with the warning that

- 77 -

this area was off-limits and if there was to be any search for mineral deposits it would have to be with Señor Fraga's permission.

On our way back to the village Aldomar reminded me of our agreement to meet in the local church and he thought it would be a good idea for us to keep that appointment. It may have been an act of piety, or he may have wanted me to see a local tourist attraction. When we entered the church Aldomar knelt in silence for several minutes. The little church, like the one in Amparo, was decorated with multiple statues and paintings. A couple of women kneeling side by side were whispering their rosaries in the semi-gloom. The prayerful atmosphere, combined with my own gratitude for having escaped from I-don't-know-what, made the visit to the church seem entirely appropriate. I was curious however about how Aldomar squared his evident piety with his skill at improving on the truth; and I was distracted by a question: Should I be thanking God that my large friend's well-crafted falsehood had very likely saved me from serious harm, or would I have felt better if he had resorted to violence?

When we emerged into the full light of the afternoon Aldomar had a suggestion. "The people here do not like Fraga," he said. "I know a man here who owns a truck. He hauls sheep and other farm products from San Martin to market in Magdalena and returns with products for the grocery and hardware stores in San Martin. Maybe he can drive us out to the highway. Also, he sometimes hauls stuff for Fraga's outfit, so he should be able to tell us what we want to know about the inside of that enclosure."

Another blow to my self-esteem. There was a simple, safe way to get the information we needed.

I had probably put too much stock in western movies that portray rows of Latinos sitting idly on benches, sombreros shielding them from the afternoon sun. Talcayan had offered no such scene. Señor Camacho was busy hammering and filing on a metal piece while he talked to Aldomar. He was short, barrel-chested, with the dark, lined face of someone who spends much of his time out of doors, and the calloused hands of a man who made his living working with tools. He operated the only gas station in the village, and when the supply trucks came to fill up his tank they would usually leave several fifty-gallon drums of diesel fuel which he would later deliver to the Fraga enclosure, so he was well acquainted with what lay within those walls.

The enclosure normally contained the Leopard Tank parked against the north wall, and next to it a large truck fitted with benches in the back to accommodate a considerable number of people. Scattered around the enclosure were a jeep, a smaller truck, an armored personnel carrier and barrels of diesel fuel. Sometimes one or several automobiles would be parked within the walls.

Once Señor Camacho had finished hammering and filing he fitted and bolted the metal piece on to the hitch on a trailer that was loaded with firewood. The repair job completed, he hitched the trailer behind a truck that looked like a close relative of Aldomar's old vehicle. He left his teen-age son in charge of the single gasoline pump and we hopped into the cab and drove towards the highway.

The guards at the checkpoint were curious about why Aldomar happened to be in this area. The latter gave the same response he had given to my captors an hour earlier. Whether the guards believed the account or not, they seemed uninterested in anything that was going to complicate their lives and they waved us through. They were probably more concerned with who entered San Martin than with who left it. Aldomar and I got off at the highway where we would be picked up by the driver who had brought us there earlier. We thanked the good señor and he continued on his way.

CHAPTER TEN

The next step was to recruit thirty men who could aim a rifle and not be fazed by the fact that the enemy might be similarly occupied. Due to the diplomacy of Señor and Señora Robles, the owners or the three large estancias south of the Rio del Rey were now interested in opposing Fraga, but they had left it up to their hired hands to volunteer. Aldomar was to learn in the next several days that most of those hired hands were not eager to do battle. Seven of Sangallo's men volunteered, but no one from the Calvino estancia came forward. On the second day, however, at the Chavarria ranch Aldomar found Felipe Diaz and twelve of the gauchos ready to march. We could count on the five police officers in Amparo. To fill out the required number we had to ask Mayor Laval to lend us several members of the Marino police force for a couple of days. Since the pay was good he was able to find the required number of volunteers.

On the following Friday Will and I drove to Mendoza, dropped the Toyota off at the rental agency and picked up a flatbed truck that awaited us, already loaded, at the railway station. The largest item on board was a metal tube about thirty feet long and four feet in diameter that would become a culvert under the reconstructed road. There were also two large metal cylinders about eight feet long that had been identified quite accurately to Argentine customs as mine safety equipment. With

- 80 -

these and several smaller items on the back of the truck we drove back along the now familiar road south by southeast from Mendoza and west on Camino del Campo. The customs official at the entry point, familiar with us by now, must have been impressed by how quickly our preliminary investigations were followed by the importing of mining equipment.

Four members of the Fraga gang continued to roam the streets of Amparo, seeming to go out of their way to be offensive, taking over several rooms in Amparo's main hotel and informing the frightened proprietor that, in lieu of payment for the lodgings, they would make sure that his property would not be harmed. They took their meals in the restaurant across the square from city hall. Whether they paid for them was not clear, the owner not being as public in his complaints as was the proprietor of the hotel. The leader of the four, a tough looking, broad-shouldered, shaggy character named Juarez, who was reputed to be Fraga's lieutenant, swaggered around the town with a proprietary air that sent Mayor Robles into near-frenzy.

The four were always armed while in public, so apprehending them required some finesse. The owner and manager of the restaurant and his wife, who was the cook, lived on the second floor above the kitchen and usually began their day's work at about 6 A.M. Two waiters would normally arrive at 6:30. On a certain Monday morning the four gangsters followed their usual schedule, arriving for breakfast at 7:15. Several people who had shown an inclination to enter the restaurant had been redirected for their safety to an alternative eating place.

As soon as they had served breakfast to the four, the owner, his wife and the waiters left the building, having first locked the door leading up to the second floor. The previous evening a very heavy cabinet had been so placed as to obstruct egress from the building by the back door. The flatbed truck drove into the middle of the square and stopped opposite the front of the restaurant. On the flatbed were two large concrete slabs, and behind those slabs were six men with rifles. Five of the men had directions not to use their rifles unless something very unexpected happened. I was the sixth person and hardly needed help covering anyone trying to escape from the building; but our friends in the restaurant might not see it that way, and the presence of extra troops might help them to appreciate the wisdom of our forthcoming proposal.

Once everyone was in place several tear gas canisters were hurled through the downstairs windows, with much crashing and clinking of breaking glass. A loudspeaker informed Fraga's men that they were under arrest by authority of the chief of police of the town of Amparo, and they were to leave their weapons and come out with their arms raised. I glimpsed a face peeping out of one of the windows for a moment. There was a pause and then four figures emerged through the front door.

Three of the four were bent over, coughing or gagging and not observing the letter of our instructions concerning the position of their hands. Since they gave no appearance of carrying weapons we were prepared to be lenient. The fourth, Juarez, came out looking as contemptuous as he could manage in the face of the assault of the tear gas on his system. You can have your little game, he seemed to imply, but there will be a day of reckoning.

Aldomar made a great show of arresting the four. While they were being photographed and fingerprinted a few teen-age boys ventured from the houses, watched from a distance and then approached to get a closer look. They were followed a minute later by younger children and several mothers. There was interest, but no cheering. They were probably uneasy about where this show of defiance against Fraga might lead. A few young people fell in line in a sort of procession as the prisoners were escorted to the local jail, which had been cleaned and reinforced several days earlier. By nine o'clock the only sign that anything had happened was the local glazier happily at work on what was probably the largest contract he had obtained in some years.

Mayor Robles sent a message to San Martin informing Señor Fraga that four of his men had been arrested for illegal trespass against the explicit order of the chief of police that they vacate the town of Amparo. The two automobiles used by these four men had been confiscated as partial payment of an estimated three million pesos that Fraga and his followers had extorted over the years from citizens who were under the jurisdiction of the mayor of Amparo. Upon payment of the remainder of that amount, three of the arrested men would be released on the understanding that they would not repeat their offense. For his part, Señor Fraga should know that he would no longer be welcome south of the Rio del Rey, and he was expected, as part of the settlement, to prevent any of his employees from straying into that territory for the next two years. Mayor Robles as an expression of mercy promised to intercede on behalf of Señor Juarez when the latter appeared before the magistrate who would preside at sessions next month in Amparo.

This message was delivered to the detachment manning the roadblock at 10:30 A.M. by Aldomar, who then joined his five-man Amparo police force and several other recruits at a point near the junction of the San Martin road with the highway leading to Amparo. We worried that we might be left twiddling our thumbs for hours or even days while Fraga considered his options. Fortunately that outlaw proved to be a man of action. At 1:15 P.M. Aldomar reported to Amparo that Fraga's tank and a truck loaded with personnel had turned off the road from San Martin and headed south towards El Puente Ingles. Aldomar apparently had never actually seen the tank and was awed by the size of it and the firepower that it represented. Fortunately for his peace of mind his part in the proceedings was in San Martin. The back of the truck was open and Aldomar estimated that perhaps twenty of Fraga's men were in it, along with a number of villagers who appeared to be hostages.

At 1:35 P.M. a fire truck belonging to the town of Amparo turned off the highway and sped westwards towards San Martin. The vehicle carried a pressure tank and was used for dousing fires. It was followed by a larger fire truck on loan from the city of Marino which stopped, picked up Aldomar and his officers and followed the first vehicle towards San Martin. Approaching the road block, they turned on their sirens and men standing on the platforms on each vehicle gestured frantically to the smoke rising in billows in the direction of San Martin. The vehicles slowed down but were waved through without stopping.

Arrived in San Martin, the two vehicles did not head for the pile of smoldering tires that was producing the impressive column of smoke. The truck with the pressure tank sped to the structure that enclosed Fraga's equipment, turned and pulled up next to the wall. A man standing on the platform aimed the hose, the truck began to move

- 83 -

briskly and a stream of liquid poured out of the tank and over the wall. The truck took only a few second to complete its mission and quickly moved out of the area. Seconds later a youth from the village hurled a packet over the wall, and it was followed by a flaming missile, a rock wrapped in a gasoline-soaked rag, thrown by a second youth.

The results apparently had been impressive. The first assault on the senses was a roar as the gasoline that had been poured into the enclosure caught fire. Then there was a crackling noise as the fire began to consume other combustibles, and then an impressive blast as the packet that had been thrown over the wall exploded.

Figures began to appear at the front doors of the nearby houses occupied by Fraga's people. They could see dark smoke rising from the enclosure close by and to the east the larger of the fire engines was drawn up across the road, effectively blocking any traffic in that direction, with armed men peering out from behind the fire engine. Then a voice through a loudspeaker explained that by the authority of the Mayor of Amparo and the orders of his Chief of Police the organization of Rafael Fraga was being disbanded. Its members were hereby commanded to surrender. They would be disarmed and held in custody until police had time to identify those who would stand trial for crimes against the citizens of Talcayan. Those who were found not guilty would be released as quickly as possible. Women and children would be provided for until the situation was settled.

Those followers of Fraga who had ventured outside quickly slipped back indoors. For about a quarter of an hour the sound of the loudspeaker repeating the message competed with the crackling sounds from inside the enclosure, but there was no response from the houses. Then two women and several children ventured out of one of the two largest houses and made their way uncertainly down the road away from the enclosure. Upon reaching the large fire engine they were greeted politely by Aldomar, who turned them over to several of the women of the village. Were Aldodmar and his men interested they might have observed figures slipping away from the back doors of the houses and making their way furtively into the nearby forest. The jail in Amparo would not hold all of Fraga's followers, so there was no point in trying to arrest every one of them.

THE BLOOD-DIMMED TIDE IS LOOSED

Apparently the citizens of San Martin were more daring than were those in Amparo. A few youths had gathered to watch as soon as the two fire trucks had roared into the village, and none of their elders seemed to object. As the fire began to die down and the loudspeaker fell silent a festive mood began to prevail. There was a lot of chatter and some of the young people started to sing and dance. Aldomar was the man of the hour. A search of the residences revealed them to be empty. Two of Aldomar's officers were left in San Martin to organize and arm a few citizens of the village in case any of Fraga's followers came back to cause trouble. The rest began their triumphant return to Amparo in the cab of the smaller fire truck and in the back of Señor Camacho's vehicle. On their way back they stopped at the road block, several armed men got out of the vehicles and Aldomar informed the guards that they were under arrest

CHAPTER ELEVEN

The key to success at San Martin had been to keep it simple. The plan for the confrontation at El Puente Ingles was more complicated.

At 1:15 P.M., when Aldomar informed our people in Amparo that Fraga was on his way, I was on the side of a hill near the bridge munching on a sandwich, so my first awareness of Fraga's approach came later. I was hidden from view from below by an outcropping of rocks but able to keep track of comings and goings in the area. It had been quiet since I had taken up my position. As the road crossed the bridge to the Amparo side of the river, it ran straight for perhaps fifty yards between two hills and then turned to the right to more-or-less follow the river. The old road had been thoroughly torn up and dirt had been scraped away from the hills on either side to allow the road to follow a more gradual curve as it ascended from the bridge. The work was near completion but the ground was sufficiently uneven to slow down any vehicle approaching the curve in the road.

On one side of the unfinished road was the culvert we had trucked in from Mendoza. One end was wedged against the bank that had been cut in the hill. The other end, lying within a few feet of the new road, was covered with dirt. On the other side, closer to my lookout spot, a considerable space had been leveled. On it were parked a bulldozer,

- 86 -

a tractor with a front end loader and a truck with two fuel tanks on the back. About forty yards from the road lay a pile of lumber, mainly two-by-fours and two-by sixes of the kind used to build forms to hold the concrete when pouring a curb.

At about 1:30 P.M. an automobile and a school bus arrived on the scene from the direction of Amparo, disgorged a total of twenty four men and then returned in the direction from which it came. The new arrivals included Will McGrath, men from the Sangallo and Chavarria estancias and the officers we had borrowed from Marino, all in green-gray-black camouflage. They immediately began to climb the hills on either side. The men from the Chavarria estancia scrambled up the hill opposite to where I was, got to the top and took up positions where I could see them from my vantage point, but they were not visible from the road. They were without their leader, Felipe Diaz, who had volunteered for a more dangerous assignment.

The foliage on my side of the road was quite thick and I quickly lost sight of the men coming up towards me. In a couple of minutes there was a rustling and snapping of twigs and two of the police officers from Marino emerged from the bushes within a few feet of me. They gave me a quick wave and set about moving some branches, revealing a rocket launcher that could be handled by two men. This had been the most difficult piece of equipment for us to find. Rocket launchers were relatively easy to come by, but we needed something that could be aimed very precisely and that fired rockets with a small charge that would not injure people beyond a very limited radius. The two policemen pointed the weapon towards the road and we waited.

Although we could see the bridge, our view of the road on the far side of river was cut off by trees, so the first signal of Flores' approach was the roar of unmuffled motors and the grinding and clanking of vehicles approaching from a distance. First to come into view was the Leopard Tank, followed by the truck that served as a personnel carrier. Both vehicles stopped at the far side of the bridge. A number of uniformed men climbed out of the back of the truck and held their weapons at the ready while nine men and boys emerged. These hostages were then lined up and walked, nine abreast, across the bridge, followed by their armed escort with the tank and personnel carrier close behind. There was a large figure in the turret of the tank, occasionally gesturing and apparently shouting orders, but nothing of his voice reached us above the roar of the motor. Canvas covered the sides and top of the back of the truck, so personnel exited and entered only from the back.

As they came closer to us the two vehicles stopped. The soldiers prodded the hostages to keep going. The latter walked slowly until they were almost directly in front of us. Then apparently they were ordered to return to the space in front of the tank. About a half dozen more soldiers jumped off the back of the carrier and joined their comrades in a search of the area. They approached the pile of lumber with special caution, weapons at the ready, prepared to drop and fire if they met any resistance. They surrounded the lumber, poked through it, and deciding that it posed no threat they moved on to a more casual inspection of the rest of the site.

I was sweating as they came to the fuel truck. Would they think it strange that the seat in the cab had been taken out and replaced by a steel box? Would they be curious about either of the fuel tanks on the back? Apparently the truck did not excite their suspicions as much as had the pile of lumber. Give them something obvious to worry about, Will had said, and maybe they won't worry so much about the real threat. They paid almost no attention to the culvert, which looked completely natural on a road construction site. Had they showed enough curiosity to begin digging out the dirt at either end we would have had to revert to Plan B. I would cease to be an observer and my two associates with the rocket launcher would try to disable the tank without injuring the hostages.

Their inspection of the site finished, the men began to search the surrounding area. First they pushed the hostages at gun point ahead of them through the scattered trees and bushes on the opposite side of the road. At this point Diaz's men drew back, staying out of sight of the hostages and their guards climbing up the hill. The latter got to the top, looked around and started back down. I began to breathe again.

They began the same procedure on our hill, without the hostages, who might easily have escaped through the more dense foliage on this side of the road. The search of our hill was quick, almost perfunctory. Our men on this side were hidden high on the hill, hoping that Fraga's men would eventually realize that a search under those conditions was dangerous if they got close to any enemies in hiding and useless if they did not. They stayed on the hillside for several minutes, shouting to each other once in a while and walked back down to the road.

Most of the soldiers climbed back into the truck, and four of them went back to herding the hostages. The latter, again nine abreast, walked slowly over the rough ground that was the future path of the road, then back again. Then three soldiers with metal detectors went over the ground. That done, the procession formed up again; the hostages leading, followed by the four guards, the tank and the truck, all in close formation

At this point I was viewing the procession through the scope on my rifle. According to the often rehearsed plan, as the procession came close to the culvert Will would radio a signal to the fuel truck. A man in the box that was serving as a seat in the cab would scramble out, start the motor and back the truck a few feet towards the procession. Felipe Diaz, hidden in what looked like a second fuel tank on the back of the truck, would slip out and aim a hose at the four men walking behind the hostages, then at the Leopard tank and then at the troop carrier. As soon as he saw that the truck was started Will would signal the man in the culvert. A hatch would pop open and the man would aim his hose, in the same order, at soldiers, tank, troop carrier. All three of our men were in danger at that moment, especially Diaz. My job was to protect the two in the truck as well as I could, and hope that Fraga and his men would take a few seconds to notice what was happening. The sweat began to drip off my forehead and into my eyes, even though the day was relatively cool and the sun was behind a cloud.

Many mines, as a safety precaution, keep a supply of fire-fighting foam which, under sufficient pressure, can blast its way hundreds of feet into a mine shaft within seconds. When it's released in the open air the results are impressive. As the fuel truck began to inch backwards, for several seconds there was no sign that anyone had noticed. Then there was a loud woosh on each side of the road and instantaneously the four armed men in front of the tank were knocked off their feet and awash in a tide of white. Seconds later the tank along with the figure in the turret was smothered in foam. For a moment I thought everything was going to go without a hitch, but then there was sudden movement at the truck carrying Fraga's men. One of them apparently had noticed that the fuel truck had begun to move; he jumped to the ground and ran a few steps away from the truck to get a shot at Diaz. I followed him with the scope until he raised his automatic weapon to fire, but I fired first.

Our army instructors told us that in a situation like that you cannot afford to think. You let your training take over. I fired automatically, with as little thought as possible; but a second later reality intruded. I had not only removed an enemy operative. For the only time in my life, I had killed a man. I froze for a moment, very aware of why the army taught you not to think.

Will's instructions to Felipe had been to ignore any of Fraga's men who might come into the open. They would be my responsibility, backed up by several other snipers if needed. The fuel truck continued to back past the troop carrier, covering it with foam. I kept an eye on the scene until the foam had covered the back of the vehicle. No one else emerged. They may have seen the fate of their comrade, or they may simply have lacked the presence of mind to do anything. In any case, they saved their lives by remaining in the carrier, although in doing so they had to endure a good deal of discomfort.

The main ingredient of the foam was carbon dioxide. It douses flames, stops any internal combustion engine once it is sucked in through the air intake, and robs the human body of oxygen if it's inhaled. In addition, the gas released under high pressure is extremely cold. Our next concern was to rescue those whom we had put in danger.

Once we saw that the tank and truck were completely covered with foam the three of us in the lookout spot sped down the hill. Although we were the farthest from the site, when I arrived others were just beginning to emerge. Some were heading for the front of the tank to take custody of the four stunned guards who had been blasted off their feet by the first onslaught. Others were heading cautiously towards the truck. When I found myself the first on the scene I ran to the sprawled figure who seconds earlier had been in my sights, hoping that through some unlikely chance he had been wearing a protective vest and that my shot had merely knocked him out. He lay on his back, thrown there

THE BLOOD-DIMMED TIDE IS LOOSED

by the force of the bullet, his eyes wide open; the only movement was blood seeping through his open mouth and gushing from a hole in his chest. He was either dead or spending his last moments on this earth.

My responsibility was the tank. I had with me a blanket with a hole cut in the middle. I jumped up on the tank and by waving the blanket frantically managed to dispel the foam around the turret. I placed the blanket so the occupants of the tank could climb out and not slow things down when they placed their hands on the freezing metal. By this time one of Diaz's men had climbed on to the other side of the tank and shouted to the occupants to come out hands first. There was sounds of motion, and after a few seconds Fraga, the man who had been shouting orders from the turret, clambered out, gasping for breath. The fight had gone out of him, and we handed him down to another of Diaz's men. Another occupant followed, in even more distress. We asked him whether there was a third man still in the tank, and he nodded, yes. We waited several seconds but there was no further motion. I glanced into the interior and could make out a still figure lying on the floor. I climbed down and lifted him up high enough that my companion was able to pull him clear.

By this time our men at the front had rescued the four guards from the mound of foam in which they had been wallowing. None of them seemed to have been injured by the experience. A small bus had driven up and a couple of women and three middle aged men were taking care of the hostages, most of whom moved slowly and uncertainly. Mayor Robles walked from one group to another. He had volunteered to join us on the hillside, but we had, with some difficulty, convinced him that he would serve our cause better by supervising relief efforts.

The last task was disarming the men in the troop carrier. The fuel truck kept replenishing the foam, both over the cab and at the back of the carrier. None of the occupants had yet ventured out. Several of our armed men had taken up a position behind the truck, using as a shield the bull dozer that had been moved into position for that purpose. As I approached them, a megaphone was blasting out the message that the occupants were to come out with their hands up, and no harm would come to them, but that any attempt by them to resist would be met by rifle fire. We waited for a minute for the foam to disperse, and

- 91 -

then gradually they began to climb down and allow themselves to be handcuffed.

Mayor Robles approached in the company of one of the Marino policemen and Señor Fraga. The latter had caught his breath and was walking with as much dignity as he could muster in the circumstances. He was tall, athletic looking, with strong, rugged features. Hollywood would cast him as the commander of at least a platoon, if not of a whole regiment. I joined them as they walked over to the dead man. I thought I was maintaining my calm rather well in the face of the thought that this lump of flesh had minutes before been a living human being, but then my stomach betrayed me and I felt a wave of nausea. Robles asked Fraga the name of the casualty and he grunted an answer. Does he have a wife? Not any more, Fraga said. He hasn't lived with his wife for years. Does he have any children? Fraga didn't know. Robles signed to the guard to take him back to where the other prisoners were gathered.

As I turned away from the corpse I felt Robles' hand on my shoulder. "You had to shoot him, my friend. He would have killed Felipe. He was an evil man." I couldn't think of anything to say for a few seconds and finally blurted out, "Wouldn't it have been better for a good man to go to meet his Maker?" Robles threw up his hands. "We do what we have to do." But did I have to do it? Yes, once the plan had been put in motion, not to follow it was unthinkable. Not to act would have made things much worse. But did we have to make a plan in the first place?

The prisoners in handcuffs were loaded into the troop carrier accompanied by the police from Marino, and they took off towards Amparo. The rest of our men gathered around, silent or speaking quietly. Had it not been for the body lying there they might have been shouting, slapping each other on the back and congratulating each other on their complete victory. It may have been my imagination, but they seemed to avoid me, and to tell the truth, I would have liked to avoid myself. Robles signaled to the men who had been helping the hostages, and they came with a stretcher to remove the body.

It's not often that one can rehearse a battle, but this one had been rehearsed in detail. In spite of practice and planning there had been a fatality. At least we did not have to resort to Plan B; if Fraga's men had left the troop carrier and tried to engage us, they would have been sitting ducks as we fired on them from cover. Things could have been much worse.

Will McGrath had been supervising the loading of the prisoners onto the carrier. Now he walked over to where the rest of us were gathered and shook hands with and thanked each man, pausing for an extra minute with Felipe. That young man was trembling, hardly able to speak. When he came to me Will said simply: "Nothing happened that we didn't foresee as very possible. Everyone did what we had asked them to do. That's as good as it gets in this sort of operation."

As we were getting ready to leave for Amparo the noisy crew arrived from San Martin. Aldomar strode over to Will and announced that things couldn't have gone better. The plan worked perfectly. How did things go here? I was some ways away from the main party, stowing the weapons on the back of a truck, so when the conversation settled down to a more normal tone I couldn't make out what was being said. Aldomar's grin widened as the people around him gave their versions of the afternoon's work. Then his face took on a more sober look and he came over to me and asked how I was doing. I could easily become the object of too much commiseration, so I replied that I was fine and that we had a lot to be thankful for. Aldomar put a large hand on my shoulder. "Miguel, you and I, we do other people's fighting for them. Half the time we don't know what the hell is going on. We do our best, and we're never sure whether it's not all some hideous mistake."

I rode back to Amparo in an old school bus with about fifteen of the men. As they went over the events of the day, their tone became more jubilant. In a half-day they had broken the power of an outlaw who had been bullying them for years. By the time we reached Amparo they were ready to enshrine Colonel McGrath in a pantheon with Bolivar, Mendoza and O'Higgins.

Our vehicle was the last to arrive from El Puente Ingles, and as we debarked Señor Robles met us and announced that some of the people were going to meet in the church. The padre said a few words and led us in the rosary. Then the mayor stood in front of the sixty or so people and began by thanking everyone who had participated, directed us first of all to thank God for the results of the day. On the other hand, their troubles were not over. There were still men who would try to take advantage of the weak and helpless. It will not always be as easy to defeat them as it was today. If at all possible, they must always try to solve their problems without violence. For that to happen, they had to pray to God, they had to stand together and act as soon as a threat occurred, before an enemy became strong. It is better for honest policemen like Aldomar to handle a situation than to have to raise an army.

As we filed out of the Church the sun was going down, and a band began to play on the square. I left the scene as quickly as I could, went to my room in the hotel, fished out a book from my half-unpacked suitcase and read until I was ready to go to sleep, with sounds of revelry in the background.

CHAPTER TWELVE

Had a certain segment of popular opinion south of the Rio del Rey prevailed, Señor Fraga and his second-in-command might have been disposed of quickly. Mayor Robles however reined in the most bloody-minded of his townsmen and insisted on due process. The country's current state prevented the local police and courts from handling the case. Few judges would convict the worst criminals and thereby risk retaliation. The police, those not on the payroll of some faction or other, were not eager to detain people whom the courts were unlikely to convict and who, once free, might wreak vengeance on the officers and their families.

Some days earlier Señor Robles had asked Dolores Laval to look into the possibility of extraditing Fraga to some country, preferably Argentina, where he could be tried and, if found guilty, incarcerated. She had discovered that there was no way that any United Nations agency would take immediate action, nor did anything in the charter of the Organization of American States promise help. Señorita Laval had uncovered one scrap of useful information. A few years earlier Argentina had provided a locale for the trial, by a Talcayan magistrate, of a particularly dangerous felon whose trial, if held in Talcayan, would endanger the magistrate, the prosecuting attorney and their families.

While the rest of us were preparing for the confrontation with Fraga, Dolores Laval was arranging with government representatives of Talcayan and Argentina for Fraga and his second-in-command, Suarez, to be held in Mendoza until a preliminary hearing determined whether there were grounds for bringing them to trial. Authorities in Mendoza would provide a site for this initial hearing, hold the two prisoners and provide a site for the trial, provided that it took place within two months of the initial hearing. Talcayan was to pay all expenses and supply the magistrate, the prosecuting attorney and staff. Fraga had enough money stashed away to employ competent persons for his own defense. Should the trial lead to a prison sentence, Talacayan must find accommodations elsewhere.

Will and I volunteered to help escort the two prisoners to Mendoza, where they would be turned over to Argentina authorities. We were traveling to that city in any case to return the rented vehicles and then at last to catch a flight back to North America. This left the problem of the others who had been taken prisoner. The little jail in Amparo and a deserted house nearby had been given a quick make-over and were overflowing with detainees. Robles thought that most of them could be released rather quickly after the individual cases were sorted out. Several individuals however were guilty of crimes for which they should be held accountable, and they would be tried locally. The mayor reasoned that, while Fraga's friends might try to free him, if they could discover where he was, they were not likely to risk their own safety by trying to rescue his followers, most of whom could expect to be released within weeks in any case.

Two days after what Aldomar had begun to call "the Battle of El Puente Ingles", Mayor Robles, Will and I set out in the Land Rover for the city of Magdalena. Robles intended to bargain with Mayor Guzman for the use of his city's jail for the short term to accommodate our prisoners awaiting trial and for a longer term if some prisoners were sentenced to prison. Will accompanied Mayor Robles mainly, I suspect, to remind Señor Guzman that Amparo had defended its own interests with force when it had to. I tagged along to see the sights. Magdalena, situated at the foot of the Andes, was reputed to be the country's most

THE BLOOD-DIMMED TIDE IS LOOSED

beautiful city and its main tourist attraction, and I intended to enjoy the fine weather in congenial surroundings.

Señor Robles recommended a scenic route if we were willing to take a little extra time, so a few miles north of the turnoff to San Martin we left the main road and headed northwest into the mountains. The previous night my sleep had been troubled by the image of the dead outlaw, but this morning was different. The landscape, refreshed by rain during the night, sparkled in the sun. Once we left the main highway the road presented a new and more beautiful scene every couple of minutes as we topped hills and wound our way through green valleys, some covered with forest, others bright with the blossoms of orchards coming to life. After a gradual, serpentine climb of several kilometers Señor Robles instructed me to pull over on to a scenic lookout. We got out and looked down into a broad valley covered with orchards and gardens. Perhaps twenty kilometers away lay the city of Magdalena, starting in the valley and climbing up the foot of a mountain.

At four o-clock that afternoon Mayor Robles and Colonel McGrath were to meet with Mayor Guzman. We would stay overnight because Robles planned to confer the next day with several citizens of Magdalena about plans to keep people like Fraga from getting a foothold. For the rest of the day I was free to roam. I got out of the Land Rover at the entrance to a trail that, Mayor Robles informed me, would lead me into the city. The mayor and Will had some time to kill before meeting with Guzman, so they would stop at La Posada Alicante to reserve a double room for Will and myself. Robles would stay the night with friends. Will and I were to meet at the posada at six P.M.

The trail wound upwards for several miles to a point that overlooked Magdalena. The only sounds were birds chirping and the rustling of leaves. A couple of times I caught a glimpse of an agouti but it would never stay visible long enough for me to get a good look. Hiking along wooded trails has always seems to me like a luxury. The hush, being alone, working off nervous energy, passing through ever-changing scenery and letting one's mind wander, it never fails to lift my spirits. We spend our days complaining and fretting and feeling pressured, and then we plan and spend and travel to get away from it all, when something so refreshing is close at hand.

- 97 -

Hiking in the Canadian Rockies has recently become less relaxing because of newspaper reports of rare but occasionally fatal attacks on human beings by grizzly bears and cougars. A couple of days after each such report there is usually an editorial or a letter to the editor pointing out that we are encroaching on the natural habitat of these magnificent beasts. It occurs to me that the magnificent beasts don't show much compunction for intruding on the natural habitat of the elk, deer and big-horned sheep that make up their diet; but that must be the inner redneck in me speaking. On this day I could put such thoughts aside, having been assured that I would meet no predators that would resent my intrusion into their home territory or regard me as a savory addition to their menu.

It was only two o'clock when I arrived at the little park which marked the end of the trail. There was no reason to hurry on to the street so I sat on a wooden bench and dozed in the sun for a few minutes. I was awakened from half-sleep by a stabbing pain in my foot. I looked down and saw a small hole in the top of my shoe. Just a few feet away a man with an expressionless face was holding a pistol with silencer and looking at me as one might look at an interesting lab specimen. He was slim, perhaps forty years of age, with thinning, dark hair pulled back in a pony tail. He spoke English with a middle-American accent: "Okay, Mr. Hannigan, that was just to catch your attention. Now we're going to talk."

Jason Bourne would probably have sized up the situation, shook off the hole in his foot as a minor irritant and sprung into action. The most brilliant thought that occurred to me was that I was in serious trouble. This fellow was not a local amateur. By the simple expedient of shooting me in the foot he took away whatever advantage I might have in quickness, should I try to defend myself. After I got past the first moment of shock and started to think I reflected that he was not likely to kill me right away if, as seemed apparent, he had some reason to talk. Maybe I could overcome my lack of mobility and put my reflexes to work if I could provoke him to get close enough to take a swing at me; so I decided to indulge my anger, an easy enough task in the circumstances. My combat training had included some exercises in overcoming fear, and one of our instructors had a theory that we overcome fear through anger. Homer pictured his Greek heroes preparing for battle by working themselves into a raging frenzy.

I snarled at pony tail that he must really be proud that he had gotten up enough courage to shoot me while I was asleep. I began, very gingerly, to take off my shoe to examine the damage while describing his ancestry in terms which his mother would probably resent. He took my ranting in stride however, stayed well out of my reach and informed me calmly that it would give him great pleasure to put a bullet through my thick skull, and he might do that in a minute or two if I didn't tell him where Rafael Fraga was being held.

The irony of the situation infuriated me even more. I was ready to howl with pain, and I was probably going to die because this idiot had run me down to question me about something I didn't know. I stated that Fraga's friends must be short of money if the best they could hire was a bonehead who chased around the country asking people for information they didn't have. Several other expressions may have crept into my speech, but they did little to clarify the issue and need not be recorded here.

He was contemptuous. "Don't pretend you don't know where he is. Robles doesn't bring in a couple of heavies to do his fighting for him and then forget to put them in charge of his principal prisoner."

I answered that I had come into the country to look at a business proposition for the company I worked for. It had nothing to do with fighting anyone's battles. "Believe me, if I had been brought into the country to use a gun, first I would have learned something about the situation rather than blundering around, shooting people while they're asleep."

"Yeah, if you're the genius" he smirked, "How come you're the one with the sore foot?"

"So if I snuck up behind Albert Einstein and shot him," I said, "would that make me smarter than he is?"

"I hope you don't mind, old chap," he replied, "but shooting you in the foot is only step one. I'll keep aiming higher and higher until you tell me where you are holding Fraga."

"Let's see," I replied, "If I knew where he was and told you, then you'd have what you want and you'd shoot me, just to tie up loose ends. If I don't tell you, then maybe we argue for a while and then you shoot me. Am I missing something, or do those two choices seem rather similar?"

He paused for a few seconds, and seemed to come to a decision. "Where are you going to meet your big friend?"

"What big friend?"

"Don't be so damn stupid. The guy who organized that little ambush the other day, the one with you in the car today."

"So this is plan B. I tell you where 'my big friend' is, and you shoot me. Then you shoot him, because he doesn't know where Fraga is either, and if he did tell you, you would still kill him. You're not motivating me."

He paused for a minute. "Look. I don't give a rat's ass about what happens to you. Personally, I would as soon put you out of your misery; but I'm being paid to get information, not get rid of you, so just because I'm soft-hearted I'm making you this offer. We go and find your friend. Maybe they didn't tell a numbskull like you where Fraga is being kept, but they would have told the guy with the brains. Maybe when he sees me killing you a little at a time he'll answer my question. Then I let you go. You don't believe I'll let you go? Well, it's your one chance to stay alive, so here we go."

"Just like that," I answered. "You're going to let us go. Of course you're a trusting type. You wouldn't suspect that we might make a phone call or two and put a crimp in your plans? What possible reason would I have to do what you told me?"

"The only hope you have is to do what I say. So, do it."

I continued taking off my bloody sock. The bullet had gone right through the sole of my shoe. The amount of blood scared me.

Pony tail stood in front of me and pointed the pistol at my head and barked out, "Get up. We're moving."

I looked back at him and spoke more calmly than I had up to that point. "I have two choices. I can get up and go with you and bleed to death. I can stay here and put a bandage on this foot and go with you when I slow down the bleeding. Just on a hunch, I'll go with the second choice."

He cursed and informed me that I had a minute to get ready and that if I thought I could save myself by waiting until someone came into the park, he would be happy to shoot anyone who might sound an alarm. I believed him. I folded my handkerchief into a bandage and used a shoelace to bind it in place. I was able to get my unlaced shoe on again, and more or less staggered to my feet. My assailant remarked on what a pansy I was, letting a little thing like a sore foot bother me. A couple of women pushing baby carriages came through the gate, gave us a curious look and passed on. The gun had disappeared and its proprietor had adopted the stance of someone helping a friend who had sprained an ankle. When the women had made their leisurely way out of sight along one of the paths he pointed to a panel truck parked a few yards outside of the gate. I hopped in that direction with some slivers of a plan starting to form in my mind.

I told him that I was supposed to go to La Posada Alicante to reserve a double room for Will and myself to stay the night, and I gave him the directions to the posada that Robles had given me. He told me to toss him my wallet, he extracted my credit card and threw the wallet back and ordered me into the back of the panel truck. "I'm overflowing with kindness today, so I'm going to save you the trouble of registering for that room."

This was not what I had planned, but I didn't have a whole lot of options. He slammed the door, started the motor and we began to move. The only access to the space in which I was confined was the back door, and the inside handle had been removed. The glass in the rear window was reinforced with wires. The motor started and we drove for a few minutes. The motor stopped and driver's door slammed shut. Nothing happened for a while, then I heard the driver's door open, we drove a short distance and stopped. The back door opened and he ordered me out. There was no-one else in the parking lot, not surprising in the early afternoon. He had parked next to the room he had reserved, so I was able to hop to the door, which opened on to the parking lot.

My watch showed a little past 2:30 P.M. Hardly a half hour had passed since I sat down to doze on the park bench. I informed pony tail that Will was to meet me at 7 P.M. He ordered me to lie on the bed farthest from the door and he took his place on a comfortable chair. I had plenty of time to think of all the reasons why my fragile plan would fail. It all depended on Will "smelling a rat" when he discovered that another room had been reserved for the two of us. Maybe at the front desk the gunman had learned that Will had already reserved a room, and we were now waiting in that room for Will to walk into a trap. Or suppose part of my plan worked and when Will returned the desk clerk told him that one Michael Hannigan had reserved a room. Maybe Will would put it down to my failure to listen to instructions. Again, he would walk into the trap. Perhaps Will would learn nothing relevant to the situation from the person at the desk and simply retire to his reserved room to wait for me. That scenario might take longer to play out, but I could not imagine it ending pleasantly. However, as I had told Will a few days earlier, it's like playing bridge. When you can think of only one lie of the cards that allows you to make the hand, that's how you play it.

There was a heavily curtained window next to the door. Presumably there was another window in the bathroom, a corner of which I could see through a partially open door. There were no windows or outside doors on three sides of the room.

When I tried to convince my captor that I needed pain killers he remarked that he didn't want me to miss out on any of the experience. It would make a man of me. I tried to get some information out of him. Why was he in Magdalena? Why not try to get at us in Amparo? He had been watching us from yesterday noon, had followed the Land Rover this morning supposing that we were transporting Fraga away from Amparo. Passing us where we had pulled off the road to view the scenery, he was able to see that Fraga was not on board. I had then obliged him by following the trail. He simply drove to the Magdalena entrance and waited for me.

I quit asking questions, hoping that pony tail would doze off, but he seemed to be able to remain alert indefinitely. About five o'clock he remarked that possibly my friend might return early, and there was nothing like being prepared. He cuffed my hands behind my back, proceeded to put a couple of layers of tape over my mouth, admired his handiwork and remarked that it improved my personality considerably.

CHAPTER THIRTEEN

As my captor settled back into the chair I pondered the fact that these might be the last few minutes of my life. I am not terrified of death as such, but what comes afterwards is a concern, and I tried to pray. One might suppose that prayer would come easily in such circumstances, but pain has a way of focusing the mind on the immediate present rather than on eternal verities, and with the pain came the feeling that by now all sorts of infections were probably setting in.

Then there was the thorny issue of forgiveness. Many thousands of times during their lives Christians pray that their offenses might be forgiven as they have forgiven others. Could I really forgive this smirking criminal? Or could I forgive the as-yet-unidentified killer of Catherine? I decided that I could get as far as not wanting them to be eternally damned. I might go farther and resolve that, if given the chance, I would not choose to kill them or do them any unjustified harm. I could however imagine several forms of justified harm that I would be happy to visit upon them. Would that be enough to get me off the hook? Was it real forgiveness, or had I patched together something that just looked like it? Once free from the immediate danger of death would I revert to what was my real attitude? In war a lot of soldiers must go to meet their Maker without forgiving their enemies, especially those who, like myself, had been trained to use anger as an antidote to fear. Is there some special dispensation for those who die in battle?

As my mind wandered I thought about Corporal Henri Robichaud, who during my time in the armed forces had generously offered to help me raise the level of my French from atrocious to merely bad. He had probably read more existential philosophy than was good for him, and spoke earnestly of the need to be engagé. Well, I had become engagé, and a fat lot of good it had done for me, or perhaps for anyone else.

Maybe the best I could hope for, if Will were forewarned, was to become a pawn in a stand-off. That thought alternated with a desire to get some relief from the pain. I began to shift my injured foot into different positions, because each time I did so there seemed to be a moment before the pain came back in full force. I was in the midst of one of these maneuvers when a motorcycle close by began to rev up noisily. When the noise continued for a minute pony tail went to the window, pushed back a curtain with the end of his pistol and then returned to his chair without comment.

Perhaps the motorcycle noise was to cover up some other activity. I was listening intently when there was a crash of breaking glass. Any intrusion by rescuers would have to come through the front of the room, and I immediately rolled off the bed on the side away from the door, managing to land on my good foot and then rolling part way under the bed. I was half way through this maneuver when there was a brilliant flash and an earsplitting explosion in the room itself. Although I was turned away from the flash I was blinded for a moment. A couple of seconds later there was another flash and another explosion. The second explosion was followed almost immediately by a gunshot. It was not from a gun with a silencer. I heard footsteps, some words shouted in Spanish and then my uncle's voice asking whether I was there.

With the tape over my mouth the best I could do was to groan and begin to climb up off the floor. As I recovered some sight I could make out a couple of officers in the room with Will, who had his back to me. Two white-uniformed men ran in with a stretcher, went over to the far side of the other bed and began to work on pony tail's prone body. Will turned around, noticed me and began carefully to pull the tape away from my mouth. He was asking me about a key but for a moment it didn't register what he was talking about. Finally I indicated that the gunman had the key to the handcuffs in his pocket.

The whole mess was sorted out with a speed that suggested that no one wanted to hang around to explain. The ambulance attendants, having slowed the bleeding where the gunman had been shot in the hip, carried him out on the stretcher, accompanied by two policemen. I was more or less carried to the Land Rover and lifted into the back seat. Will got into the driver's seat and in seconds we were out of the parking lot and on the street. The prisoner would go, under guard, to the emergency room at the local hospital, but the prevailing view was that I would get more prompt treatment at a clinic in the immediate neighborhood.

I explained to Will, apologetically, that while I knew that there was a risk that my plan would lead him into a trap, the chances seemed just as good that if I did nothing the gunman would hunt him down and attack him. Will did his best to reassure me that I had used good judgment. When I remarked that it was lucky that Will caught on that something was amiss, he explained that I need not have worried about that. "After your friend made the reservation and was walking back to the truck the clerk remembered that he had already rented a room for two people, one of whom was a Michael Hannigan. He was ready to go out and tell the guy, but he saw him drive across the parking lot, stop and open the back door of the van. Then he saw you hobble out and into the room."

The clerk thought of calling the police, but for all he knew this might be a police operation, either on the level or illegal, and decided to wait for Will's return. The colonel had arrived early, and after hearing the clerk's story had realized that he could do nothing without police help. He called them, explained the situation and suggested that they bring with them several stun grenades. These would explode on contact and produce lots of noise and light without being likely to cause permanent harm, although they could cause a nasty burn if you were too close.

The tricky part was to get everyone in place without alerting the gunman, including getting a man with a sledge hammer with his back to the wall next to the window, where he would begin operations by smashing in the window. The curtain drawn across the window was a problem, so someone had crouched under the window and reached up with a garden rake to lift the curtain while another tossed in the two grenades. Before my captor could recover his vision the door was opened, an officer crawled through behind a protective shield and Will stood up and peeked into the room from the side of the door and winged the gunman on the hip as he was staggering towards the back of the room.

We waited almost an hour at the clinic before a doctor was free to see me. It took more than an hour for him to make the necessary repairs to my foot. There was no anesthetist at the clinic, so the best they could do was to use a local anesthetic, which no doubt reduced the pain but retained enough of it, as my erstwhile tormenter might have said, to help make a man of me. The operation complete and a cast having been applied, the physician assured me, with a let-that-be-a-lesson-to-you expression, that the foot would be very painful and that I could not walk for several months. He probably thought that any foreigners intruding into his country deserved everything that they got, and I was inclined to agree.

Later that evening we dropped by La Posada Alicante to reimburse the proprietor for the damage and leave a gratuity for the clerk, who may have saved our lives. We moved to a different posada for the night and double checked the locks on our door. As we left the next morning Will was not in a jovial mood and grumped, "I've had about enough of this place. I can't wait to get home."

Señor Robles had learned about my misadventure when Will called him the previous evening. When we picked him up at his friend's home he was still alarmed about the hardship and danger I had undergone and apologized as though he had caused them. We reminded him that it was we who had initiated the action against Fraga, but this hardly muted his protestations.

Robles called off the meeting he had planned for that morning and the three of us headed back to Amparo, this time by a more direct route. After a half hour or so we were clear of the foothills and the mayor became more reflective. His guess was no better than ours about who had hired the gunman. The remnants of Fraga's gang that Aldomar had allowed to escape from San Martin could hardly have located and hired an American hit man and have him on the scene within such a short time. It had to be someone higher up with more resources and organization. We had invisible enemies.

"I wish we could have questioned the guy," Robles mused. "I called the police station this morning, identified myself and talked to the chief. He had about one minute to give me. No, it would not be possible for me or any of my people to speak to the prisoner. That person, in bed in a local hospital, is being represented by a foreign lawyer who is making sure that no one other than the local officers sees him. Who knows what's going on? Maybe it's the lawyer. Maybe it's the local police. Anyway, someone with power is keeping us away from the prisoner."

"I doubt that it's the local police," Will said. "They gave me everything I asked for yesterday. They couldn't have been more cooperative."

Señor Robles looked at Will, who was driving, and then at me in the back seat.

"Those officers with you last night were just answering a call. They had no idea that the man they were dealing with was connected to anything. They had no orders from higher up. Besides, when they found out who you were they would be impressed and maybe a little bit scared. Word gets around fast. You two are famous in Talcayan, whether you like it or not. You could see it yesterday. Until now, Guzman wouldn't give me the time of day. Yesterday he was all smiles. Marco Robles has these two operatives from the north. One is a military genius and the other is the most dangerous shooter in Talcayan."

Other than target practice, I had fired two shots since entering the country. If I had gotten off four or five rounds I might have become a legend.

Word of our misadventure had preceded us to Amparo, and about twenty people were waiting for us in the town square. My exit from the Land Rover on crutches confirmed for them that something dramatic had happened. A variety of fanciful accounts had already begun to make the rounds. Will and I tried to get them back to the facts, but I doubt that it made much difference. Reality, it has been said, is a crutch for people with no imagination. Aldomar had brought his wife to join the reception. Señora San Pedro (I finally found out Aldomar's last name) was as gregarious as her husband. We were introduced to two of their children, boys about eight and ten years of age who would probably brag to their classmates that they had actually been present at the return of their father's two friends who had survived who-knows-what perils in Magdalena.

With our enemies looking to free Fraga, we needed to review our plans for his transfer to Mendoza. The first suggestion was to spirit him and his lieutenant out of the country by night, but when I began to imagine the trip I wasn't so sure about that strategy. Fraga's friends hired one man to go after Will and me. Why only one? Presumably they were not in a position to mobilize a large force on short notice. If that held true also for efforts to free Fraga while he was being moved, then we should worry not about a major attack but about an ambush by one or at most a very few people. It's easier to deal with an ambush in broad daylight than in the dark.

We left Amparo the next morning, Aldomar leading the way in the Land Rover with me next to him with a loaded rifle. Someone questioned whether it was prudent for someone on crutches to be acting as the armed escort, but I figured if the important thing was to keep my eyes open and remain alert, the pain in my foot might actually help. We were followed by a police car from Amparo with two of Aldomar's men in the front and the two prisoners, suitably restrained, in the back. Will accompanied by another police officer brought up the rear in the flatbed truck loaded with the two containers for the foam that had smothered Fraga's Leopard tank. Anyone trying to attack us from behind would have a hard time disabling or getting by the truck if Will spotted him on time. At Marino Aldomar would be replaced by Mayor Laval, who would represent the Talcayan government dealing with authorities in Mendoza.

The trip as far as Marino was uneventful. Aldomar talked about the danger from Fraga's allies who were still at large, and I began to feel like I was deserting my friends in their hour of need. But Will and I had already stretched our stay well beyond the original plan and beyond what my relatives in Edmonton had expected. I didn't relish the thought of hobbling off the plane on crutches and having to explain how this happened on a trip that I had so airily predicted would be a piece of cake. I was neither enjoying the moment nor looking forward to what was to come. Were I in a better mood this would have been a time to practice my Spanish, but I was a mostly silent and dull travelling companion.

As we pulled off the road into an empty yard just outside of Marino, Aldomar held out his hand. "Sir, it has been an honor to serve with you. We will always be grateful for what you and the Colonel have done. I hope you will come back to visit us." I assured him that it had been an honor for me, and that if Hannigan Industries opened up mines in Talcayan I would almost certainly be back. I felt sorry for the big man as he ambled back to take his leave from Colonel McGrath, burdened with the responsibility for the safety of the citizenry of Amparo.

CHAPTER FOURTEEN

The figure that emerged from the taxi parked across the yard was not Mayor Laval, as I had expected, but his daughter, who stopped to exchange a few words with Aldomar. She seemed almost hesitant as she approached the Land Rover, without the confident stride with which she had entered our meeting with Señor Laval a few days earlier. She came up to the window on my side of the vehicle and said in her careful English, "I'm sorry to hear about your injury. It must be painful." Assured that the painkillers took care of most of that problem, she went on. "Papa cannot come. Only Papa and I are authorized to act as agents of Talcayan when we hand over the prisoners, so I must come with you."

She got in behind the wheel, took a look at my foot in the cast, put the vehicle in gear and pulled on to the road without hesitation. Keeping her eyes on the road, she said, "I heard only a little about what happened to you in Magdalena." I gave her the condensed version that by now I had practically memorized. I asked whether her father was ill. She shook her head. "Papa received a telephone call this morning. The caller did not identify himself. He said that if Papa takes any part in the prosecution of Rafael Fraga, a bad accident will happen to him and Mama."

- 110 -

"Did the people who contacted your father say anything about our trip to Mendoza today?"

"I think not. They did not talk about Fraga being moved out of the country. They only warned Papa not to take part in prosecuting him."

"If you take your father's place on this trip, does that solve anything? Won't they still attack your family?"

"They seem not to know much. They probably never heard of me. If Papa is away for a day or so and they learn that Rafael Fraga has been moved out of the country, that would be bad. Anyway, one of us must go. How fast do you want me to go?"

"We've been going about seventy kilometers per hour. Any faster on this road and you raise dust and throw up stones so that the vehicles can't stay close to each other."

We entered Marino shortly and had to stop or proceed slowly at each intersection. Traveling through the city made it impossible to spot all the places from which we could be ambushed. On the other hand, a small attacking party would probably not make a move in the middle of a city. Once clear of the town she asked, "You have your rifle beside you. Do you expect trouble?"

"We don't expect trouble. Then, we didn't expect trouble in Magdalena either. It's best to be prepared. Does me having a rifle bother you?"

"No. It does not matter one way or the other."

Then she abruptly changed the subject. "Do you go to church regularly? People in Amparo say you and Colonel McGrath go to Mass on Sunday."

"Yeah, we go whenever it's possible. Why? Does that surprise you?"

"Well, it is not what one expects . . . for someone in your occupation."

"What do you think is my occupation?"

"I am sorry. It was very impolite of me . . . to ask such questions."

"All my life I have been a fairly conscientious Catholic. For a number of years I was a soldier. Lots of soldiers go to Mass on Sunday. Now I'm a security officer. I try to make sure that my uncle's mines use all the proper safety measures. I am not a gunman, if that's what you think."

For the first time she looked towards me. "I am sorry. In this country they think you are a . . . a hired gun. You have a reputation. I should not jump to conclusions."

"That's okay. If I stay in this country much longer I'll start thinking of myself as a hired gun."

"I hope not. But you are very good at it, they say."

I shrugged, and we were quiet for while. Then I recalled an earlier conversation. "Your father said he thought you should be an opera singer."

She nodded. "Papa spent much money so I could have a teacher of voice. I learned much . . . a lot of music. But I would not be a first class opera singer. My voice is good but not great."

"Do you sing when you are driving?"

"Not usually. Do you?"

"When I was young my mother and I would sing when we drove. She has a good voice. I can carry a tune. If they gave prizes for volume I would do well, but no one ever suggested I should sing opera."

We began to alternate songs. Dolores had a rich, alto voice that seemed to justify her father's evaluation of her career possibilities, although a Land Rover with the wind whistling and the gravel clattering against the undercarriage is perhaps not the best place to assess vocal talent. My own repertoire had not expanded much of late, so it still owed much to my mother's tastes, which ran to Irish ballads and Broadway musicals. Dolores, probably in order not to show up my limitations, at first confined herself to popular Spanish and South American songs, but with a little encouragement she launched into several arias. We discovered a few songs we both knew and relaxed a bit.

A couple of automobiles passed us, impatient at our measured pace. At one point my CB radio crackled into life and Will's voice interrupted my rendition of something from Brigadoon. "There's a big semi in a hurry back here, and I'm pulling over a little to give him room. You might want to do the same. Maybe slow down. The galoot could throw a lot of gravel at you if he hits that ridge in the middle of the road."

THE BLOOD-DIMMED TIDE IS LOOSED

The truck passed, pulled back on to our side of the road and, sure enough, showered us with gravel. Once clear of that problem Señorita Laval asked, "What is a galoot?" When I hesitated she asked again, "Is it a bad word? Would I insult someone if I called him that?"

"It would depend," I said. "If you brought your boy friend home and your father referred to him as a galoot, that would not be a good sign. It would mean he was not impressed. But if there are two friends, and one does something the other doesn't agree with, and the other called him a big galoot, that would be more like a joke than an insult."

"So if someone does something I do not agree with, I could call him a galoot and it would be okay?"

"Something like that, if you were friends."

"Are galoots always men?"

I had to admit that I had never heard the word used of a woman. She was quiet for a few seconds and then: "Galoot. I like that word. So . . . if someone has an injured foot and he should be resting, but instead he is driving across the country with a rifle beside him in case someone wants to shoot at him, could such a person properly be called a galoot?"

"Well if this person has to aim a gun with his feet then he might be a galoot."

She broke in, still in a slightly jocular tone but her words came out in a rush. "And if someone starts shooting at this person, he is going to walk on his hands to get out of the line of fire?"

"Well," I said, "We're talking about a hypothetical situation here, so let's imagine that this injured person doesn't have to hide from the attackers. They have to hide from him."

She put on a wry face that probably meant "Isn't that just like a man?" I assured her that I was joking and that I was not really inspired by bravado. She was not satisfied. "Really, it is dangerous to be overconfident. You are not indestructible."

I pointed at the cast on my foot. "So it would seem."

We passed a sign that indicated that the Talcayan-Argentina border was one kilometer ahead. While Will had been scrutinizing the traffic overtaking us, I had managed to stay alert and had detected nothing of a threatening nature ahead.

- 113 -

Mayor Laval had informed Argentina Customs and Immigration that we would be passing through with prisoners bound for Mendoza. The truck and police car stopped in a clear area well short of the Argentina customs office while we in the Land Rover approached the office to deliver the required documents. Señorita Laval parked in one of the spaces next to the office, grabbed a large envelope with the documents and was about to get out when she turned back to me.

"Do you see anything that worries you?"

"No. All clear as far as I can see." There were two cars ahead of us, the driver of one was talking to the agent in the booth, the other vehicle was waiting in line. There was nothing to arouse suspicion, but of course it's always a guess. "How long do you think it will take to get through the red tape here?"

"Only a few minutes," she replied. "All the papers are correctly completed."

"I've gone through immigration offices with all my papers in order, and that just seemed to present a challenge for the officials to find some other way to delay me."

"Ah, but you see, you are not a lawyer."

"So why is a lawyer going to do any better?"

"What do you think we lawyers study for three years in law school?"

"Just on a hunch, I'm going to guess you study the law."

"Nooo." She sounded like a school teacher disappointed with a student. "We learn in law school that there are too many laws for anyone to know them all. So in a situation such as this you say whatever you need to say, and you say it with authority, because there is a very good chance that there is some law somewhere that agrees with you. Just watch." And she strode off towards the office.

She was back out in less than five minutes with a self-satisfied look and waved to the drivers of the other two vehicles to approach. The border officials did a cursory examination of the three vehicles and checked the passport pictures of everyone against their actual appearance. Everything was in order. In a very few minutes we were back on the road.

- 114 -

As we pulled away I took what might be my last look at Talcayan. A mile or two across the border we pulled off into a shaded spot, spread a clean canvas on the ground, pulled out two picnic baskets that the cook in the Robles household had prepared, and we lunched at leisure. The two prisoners even dropped their sullen expressions for a few minutes. Had I been in their place I think that the very ordinariness of the experience of a picnic lunch might have brought home the inevitability of my fate. It was the everyday world, without the intervention of gangs and guns and desperate gambles, the wheels of justice grinding slowly and inexorably.

When we were back on the road Dolores asked: "Now that we are in Argentina, is it probable that someone will attack us?"

"I think not," I replied. "If our enemies knew we were transporting the prisoners, I think they would have intercepted us by now. But not many people knew about this trip. Our enemies probably have no idea of where Fraga and his pal are."

"I have been watching you," she said. "Even when we were singing, your eyes were going back and forth from one side of the road to another, out the side window, in the rear view mirrors. I am not objecting. It makes me feel more safe. Watching. Is that something else they taught you in the army, along with marksmanship?"

"No," I answered. "I don't remember any courses on watching. I guess we did have some training on spotting anything unusual in a situation. It helps to concentrate the mind if there is even a small chance of an attack, of course."

Dolores changed the subject again. "Have you always been religious?"

"I wouldn't say I'm super religious," I answered, "but I didn't go through a rebellious phase as far as religion was concerned. It's probably my mother I have to thank for that. She had these books that she had studied in school, back, she would say, before the experts decided that religion for the young is a matter of nice pictures and feelings. So she got me reading those books. By the age of twelve I knew about the proofs for the existence of God. By the time I reached grade eleven I had read about the debate concerning the historical value of the gospels. So I never got around to wondering whether the Catholic faith has a firm basis or not. Those books got me thinking about it even before the questions would normally have occurred to me. I used to wonder at some of my classmates who thought that religion was a bunch of rubbish. And then when I joined the armed services a couple of the padres gave me more stuff to read, and we would spend quite bit of time talking about it. They were happy to find a soldier who wanted to talk about religion."

She thought about that for a while and then asked: "So now you know all the answers?"

"I don't have nearly all the answers. Not at all," I said. "The way I see it—well, the way it is—we have limited minds. In the midst of a huge world we know a tiny bit. So what most people seem to do, they try to base their lives on the basis of that tiny bit that they think they know. But it doesn't work. Some of the most important things affecting your life fall outside of that tiny amount. Why does the world exist? What does God want us to do? What happens to us after we die? So you look around to see if anyone can help you with all of those things that fall outside of your tiny circle of clear knowledge. As far as I can see, the Christian faith and the Catholic Church do a much better job of pointing to some way of navigating in this mysterious world than any of the alternatives."

"You sound pretty confident," she said. "What about all those objections? Why would God let little children suffer from hunger and earthquakes, and so on?"

"As I said, I certainly haven't figured everything out. I don't know why God allows evil. But I'd be a little surprised if, with my mind, I had figured out every mystery. I'd be suspicious of any religion that makes everything clear. It would have to leave out a lot of reality. My assistant at Hannigan Industries, he's a lot smarter than I am. He's an atheist, and he has the confidence of the village atheist who can show off his superior knowledge without expecting to be challenged. He presumed that since I'm a Catholic I've never heard all of the stock arguments against religion. So I responded with the 'dead body in the parlor' argument. Do you know what I mean?"

She shook her head.

- 116 -

"Okay. You have an Agatha Christie murder mystery. A dead body with a bullet hole in the temple shows up in the parlor of a country house. The detective Hercule Poirot is on the spot and questions the house guests. One of the guests tells him that he's wasting his time. The body was just in the library. That's all there is to it. Why do you suppose there has to be a cause? Poirot is not likely to accept that sort of answer. But if the body in the library needs an explanation, doesn't the existence of the universe need an explanation?

"Now of course this doesn't stop my atheist assistant. But at least it puts him on his guard. We haven't changed each others' minds much. He seems bewildered that even though I'm not nearly as intelligent as he is, I can hold my own in the argument. Of course I cheat. I steal ideas from people like Thomas Aquinas."

CHAPTER FIFTEEN

I began to ask Señorita Laval about herself, her education, how she had ended up working as assistant to her father, etc. After a third question she was quiet for a moment and then said rather tentatively: "It is a complicated story. Some people—you ask them how they are and you get their medical history. I do not want to be like them."

I observed that we had about a hundred and twenty kilometers to go, and we were puttering along at seventy kilometers per hour. We probably had time for the short version of her life story. She hesitated a little while longer, finally shrugged in a sort of "Why not?" gesture and said: "If you are going to hear my life story, you should start calling me Dolores. Okay?"

"Okay, and you call me Mick."

"Mick. Is that your real name?"

"No. It stands for Michael."

"Michael. That is a good name. Miguel. Is it all right if I call you Miguel?"

I agreed to that, and she launched into her account.

"First of all, I am the daughter of Rodrigo Laval. I am not the daughter of Señora Laval. I was born in France before Papa had even met Mama Laval. My mother's parents were rarities—Algerian Catholics. They

- 118 -

emigrated to France and set up an épicerie in Bordeaux. They wanted something more for their daughter, so they sent her to do higher studies in Paris. There she met Papa, who took some of the same classes as she did. Within weeks they had begun to live together. It was the kind of thing you did if you were a student at the university in those days.

"One day my mother and father quarreled. I never learned why. My mother angrily left the apartment where they were living and never returned. A week later she discovered that she was pregnant. Rodrigo Laval was the father, but my mother was too proud even to let him know. As they say, trying to make it sound better, I was a love child. My mother was also too proud to ask for help from her parents in Bordeaux. They probably would have helped her, but they would be unhappy that their daughter had been living with a man and had become pregnant.

"Mother finished her year at L'École Polytechnique, intending to go back later, but she never did. Nor did she ever marry. My earliest memories are of my mother picking me up after working all day as a salesperson in a clothing store. We were not poor. Mother always earned enough to pay the bills. We lived in a small apartment in a working class part of Paris. It was a happy enough childhood. Once I began to attend school the schedule was regular. After school I would walk with a classmate to her home, and I would stay there doing homework, but mainly making noise, until my mother took me home. On Sundays Mother and I walked. Paris is a wonderful city in which to walk. We took the Metro to many places that I had never seen before.

"In my teens I started the usual silliness of fighting with my mother about unimportant things. There was one thing that especially bothered me. She was always careful about money. We never lacked necessary things, but only rarely did Mother buy anything fancy. Then one day she had a fur coat that she wore proudly, in spite of what Brigitte Bardot might have said; and we got an expensive new television set, and after that we took a vacation on the Côte d'Azur and stayed in an expensive hotel in Nice. Later I asked Mother for money for a pair of shoes that were very fashionable at the time and she said they were too expensive. I pointed out that we must have quite a bit of money, because she had a fur coat and we had a big television set and we had taken an expensive trip. She answered that those had been gifts. I did not know we had rich friends who could give such gifts.

"One day at school two girls were angry with me and said that my mother was nothing but a prostitute. I became very angry with them and I denied it loudly, but they pointed out that my mother took gifts from rich men. This silenced me. As it turned out, my mother had been the mistress of more than one wealthy man. Until then our arguments were probably not worse than those between other mothers and daughters. From then on our whole relationship was . . . not good . . . strained. We never talked about her relationship with these men, but I think she suspected that I knew. I began to despise her and despise all the advice she gave me. Believe me, I could have given lessons in stupidity to the three stooges.

"When I was fifteen, my mother was diagnosed with breast cancer. She lived almost a year after the diagnosis. We became closer during that time. As it became clear that she probably would not recover she began to make arrangements for me. She sold the fur coat and the television set. She tried to save money, but when she had to quit her job the welfare payments covered only part of our expenses. Then she moved into a private care facility. That was the only help she got from any of her former lovers. I think one paid for her stay for a couple of months in a hospice. Before her death Mother arranged for me to stay with a family.

"A couple of weeks before she died we talked about what was going to happen to me. She was crying and saying that she had so little to pass on to me, not even a good reputation. She said I had three choices. She had sold our apartment and most of that money was earning interest in a bank. I could continue to live with the family, friends of my mother, who had taken me in when Mother went to the hospital. I could continue to use the bank account to pay my expenses until I was old enough to begin working steadily. I could contact my grandparents in Bordeaux. They knew about me, but because my mother had stayed away from them I had never met them; but Mother said that they would help me if I asked. The third choice was Rodrigo Laval. Mother knew he was from Marino in Talcayan, so it had not been difficult for her to discover where he lived, but she had never contacted him. She said that if things became very bad for me I should write to him. He didn't know that I existed but Mother said he was a kind man and would very likely help me until I was old enough to get a job and take care of myself.

"One of the last things my mother said to me was that I must not make the same mistake she had made. She had been too proud to go to her parents or to get in contact with Rodrigo Laval. If she had not been so proud I would not now be left so alone in the world. I should ask for help when I needed it. After Mother died I continued to live with this couple. They had two children younger than I, a boy and a girl, and part of my job was to babysit them when their parents went to a movie. I did not like living there. They acted as my foster parents and tried to impose stricter rules than my mother had given me, so after several months I moved out.

"I had already been hanging out with some wild kids a little older than myself. They were into drugs and sex; and I found out that my money didn't last very long, and I began to exchange sex for cash. Then one night I got beat up. I limped back to the rooms where I lived with three other girls like myself. As I came in the door and began to tell my story, none of them seemed interested, and then I realized. It had happened to them. You say in English, 'no big deal'? That is who I was, an underage prostitute, risking my health and even my life, on the way to destroying myself with drugs, painting myself with make-up to cover up how I looked.

"I was trapped and didn't know how to get out of the mess or how to support myself honestly. I had rejected all three of the choices my mother had pointed out to me. Finally I listened to her advice: do not ruin your life by being too proud to ask for help. I told my three roommates that I was leaving, used the money left in my bank account to rent a miserable little room and sat down and wrote about a dozen versions of a letter to Rodrigo Laval.

"I was impatient for a reply even before my letter would have reached Marino. I had no telephone. My money was running out. Then one day I got a telegram. Señor Laval would arrive at Orly Airport three days later. He gave me the flight number and arrival time, and said that if I cared to meet him I could recognize him. He was of medium height, dark wavy hair cut short, would be wearing a light colored suit and the loudest red tie that I was likely to find in the airport that day and carrying a briefcase with an Aerolineas Argentinas sticker on the side.

"For two days I fretted. I could not bring him to my shabby room. What do you do with a visitor when you cannot offer him hospitality? What would he think of me, claiming to be a daughter that he had never heard of and asking for help? It might be a scam. Even if I could prove that I was who I claimed to be, his last contact with my mother had been a serious quarrel. He was a married man with a family and a good reputation in the community. He would not like this complication in his life. What would his wife think if she found out? On the other hand, he had responded quickly to my letter, and not tentatively but by flying to Paris.

"Anyway, I went to Orly to meet the plane, so nervous that I was trembling. I will never forget my first sight of the man with the bright red tie, in the middle of the line coming into the arrivals area, looking around anxiously. I caught his eye and his face brightened when he saw me. That was the end of the prologue and the beginning of my real life."

Dolores' eyes had moistened and she smiled rather sheepishly. "Anyway, that's the climax of my story. I thought that the most I could hope for was some financial support so I could finish at the lycée. Papa asked whether I thought I needed to make a new start. I wondered about how much he had guessed about me, and I said yes. Then, he said, a new start is much easier in a new place. I should return with him to Talcayan. I was so glad to find him and to have that kind of support, I agreed.

"Papa asked whether I would like to live with him and his family. When I looked doubtful he guessed correctly that I was worried about how Señora Laval would react. Papa said that he was fortunate to have known two good women in his life, and he had had the good sense to keep hold of the second. Señora Laval had learned about my existence a few minutes after Papa had read my letter. It was she who had insisted that her husband must not simply reply. He must fly to Paris and bring me back with him. If I would be content with a noisy Talcayan household with four children I would be welcome. So that was settled.

"Mama Laval has treated me less like a step-daughter and more like a younger sister. She gave me responsibilities in the home. She asked my advice about what was going on with 'this younger generation' and we had long conversations. My brothers and sisters never showed any resentment. I think they had so much confidence in the love of their parents that they did not feel bad because it was extended to one more. Mama and Papa were careful that I did not get different treatment except what was justified because I was older. I had become wise, and I paid attention to all the advice that my new-found parents gave me."

Dolores looked over at me. "Well, you asked for it, didn't you?" There was silence for a minute or two, and I would like to have broken it with appropriate words, but none came. I hadn't had much practice. Most girls, or women, whom I had dated were usually busy impressing me and I was usually busy trying to figure out what they were really like, so no conversations like this had ever taken place. Finally Dolores continued. "I've never told the whole story to anyone. There are parts of that story—you can guess which ones—that I haven't even told Mama or Papa." She paused again for a moment. "Maybe it is because you are going away."

I guessed that she was feeling embarrassed about confiding so much to a comparative stranger and I finally found some words. "I'm flattered that you told me. It's a remarkable story. You should be proud. You didn't give up. You made use of your opportunities and I am sure you have made the Laval family proud of you."

Stilted perhaps, but better than just sitting there like a dummy.

Our conversation wandered over many subjects after that. Dolores had been baptized as an infant, but her mother had never attended Mass. Dolores knew that her grandparents in Bordeaux were Catholic and she had a vague feeling as a child that she should be a Catholic. Once a part of the Laval household, she willingly attended Mass with the family, but she explained to Mama Laval that she could not go to communion because she wasn't sure about this whole religion business. The good woman had assured her that she was making the right decision. Some day, she said, she might see her way to become a fully practicing Catholic. Meanwhile, there was no point in pretending. But she could pray and listen to the readings.

Dolores continued. "I had been studying English and wanted to continue, so Papa enrolled me in a special school where they taught English. Then he paid a lot of money so I could attend Stanford University. The last year and a half at Stanford I lived with a man—an engineering student. When I graduated, we said good bye. He did not seem to be very sorry about it. I was angry. I had given him a year and a half of my life, and then suddenly it was over. No fuss, no pain. Then I realized that I was not very different from him. I really did not feel very sad about ending the affair. I was angry because I wanted him to care, not because I cared much. But if we could live together and be intimate for a year and a half and bring it to an end without missing anything, where was it all leading? Nowhere. What do you think of that? The agnostic university student coming to a realization like that?"

Again, I didn't know what to say. General formulas could sound smarmy. Reading the very particular state of her mind was beyond me, and the possibility that someone might actually expect me to have something wise to say was unnerving. So like a good coward I took refuge in a question. "Do you still think that way?"

"No. Yes. I am not sure. By twenty nine years of age should I not have some answers? When I went to Buenos Aires to study law, at least I knew that there was more to life than sex and passing exams in order to get a good job and make money. I made some good friends, and I actually worked at being a good friend. I went to church a little, maybe once every two months, but I still did not think of myself as a Catholic. But if I completely rejected Catholicism I would not have anything else to turn to. My brothers after they left home still claim to be Catholic and they hardly ever go to church, and I think maybe they do not pray. I pray and go to church and I do not know whether I am a Catholic. I guess that is what you call being messed up, right?"

"Does anyone who knows you think you're messed up?" I asked.

"No. Mama and Papa and others think I am solid and reasonable and a good person. Maybe I am the only one who knows I am messed up."

I replied that there was a difference between being messed up and being an intelligent person who wanted to think things through. Her parents were surely right.

I continued to scan the landscape ahead for any signs of possible trouble, not really expecting any but anxious not to be caught napping. After several minutes Dolores broke the silence. "I hope you will forgive me. When you first came to Marino I thought you were probably someone whom people hired to do their fighting for them, and that you were coming to Talcayan to bring us your form of justice, and I was very impolite. I really made the colonel angry. Today I insulted you by saying I was surprised that you would go to Mass. But now I have told you more about my life than I ever told to my parents or to a priest or to anyone."

"Well, as it turns out, you were at least partly right," I replied. "I have ended up doing someone's fighting for them."

She just shook her head and we drove in silence for a while. Before long we were among the beautiful hills and vineyards and orchards near Mendoza. Our three vehicles pulled off to the side of the road. The officer who had accompanied Will got into the back seat of the Land Rover. Will pulled out onto the road and headed for the railroad yards where we had picked up the truck. The other two vehicles proceeded to the prison where we would deliver Fraga and Suarez to the Argentina authorities. When we stopped at the prison I asked Dolores whether she would write to me to keep me informed of events. She replied that she would like that very much. "When you come back, bring your mother. We will go for a drive and sing."

Then a handshake and she was out of the vehicle and giving directions to the two police officers in the other car. The third officer, who had been riding with us for the last several miles, moved into the driver's seat and we were off to the rental agency to drop off the Land Rover. He would wait there to be picked up by the Amparo police car on their way home. I would take a taxi from the car rental agency, pick up Will at the railroad yards, and we would proceed to the airport.

CHAPTER SIXTEEN

Experts warn us that on longer flights we should get up and walk around to prevent circulation problems. That presents a considerable challenge when one is on crutches in aisles ten inches wide, so Uncle Hugh's secretary booked us in first class. The first night we stopped over in Bogota and the next night in Miami before flying on to Toronto. I attracted attention in the respective terminals as I hobbled around rather than use the proffered wheel chairs.

Uncle Will believed in learning from both successes and failures. We were scarcely airborne from Mendoza when he launched into a review. "Well, lad, what did we accomplish in Talcayan?"

I had been concentrating more on getting through each day than on accomplishments, so I was silent for a while before suggesting that it had been disappointing.

"Okay," Will said, "Our first purpose was to find out about what happened to Catherine and her husband. Let's start there"

"Well, we didn't find out who killed them."

"What did we find out?"

"From your telephone conversation with Captain Langer we already knew that he was helping Officer Costa to keep information from us. Now we have reason to believe that the crime didn't take place at Cantal at all, but probably in the area of Valdez, and someone there

- 126 -

is the real source of the cover-up. Very likely Costa doesn't know the identity of the murderer, or murderers. If anyone knows, it's probably someone in Valdez, possibly Flores or Langer or both; but it's going to be just a tad tricky getting information out of them without getting our heads blown off."

"Anything else?"

"That's about it," I said. "What have I missed?"

"To start with, what are you going to tell Hugh to do?"

"I'll have to tell him that we can't go any farther at the moment. There are no officials in Talcayan willing and able to investigate further, and we can't do anything ourselves without stirring up a hornet's nest. Uncle Hugh could hire a private detective to nose around further, but I don't think that's his style."

"Sounds right so far. What else can you tell him?"

"I suppose we could say that the political picture could change and someone with more clout and the desire to fight corruption could come to power."

"And?"

"I can't think of anything at the moment. Maybe when we get back and I have more time . . ."

"If the situation were to change and you took up the case again, where would you start?"

"I'd start with Antonio Rossi."

"Yes. Probably the key is there. What Rossi knows about Flores and Langer would give you a start, and you might eventually get to the bottom of the whole mess. We know quite a bit, and we can tell Hugh with some assurance that there's no point in going further right now. Hugh will know what he needs to know to act reasonably. Now for the second purpose, to find out the lay of the land before deciding whether Hannigan Industries should go into Talcayan. What have we learned?"

"It's probably less work for you to give the answer rather than try to drag it out of me. My mind seems to be on a sympathy strike with my foot."

"Okay. Along with what Dieter has discovered, we've found out quite a bit. We thought that a major problem was the Fraga gang. We eliminated them, at least for now, but there seems to be someone higher up who's calling the shots, or at least is mightily interested in supporting Fraga. What do you think is going on there?"

"My guess is that someone wants Robles out of the way and replaced by one of his own people."

"That's what it looks like," Will replied. "If that's the case, then the situation is worse than we thought. So we have to advise Hugh to stay out of Talcayan for the time being. But we're not flying completely blind here. We have several allies, including some who are probably reliable sources of information: Robles, Aldomar for some of the details, Señor Laval, . . . and Señorita Laval, lest we ignore the lady."

"I applaud your gallantry in giving due attention to that blasted woman," I said.

Will's cleared his throat. "That's a habit you're going to have to get over, lad, I mean listening to me too closely. It could get me into trouble. On the trip to Mendoza did you learn any more about where she stands and whether she can help us?"

"When we arrived in Marino," I replied, "she thought we were a pair of adventurers interfering in her country, so she was a little peeved. I think she's gotten over it."

"Good. Does she agree with her father about avoiding of violence, do you think? Not that I disagree. In the circumstances he seems to have been right. Our little experiment in limited violence did exactly what he might have predicted. We removed one evil and then uncovered another that has us stymied."

"I'm not sure how much she agrees with her father. Certainly they're close. My impression is that he has a lot of influence on her.

"Would she help us if she could do so without getting her father in trouble or going against him?"

"I think so. She's bright. I think her judgment would be sound. She may be a little prone to jumping to conclusions and speaking before getting all the facts, is all."

"Okay," Will went on. "What do we know besides the fact that Hugh should keep Hannigan Industries out of Talcayan for the time being? We have made friends with two of the mayors, and both of them are smart but neither of them has a lot of power in the country as a whole. We have an inkling of what it would take to get some of the honest citizens to assert themselves. They are cowed by those who are willing to use force. They would join in an effort to get rid of the thugs if it had a reasonable hope of success. At least that's my guess about the estancia owners in the Amparo district."

I agreed that his account made sense, but it was a catch-22 situation. To attract enough followers you need already to have a lot of followers. There were only a few, like Aldomar, who wouldn't wait to be assured of victory before taking action.

"That's another thing," Will added. We have some idea of people we could work with. Besides the two mayors, there's Aldomar, there's Antonio Rossi, and I admire that other guy—the Chavarria son-in-law. So we have a few contacts that we can trust, after only a few days. I'd say that's not bad. Now get some sleep."

I would have liked to go to sleep, but I had something else to think about. Someone who has airily dismissed his relatives' concern about the dangers of a mission and returns later on crutches and a bullet hole through his foot cannot help but feel at a disadvantage. It's the kind of situation that might tempt someone of imperfect virtue to invent a cover story. I was saved from utter mendacity by the fact that I couldn't think up a plausible lie. The picture of a marksman with a closet full of trophies explaining that he had accidentally shot himself in the foot, if it had the slightest chance of being believed, would have provided my cousin Ellen with enough ammunition to embarrass me well into the next millennium. Were I to claim that a colleague had accidentally discharged a firearm into my foot I would have to explain how I had gotten mixed up with the gang that couldn't shoot straight. So there seemed to be no way to avoid admitting that the wound had been inflicted by someone who wished me ill, a precarious lurch toward veracity. I think I heard a quote somewhere: "When all else fails, tell the truth." But how much truth? Historians assure us that no account of the facts can completely describe any event. So I decided to provide a stripped down version of the facts. Aldomar could have invented a more plausible and interesting story, but I lacked that admirable officer's special gift.

Colonel McGrath's destination was Toronto. As we waited at the baggage carousel I expressed the hope that he would recover quickly from the Talcayan adventure, which must have been a little more than he had bargained for. "I'm almost ashamed to say it, Mick," he said, "But in a way I enjoyed it. I haven't been so fully involved in anything for years. If it weren't almost criminal even to think it, I would be inclined to look for some adventure like that every year. Maybe it's an occupational hazard. Soldiers are trained to meet crises, so maybe some of us old crocks need a disaster every once in a while to get the blood circulating. Running a nursery doesn't do it. That's why I chose it when I left the military. I didn't think I'd miss the action. Not that I'm disappointed to be home. I'm going to enjoy a little peace and quiet."

It was the first time I had spent much time with Uncle Will and really gotten to know him. What we had gone through together would have forged a bond in any case, but besides that I had come to admire his sense of fairness and his calmness under pressure; and I was in awe of the ease with which he could take charge of a situation and organize what needed to be organized. Granted, he could be a mite testy with people like Bishop Kendel who he thought were accusing him of being in the wrong. He could be overpowering and was not above throwing his weight around; and it wouldn't kill him to consult with others now and then. But those are peccadilloes to which the super-competent are probably prone. Some people, when you get past the veneer there's not much there to like. With Uncle Will, when you get past the veneer you find a genuine person.

I was met in the late evening at Edmonton International by Mom, Uncle Hugh and Aunt Phyllis. They were mercifully brief in their expressions of concern, and there was not a single "I told you so" voiced in the flurry of hugs, handshakes and grabbing of bags off the conveyer. My injured foot and my account of its genesis were accepted without cross-examination. They were still preoccupied by the loss of Catherine, I'm sure, and less inquisitive than would otherwise have been their wont.

Of course they were all for subjecting me to as much medical attention as I could endure and maybe a little more. I agreed to consult a podiatrist to get an opinion concerning whether I needed further treatment, so at 7 A.M. a day and a half later Dr. Wentzel took a look at my cast and, using a tool that looked like the kind of thing they use to trim horses' hooves, he cut through the plaster and only a little of my epidermis. My naked foot didn't seem to reveal much more to him than the cast did, but I was glad to attend properly to the itch that for the last while was as big a nuisance as the pain. I was directed to the x-ray clinic in the same building, where I had time to regret that I had not brought along a copy of *War and Peace* for a quick read-through. Then it was back to the office where Dr. Wentzel examined the X-rays, nodded and assured me that the surgeon in Talcayan seemed to have done his job well; the bones apparently were mostly where they were supposed to be and should heal properly without any further surgical interference. Before I had properly given thanks for this news he informed me that there was some infection, I would need some antibiotics and he wanted to have a second look when the swelling went down. I should stay in the University Hospital for a day or two while he kept an eye on it. By two P.M. I was ensconced in a noisy ward on the third floor. I had managed to miss lunch, and inquiry revealed that nothing short of an act of the provincial legislature would move the powers-that-be to allow food to be transported from the hospital cafeteria to a patient at that hour.

Hunger was only a temporary problem; but once in the hospital I was a stationary target for the sympathy of my female relatives. As soon as Mom's workday was done advocating for patients at Misericordia she crossed the river to make sure that similar weight was being given to the care of her son at University Hospital. I could have used her services earlier to help me ward off starvation, but by the time she arrived I was enjoying (if that is not too strong a word) the evening meal. She let me off easy for the mistake of getting a bullet through my foot, perhaps considering it the sort of thing to be expected of males in general and male Hannigans in particular.

The next morning Ellen breezed into the ward and eyed my new cast. "It's so reassuring to know that all that worry about violence on this South American escapade was just the imagining of hysterical women." She paused a second and went on. "Now, I'm here to offer you all the kindness and sympathy you can stand."

For a few minutes I answered her questions about what had really happened. She seemed skeptical, not without reason, of certain details of the edited version. Then she added: "Now to the important question. Did you find a suitable companion to share your declining years?"

I replied that I had seen a number of candidates worthy of further attention, but I had been busy with one thing and another and had no opportunity to subject them to my charm. Besides, I had been looking after her interest in locating a suitable young man.

"Oh, that," she said. "You don't have to worry about that. I've taken the matter into my own hands. If you want the job done properly, etc., you know. Anyway, I've found my mate for life. You're the first to know. I haven't even told him yet."

"And who is this . . . fortunate man?"

"His name is Cyril Kostiuk. He comes complete with family. He's not married, if that's worrying you. And don't look at me in that supercilious way, or whatever way it is you have of looking. The two kids are his sister's daughters. Her husband left the sister a couple of years ago. A real gem, that one—the husband I mean. If I locate him I may call on you to put your karate skills to use in his regard."

"I don't do karate," I replied.

"Well, you do something masculine and destructive, and that's what's called for this case. But anyway, Cyril's sister died of cancer three weeks ago and Cyril is taking care of the kids."

I asked her how the daughters would react when she revealed her plans to marry their uncle. "Oh, I can count on them to be on my side. I got to know them when their mother was in palliative care. Cancer is a curse—that poor woman. I go down to Palliative Care almost every day—like to keep an eye on it, watch for burnout among the staff. Anyway, I got to know the two daughters. Of course they are going through a miserable time. It was terrible for them to see their mother that way."

"What does Cyril do for a living?"

"He's a master carpenter. Actually I don't think he does much hammering and sawing any more. He's a site foremen or something. He probably makes more money than I do."

"And do you have any evidence that he won't head for the hills once you unveil your plans for him?"

"The man's crazy about me. I mean, how could he help it? Besides, I figure he'll be desperate to find a mother for those girls. And I'm desperate to do penance for my sins by becoming responsible for two children who in a frighteningly few years will be teen-agers. It's a match made in heaven."

"Ah, a marriage held together by desperation."

"Exactly. Actually, Cyril is a real find. You've got to meet him as soon as I can arrange it. I'm counting on you and Dad. If Cyril begins to get the impression that I'm no great bargain, then I'll need to convince him that joining up with me will at least net him a couple of interesting male relatives."

"You can count on me," I assured her. "Just tell me what to do and I'll be so nice you wouldn't recognize me."

She paused for a moment and then continued more slowly. "Wild horses couldn't get me to admit this to anyone but you. But maybe, unconsciously, I've been waiting for someone who could go with you and Dad on those crazy fishing or hunting expeditions up north and come back and boast about how you damn near froze to death. Maybe I'm looking to marry someone like my father. How do you like that, eh? Do you think there's any hope for me?"

"Ellen, you'll be fine. All you need is a couple of years in psycho-analysis."

She considered that for a moment. "No, I don't think so. I'm quite sure I'm crazy enough already."

I asked about the two girls. "They're eight and ten. They're a bit spoiled, I suspect, but they're easily bribed, and that's the important thing, don't you think?"

She put on her rain coat but turned back at the door. "By the way, is this hospital infested with any of those tough, man-hating, Valkyrie-type nurses roaming the halls with large hypodermic needles? They're a common sight in hospitals at night, you know."

I replied that the nurses that I had to deal with were mostly small and oriental, and depended more on guile than brute force to bend us patients to their will.

"Just so you know not to trust them either. And watch out for the doctors. Imagine, entrusting your health to people who would be out of a job if everyone got well." She fiddled with an ear ring, usually a sign that she really intended to leave. "Well, anyway, give me a shout any time you need someone to come cheer you up. See ya."

- 133 -

CHAPTER SEVENTEEN

I left hospital the next day. A couple of days later Uncle Hugh called to say that when I thought I was up to it he would drop by and I could bring him up to date on the goings on in Talcayan. He was dubious when I proposed instead to go down to his office. "I can only read so much, and then I have to move," I protested. "I've finished *Das Kapital* and I'm half way through *The Oxford English Dictionary.* I'm getting cabin fever."

"More likely you've just run out of copies of *People* magazine," he said. "But we've got to keep you mentally healthy, so if you're sure you can manage it without getting into trouble with the doctor, come on down. We can meet over lunch."

I should explain how I happened to be working for Hugh Hannigan. I had hardly moved back into my mother's house after leaving the army when Uncle Hugh showed up and, over the first cup of coffee, looked at me from under those bushy brows and asked how many offers of employment I had received. The question was facetious, but I suspected there was something serious behind it so I refrained from making some smart-alec remark. I would start looking for work in a day or two, after I got used to wearing civvies. He leaned back and asked, "How would you like to be my Director of Security?" That sounded like an exalted title for some sort of guard duty, but it turned out that he wanted me

- 134 -

to be in charge of safety and security for all of Hannigan Industries, which included seven mines in four different countries, odd bits of real estate, a hydro-electric operation in Manitoba and other odds and ends that Hugh had picked up and salvaged over the years. The job involved overseeing the installation and conscientious use of safety measures in all operations, but extended also to protection against theft and vandalism.

My first response was that my main accomplishment was marksmanship and that didn't really make me an expert on safety. Hugh was not so easily put off. I would apprentice with the Director of Security at a larger company for six months. I would spend another six months inspecting all the Hannigan holdings to familiarize myself with the safety measures already in place. After that I would become "Field Inspector for Security" until the incumbent director retired, at which point I would take his place.

Like most of Hugh's plans, it worked. Not long after I completed the inspection tour and learned a lot about the business from our own Director of Security, he retired and I took over his position. I found Alex Brosky, a young genius working at the head offices of Hannigan Industries, and convinced him that it was more fun analyzing real safety systems and designing new ones than playing computer games, and I hired him. Brosky apparently had studied diplomacy in the school of Vlad the Impaler, but on the job he dealt with computers and I dealt with people. Within several years three other companies tried to hire either Brosky or myself, but neither of us was ready to work for someone not named Hugh Hannigan.

I left a note to let Mom know that I had not run away from home, in case she returned before I did, caught a taxi and at 11:57 A.M. presented myself at the head office. By the time I had weathered the welcomes of the staff and parried their inquiries about my crutches it was 12:15. Uncle Hugh led me to the restaurant in the mall that served more or less as the lunch room for the office. They put us at a corner table and we began with a review of what had been going on in the business since I had been out of touch. The situation apparently had not lacked drama.

"I don't know how you put up with that Brosky individual," Hugh groused. "I've tried to do a little smoothing of ruffled feathers for him, but it's turning out to be a full time job. You ask him a question, any question, and he searches around for some way of proving that if you had any sense you would not have asked it. Suggest that two plus two equals four and he'll explain that there are alternative systems in math where that's not true. If they discover how to transport people to one of these alternative universes they're starting to talk about I will personally pay for the ticket to get him there. I'll be glad when you're back and can take care of him."

I had been waiting for that opening. "I'll be back at work on Monday."

"Some Monday, yes. Just not this Monday. Aren't you supposed to stay off that foot?"

"I am off the foot. Walking on crutches puts no more pressure on it than watching television would."

"It's your choice. If you get into trouble with your mother, just make sure you let her know that I fought tooth and nail to keep you from coming to work."

Other things had been happening at Hannigan Industries. Dieter Helfrich had reported on his return that there was a good chance of finding substantial reserves of silver and cobalt in the south western corner of Talcayan. He reported that an Australian company, Perth Resources, almost certainly had more solid information, but that this information would not be available for several years. Perth had spent substantial amounts of money on surveys but had not bought up the mineral rights to the area. This might indicate that they had not discovered sufficient resources to justify further investment, but Dieter, usually a cautious advisor, guessed that Perth lacked the funds to buy the mineral rights and begin operations right away, and so were temporizing, hoping that no other company would, as it were, jump their claim.

Dieter's advice to wait several years sounded too cautious to Hugh. Within several years Perth might simply start development and exclude all other interests. Hugh had directed one of his accountants—one whose interest was as much in other company's books as in ours—to find all that could legitimately be found on Perth Resources. The accountant had discovered that Perth seemed to have been short of cash for several years after over-extending themselves in explorations in Bolivia and in Western Australia. Armed with this knowledge, Hugh had approached Perth with an offer. In exchange for an infusion of cash by Hannigan, Perth would turn over what they had discovered about mineral resources south of El Rio del Rey, on the understanding that the information would be kept in strictest confidence and that any future development of the resources would be done jointly by the two companies. Hannigan and Perth would share all information and share profits according to the amount each invested in a particular mine.

I gave my opinion, shared by Colonel McGrath, that the political situation was sufficiently threatening that it would be unwise to open up any operation until things improved considerably. Hugh remarked that he expected that to be the case, but that what had been done thus far meant that Hannigan Industries could move quickly if the opportunity presented itself. There were other details and guarantees that I didn't quite follow, but I knew that Hugh would neither cheat nor be cheated. The people at Perth were studying the offer. The speed with which Hugh moved things forward took my breath away. He added that among the points helping to sell the deal to Perth was that Hannigan Industries had the resources and the record to guarantee the highest available level of safety, and also that we were ahead of the game in studying the political situation in Talcayan; we would continue to monitor that political situation. "So let's start with what you've found out about all of the players."

I summarized what Colonel McGrath and I had learned, the personnel involved and our impressions about the situation. When I was finished Hugh took me through all of the names again. What did I think about so-and-so? Could he be trusted? Was he bright? Was he in a position to know? It was two o'clock by the time we finished. I had talked a lot and not all of what I said was provable, but that didn't worry Hugh. "You've given me your opinion about things where nothing more than an opinion is possible. It's fallible, but it's better then guessing, which is what we would be doing if you hadn't gone there."

I was able to communicate in five minutes what we had found out about the Tipping murders. We were, apparently, at a dead end for the time being.

My restlessness after returning from Talcayan drove me back to work, but returning to work didn't cure it. That was not surprising. I've never been fond of paperwork. By Saturday morning I had caught up on correspondence, returned all my telephone calls, substantially reduced the clutter on my desk and made arrangements to do a site visit at a mine north of Sudbury, Ontario. My practice was to visit every site at least twice a year to meet with the local safety committee, check that safety regulations were being followed and lend a fresh pair of eyes to the search for overlooked hazards. Getting out of the office a week after I had fled into it helped a little. The difficulty of getting around on one leg kept me even busier than I would normally have been on the visit, and that probably helped my mood. When I got on the plane to fly back to Edmonton, however, I was still not feeling that good about life.

I was, of course, still mourning the loss of Catherine and Richard and disappointed that we had found out so little about those responsible for their murder, but that didn't explain it fully. Had I caught the disease that Colonel McGrath had talked about? Had the adventure in Talcayan spoiled me for humdrum, everyday activity? But in no way had I enjoyed the prospect either of shooting or being shot at, either at the time or in retrospect. There was some feeling of satisfaction at our success in removing Fraga from circulation, but that surely didn't compensate for the danger, or being in a position in which I might have to kill, or the feeling that dealing with one evil seemed to provoke another. Were I ever to enter into such a situation again it would have to be from a sense of duty, not because I found it exhilarating.

As Mom and I sat down to dinner the evening I got back from Sudbury there was a letter next to my plate. It was addressed to the office, but the mail sorter there, not knowing I was back at work, had sent it on to the residence. I could feel Mom's eyes on me as I picked it up, read the return address, and with studied casualness set it aside for attention later.

"The letter is from Talcayan," she said. (Translation: "Are you going to tell me about it willingly or am I going to have to drag it out of you?")

"Yeah," I said. "Uncle Hugh wants to be kept informed about the political situation there, because if it doesn't settle down he can't invest. So I asked several people in Talcayan to let me know what's going on."

"Your informant writes with a very delicate hand." Mom was wearing the smug look she reserved for these inquisitions.

"Okay, I confess. It's a woman. I've been consorting with a regular Mata Hari down there."

"Ah. A professional spy. That's accounts for why she would have discovered something important to tell you so soon after you left the country. How old is this Mata Hari? I wouldn't want my son consorting with an older woman spy."

"She's twenty nine." As soon as the words were out of my mouth I knew I had lost Round One. You might as soon expect Mike Tyson to ease up on a stunned opponent as that my mother would ignore a tactical slip like that. "I think it is commendable," she replied primly, "that you find out details about your informants—their exact age, for example."

"I think it's important to check the facts about all of the women with whom I have affairs," I replied.

"Aha. And this affair explains your injury. Apparently jealous suitors in Talcayan have this quaint custom of shooting their rivals in the foot. And what is this gorgeous gold digger's name?"

"Gold digger? On the contrary, I'm relying on her to support me in my old age."

"Ah yes. My son as a kept man. Now, about this lady's name. First I have to warn you. When I saw the feminine handwriting I could not contain my curiosity and I let my eyes stray to the return address. I know. Prying into my son's private life. I'll go to confession. If you see me climbing the front steps of St. Vincent's on hands and knees before the 10 A.M. Mass you'll know I caught Fr. Molnar in a bad mood. Anyway, I did see the name 'D. Laval' before the return address. So that narrows down your scope for invention."

"Okay, here's my fall back story. Her name is Dolores Laval. She speaks fluent English and French along with Spanish. Miss Laval has a law degree, but at present she is the assistant to her father, who is the mayor of a city in Talcayan. Our acquaintance consists of conversations on two occasions. Anything else?"

"One more question. Now I realize that you are quite indifferent to her; and she probably had to check her notes to remind her of your name before writing that letter. But just supposing that things were different and you were to bring her home to meet your mother, would I like her?"

It was difficult to gauge the seriousness with which it was asked, but the question had actually occurred to me, though at the time I would have been embarrassed to admit it, even to myself. Characteristically, I answered without giving the matter much thought. "I think the two or you might actually get along. You agree on at least one thing. You both like to give me a hard time."

My mother's eyes widened and after a second she burst out. "Michael, Michael. This woman has you in her gun sights. You either surrender or you run for your life."

I groaned. "I think I've just remembered why sons don't confide much in their mothers on the subject of women."

She arched one eyebrow, which was about as close as she was likely to get to acknowledging that I had scored a point. "Now, now, Michael, I'm just filling in a gap in your education. I've neglected to teach you how to protect yourself against the wiles and machinations of predatory females; except in this case I may just be on the side of the female."

"I think you considerably overrate my charm in this case. Señorita Laval has more important things to do than to cavort with a stranger from what probably strikes her as somewhere near the North Pole."

"Rubbish." The tone suggested that my mother was about to deliver the last word in this subject. "I'm just giving the woman credit for being able to recognize a good man when she sees one."

After a few seconds of silence, Mom continued in a more serious tone. "Michael, since you have come back you've been a bit moody. At first I thought it might be that you have to get around on crutches and you usually like to do things in a hurry; but I don't think that's the reason. Your usual reaction to adversity is to dig in and lick it. You enjoy the challenge. Tell me, your mood these days, is it something like what you felt in your last years in the army?"

"I've thought about that, Mom. I realize I've been grumpy and feeling low. It's a bit like what I felt before I left the army. I don't know why. It probably has something to do with Talcayan. I guess I feel that in a way I let them down, leaving them in their hour of need."

"And maybe Dolores Laval is one of those you think you let down?"

"It's possible, I suppose. But it may be what they call post-traumatic stress syndrome, or some such thing. I'll try to get over it."

"Michael," she said slowly. "Don't misunderstand me. I certainly don't want to be one of those people who tell you to cheer up, as though you could just flip a switch. Don't worry. A Michael Hannigan who's grumpy now and then is okay with me."

CHAPTER EIGHTEEN

My level of culinary skill qualifies me to put dishes into the dishwasher, cram leftovers into the refrigerator and generally tidy up the kitchen, so it was a few minutes before I satisfied my curiosity about the contents of the letter. Shortly after we left Talcayan Señorita Laval had contacted the police in Magdalena. The U.S. passport found on the person of my assailant identified him as Martin Lederer and his place of residence as Richmond, Virginia. Inquiry showed that no passport had been issued to anyone whose name, age and place of residence agreed with the passport. The man stuck to his story that the passport was valid and that he had no idea about who hired him, insisting that he had dealt with an anonymous contact person who had given him some money and instructions to discover the whereabouts of Rafael Fraga. Presumably he was to receive more money on completion of his task. He also insisted that his job was only to find out where Fraga was being held, and he had no intention of harming anyone beyond whatever intimidation might be necessary to achieve his primary task.

Dolores had spoken with Mayor Guzman of Magdalena and he had assured her that the police were continuing to try to discover the man's real identity, that efforts were underway to expedite his trial and that Mayor Guzman expected no problem getting a conviction.

- 142 -

THE BLOOD-DIMMED TIDE IS LOOSED

Colonel McGrath and I had left depositions and these, along with the testimony of the police who had arrived on the scene in Magdalena and the clerk at the hotel, should suffice to prove "Lederer" guilty of forceful confinement and bodily injury. The mayor would keep Señorita Laval informed of further progress.

Dolores' letter was business-like and factual. The only element that even faintly accorded with Mom's imaginings was a closing "I look forward very much to seeing you in Talcayan before long," and that was hardly more than a polite convention.

A few days later Mom and I were invited to dinner at the home of Uncle Hugh and Aunt Phyllis to meet Cyril Kostiuk. Cyril turned out to be a lanky, pleasant man about thirty years of age. Ellen had obviously been joking when she implied that Cyril was like her father. Where Ellen and Uncle Hugh were talkative and loved to play with language, he was quiet. Where they were impetuous and spontaneous, he was soft-spoken and careful, with an aura of gentleness. Where each of them had a fund of stories, usually funny and not always complimentary to the persons portrayed, Cyril's contributions to the conversation were usually brief and good natured rather than humorous. However, it was probably true that he would fit nicely on one of our crazy hunting trips, and he seemed to enjoy the repartee of the Hannigan tribe. He was well informed on a variety of subjects and showed an apparently unfeigned interest in Mom's work and mine.

Cyril's nieces were in attendance and popped into the living room every few minutes to inform him of the progress in the kitchen, or how they were helping out Mrs. Hannigan, or what they had discovered on their visit to the basement. The two were obviously fond of Ellen and had probably already assessed her favorably as a prospective step-mother. Mom summed up the encounter nicely as we backed out of the driveway to head for home. "Trust Ellen to get it right, even down to choosing a fiancé."

In the weeks that followed I graduated from crutches to a more dignified cane. Lest my conditioning become further eroded I consulted Dr. Wentzel about appropriate exercises. He suggested swimming as something that would put minimal stress on my foot and would not be very painful, so I began to spend time every day at the YMCA pool,

- 143 -

outfitted with a rubber sock to protect the wound and the dressing around it.

After a week or so I found that I hadn't lost my aversion to aquatic sports, which as a pastime I rank right up there with lion taming and walking barefoot over hot coals. My specific gravity must be considerably greater than that of water, and most of my energy in the pool is spent struggling to the surface and gasping for breath; so I began to look for a milder form of penance. Since leaving the army I had worked at keeping up the skills I had mastered, so I contacted a physical therapist and we worked out a regimen that would keep me more or less in shape without retarding the slow healing of my foot.

The cool of autumn passed into the deep frost of Edmonton winter. People from milder climes are markedly unenthusiastic when they first encounter winter on the Canadian prairies and ask tactless questions about why any sane person would freely choose to live there. But for us natives, striding along in the face of a gale that drives the wind-chill factor down to -40 degrees is an expression of something basic to human existence—the need to defy and transcend nature. The true Edmontonian does not cower indoors. We treasure the experience of coming in out of the cold, stamping our feet to get rid of the snow, peeling off layers of clothing and settling down to refreshments. Shallow persons might suggest skipping the preliminaries and proceeding directly to the refreshments; but there is nothing like exposure to the elements to help one savor the comfort and satisfaction of a warm chair, a hot drink and a good book; and there are people who travel thousands of miles to "get away from it all" when they need go no further than the street during a snow fall to experience a profound and quiet peace.

Taking up life again in Edmonton involved hockey. My foot injury might rule out active participation in the game, but it presented no obstacle to resuming support for the Edmonton Oilers, at that time seeking to recover their glory years. One hears complaints that the sport of ice hockey lacks a certain politesse, and the sport has provided evidence to support this view. Although it may have gotten worse recently, there seem always to have been performers whose skill consisted mainly in slamming more accomplished players into the boards or impeding their progress by using the hockey stick as a shepherd's crook. The troglodytes on the ice usually find support from a few relatives in the mass media for whom the attraction of the sport seems to be the spectacle of apes on skates, not the artistry of the likes of Beliveau, Lemieux or Crosby.

As anyone can attest who has watched the college game at a high level, hockey can be played at great speed with plenty of bodily contact without the silliness of millionaires supposedly skilled in one sport trying to prove their superiority in another sport in which they would be acutely embarrassed by any moderately accomplished welterweight. I can personally attest, however, that few experiences in life are more satisfying than up-ending one's opponent and then receiving absolution from the referee who rules that it was "a good, clean check". Some may cavil about the use of these two adjectives in this context; but the real masters of a language, we are told, are the masses who speak it, and those masses obviously have detected qualities of goodness and cleanliness in a well-executed body check.

After several months I was able to take up again my participation in an over-the-hill league, membership in which entitles you to rise at 5 A.M., scrape the snow off the windshield of your car while your hands slowly freeze, drive over rutted, snow-packed streets into an icy parking lot, enter a scarcely heated dressing room, pull on cold hockey equipment and then take to the ice and try, occasionally with success, to avoid serious collisions as a dozen men, armed with wooden clubs, engage in the high speed pursuit of one small, hard, rubber object. It says something about the state of my social life that, except for occasional dinners where I would play a poor man's version of Bob Hope for some organization that couldn't afford a proper Master of Ceremonies, my main social outlet during the winter was the good-natured pre-game and post-game banter in the dressing room.

By February Perth Resources had accepted the offer from Hannigan Industries and the two companies had worked out an agreement to share information, resources and profits from any mining operation in Talcayan. Dieter had been correct in his guess that what had held Perth back was lack of cash along with concerns about the political situation. Dieter had also been right about what Perth had discovered, except that along with silver and cobalt, the most promising deposits that were found were of copper. This suited Hugh, who was skeptical about diamonds, gold and even silver. He argued that because their market value was not based mainly on their usefulness, their value could drop if people decided that their jewelry should be made out of zirconium or bismuth or whatever else might come into style.

Typically, Hugh wanted to move forward. The political situation in Talcayan was still unsettled. Sergio Gracida continued in office because the opposition was too fractured to agree upon an alternative. However, there had been no news of violence or threats of violence since Will and I had left the country. After consulting with several of us, Hugh decided to send an assay team to finish the exploration begun by Perth. He arranged for a security firm to send four of its agents with Dieter's crew, because Hannigan Industries didn't want to take corporate responsibility for security in a country about which they had limited knowledge. I was a little disappointed about not getting a trip back to Talcayan, but the decision made eminent sense. So in late March Dieter, a geologist and two engineers left Edmonton for Talcayan. Dieter as usual predicted the worst, but he protested indignantly when Hugh suggested he stay home and let his well-qualified assistant lead the team.

About this time there was an incident that, Sherlock Holmes might have noted, possessed certain points of interest. It began as I returned victorious from the hockey arena at about seven A.M. one day in late March and the phone rang in the kitchen. Mom answered but quickly handed me the receiver and whispered, "I think he's speaking Spanish."

The man at the other end of the line identified himself as Carlos, a clerk in the office of Mayor Guzman in Magdalena. Apparently my assailant, alias Martin Lederer, who had been serving a seven-year sentence for kidnapping and assault, had been unexpectedly paroled. I was not able to catch the nuances of the rest of the message, but I did understand that Carlos was warning me that this parole could mean that Colonel McGrath and I were in danger. This sounded improbable and I was afraid that I might have misunderstood some parts of the message, so I arranged to call Carlos back as soon as I was able to get an interpreter.

There seemed to be no way to hide any of what was going on from my mother. After I had explained what I understood of the situation she showed less agitation than I expected, merely thanking me for keeping her informed. I called Colonel McGrath's number and his secretary informed me that he was traveling and planned to return to the office that afternoon. I told her to have him call me as soon as he got in. When I mused about who I could get as a translator Mom pointed out that Sister Lenore with whom she worked at Misericordia Hospital had spent twenty two years in Central America. She had returned from Guatemala a few months earlier and was spending her retirement visiting the sick. I called Uncle Hugh to alert him to what I knew of the situation, and in a very few minutes Mom and I were on our way to pick up Sister Lenore at her convent.

The sister turned out to be a lively, bird-like seventy-year-old who seemed delighted to be involved, even at a distance, with an adventure. We settled in at my office, and she called Carlos. The officials in Talcayan had found out that the real name of the man who called himself Martin Lederer was Maurice (Maury) Archer. He had been paroled, almost certainly because those who decided on parole had been given a confidential offer that they couldn't refuse. Mayor Guzman had tried to keep Archer in custody pending an appeal but had eventually withdrawn his opposition to his release.

At the time of his incarceration it had been apparent to police and lawyers dealing with the case that Maurice Archer had the backing of someone who had financial resources and was willing to exert pressure on officials in Talcayan. This was enough to make Mayor Guzman uneasy. A prisoner who spoke English had been transferred from another jail to the one in Magdalena and assigned as Archer's cell-mate, having been promised early parole if he found out who was supporting Archer and why. This prisoner discovered nothing on that score, but did report that well before Archer's case had come up for review he had boasted that he was going to get out early. When his case was unexpectedly scheduled for review Archer had crowed that the fools who thought they could hold him in prison were going to find out who was really calling the shots. Subsequently Archer had let slip that he was going to get a good sum of money for "settling a score".

- 147 -

Judging from Archer's invectives against McGrath and Hannigan, it was suspected that the score he had to settle might be with us. So, Carlos concluded, Mayor Guzman had decided that we should be informed about what had taken place. That some anonymous and powerful person had intervened at this point to get a not-very-important criminal out of jail reinforced the impression that Archer was being freed in order to carry out some task within his professional specialty. It was at least plausible that the people who brought Archer from America to hunt down Will and me in Talcayan would employ the same person to attack us in Canada.

Although this was guesswork, we had nothing else to go on. If we were going to trace Archer's movements the first places to look were passenger lists, and for this we needed police intervention. Uncle Hugh spent a few minutes on the phone, and soon Sister Lenore and I were heading East on Highway 16 to the district office of the RCMP located in Sherwood Park, where we were to meet with Superintendent Novak. Like many Edmontonians, I had heard of the superintendent, whose exploits as a criminal investigator in earlier decades had made him a local celebrity. Tall and as lean as he had been when he played tight end for the British Columbia Lions, Novak looked fit enough to be out chasing bad guys except for a pronounced limp. He asked about Hugh Hannigan, listened to our story, then took a few minutes on the telephone to get the necessary authorizations, and we had access to airline passenger lists for the days following Archer's departure from Talcayan.

Thanks to computers and the requirement that passengers supply identification, it wasn't difficult to trace Archer's path from Talcayan back to United States. He had no particular reason to hide his movements that far. Even if he were up to no good he would know that we would expect him to return to the U.S., so why take the trouble of keeping us in the dark about that? He had flown under his real name and with his legal passport from Mendoza to Santiago and from there to Miami. After that the trail disappeared. Either he was still in Miami, or he had flown out under an assumed name, or he had found some kind of ground transportation. There was no point in trying to cover all of those possibilities.

It looked like Archer was beginning to cover his tracks, and that was not reassuring. Superintendent Novak recognized that he might be a real threat, but there was not much else he could do for us. A check with the police in Columbus, Ohio, Archer's home town according to his legitimate passport, uncovered no record of criminal activity or arrests for any reason. Through mysterious contacts of his own, the superintendent was able to discover that the FBI had no record of the man. As a gun for hire, Archer had been remarkably successful at hiding his chosen calling from the authorities. Because he was not a fugitive from justice there were no grounds for putting out an "all points bulletin" on him. Superintendent Novak urged me to keep him informed, and if anything turned up that would allow police intervention he would be happy to help.

Late that afternoon I got in touch with Colonel McGrath. He didn't sound worried but advised me that he would be on his guard. I told him that I would try to find out what was going on and keep him informed. At Valdez, at Magdalena and at San Martin I had run into trouble because I had underestimated the threat, partly because we knew so little about who our enemies were and what their real purposes might be.

If I was to do more than wait and worry, the starting point was the address on Archer's valid passport: 1704 Crest Road, Columbus, Ohio. So two days after the call from Carlos I flew through Chicago to Columbus with a letter in my pocket signed by Superintendant Novak. It requested the Columbus police to cooperate with one Michael Hannigan, who would be making inquiries about the whereabouts of a certain Maurice Archer, a person of interest to the Royal Canadian Mounted Police. Novak had also called the captain of the local precinct in which Archer was reputed to reside to inform him that I would drop by.

In Columbus I picked up a vehicle at Rent-a-Wreck. Ellen would say I was indulging my inner cheapskate. The next morning I located Crest Road in a slightly shabby part of town. A leisurely drive revealed a street of mostly small to medium sized bungalows with one-car garages, most of them well maintained, a few abandoned. Where 1704 Crest Road should have been there was a non-descript strip mall stretching the whole block. A couple of what had been small shops were now empty. I didn't want to draw attention to myself by stopping for a closer look, but it appeared that if Maurice Archer lived at that address he must occupy space on the second floor above a store; or maybe he lived in what had been a store and now looked deserted. In any case, his line of work was not providing him with a penthouse lifestyle.

The next stop was the local precinct station. I introduced myself to Captain Baker, an easy-going African-American who looked too young to be a captain. He examined my letter of introduction and signaled me to follow him into what I suppose would be called the squad room, where a few officers were working at desks or conversing quietly. With admirable brevity Captain Baker explained who I was and what I wanted. The name Maurice (Maury) Archer did not register with any of the officers. Baker then sat me down at a desk and asked the woman behind the desk to run the name against recent arrests or inquiries in the precinct, and if that led to nothing, then ask the neighboring precincts to do the same.

The name came up in one report as a "person of interest" in an assault a couple of years earlier. He had been questioned but not charged. The officer on the case was now retired and a quick check indicated that he had moved to Florida. I would have to come back later to see if the searches run by other precincts had turned up anything, but it was becoming clear that our Mr. Archer had been flying under the radar. The telephone directory did not list a Maurice Archer, and none of the M. Archers, or any other Archers for that matter, listed an address on Crest Road.

About noon I was back in the neighborhood of Crest Road and pulled into a bar and grill where the number of parked vehicles suggested that the food and drink were acceptable to non-discriminating palates such as mine. I sat at the bar and ordered a beer to establish my working class credentials. There were only four others at the bar. At that hour presumably only the more dedicated patrons were in session. My exchange with the beefy, pock-marked individual behind the bar was brisk and to the point. I began by showing him my business card, which indicated that I was Mick Hannigan, Director of Security, Hannigan Industries, and asked him whether he had seen Maury Archer recently. He asked why he should give me that information. I replied that I was ready to pay for it. He inquired further as to how I would know whether his information was accurate. I suggested that if his information turned out to be incorrect I would return to reclaim my money and I would bring my friend who was even bigger and uglier than he was. He made noises that suggested that I had failed to appeal to his better nature. It's possible that my approach had lacked subtlety.

I finished my drink and was on my way back to my rent-a-wreck when a figure approached with as much speed as seemed to be within his capacity. He looked to be in late middle age, but time at the bar may have hastened the aging process. He wanted to know whether I was still in the market for information. Being assured that I was, he told me that Maury Archer had been away but had returned recently. My informant had seen him leaving his living quarters on Crest Road the previous night. I asked him what Archer had been wearing, whether he was limping or showing any sign of injuries, whether he looked pale or had a tan. None of this information was of much use to me but my informant's answers might indicate whether he was recalling facts or making them up. If he had reported, for example, that Archer after months in jail was sporting a healthy tan I might have been suspicious. However, he gave no clear sign of duplicity. I gave him twenty dollars. Judging from the purposeful way with which he shuffled away, that twenty dollars would soon be in the custody of my pal the bartender.

CHAPTER NINETEEN

For the foreseeable future that gentleman would not be including me on his most-favored-customer list. If he could recall my name and if he were a friend or even an acquaintance of Maurice Archer he might well warn him that a certain Mick Hannigan had been asking about him. In other words, I may have as much as announced my presence to a hit man who was looking for me. Devising tactics for periods longer than thirty minutes has never been my strong point.

After a lunch at an eatery where I tried not to antagonize any more of the locals, I drove back to Crest Road and paid for a spot in a parking lot across the street and down a half block from what, in the absence of a sign to that effect, I had concluded to be 1704 Crest Road. With the help of binoculars I was able to get a good view of the entrances along the front of the two-story row of shops, and I paid particular attention to what looked like the door to a stairway leading to the second floor. By sitting in the back seat and slouching a bit I could avoid undue attention from passers-by.

Fastening one's eyes on a shabby doorway hour after hour may provide aesthetic stimulation for certain *avant-garde* cinematographers, but my sensitivities have not yet been developed to that level; so as darkness closed in I began to find reasons why this was a useless exercise. Suppose I found out that Archer was here. What then? I would

- 152 -

have merely confirmed what the old guy from the bar had told me—that Archer was back in town. Was it worth hanging around for days just to accomplish that? But I had come a long way to discover whatever I could, and tomorrow I could find out whether any other precincts had information about Mr. Archer.

The next morning, back at the precinct station, I learned that a search of files at other police stations had yielded no references to Archer. There were three officers who had not been present the day before, but none of them had heard of him. However, one of them suggested that those most likely to have heard of the gentleman would be the uniformed officers on the street. So, not having anything more promising to do, I brought Novak's letter with me on to the streets and managed to engage several policemen in conversation. One of them had heard of Maury Archer but knew him only as a shady character who had served as muscle for a suspected dealer in illegal substances and had eluded arrest.

I bought a take-out hamburger and coke and returned to my vigil on Crest Road. This time I reconnoitered the building and discovered several back doors opening on to the alley behind the strip mall. There was no vantage point from which I could observe those entrances unseen unless I hid in one of the garbage containers that were stinking up the environs. I had visions of doing an Inspector Clouseau impersonation, emerging from one of the bins wearing a banana peal on my head and chased by a half dozen alley cats drawn to the rancid grease soaking into my trousers. The only other place that provided any cover was a recessed doorway where the rusted hinges and level of debris suggested that it was not much in use. Even that vantage point was too suggestive of Clouseau to be attractive, so I went back to my automobile a half-block away

I had been there a little over an hour when the door I was watching opened, and there was the joker who had shot me in the foot a half year earlier. I would not have recognized him had I not been looking for him. He had replaced the pony tail with closely trimmed hair. All it took was a haircut and he had an effective disguise, at least for the casual observer; but I had not spent those hours with Mr. Archer as a casual observer.

He had one piece of luggage with him and a topcoat draped over his arm. He got into a taxi that had parked a few yards from the door, the cab pulled away, turned in my direction and passed within a few yards of me. I got my Rent-a-Wreck in gear and followed. They say that developing new skills helps to keep you young. Certainly tailing even highly visible yellow cabs was a new skill for me, but I can't say it retarded the aging process noticeably.

The luggage suggested an airport destination. The fact that he was carrying a top-coat on a relatively warm day pointed to a north-bound flight. Not wanting him to notice me, I lagged well behind the taxi and as a result lost it, but was able to find it again simply by speeding up a bit and taking the route that the signs said would take me to the airport. If Archer noticed he was being followed he must not have been concerned, because the cab took no evasive action but went straight to the airport. I could park and go into the terminal, but I wouldn't accomplish much without Archer recognizing me and that didn't seem to be advisable. I drove to the motel where I was staying, grabbed my bag, called a cab to meet me at the Rent-A-Wreck place, checked out, and in an hour and a half was back at the airport. An obliging young lady charged me only an arm and a leg to put me on the next flight to Edmonton, through Chicago and Calgary.

United Flight 5831 to Chicago was uneventful, but my trip took on added interest at O'Hare. The sheer size of the place intimidates some people but it impresses me. I had checked my bag through to Edmonton, so I was free to wander around and stretch my legs until the 6 P.M. flight. At about 5:30 I ambled in the direction of the gate where, according to my boarding pass, Air Canada Flight 4039 to Calgary would be taking on passengers. I had just moved into the waiting area when I stopped short. There, with his back to me, was Maurice (Maury) Archer. Any doubt about his identity was removed by the sight of the tan jacket he had been wearing when he had emerged from 1704 Crest Road.

I ducked back out of sight quickly, wanting him on that plane and not wanting to spook him. I loitered in the area, close enough to hear when they announced that they were boarding passengers, and at the last minute I joined the short line of stragglers submitting their boarding passes and IDs to scrutiny. I had been assigned a seat in the front half of the cabin, and proceeding down the aisle of the 767 to Seat 12C with eyes cast down I hoped I was exposing only the top of my head to the view of anyone seated farther back. I was able to ascertain that Archer did not occupy any seat in front of the fourteenth row. The seat next to me was occupied by a fidgety boy perhaps four years old, with his mother in the seat next to him. Ordinarily the arrangement would not have appealed to me, but relaxation was not my main concern at the moment.

With the aircraft aloft and the seat-belt sign off I got up, stretched and made my way towards the back of the cabin. Maury Archer was in seat 24A. The two seats next to him were occupied. Although I looked directly at him as I approached, he was looking down or out of the window, maybe deliberately. I proceeded to the back of the cabin and then back up to my seat. I motioned to the nearest flight attendant and asked to speak with the captain. She seemed perplexed and I added, "Please just ask the captain. I have some important information for him."

In a couple of minutes Captain Lovett was at my seat. He was a big man, a bit more corpulent than your usual airline pilot. He was probably near retirement, gray-haired, with a no-nonsense manner that made me wonder whether he would take my concern seriously. When we had moved up near the galley I explained that the passenger in seat 24A was a Maurice Archer, who had been convicted of assault on myself and been recently paroled, and I had reason to believe his presence in Canada would pose a threat to myself and another person. I suggested to the captain that he check the passenger list to see if Mr. Archer had used an ID with another name. I also gave him the name and telephone number of RCMP Superintendent Novak, who was informed about the general facts of the case and could vouch for me. Failing that, he could call the numbers of Hugh Hannigan or Colonel McGrath, either of whom might in a pinch carry enough weight to reassure the captain that he was not dealing with a complete kook.

As he turned away I couldn't tell from Captain Lovett's face whether he was on his way to check out my story or to find a straight jacket. For a space of about fifteen minutes I imagined him rummaging through a drawer looking for the manual dealing with passengers who suffer delusional episodes. Eventually however a flight attendant dropped by to tell me that the captain wished to speak with me at the front of the first class section.

"Superintendent Novak supports your story," Captain Lovett began, with a worried expression. "The gentleman in seat 24 A identified himself as Henry Mortensen and presented a passport in support of that claim. From what you say, I gather we are dealing with a dangerous character. I presume the man is not armed, after going through airport security; but if he gets the impression that he's in trouble, might he try to hold some defenseless passenger hostage? If he is, as you indicate, a hit man, he probably doesn't need a weapon to endanger someone's life."

I told Captain Lovett about my episode with Mr. Archer in Talcayan and his subsequent imprisonment and surprisingly early parole. "But if we don't do anything to alarm him, there may be no problem. The first he need know that anything is amiss is when the police grab him as he exits the plane. Thus far the only thing with which Canadian authorities could charge Mr. Archer concerns his use of a bogus passport. Is he likely to make matters a lot worse by trying something desperate?"

"I'm afraid Mr. Archer already suspects something," Captain Lovett replied. "I talked to the flight attendants about him, and one of them reported that he came up the aisle apparently to get a better look at you. We have no security guard on board. I could get an attendant to let the young mother and little girl next to him know that they have been upgraded to first class and get them out of harm's way."

I replied that with the help of an excellent instructor in the Armed Services I had achieved some competence in hand to hand combat. I would be happy to sit close to Mr. Archer and keep an eye on him.

"Inspector Novak informed me that in a pinch you might come in handy that way," Lovett said. "But do you really want to sit next to someone who, if you read the situation correctly, will become considerably richer if he puts you out of commission? Besides, well . . . I don't want to precipitate anything. So thanks, but . . . I think we'll just move the mother and child and let it go at that."

The two passengers were moved to first class without incident. A few minutes later a flight attendant asked me to come forward again to meet with the captain. "I've changed my mind," he said. "If you are willing to do it and are confident that you can handle anything that arises, then you would, I think, be doing us a favor if you would sit close enough to Archer that you can intervene if he becomes aggressive."

I took a few minutes to plan my approach, then strolled back and took my place in seat 24C without comment. Archer was apparently absorbed in a newspaper. We remained in silence, during which I was not able to give of my best regarding the New York Times crossword puzzle, what with keeping one eye on my seatmate. After a while I decided to find out whether Mr. Archer had retained the sense of humor he had displayed during our previous encounter. I had the vague feeling that I might be once again stumbling into some sublimely stupid behavior—but it was, as I say, only a vague feeling.

"Excuse me sir," I broke into his concentration. "I've been admiring your shoes. Are they comfortable?"

He looked at me with an expression between perplexity and irritation, but remained silent, so I continued. "The reason I ask, about six months ago some moron shot me in the foot and since then I've had the devil of a time finding comfortable shoes."

This elicited no comment. "Do you believe in reincarnation?" I asked, in the interest of keeping the conversation going. "Do you think maybe Shirley MacLaine is on to something?"

"Nope." He didn't look away from the Chicago Tribune.

"Well I hope there's reincarnation," I replied. "I want that guy who shot me to come back as a statue in a park somewhere, and I'll come back as a pigeon, maybe the leader of a flock of pigeons. That more or less sums up my sentiments about that blockhead."

Some item in the newspaper was apparently even more engrossing than my conversation, but I was undeterred. "Where are you headed?"

This time he responded. "I'm thinking of landing in Calgary about the same time as this plane does."

"What a coincidence," I replied "I'm going there myself. You wouldn't by any chance be going on to Edmonton? I could give you a lift."

He shook his head ever so slightly and elaborately turned over a page of the paper.

- 157 -

"Sir," I said. "Don't you feel that there is a sort of bond between us—like maybe we knew each other in some other life? Here we are back on the subject of reincarnation."

Archer remained as chatty as a clam. Was this his first visit to Calgary? More silence. I continued: "There are several things that first time visitors to Canada should know in order to make their stay more enjoyable. For starters—the immigration officials. You may have heard that Canada has come under international criticism lately for being lax about passports. As a result our immigration officers have taken on the personalities of a pack of starving Dobermans. If a person were to try to enter Canada with a false passport, for example, my advice to him, or her, would be to come clean, just beg the officials for mercy. They become enraged if they think you're hiding something; and the only thing worse than a false passport is two passports. You wouldn't believe the damage one tiny woman on the scent of a second passport and armed with nothing more than a razorblade can do to a fellow's clothing and even his luggage."

I paused to give Maury a chance to start holding up his end of the conversation but he seemed disinclined to encourage me. So I continued. "Of course something like passport fraud would have to be handled by the Mounted Police."

Archer broke his silence. "Ah, the Mounted Police. They're the ones who always get their man."

"Not at all," I replied. "You are probably thinking about the olden days, Nelson Eddy and Jeanette MacDonald and maybe Sergeant Preston chasing mad trappers through the north woods. Actually even in the old days I think the Mounties got a lot of credit that really should have gone to the black flies. It may be a perfectly sane trapper who flees into the forest at 6 P.M., but I can guarantee that if it's black fly season it will be one really mad trapper who emerges from that forest the next morning, and that puppy is going to head for the nearest RCMP station and beg them to take him in.

"Now what our Mounted Police are really good at is waiting. It goes way back in our history. You probably never heard of the Riel Rebellion. Well, like much of what you'll find in Canada, our rebellion was a modest affair. But the rebels had a real smart military leader named Gabriel

Dumont. This regiment from Eastern Canada went out west to put down the rebellion and they met the rebels at a little place in Saskatchewan called Batoche. The rebels were mostly Métis, half white, half native. The leader of the army from Eastern Canada knew that time was on his side. His men could sit on their backsides week after week and draw their regular pay. The Métis were farmers or had other jobs and they had to get back to work or their families would go hungry. So the army just sat there and drew their pay and gradually the Métis drifted away, which reduced the number of casualties considerably.

"That experience taught the Mounties a valuable lesson. You know that mess at Waco, Texas several years ago? The government moved in and all sorts of people got shot. Well, a while ago we had a stand-off at a Native People's reservation near Montreal. The guys on the reservation blocked a highway. What did the Mounties do? They just waited and drew their pay, and eventually the people on the reservation got tired and went home. Now in the U.S. the government troops would have been tempted to move in and show those guys who was boss.

"Actually we Canadians would probably be as good as anybody at showing people who is boss, but we're not sure ourselves. For years we thought it was the queen, or at least someone in London. Now we think it might be the people in Washington, or maybe Wall Street. But you're not going to get a lot of Mounties excited about showing our criminal classes that the real boss is the U.S. congress, or Walmart, or J.P. Morgan Trust."

Archer apparently did not find my loquacity nearly so diverting as I did. He turned towards me. "Is it just me, or is it terribly noisy on this aircraft?"

"You're quite right," I replied. "I got side-tracked. What I really wanted to tell you about is the present-day Mounties. They have nothing against getting their man, or their woman for that matter. But more and more, they've taken to outsourcing as a way to save money. You know how police forces are usually underfunded. Here's how it works. Suppose—just a hypothetical case—I'm suspicious that a certain person intends to harm me and I bring my concerns to the Mounties. They then bring this person in for questioning. At this point he hasn't committed a major crime, just something minor like passport fraud. But this is a person of dubious reputation. So the police are in a quandary. They can't hold him for more than a year or so for a passport infraction but they don't like the thought of him roaming around getting into mischief.

"So this is where outsourcing comes in. The RCMP might give this person and myself a chance to work out our differences. We would negotiate. I might suggest, for example, that he tell me who is paying for his trip. Then I would agree not to testify to the police that his real name is not the one on the passport he has been using. The police are busy and they're not looking for extra work, so they let this person return to his home base. So everyone's happy. Well, not quite everyone. The generous people who paid for his trip might feel that they aren't quite getting their money's worth."

At this point Archer became almost voluble. "Suppose, just hypothetically, that you are mentally unhinged, that the whole thing is an invention of your fevered brain. Are you telling me the RCMP are going to act on your wild accusations?"

"Ah," I said, "You've missed the beautiful part of outsourcing. In this case the RCMP are precisely not acting."

He kept his voice low. "Listen, I've heard enough of this nonsense. I don't know what your problem is, but you have no business verbally assaulting a stranger on an airplane with this drivel. There's got to be legal protection against this kind of harassment, and I intend to report this to the proper authorities; and if the Canadian authorities don't act I'll report it to the American consul the first chance I get."

"I quite appreciate your point," I replied. "A chap has a reasonable expectation to be left at peace when he pays for a seat on an airplane, or for that matter even if someone else pays for his seat. But you should know, there's a special assistant in the office of the Minister of External Affairs in Ottawa who does nothing else from dawn to dusk but shred stiff letters of protest from foreign consulates. Of course the consuls have to write letters, but what then? If they start insisting on action . . . you can guess what happens the next time someone from Washington asks Ottawa for information about this or that crime syndicate or drug ring. They'll be lucky if they get accurate directions to the nearest john."

I was on a roll. I had just calumniated the RCMP and the Ministry of External Affairs and created a peculiar history of the Riel Rebellion. I had used up much of the material from two of my better routines and had added a couple of touches which, with a little tweaking, I could work into the mix the next time I was called upon to liven up a program of after-dinner speeches. But I was running out of material and a tiny voice of reason was suggesting that this might be a good time to throttle back. Every once in a long while I listen to that voice, so I joined my seatmate in contributing to the silence in our section of the airplane.

CHAPTER TWENTY

When we landed in Calgary Mr. Archer seemed to be playing it cool as he pulled his bag from the overhead bin and joined the procession of debarking passengers. As he left the plane a burley representative of the Royal Canadian Mounted Police stepped forward and explained that there was some complication about Mr. Mortensen's identification. Would the gentleman please come with him to get it straightened out? Without being asked I included myself in the welcoming party, so we proceeded down the passageway in single file, reading from front to back: officer, Archer, officer, Captain Lovett, Hannigan. Once in the terminal we proceeded through a door marked "Airport Personnel Only" and down a hallway to a windowless office with a table and six heavy wooden armchairs around it and four similar chairs against one wall. Captain Lovett departed and the senior officer bade Mr. Mortensen and me to be seated at the table. The officers sat on chairs against the wall, and we waited.

After a few minutes there were noises in the hallway, the door opened and Superintendent Novak entered accompanied by another RCMP officer. Novak's limp seemed to be more pronounced than it had been when we had previously visited him. It might have been the effects of a hurried trip to Calgary from Edmonton, but I suspected that the superintendent was not above using it as a stage prop.

- 162 -

He was quiet, business-like, apparently preferring to give people enough rope to hang themselves rather than use the sweating process popular in TV police dramas. He explained that the guest was not under arrest, because whenever possible the superintendent avoided arresting foreign nationals. However, Mr. Mortensen's presence was required until certain questions were cleared up. Was he willing to remain and answer questions?

Archer, alias Mortensen, replied that he was happy to answer questions, but this person—he pointed at me—had violated his rights by making frivolous charges. Superintendent Novak replied that if it should be shown that Mr. Hannigan had made false accusations he would be dealt with severely. Archer then stated that he wished to get in contact with the American consul in Calgary. Novak pointed to a telephone on the table. "We have been in contact with the consul-general. He has agreed to be available to take your call. Here is the number. The rest of us will vacate this room while you speak with him. It may be best if you have him suggest a lawyer who will represent you at these sessions."

We left quietly. Novak took me by the elbow and guided me to a room across the hall, and during the next few minutes I filled him in on the events of the last couple of days and the meager store of reliable knowledge I had gained. Presently Archer informed the two guards outside of the room that he had finished consulting the consul. On the way back to the interrogation room the superintendent asked me whether I played poker. When I indicated that I had never played the game he continued, "You should get your uncle to teach you. He could bring you along to the Legion on Tuesday nights to help him carry home the money he takes off us poor people."

Asked whether he wished to have legal counsel present, Archer replied that he did, and that the U.S. consul had recommended Mr. Gregory Dale of the Calgary office of Wilson, Horvath and St. Pierre. Novak said that we would meet again at the earliest convenience of Mr. Dale. Mr. Mortensen would be housed in the Palliser Hotel, where, if he were allowed free run of the place, he might rub shoulders with some of the elite of the Alberta energy industry. The superintendent was not cooperating with my effort to impress our guest with the callous character of the RCMP, but he did indicate that two policemen would be available to guide Mr. Mortensen on any excursions he might take outside of his room.

We gathered at 10 A.M. the next morning at the RCMP station in downtown Calgary, Counsel Gregory Dale being added to the company. Superintendent Novak began: "Mr. Mortensen—I will use that name until we sort out this whole matter—before we get to the question of passports I want to comment on the other issue that you have injected into this hearing. You alluded last night to the fact that Mr. Hannigan has claimed that you were traveling to Alberta with the intent to do him harm. On the surface, this seems implausible. For one thing, for the past few years we have been blessedly free of the sort of organized crime that gives rise to contracts and hit men and that sort of thing. Of course Mr. Hannigan has been out of the country recently and he may have picked up some unsavory associates."

A flicker of a smile crossed Novak's face as he consulted his notes, fixed his eyes on Archer and continued: "The second reason to wonder about Mr. Hannigan's charge is that it seems unlikely that someone sent to harm him would so quickly become involved with the police. The only way in which the accusation becomes plausible is if this is an instance of what we here call a Zeidl hit. Mr. Mortensen, have you by chance ever heard of a person named Harry Zeidl?"

Archer shook his head, looking bewildered.

Novak continued. "No, it's not likely you would have heard of Harry. He was Canada's own small contribution to underworld lore. Harry hated to spend money, so he developed this economical way of getting rid of people. He would not, as they say, put out a contract on them. Instead he would give them a contract. Let's say Mr. X is a criminal who has the sort of knowledge that is, one might say, negotiable. Harry doesn't want to take the chance that Mr. X might be arrested and then plea bargain by giving police information that could put Mr. Zeidl behind bars. So Harry tells Mr. X that he can earn fifty thousand dollars if he knocks off a certain enemy of Harry whom we shall call Mr. Y. Now Mr. Y was always someone who has some of the same skills in self-defense that Mr. Hannigan here possesses, although lacking those elements of conscience that Mr. Hannigan seems to have retained."

THE BLOOD-DIMMED TIDE IS LOOSED

The inspector took a quick glance in the direction of that person who seemed to have retained some elements of conscience, and then went on soberly. "So Mr. Zeidl has someone get the word to Mr. Y that Mr. X is gunning for him. Just like that, Harry gets rid of Mr. X without paying a cent. I'm telling you this story, Mr. Mortensen, because of a curious fact in this case. Mr. Hannigan here claims that he was tipped off that a certain Maurice Archer was intent on doing him harm. That is why he was able to have what he claims to be your residence under surveillance before you even left to come here. He was able to accompany you on the plane and deliver you into the hands of the police when you arrived. Mr. Mortensen, if in fact you have been hired by someone to harm Mr. Hannigan, you might check to see whether that someone wishes you ill."

The superintendent was laying it on a bit thick, and Mr. Dale protested. His client had agreed to cooperate with the police, but the superintendent was making certain absurd accusations the basis of his interrogation. If the questioning were to continue on this prejudicial basis Mr. Dale would have to advise his client to cease cooperating with the police.

Novak waved dismissively. "My point, Mr. Dale, was that Mr. Hannigan's accusations, as your client has reported them, seem far-fetched. I would consider that a point in your client's favor. But I do not intend at this time to continue on the subject of Mr. Hannigan's reported allegations. My primary interest this morning concerns a possible breach of Canadian immigration law because of some confusion about a passport."

That narrower focus for the session still left much to interest an observer, but a receptionist knocked at the door, entered and handed me a note that drew us into a whole new phase in the Talcayan affair.

"Call immediately." The message was from Uncle Hugh. The receptionist led me to an empty office with a telephone. Uncle Hugh picked up on the first ring. "Mick, get back here fast. Bad news from Talcayan. Dieter and his crew and their security people have been taken captive by some outfit. The same people have kidnapped some of your friends in Talcayan. The news is still murky, but I have one very bad item for you. . . . Your friend Aldomar has been killed."

- 165 -

Uncle Hugh said some other things before he hung up but I was hardly paying attention. I was thinking about Aldomar: meeting us when we first arrived at the border, explaining to the customs officer that while he, Aldomar, was the most reasonable of men, he was under orders from this tyrant, Mayor Robles; the big man talking Fraga's goons into letting me go when I had fallen into their hands in San Martin; my last sight of him trudging away from the Land Rover outside of Marino. My feeling on leaving Talcayan that I was abandoning friends was very much a feeling that I was abandoning Aldomar.

First Catherine and her husband murdered, now this. Was the country under a curse? I reminded myself that now of all times one had to be calm and reasonable, a reminder that was more irritating than helpful; and if our past actions had yielded such messy results, what could we accomplish now?

I went back to make my excuses to Superintendent Novak. He already had drained me of whatever useful information I had, so my presence at the interrogation was not important. Within less than two hours I was on a shuttle flight to Edmonton. When trying to deal with something like this I want to pace or jog until I'm exhausted, so being strapped into an airplane was not the most congenial circumstance.

I was surprised that it was Uncle Will who met me at the Edmonton airport. As it turned out, Señor Robles had tried to contact me, and having learned that I was out of town he had called the colonel. Will had relayed the news to Uncle Hugh, who had been unable to locate me until this morning. I had called my mother the night before to explain that I would be held up in Calgary to attend a police interrogation the next day but neglected to give her a phone number where I could be reached, and Hugh's secretary had taken a while to discover the venue of the interrogation. Uncle Will had taken an overnight flight from Toronto to Edmonton. He was the right person to have on board, but we Hannigans were taking up a lot of his time. Maybe he had been serious about needing some action once in a while to get his blood circulating.

For the rest of the afternoon there was a council of war at the headquarters of Hannigan Industries, beginning as soon as we got in from the airport: my uncles Hugh and Will, my assistant Alex Brosky, a couple of senior people in the company whose judgment Hugh trusted,

THE BLOOD-DIMMED TIDE IS LOOSED

and myself. It was clear that we needed the co-operation of the Canadian military. The meeting was suspended while Hugh went to one telephone to reach his political contacts and Will went to another to confer with former colleagues in the armed services. The rest of us wandered back to our offices. Some may even have gotten some work done. A while later we were summoned back. Will had gotten a sympathetic hearing from Colonel Manion in Ottawa who was an aide to General Forget, who would have a great deal to say about any deployment of Canadian military personnel outside of the country. Manion cautioned that what was being proposed would ultimately require a political decision, and the Minister of Defense might prefer to have nothing to do with the complications we were proposing.

Hugh reported that R. D. Lansinger, a backroom presence in Canadian politics, thought that the atmosphere in Ottawa might in fact help us. Several weeks earlier the Leader of the Opposition had hammered the Minister of Defense for several days during Question Period in the House of Commons about cuts in the military budget. The Opposition Leader charged that Canada was failing to live up to its commitments as a member of NATO, which is after all a military alliance. He went on: Canada has become a laughing stock, depending on the Americans for defense while criticizing American foreign policy, trade policy and whatever other policy needed to be criticized in order to catch headlines. We lack even the military resources to assert sovereignty over the waters adjacent to our Arctic coast. When, he asked, would Canada be able again to hold up its head in pride as a country that fulfills its obligations and fights its own battles?

Lansinger advised that in this atmosphere the Minister of Defense might be shamed into doing something lest he supply his inquisitor with further ammunition. News of the capture of the assay crew would quickly make the front page of the major daily papers, and it was not likely to go away as long as Canadians were being held hostage in a foreign country. The term "hostage" would inevitably be used, although thus far there had been no word from the captors about ransoms or conditions for release of the prisoners.

Manion and Lansinger were each deputed to talk to others. After a few minutes of firming up what we wanted the government to do, Hugh

- 167 -

and Will went back to their telephones. By six o'clock my two uncles had cobbled together a plan that had a chance of being approved by both the politicians and the military brass. Comparing myself to those two, one on each side of the family, I wondered where the gene that determines organizational ability had gotten lost.

Within a couple of days wheels had turned within wheels and wise heads had nodded in agreement. The Minister of Defense rose in the House of Commons to spike the guns of the Leader of the Opposition by announcing that Canadian ground forces, responding to a request from the Government of Talcayan, would cooperate with that nation in freeing the kidnapped Canadian personnel. I wasn't happy with the limitation of the operation to the freeing of Canadian personnel, but maybe while in the neighborhood the soldiers would also rescue whoever else had fallen into the hands of the outlaws. Matters would move forward "with all deliberate speed", the emphasis being on "deliberate", since the military personnel would not be in place for two weeks. With due regard for the egos of all concerned, the machinery of government and the armed services clanked and creaked and groaned into action.

In the short term what was needed was what military people like to call "intelligence". Most military fiascos result when officers don't know the pertinent facts and maybe don't even know what questions to ask. So within four days of my return from Columbus, Ohio I was in the air again. With me were Captain Albert (Alberto as the occasion demanded) Tamayo, a slim, handsome, forty-year-old military policeman whose special qualification for this mission was that he spoke Spanish, and Major Jason Knobel, who was neither slim nor handsome, whose specialty was assessing situations from a tactical or strategic point of view.

The day before taking off I had visited Superintendent Novak to find out what was happening in connection with Maury Archer. That gentleman had been informed that using a false passport and travelling under an assumed identity were offences that could land him in jail for a considerable period of time. Judges in such cases have considerable latitude. Mr. Archer had not been able to provide a convincing reason why he had travelled to Calgary on his way, as his ticket indicated, to Edmonton. This lent credence to the accusation that he did indeed plan harm to Mr. Hannigan. In view of this, the crown prosecutor would probably be moved to ask for the maximum sentence provided by law for Mr. Archer's provable offense. While he was serving this sentence officials would be digging into his background, sources of revenue, record of travel—in fact moving heaven and earth to find out whether there was any truth to the rumor that he had been making a living in an occupation that would not be regarded kindly by the law on either side of the Canada-U.S. border. On the other hand, if Mr. Archer could provide information that would enable the police to identify malefactors on a higher level, his cooperation would be taken into account by the sentencing judge.

At first Archer had maintained that his trip to Canada was innocent. On the second day, however, after consultation with his lawyer, he decided to answer questions. He admitted that he had travelled to Canada at the behest of the same people who had hired him six months earlier to try to locate where Rafael Fraga was being held. He insisted that he did not plan to harm either Colonel McGrath or myself, but had been commissioned to "throw a scare" into us in case we were minded to interfere again in the affairs of Talcayan. As to who had hired him, Mr. Archer was less forthcoming. He had dealt with a man who had not given his name. At this point Superintendent Novak had called in a police artist to work with Archer to provide a recognizable sketch of this unnamed person.

Superintendent Novak showed me a copy of the sketch, remarking that it might be worthless, but if that were so then Mr. Archer was looking at a considerable stay at the expense of Canadian taxpayers. I took one look at the sketch and realized that for the first time in this wobbly search for clues we might have arrived at something solid. The sketch was not particularly detailed, but the flash of white hair was unmistakable.

"I suspect that this time Mr. Archer has actually done something honest," I said. "This is a sketch of a man named Julio Lara. He's an officer of the Valdez Police Department, and I have had the pleasure of disarming him and his partner before they got around to disposing of Colonel McGrath."

If Lara was involved in both cases, that seemed to confirm that the people working to free Rafael Fraga were the same ones who were in power in Valdez, who were involved in the cover-up of the Tipping murder if not in the murder itself. That didn't solve any mysteries but it suggested that at least we were involved in only one wild goose chase rather than several.

Knobel, Tamayo and I flew through Atlanta and Santiago to Mendoza, and by the time we landed, stiff and sleep-deprived, the two officers had pretty much exhausted my knowledge of Talcayan, its history and geography, its politics and the events of the last few months. As I began answering their questions I congratulated myself on how much I knew about the place. As the major continued to probe it became clear how much I didn't know. Knobel, who was in charge of our operation, had as yet no plan of action, so at first we would be making it up as we went along.

The final leg of our journey was a flight from Mendoza to the field south of El Rio del Rey where the plane had landed that had hurried Dieter and his crew out of the country six months ago. We flew on an ancient but airworthy Canadian Forces Twin Otter aircraft that happened to be in the general vicinity and had been commandeered to get us to our destination quickly. When travelling on a Twin Otter it's a good idea to bring along ear plugs, but to my mind that is more than offset by the fact that, judging from its record, when properly maintained the aircraft is close to accident proof.

We brought with us three Harley-Davidson motorcycles, property of the Canadian Armed Services and adapted to carry a certain amount of firepower without it showing. We also took with us, courtesy of Hugh Hannigan, more cash than the average three-man force would carry on a mission. It was mid-morning when we waved good-bye to the crew of the Twin Otter and set out on the journey north. The sun was shining, the temperature was about 15 degrees Celsius. We wore biker style leather jackets and looked forward to a ride in the fresh air. For several miles we bounced over open ranchland with clumps of trees here and there, and then turned north on the road leading to El Puente Ingles. On the road our ride became only marginally smoother, but we were impatient and opted for speed rather than comfort.

We didn't have to wait long for our adventures to begin. Within minutes an automobile approached from the north. We wheeled off to the side to escape the worst of the dust as it passed. The car did not pass, however. It stopped and two men stepped out, dressed much like ourselves but wearing sunglasses, with obvious holsters and pistols on their hips, and one of them was carrying a rifle. This definitely was not good. They were not members of the Amparo police force, which was the only legitimate police presence south of the Rio del Rey; so they very likely belonged to the gang that was terrorizing the countryside. I nudged my vehicle forward and dismounted. I could have deferred to one of my companions to take the lead, but I was furious at the thought that we might be put out of operation before we got started and I was going to do whatever I could to prevent that from happening.

One of the men stood directly in front of me, the other, pointing the rifle downwards but in our direction, stood slightly behind him and to one side. The one in front of me demanded that we produce identification. Trying to keep my voice mild and conciliatory, I asked him to produce his policeman's badge or other identification. The man with the rifle stepped up to me and jammed the weapon into my ribs.

It was not the move of a practiced combatant. Tests show that in this situation a person with quick reflexes can usually deflect a weapon before the holder can fire it. Of course that word "usually" is bothersome. I turned towards his companion and asked loudly who was in command. As expected, the man in front of me turned his eyes momentarily towards the other. That gave me an extra split sentence to grab the end of his rifle with my right hand and point it away from me while with my left I pulled the Berretta from its shoulder holster. I advised the two of them that they should raise their hands slowly, and they did. Without a word, Captain Tamayo came up behind them and relieved them of their weapons.

The two had nothing on them to identify them as police. We had discussed the possibility of establishing some kind of hegemony for ourselves and the Amparo police south of the Rio del Rey so that we could move about in relative freedom in that part of the country. North of the river we would probably have to travel cautiously while we surveyed the situation. It was only a suggestion, and we intended to discuss it with Mayor Robles and his police, but by taking the two men into custody we seemed to have already begun to implement the plan.

To delay hostile reactions from our enemies we needed to keep our two new acquaintances out of circulation for a while. Talcayan law would probably allow them to be held on charges of impersonating police officers. We stashed two of the Harley-Davidsons in a ravine a half mile or so off the road and proceeded on our way, myself on a motorcycle, my two associates in the front seat of the automobile and the two prisoners, suitably restrained, in the back.

CHAPTER TWENTY ONE

At the City Hall in Amparo Major Knobel and Captain Tamayo remained in the automobile while I hurried in and was greeted effusively by Mayor Robles. His receptionist poked her head around the corner to say that the mayor's wife was on the phone, would he like her to call back? Robles picked up the phone. "Maria, wonderful news. Miguel Hannigan has arrived with two of his friends. I must go out to meet them. I'll call you back in a minute." He listened for a moment, put down the receiver and announced, "Maria is delighted and says you must come to visit us at our home as soon as you can."

I led the mayor out to the curb, where Major Knobel and Captain Tamayo got out of the vehicle to receive their formal welcome to Amparo. The mayor then inquired about the two passengers in the back seat. When we explained how we had picked up two guests for his jail his eyes widened. "By heaven, you fellows don't waste time getting to work!"

Mayor Robles was of course shaken by the murder of Aldomar, but our arrival seemed to give him heart to get back into action. After we had stowed our two captives in the jail he filled us in with what he knew about the situation. People who lived along the road to the site where Dieter and his crew were working were well aware of their comings and goings. Several days earlier they had observed two unfamiliar vehicles

- 173 -

driving up into the foothills towards the site: a jeep and a personnel carrier. Several hours later the two vehicles passed by in the other direction. Word went around that some of the Canadians were seen in the personnel carrier. A lad who owned a motor scooter visited the site and confirmed that it was deserted, though the crew's equipment remained. When the crew had not returned a day later the local people began to suspect that something serious had taken place.

In the next two days a number of citizens of Talcayan had been kidnapped. These included Felipe Diaz, foreman of the Chavarria estancia and son-in-law of the owner. Felipe it had been who took the most dangerous part in our confrontation with Fraga. Also kidnapped were Dolores Laval and Antonio Rossi. On the second day Emilio Flores, the son of the mayor of Valdez, drove into Amparo with three of his friends. Within an hour of their arrival the owner of a taberna had complained to the police about the disruptive behavior of the four. Aldomar and another policeman had entered the taberna and had tried to talk them into changing their behavior. They defied him. When Aldomar stated that they were under arrest they remained sitting and smirking contemptuously. When Aldomar reached for his gun Emilio shot him twice. The four of them then stepped over the dying man, swaggered out to their automobile and drove off. Aldomar died before the local physician arrived on the scene.

"It has been very systematic." Señor Robles was almost weeping in frustration. "They have tried to immobilize anyone who might oppose them. They killed my police chief and kidnapped the one man from the estancias most likely to take the lead against them. They have tried to terrify Mayor Laval by kidnapping his daughter. They have removed their main newspaper critic by kidnapping Antonio Rossi. What we are seeing is an effort to take control of the country."

"And who are 'they'?" I asked.

"Nobody has come out and claimed to be leading the movement," the mayor replied, "But Miguel Flores from Valdez must be either the head of it or one of the leaders. The only other mayors who could be behind it are Guzman in Magdalena and Rendon in San Isidro. I saw Rendon yesterday, and he is as worried as I am. Señor Guzman called me when he heard of the death of Aldomar and the kidnapping of Diaz, and my impression is that his main purpose was to rally support against this outrage.

"What is most worrisome is that whoever it is—probably Flores—has been at work at this for some time. Both Rendon and Guzman suspect that some of their own police are in his pay and will openly join him when the time comes. For all I know, some of my own officers are working for him. One thing is clear. Since Aldomar's murder my officers are unwilling to take action against the outlaws. I have asked two them to take the job of Chief of Police and both of them have declined. Even now, probably my men are worrying about having those scoundrels in our jail, afraid that their friends will come and shoot up the town and free the two prisoners. The fact that you are here now and there is a promise of soldiers coming later is tremendous good news, but we have hard days ahead before the others arrive."

Where were the people who had been kidnapped? On this point Señor Robles had to admit ignorance. His only clue was a rumor that some prisoners were being held on the Sangallo estancia in a hamlet so small that it didn't merit a name. As Tamayo translated this information to Major Knobel the latter began to shake his head. Usually kidnappers hide their captives. Why would they hold them some place where they might easily be found and where there was no particular obstacle to mounting a rescue operation? Talcayan has plenty of territory where detection would not be easy, mountainous regions covered with forest and with few inhabitants.

Señor Robles thought that the most likely explanation was that Flores and his gang were not very smart. After some thought Major Knobel mused that maybe Flores wanted the prisoners to be found. He might be counting on Canada not sending troops. Then the only people who would get involved would be local citizens and the number willing to risk their lives by opposing the bandits would probably be small. So Flores might be luring the opposition into trying to rescue the prisoners, and then he could attack and demolish them once and for all.

To defend Amparo against a concerted attack we would have to make the town into a fortress, and that was out of the question. The houses were scattered and the disheartened local police were not exactly spoiling for a fight; so we had to move the prisoners. They could not be accommodated in the cabin on the Chavarria estancia where Fraga and his lieutenant had been hidden while awaiting transportation out of the country. In kidnapping Felipe Diaz the outlaws had as much as declared war on the Chavarria family, and their property would be too obvious a place to stow the missing agents. Señor Robles was going to ask Rodrigo Laval whether he could accommodate the prisoners in Marino.

"Marino!" I said. "I thought that Mayor Laval wanted to avoid conflict. This would just be an invitation for the outlaws to attack him."

"Since his daughter has been kidnapped," Robles replied, "Mayor Laval has decided that he cannot remain on the sidelines. Besides, there is no need to let anyone know where the prisoners are. We may not have to hold them for very long, and in that time their friends won't be able to check out even the likely places like Amparo. They probably won't bother Marino until they thoroughly investigate the estancias south of El Rio del Rey."

Robles left to call Marino and returned in a few minutes. Mayor Laval was delighted to hear that we had taken a couple of the outlaws out of circulation and would be happy to provide a place for them. Because our presence in Amparo might put that town in danger, the next question was where Knobel, Tamayo and I should locate. A half-dozen possibilities were discussed and rejected, and we finally decided to set up camp in a secluded ravine on the north bank of El Rio del Rey not far from Marino.

Before leaving Amparo I visited Aldomar's widow. The funeral had already taken place, but the local practice was that after the funeral the bereaved would still receive visitors, and usually women in the neighborhood would stay with her to help with the cooking and housekeeping for a while. It made more sense than smothering the family with attention until the funeral and then leaving them alone. The widow, dressed in her Sunday best to receive guests, thanked me for returning to Amparo to help out. She started to tell me something about Aldomar but stopped when she felt herself about to break down and whispered: "I'll talk to you about it later."

Five minutes after leaving the San Pedro home I was on the road with a townsman who owned a truck that was a match for Aldomar's. We made our way to a merchant in Marino who in North America might be called an "outfitter". I bought one medium-sized tent, three inflatable mattresses, three sleeping bags, several plastic containers for water, a camp stove, pots, pans and a supply of propane. Then we stocked up on food at a grocery store and headed for the ravine where we were to set up camp. I would have liked to confer with Rodrigo Laval, but if Flores had spies in Marino it would do the mayor no good for me to be seen in the vicinity.

My driver and I had scarcely unloaded our purchases when Knobel and Tamayo arrived, having retrieved their motorcycles, and we set up camp in a semi-festive mood. Having spotted no one as we crossed the grasslands on the way to this secluded spot, we felt safe for the time being. Most soldiers seem to be able to enjoy a moment of peace even though there is danger not far away, or maybe because there is danger not far away. Major Knobel was elected cook by acclamation and set to work to produce something edible while Captain Tamayo and I put up the tent and set the rest of our stuff in order. Once the food was ready we took it up the hill out of the ravine so that we could keep track of any movement in the area. As we ate the two officers quizzed me further about Talcayan, Knobel absorbing information like a sponge and never backtracking to ask about anything that we had already covered.

After supper I rode on the back of Tamayo's Harley-Davidson to Amparo, followed by Knobel. The two of them would dump the confiscated automobile far enough from Amparo that our enemies would not associate the disappearance of their two colleagues with that town. My job was to accompany the two prisoners on their journey by panel truck to Marino. Mayor Robles insisted on coming along. I think it embarrassed him that his own police were supine while the three Canadians did the work and presumably took the risks. Our driver was the elderly owner of the truck. I expected to ride in the back with the prisoners but Señor Robles insisted that I had the practiced eye to watch for danger on the road; so he sat in the back, on the dusty floor in his neat, dark suit, his back against the front of the compartment, his short legs straight out in front of him, glaring balefully from one prisoner to the other. It was unsettling that the man had so exposed himself to possible retribution, but he seemed to think that this was no time even to appear neutral. It did mean however that we couldn't set these two free in the next few days.

Our trip through the dark seemed longer than the hundred kilometers or so from Amparo to Marino. At about 10 P.M. our driver pulled over to the side of the road, stopped, pulled out a flashlight and consulted a page of directions. Satisfied, he pulled back on to the highway and almost immediately turned right on to a rutted dirt road. We bounced along for a few minutes and then stopped next to a large stone house.

A uniformed policeman emerged from the house and directed the three of us towards the front door while he stayed with the vehicle. Inside the house we were met by a somber Mayor Laval. He greeted Robles like a comrade-in-arms, which approximately described their current relationship. Laval greeted me with similar warmth and thanked me not only for coming myself but for helping to arrange for military help from Canada. I assured him that this arrangement was entirely the work of Colonel McGrath and Hugh Hannigan. The mayor left no doubt about his feelings. To do nothing was to allow the worst sort of criminal to tyrannize over good people. They must be stopped, even though, he regretted to admit, there would almost certainly be bloodshed. The mayor reminded me now not of a Vince Lombardi quieted into elderly pacifism but a Coach Lombardi before whom 260 pound football players cowered when they missed tackles or broke curfew. If Flores thought that kidnapping his daughter would immobilize the mayor of Marino he had miscalculated.

I told Laval that it seemed that we would have to keep the prisoners incarcerated for more than a few days in order to protect Señor Robles. That was not a problem. The officer led us as we walked the prisoners not into the house but down an exterior stairs and through a door that let into the basement. There Señor Laval pulled on a row of shelves and part of the wall swung creakily out and revealed a room within. The space looked more like a place for people to hide than a place of incarceration. The rancher who had built the house many decades earlier had feuded with several of his neighbors to the extent of fearing for the safety of his family, and so in constructing his new home he had included this hiding place.

The room was large, with a couple of beds, an attached bathroom, television set, bookcase with a variety of reading materials, sofa, writing desk, refrigerator, several chairs, and other conveniences. Mayor Laval left us, we took the handcuffs off the prisoners and left them to make what they would of their new surroundings.

Upstairs we talked to the couple who were the proprietors of the residence. The husband ran a welding and repair shop in Marino. When the police or courts of Marino were not using the facility, his wife spent her spare time keeping his books; but when they had "guests" she stayed home, transferring food to the occupants of the lower suite on a dumb waiter and listening to their complaints on the intercom.

It was a relatively short trip from there to the site where we had set up camp. With my irrational fear of the dark, I was nervous walking into the camp alone at night after Robles and the driver had dropped me off. Since being blindsided by Archer in Magdalena I had become more than usually cautious, and it was possible that in spite of our precautions a Flores spy had spotted the camp. If by any chance a trap had been set, the enemy would have had plenty of warning of my approach, because the muffler on the panel truck in which I arrived muffled very little.

I positioned myself on the edge of the ravine from which I could see our camp in vague outline, and settled down to listen. I couldn't tell whether the background noise came from crickets close by or from frogs down by the river. Occasionally there would be a rustling sound in the general direction of the camp, but it sounded more like wind in the trees or a small animal in the dry grass than like anything heavy moving in the ravine.

After a few minutes I stole into the camp, keeping as quiet as I could while stumbling in the dark, and maneuvering so that if the weak moonlight cast a shadow it would not be cast in the direction of the tent. When I got to the tent I let out a loud whoop, which might have qualified me for a straightjacket had there been an audience, but I had a notion that a sudden sound might provoke some involuntary movement from anyone in the tent. My caution was wasted. An examination of the

- 179 -

tent and the clump of trees between the tent and the river revealed no intruders more sinister than an owl, which with some justification objected to my disturbance of the peace.

Back on the edge of the ravine waiting for the return of my colleagues, I had time to ponder the situation. The operation from the Canadian side was focused on freeing the kidnapped people. The mayors of Amparo and Marino, hitherto pacific, now seemed poised for a decisive battle for control of Talcayan. How did we foreigners fit into that picture? If the Canadian prisoners were mixed with the citizens of Talcayan who had been kidnapped, presumably the rescue operation if successful would free all or at least most the prisoners. That would certainly be gratifying to Mayors Robles and Laval, but it would not solve all of their problems. Was there any chance of the Canadian forces remaining to restore some order in this chaotic situation? A reliable answer to that question required a mind more versed than mine in politics. Probably the Canadian military incursion would limit itself to freeing captives. Anything further, no matter how eagerly sought by certain Talcayan authorities, could be viewed as unwarranted interference in the internal affairs of another nation.

I expected that Knobel and Tamayo would announce their arrival with the noise that one associates with Harley-Davidsons, but they were within a couple of hundred yards of the camp, lights out and the motors put-putting quietly, before I noticed them. It had been a long day, and within minutes we were breaking in our new mattresses.

CHAPTER TWENTY TWO

We set up a communications room in Marino with a telephone so we could keep in daily contact with Canada. After a week of travel and inquiry we still had relatively little to tell. The hamlet where, according to rumor, some prisoners might be held, lay on the Sangallo estancia. From that family we learned that there was a building in the hamlet where farmers stored animal fodder. A couple of months earlier a stranger had bought the structure and renovated it. If there were prisoners being held in the vicinity, that was where they were. Major Knobel and I got close enough to take some photographs of the hamlet without provoking any hostile reaction, but that constituted a very modest addition to our store of useful knowledge.

The most useful thing we learned that first week was that just a few miles north of San Martin there is a stream flowing out of the mountains through what is called the Valle Colorado because of the reddish hue of much of the rock along its course. Most of the valley is uninhabited, being too rocky to tempt anyone to cultivate it or even use it for pasture. It contains forest and a few open spaces where the ground is not hospitable even to the hardy trees that elsewhere cling to the slopes on either side. If you proceed upward several kilometers you reach the end of the valley. To go any farther you must climb the mountain. At this point many years ago an eccentric and wealthy

- 181 -

man had built a sort of castle. This gentleman seems to have been a forerunner of current entrepreneurs like Rafael Fraga. Not content with the income from his estancia, he had apparently helped himself to cattle from his neighbors' herds from time to time, charged usurious interest on loans to people who were not considered good risks by the banks, and in general preyed on the population of central-western Talcayan. Several of his neighbors began to retaliate, and this gentleman in his later years decided to build himself a fortress in which he could spend his nights in tranquility. The locals called the place El Alcázar. Since nobody else in Talcayan had bothered to build a castle, the common noun served quite well as the proper name of the place. After the death of its builder the fortress had been abandoned.

Reports had reached San Martin a few weeks earlier of activity in the upper reaches of the Valle Colorado. A road had been built where there had been only a trail. Some curious youths had ventured up the valley but were turned back by armed men before they had gone half a kilometer. Their curiosity piqued, they returned later through the forest and reported back that there was work being done at El Alcázar, refurbishing the building, adding to it and clearing a space around it. Several of our informants were convinced that this site was being prepared to serve as Flores' stronghold. After Major Knobel had relayed this bit of information to his superiors I called Uncle Hugh to report on our progress or lack thereof. He was not at that moment possessing his soul in patience.

"Imagine!" he exploded. "The troops would be ready to go tomorrow. What's holding things up is that the Canadian forces don't have aircraft available to transport them and their equipment to Talcayan. So we have to wait until the Americans can spare us some planes. On Monday we tell the Americans that they're a bunch of bullies who spend too much on the military. On Tuesday we go cap in hand and beg them to bail us out because we don't spend enough. No wonder they don't bust their butts to give us what we want exactly when we want it."

The next day I travelled to the Valle Colorado to get a look at this new place of interest. Near the entrance to the valley I spent a boring several hours and added to my fund of knowledge the fact that in that time two trucks and an automobile had driven up the road into the valley, and one of the same trucks, a dilapidated school bus, a different automobile and an open jeep with a youthful driver passed in the opposite direction. From my vantage point I got a good look at them with the help of binoculars but couldn't say that I discovered anything instructive.

That afternoon I moved several kilometers northwards to the Valle Palencia, which ran more-or-less parallel to the Valle Colorado. I hiked along a gravel road that followed a stream flowing down from the mountains. From this road several paths led off into the forest to the south. Passers-by with whom I spoke seemed not to know much about these trails, and several even gave the impression that there was something scary about them. No one answered the crucial question: Did any of these paths lead to the Valle Colorado and El Alcázar?

The next day Major Knobel left to examine the likely route that a Canadian contingent would have to take to get close to the hamlet on the Sangallo estancia. Captain Tamayo rode to the house where we had imprisoned the two pseudo-policemen. I ended up at the same place after a quick trip into Marino to pick up a copy of the morning newspaper that contained an item Mayor Laval had arranged to have published. As we entered their underground quarters the two prisoners were finishing their breakfast and looked up in a casual way that suggested that resisting their captors was not a current priority.

We started with the older of the two, the one who had done the talking when they accosted us on the road just after our arrival. He looked to be in his mid-forties, short, very dark, with long hair just beginning to turn gray, and wore thick glasses. We brought him upstairs and we sat around the kitchen table. Captain Tamayo was the good cop, leaving me with the role that fit my mood. Albert's solicitous inquiry about how our prisoner was getting along elicited predictable complaints about being illegally detained, with threats of dire consequences when his friends inevitably hunted us down. Albert reassured him that his detention here was temporary, that in a couple of weeks the whole matter would be resolved, and that Albert wanted to spare him the dangers that would arise when foreign troops arrived to free the prisoners.

The captain then tossed the newspaper on the table and asked him to look at an item on page four. It was a three-paragraph story indicating that the Prime Minister of Canada had announced to parliament that, in response to an invitation from the Government of Talcayan, he was sending troops to free the Canadian citizens who had been detained. Of special relevance to our purpose that morning, the second paragraph quoted the prime minister to the effect that the force sent on this mission would be large enough to overpower any opposition and assure the freeing of the prisoners with as little risk as possible to Canadian troops while bringing to justice those responsible for the kidnapping.

Then Albert leaned across the table and said softly, "We have to talk about what happens to you when those troops arrive. They intend to bring the kidnappers to trial, not just the leaders, everyone responsible. Are you ready for that?"

Our prisoner said nothing for a few seconds and then protested that he had nothing to do with any kidnapping, and we couldn't prove that he had. Albert shook his head sadly and pointed out that his only hope was to be honest. The automobile he had been driving had been seen often in the hamlet on the Sangallo estancia. It did not belong to the residents of the hamlet. We had to presume that it belonged to the people who had invaded the premises and were holding the kidnapped people there. Furthermore, if he was not working with the captors holding the prisoners, why would he have stopped us on the road?

I growled to Albert: "This guy is wasting our time. I say we knock him on the head and show his body to his pal downstairs. Maybe it'll loosen his tongue. We can't spend all day here."

Albert begged me to give him another chance to get the information we needed before doing anything drastic and then turned back to our prisoner. "I can't help you," he said, "if you don't cooperate." He then reminded him that he was guilty of impersonating a police officer and emphasized the hopelessness of his position. Our prisoner repeated that it could not be proven that he had taken part in the kidnapping. Albert pointed out that if you are part of a group that commits a crime, Canadian courts will hold you responsible even if you did not personally perform the criminal act. Our prisoner protested that Canadians had no legal right to try citizens of Talcayan. Albert in a regretful tone explained that it would depend on the decision of a judge in Talcayan whether the accused would be extradited for trial in Canada. "But remember," he added, "You will be in the custody of Canadian troops. You could be spirited out of the country before any authorities in Talcayan even know that you exist."

There was a long silence. Then Captain Tamayo explained that he had a proposal. He was not asking anyone to betray his friends. He only wanted some information that would help to save lives when the Canadian troops arrived. First, who exactly was imprisoned in the hamlet? The prisoner claimed not to know. At this point I interrupted angrily. How could he have spent time in a small building with the prisoners and not know who they were? The prisoner was a bit rattled and asked how he could possibly know who was being held there when they didn't even speak Spanish.

Albert took over smoothly. "Do none of the prisoners speak Spanish?"

"Only one of them, and he speaks very badly. He translates for the others."

"All the prisoners are Canadians then?"

"Yes, of course, that follows, doesn't it?"

"How many prisoners are there?"

The man thought for a moment, aware perhaps that if he knew that the prisoners spoke no Spanish he could not plausibly deny knowing how many there were. He may also have thought that while his captor who spoke Spanish fluently seemed to be a kind and patient person, the Canadian soldiers when they arrived might be more like this churl who spoke with an ugly accent and who seemed to be in charge. He mumbled that there probably were eight or ten prisoners. He hadn't counted them.

A few more minutes of questioning yielded only the information that Flores' garrison in the hamlet varied in size between ten and fifteen men, depending on the day and whether there was any special work to be done. Albert by questioning him on related matters gave him a couple of opportunities to slip up on the information he had provided already, but each time he reaffirmed that there were eight or ten prisoners and only one of them spoke Spanish. On the question of who was his boss, who was calling the shots, he clammed up so completely that any further time spent with him would be wasted.

A half hour with the other prisoner brought no results at all. He could have been brain dead as far as answering questions was concerned. Unless we were willing to resort to torture, that strategy was probably as effective as any.

That evening Major Knobel was delighted with the information we provided. It looked very much like all the Canadians were being held in one place, a place not easily defended. All that remained was to design an approach that made it clear to the captors that they could neither hold out nor escape, and therefore their only logical option would be to surrender and, in the meantime, treat their prisoners humanely.

Major's Knobel's analysis made excellent sense from his point of view. It presented some drawbacks for those who had the welfare of Talcayan at heart. With their own nationals freed, Canadian authorities would most likely view the job as finished. My dream was fading of Canadian soldiers searching for prisoners from one end of the country to the other and in the process routing the outlaws. I reminded the major that the prime minister had talked about bringing to justice those responsible for the kidnapping. That would not be achieved simply by freeing the prisoners and arresting their guards. Major Knobel granted that my argument had a certain force, even in terms of Canadian self-interest. He was not at all sure that the people in Ottawa would see it my way, but he agreed to present my case to them.

The major was anxious to inform his superiors in Ottawa as quickly as possible of our bit of "intelligence", so we repaired to our communications room in Marino. Of course the officer in Ottawa was elated that the kidnapped Canadians apparently were so situated that a relatively simple and short rescue operation should be successful. Knobel added, "There is another angle to this. If we free the prisoners and take their captors into custody, we would still probably not have the ring leaders who are responsible for the whole thing. For that we would have to keep a force in Talcayan long enough to root out the whole gang that is presently terrorizing the country, or at least until we identify and capture their leaders. I take it that our goal is to bring the leaders to justice?"

The major had put the case with his usual brevity. The rest of the telephone conversation was one-sided, Knobel putting in a few words only now and then. After he hung up he explained; Colonel Marchand, with whom he had been speaking, was not impressed with the argument that the Canadian forces should stay until the leaders had been apprehended.

"Why not?" I asked. "The prime minister said the purpose of the expedition was to punish the perpetrators. Has he changed his mind?"

Knobel thought for a while. "The way a politician is likely to see it, once the prisoners are free the public will lose interest. If Canadian troops stay in Talcayan in what looks like a military operation, the only way that makes the news is if peace advocates get hold of it and claim that Canada is interfering militarily in the internal affairs of another. The prime minister is probably afraid of losing the peacenik vote to the New Democrats."

"So," I said, "While the victims are imprisoned it's all right to promise to go after the perpetrators, but it's not all right to hunt them down once we know the captives can be freed. Do I have that straight?"

"Precisely," he answered. "You should have sympathy for the poor politicians. They tie themselves into knots because most voters have the attention span of fleas. That's democracy. As the great man said, it's the worst form of government except for the other ones. Being ruled by public opinion in the military is like depending on a chain saw operator to perform heart surgery. I can see why you might have been uncomfortable had you stayed in the Canadian Armed Services."

Were it only a matter of dealing with the ten to fifteen men guarding the Canadian prisoners, a small contingent could do the job. But the rescuers would also have to protect themselves against an attack from outside. Because we had no idea of how many men Flores might be able to muster, playing it safe meant bringing in heavy equipment and a considerable number of soldiers. Major Knobel's concern turned to logistics. The nearest airport that could handle the big planes was at Mendoza. The problem then was to plot the safest route from Mendoza to the hamlet where the captives were being held. One part of the route was predetermined—from just north of El Puente Ingles to the hamlet. Knobel and Tamayo left to spend the rest of the day touring that route with a view to safety. The major was especially concerned about the

- 187 -

possibility of the road being mined, either with landmines set off by pressure or ones exploded by radio signal. He needed to devise some way in which local people could keep an eye on the bridge and the route south from the bridge to detect suspicious activity.

CHAPTER TWENTY THREE

With Knobel and Tamayo busy planning the rescue of the Canadian prisoners, I had time to make inquiries at Flores' home base and possibly get some leads about the murders that had initially brought me to Talcayan. I had to start somewhere. There were two people in Valdez whom I could presume to be friendly to Antonio Rossi—Señora Rossi and the editor, Señor Gallego.

There might be a spy at the newspaper, so calling the editor's office and identifying myself as Mick Hannigan could get both of us into trouble. At 8 P.M. my telephone call interrupted the evening repast of Mayor Robles as I searched for some pretext to get in touch with the editor. The mayor was helpful, as usual. Along with his newspaper work, Señor Gallego had a small stable of racehorses. Another call to Uncle Hugh in Edmonton gave me the name of a reputable thoroughbred owner named Archibald Manley, and it took Hugh only a few more minutes to get in touch with that person and get his permission for me to pose as his agent to approach a breeder in Talcayan, being careful of course not to transact any business.

Early the next morning I motorcycled to Valdez, arriving at about 9 A.M. I telephoned the Gallego office, identified myself as a certain Ronald Bernard, agent for Archibald Manley and inquired whether the good editor might give me a half hour of his time to discuss horses.

- 189 -

The receptionist was away from the phone for a couple of minutes and reported back that her boss would be happy to see me if I could appear at his office at eleven o'clock.

On entering that office at eleven o'clock sharp I was confronted with a short, rotund individual with a full grey beard standing somewhat precariously on a plastic chair with watering can in hand. He beamed at me, took a second to finish watering a potted plant that hung from the ceiling, stepped down rather heavily from the chair and held out his hand. "Ah, Mr. Bernard, the agent for Manley Stables. Welcome to Valdez."

I was about to come clean about my identity but he put a finger to his lips, kept chatting, turned up the volume on a CD player, then ushered me out of the office and down the hallway, chuckling like a schoolboy who had just put a frog in the top drawer of teacher's desk. He led me on to a patio where he turned and shook my hand again. "As far as I can tell, the bugs in my office are sound activated; so I keep some noise going all day long to keep my auditors busy. When I leave I like to expand their musical horizons by playing a CD of someone like Philip Glass."

He continued when we had settled into a couple of lawn chairs, still reminding me of a lad up to some mischief. "As it happens, there are only two thoroughbred owners in Canada whom I know about, and one of them is Archie Manley. My guess is that Mr. Manley doesn't need to import stock from a humble operation in the middle of South America, so when you called it struck me that you might have something else on your mind. Am I right?"

In the ensuing conversation the editor left little doubt that, after the kidnapping of his assistant, the time had come for action. Having decided that he was not yet in a position to come out publically against the mayor, he was delighted that there was now some organized opposition to Flores and he was anxious to provide whatever help he could.

"Just as the mayor probably has a spy or two in my office," he grinned, "I have a spy at city hall. Maria's not part of the inner circle of course. She's a computer technician. That doesn't allow her to get into any confidential documents, unfortunately, but she's a bright girl. She picks up stray bits of information here and there and lets me know what is going on as much as she can."

Señor Gallego knew no more than I did about the circumstances of Antonio Rossi's disappearance or his present whereabouts. I told him about Colonel McGrath's adventure with the two officers six months ago and asked him about Julio Lara.

"Officer Lara," the editor mused, "He's the person whom Flores and Langer use to do their dirty work. A scary man. You don't want to have anything to do with him. He's very competent, and he doesn't like to be bested. I suspect that he thinks he has a score to settle with you."

Señor Gallego had not heard about the murder of the Tippings. I asked him whether he could hazard a guess about who was capable of such a crime. Could it have been Lara?

The editor was silent for a few seconds. "No, it's not the kind of thing I associate with Julio Lara. No doubt he is a wicked man, and he is guilty of crimes, but not of senseless crimes. It's hard to say who it might be. It had to be someone who had enough influence to get the police to cooperate. It could be Mayor Flores' son, Emilio. It's the kind of reckless, completely callous thing that he could do, and Papa is in a position to order the cover-up. But there are others in that bunch just as bad. I couldn't give you all their names and what I know about them is hearsay."

Gallego stroked his beard for a few seconds and then put up his hand like an orchestra conductor preparing to launch into the next movement of a symphony. "Let's look at this systematically. Who would know the identity of the murderer, besides the guilty party himself? Presumably Lara would know, though not necessarily. He could have arranged the cover-up without approval from anyone up higher. But my guess is that the order would originate with either Mayor Flores or Chief Langer. Maybe a friend of the perpetrator would know, or some drinking buddies. . . . Problem is, even if we could identify them we very likely couldn't get them to talk."

Another pause. "There's another angle. If some innocent party found the bodies he would probably call the central police station in Valdez. Maybe we could find the person who reported it. Maybe the call was received by someone who is not a one of Langer's henchmen. The officer sent out to investigate might be an honest man. There are those who have been on the police force from the time before Flores and Langer took over, and some of them I think have stayed honest. If we could identify anyone who was involved in the process, he or she might not know who committed the crime, but it would give you a place to start.

"How about this? I'll get Maria to nose around. Nothing dangerous. Just look at some files and schedules and reports. See what she finds. Give us a few days, and let me know how to contact you."

What did Señor Gallego know about the forces behind the recent kidnappings?

"On that topic," he explained, "I may not know anything that you haven't heard already. As far as leadership is concerned, the only name you hear is Miguel Flores. He has never presented himself publically as the leader, but his is the only name that you hear, so we tend to assume he's in charge. He could be a front for one or several others, but he certainly is involved at a high level. Since the kidnappings he's been away from Valdez more than he's at home. His police chief, Langer, has actually resigned his position here, probably because he's busy elsewhere, and Officer Lara seems to be in charge in Valdez. As to the whereabouts of the prisoners or where there might be a concentration of pro-Flores forces, I presume you know about El Alcázar, and if you do, you know as much as I."

My last question concerned getting in touch with Señora Rossi. Señor Gallego agreed that her telephone might be tapped or her home under surveillance. When I assured him that I would be free to meet her whenever and wherever was convenient for her, the editor said "Wait here a minute," got up and left the patio.

He was back shortly. "I have been talking to Señora Mendez, who lives close to Señora Rossi. She is going to run over to her house to borrow a cup of sugar and find out whether Señora Rossi is willing to meet with you, and if so, when and where. I'll give you the Mendez telephone number and you can call in an hour or so. Now if you don't mind, let us go back to my office and we can discuss my excellent thoroughbreds for the benefit of those people who go to the trouble of recording my conversations. You understand of course that I am notorious for overvaluing my horses and demanding outrageous prices."

Señora Mendez when I got in touch with her an hour later was brief and to the point. Señora Rossi was willing to talk to me at a particular eating place at two o'clock if I could get there without attracting the attention of the local police. I was there by a little after one o'clock, having spotted no suspicious followers in my rear-view mirror. The place was a Talcayan version of a fast food outlet. It was six hours since I had eaten breakfast, so I ordered something substantial and as unfried as I could find on the menu.

From where I sat I had a good view of most of the parking lot, including the spot where I had parked my vehicle. As far as I could tell, nobody in the area was interested in me, except for a toddler in a high chair at a table kitty corner to mine. He was engaged in the serious business of dipping French fries in a puddle of Ketchup and transferring the dripping mess more or less successfully to his mouth, and he would gaze at me meditatively from time to time while masticating that portion of the food that had not ended up on his cheeks and chin.

The restaurant was almost empty and I was loitering over a second cup of coffee when a car drove into the parking lot and two women got out. At first I didn't recognize Señora Rossi. Her hair was darker, probably closer to its natural color than the chestnut hue it had been a half year ago. She wore a blouse and blue jeans; her face seemed thinner and very somber. The two hurried across the parking lot and into the restaurant, paused briefly at the entrance and came quickly to my table. I was half way onto my feet to greet them when Señora Rossi slipped quickly on to one of the chairs opposite, reached across the table to shake my hand, and introduced her companion as her sister-in-law, Fernanda Rossi.

Hoping to allay her nervousness, I said I had been watching carefully and had seen no sign of her being followed, nor had anyone paid any attention to me. She explained that on the way she had ducked into a department store, walked through to the back door and been picked up by her sister-in-law. "I hate having to go through all this hide-and-seek stuff. It makes me feel like some kind of thief."

- 193 -

Señora Rossi knew very little about the circumstances of her husband's detainment. He was usually home from work by six P.M., and one day when he had not appeared by nine his wife had begun to make phone calls, including one to her cousin who was a member of the police force. He had told her he would look into it. After a restless night she had tracked down her cousin about noon, and he told her that Antonio had been detained because he had made false accusations against Mayor Flores and Captain Langer. No information was being given as to where he was being detained. Her cousin had said only that he was not in danger.

Señora Rossi was near to tears. "I trusted my cousin. Now it turns out that he is on the side of Captain Langer. He has turned against his own family."

I asked her whether she was aware of an influential person outside of the country whom her husband saw as his protector. She was not, nor had Antonio talked to her about the murder of the Tippings. Casting around for some sliver of information she might be able to provide, I asked her whether Antonio had said anything that would indicate what he was working on before his capture. At this point she stopped me and remained thinking.

"During the week before he disappeared, Antonio asked me about two people," she said after a few seconds. "The day he disappeared, that morning he asked me whether I knew anything about a woman, Veronica someone-or-other, Contreras I think. Yes, Veronica Contreras. I had never heard of her. He didn't say why he was interested in her. A couple of days earlier he had asked whether my cousin in the police might know a man named Garza. I forget his first name. My cousin said he knew Officer Garza quite well, but Antonio disappeared before I was able to tell him that. I don't suppose it was very important in any case. I'm sorry I can't be more helpful."

I assured her that whatever she said had helped, at least to give me new avenues to investigate. As I rose to leave she said a little desperately, "Do you think you can find him? Have you made any progress?"

The most I could say was that we had only begun to work on the problem, but we expected to get help from outside of the country to free the Canadian captives, and when that happened we might learn more about who was responsible for the kidnappings and perhaps about where the prisoners were being held.

The most promising lead that Señora Rossi gave me, and it was a vague one, was the name Veronica Contreras. The search for a telephone number indicated that there was no lack of people in Valdez named Contreras but none of those listed had the initial "V". For the moment I could think of nothing else to do but return to camp and wait to hear whether Maria in the mayor's office had picked up any information that Señor Gallego thought worthwhile to pass on to me. Parts of my anatomy balked at the notion of hours more on the Harley Davidson, and I had been up since 6 A.M. However, Antonio Rossi had warned us six months ago that if we turned in our passports at any hotel in Valdez the police would know about it. Probably whoever at the police station looked at the names would not remember anything about a Michael Hannigan, but one couldn't be sure.

I decided to make the shorter trip to Avila and stay there overnight. On the way I passed through the village of Cantal, and that brought back memories of our visit with Officer Costa. The building where we had met him appeared to be closed for the day, so I kept going and resolved to return the next morning.

Fourteen hours later I found Officer Costa in his office alone and shuffling papers. He looked up incuriously at me at first, but when I gave my name he furrowed his brow a bit, aware probably that he had heard it somewhere before. Reminded of the occasion of my last visit accompanied by Colonel McGrath, he looked like a rabbit cornered by a coyote, but he mustered up enough spirit to growl; "And what's your problem now?"

I replied that I didn't have a problem, but he might have one. The government of Canada was in the process of sending a military force to Talcayan to free some recently kidnapped people and bring the perpetrators to justice. Mayor Flores was implicated in the kidnapping, and this meant that Capitan Langer was probably involved as well. So the two persons whom Officer Costa had to fear regarding the murder of the Tippings were themselves about to come upon hard times. If Officer Costa did not wish to be brought down with them, now was the time to dissociate himself from them, and he could do that by giving me information, either confirming points that I already suspected or giving me new leads.

Officer Costa's first ploy, probably in an effort to convince himself, was to argue against the likelihood of Canadian troops arriving in force. Eventually he threw up his hands. "I have very little to tell you. I already told you and that big fellow who was here with you that I filed a report at the insistence of higher authorities. I know nothing of the real circumstances of the crime. I didn't even see the bodies. The report that I have on file here is the same one that was sent to Canada. You already know all this."

"There is one point that you can clear up," I answered. "We know that Officer Lara was involved in some way in the cover-up. Was it Officer Lara who told you to make a false report?"

Costa hesitated, then apparently decided that less harm would come to him from telling the truth than from lying. "Yes, it was Officer Lara. He didn't just call me on the phone. He came here with the report already typed out and had me sign it. Around here you do what Julio Lara tells you to do."

"When he was talking to you, did Officer Lara say anything that might indicate who had committed the murder? You realize, Officer Costa, that if you can help us solve that crime you will have done something very important for the Canadians who are coming, and Colonel McGrath and I will change our minds about you and do what we can to protect you from any effort to implicate you in the crimes of the mayor or police of Valdez."

Casta paused, and this time, I suspect, he was really trying to remember something helpful rather than find an answer to mollify me. "I can't remember anything special that Lara said. He is a careful man. He would not give out information by mistake. What I remember mainly is that he was angry. Maybe he was angry at whoever committed the murder. I don't know."

A few more minutes of my inexpert questioning brought no particularly useful information. All that Costa had given me about which to ruminate on the long road back to camp was that Officer Lara had been angry. That sounded like confirmation that he was not himself the perpetrator of the crime. Maybe it had some further significance.

The next two days I ran errands for Major Knobel. The authorities in Ottawa promised to "take under advisement" his urgent request for a reconnaissance plane to allow him to do his job properly. Then the situation suddenly changed. One morning we were finishing breakfast at the camp when a lad came bouncing over the field on a bicycle and handed us a note from Mayor Laval. Very early that morning people in the hamlet on the Sangallo property had been awakened by the noise of vehicles starting up and driving away. The first to emerge from his house noticed that the cars and van had disappeared that had been parked at the building where we knew the prisoners were being held.

With much shouting back and forth, contact was made with those inside the building. None of those outside spoke English, and the one person on the inside who spoke Spanish had difficulty making himself understood. It was eventually established that all the captors had left the scene but had left the door to the building locked. The longest ladder available reached several feet short of the only windows that were unbarred. A wagon was wheeled into place, the foot of the ladder placed on the wagon, and the eight captives made their way cautiously but safely to the ground.

Someone in the hamlet had telephoned the Sangallo ranch to convey the news. Someone there had called Mayor Robles, who passed the word on to Marino, and Mayor Laval had his messenger out to our camp by 7:30 A.M. We had a communication system. What we needed was a fighting unit to go with it.

I hurried into Marino to contact Uncle Hugh before Major Knobel reported to Ottawa. Besides being delighted at the news, Hugh was of course anxious to know the condition of the former captives. We had been told nothing about that, but if they all escaped from a third story window by means of a ladder and there had been no mention of any difficulty, it might be presumed that they were not in terribly bad shape. Hugh's instructions were to keep the eight men together, and he would have a plane there to evacuate them as soon as possible.

Before Knobel phoned in his report I let him know that Hugh Hannigan was already making arrangements for the transportation of the former captives back to Canada. I expressed my concern that, even though the Canadian captives had been released, the military intervention should still be carried out in order to apprehend the leaders among the kidnappers. The major was skeptical but promised to convey my concerns again to his superiors.

A few minutes later he came out to where Albert and I were sitting in the sun that was beginning to take the chill off the morning air. As expected, the Canadian military authorities would not hear of any further involvement now that the captives were free. I went back to the telephone, called the office Colonel McGrath had been occupying for the last few days and was told that the colonel was out but was due back in an hour or so. Would I like to call back? I gave the man at the desk our number and an urgent message to the colonel to call me as soon as he came in.

When I returned to the lawn where Knobel and Tomayo were figuring out their next step I had a question. Flores, or whoever was giving orders, had captured the Canadians and had not taken normal steps to hide them. He must have realized that there was a good chance of the Canadian government sending troops to free them. What did he expect to accomplish by capturing them in the first place?

The major shrugged. "And what happens to the mining venture now?"

I supposed that Hannigan Industries would pull out its crew, so the project was dead for the foreseeable future.

"So," Knobel said, "without firing a shot, Flores has put a stop to the operation. Isn't that probably what he wanted to do? If there's money to be made in mining and he thinks he is going to be in control, he'll want to make his own deal. He may not have had all that figured out ahead of time. At first he probably just wanted to extend his control into another part of the country; but at some point he probably saw that he could let the captives go and still come out ahead."

Knobel and Tamayo left to see to the welfare of the former prisoners and report about their location and health. Colonel McGrath called within the hour. He had just heard about the release of the captives and was still digesting the information. I asked him about the possibility of continued Canadian military involvement to search out and bring to justice the people who were responsible for the kidnapping. He was as negative about the prospects as Major Knobel had been. A major newspaper, one that opposed the government, had as much as accused it of international banditry, sending in troops rather than going through international channels. I suspect that the latter alternative could have allowed the prisoners to grow old in captivity. A newspaper that favored the government warned that Canadian troops on foreign soil must be very careful not to do anything that might provoke a wider reaction. The nature of the feared reaction was left vague. The supposition seemed to be that the kidnapping was the result of some anti-North-American feeling. No need to have observers on the ground when you can deduce the facts while sitting in your office. With both friendly and unfriendly newspapers insisting on caution, the prime minister would avoid any move that might attract journalistic attention.

I then asked Will how much the military could do without bringing the prime minister and the cabinet into it. He wasn't sure but would ask around.

A little later, on the road south from El Puente Ingles, I met a cavalcade heading north. We stopped, and Dieter stepped out of one of the automobiles and greeted me as effusively as he ever allowed himself to be. He now had a rich vein of disaster to be mined and he wasn't going to squander the opportunity. I joined the procession as it continued on its way to Amparo to provide the freed captives with food and temporary accommodations.

When Major Knobel reported to his superior officer that evening he was told that his duties in Talcayan and those of Captain Tamayo were completed and the two of them were to return to their previous postings. The next morning the two of them collected their gear from our temporary camp and left on the plane with the eight freed captives. I accompanied them to the field where the plane was set to take off. Dieter took his leave with the announcement: "You know when I come back to this place? Never. That's when. If they want someone to develop their mines they better quit kidnapping them. I told you, Mick Hannigan. It is foolishness to come down here among these madmen."

CHAPTER TWENTY FOUR

I have never felt more alone than I did after the plane took off. It would have been simpler to have flown home with the rest, but I was angry and frustrated. Most of the captives, including three people whom I knew and admired, were still imprisoned in unknown conditions. Two days ago I had a lead regarding the Tipping murders and not to follow it up seemed like a betrayal, if not of Catherine then of her family. I had not yet heard from Señor Gallego whether Maria had discovered anything useful. That was enough excuse to keep me in Talcayan.

Mayor Robles had organized a crew to salvage the equipment at the assay site and prepare it for shipment back to the owners from whom it had been rented. I borrowed a truck and made my way to our temporary camp. Although we had been there for only a few days, as I took down the tent I had a feeling of loss akin to nostalgia. When I had been there before it had been with two companions; we had shared a common goal and developed a sense of comradeship.

I hoisted the tent, the camp stove and the other stuff on to the back of the truck and drove to Marino to drop them off at a warehouse and pay rent for a storage space for the next three months. Maybe we would have some use for the camp equipment; I couldn't imagine how, but the future was so murky that I didn't want to do anything so definite as to sell the stuff or give it away. There was no one to help me unload. I drove back to Amparo with my personal belongings. When I got into the town it looked deserted. Some of the people were still on the expedition to the assay site. Mayor Robles was at the Chavarria estancia conferring with the owner, whose son-in-law remained a prisoner. I moved into a room above a garage that the mayor had invited me to use during my remaining days in Talcayan.

I was to meet with Mayor Laval that evening in Marino. I had arranged to keep the Harley-Davidson for a few days, a temporary convenience that was probably outweighed by the nuisance of having to arrange for its return to Canada. For the last while every time I had ridden on the open road I had wondered whether by that time the Flores bunch would have figured out that there were undesirables cruising the country on motorcycles. That afternoon, busy fretting about the immediate future, I didn't much care. Besides, since they had suffered the humiliation of abandoning a stronghold without a shot being fired, the Flores gang might not be flexing its muscles.

Before meeting with the mayor I dropped by our communications room and called Uncle Hugh to let him know that the captives were all in good health. I reported that Will McGrath was looking into the possibilities of some help from the Canadian military to hunt down the perpetrators of the kidnapping. It was likely that the group behind the present banditry included the person or persons responsible for the non-investigation of the murder of Catherine and her husband, so I would like to stay in Talcayan until that situation clarified itself. If nothing happened in the next few days I would return home. Hugh agreed without argument but without much enthusiasm. This time I would not be appealing to Hannigan Industries for funds. There were now at least a couple of leading people in Talcayan who were intent on bringing the culprits to judgment, and with their resources the costs would be covered for a while.

A few minutes later I got through to Colonel McGrath and explained the events of the day, ending with my usual complaint about the prime minister going back on his statement that the perpetrators of the outrage would be brought to justice.

"That windbag," Will exploded. "He was up in the House of Commons today puffing out his chest and crowing about how a firm show of force combined with diplomacy had freed the prisoners."

"Well, something good has happened, anyway," I said. "I think that what probably drove the outlaws out of their stronghold was an item in the Marino newspaper saying that the Canadian government was sending troops."

"Yeah, well don't let that get out or our glorious leader will be taking credit for placing that item in the paper. Okay, now, some questions. What are your objectives if you stay in Talcayan for a while?"

"Well, most urgently, to free the remaining captives, then to find out who was responsible for murdering Catherine and, if possible, apprehend them. I suspect that if we find them we'll also have gone some way towards finding out who is behind the kidnappings."

Will paused for a minute. "Okay. We might add to that after I explain things from my end. But first, what are the objectives of our friends Robles and Laval. You said they were fired up for action. What would satisfy them?"

"I imagine they'll want to free the captives and get rid of Flores and whoever else has been terrorizing the country."

"Get rid of them, I understand that. What else do they want?"

I hadn't thought much about that. I told Will that my guess was that they wanted to stabilize the political situation, and the most likely way of doing that would be to install Pablo Javier as president with the backing of an army capable of resisting pressure from any of the other powers in the country. I would have to talk with them to be sure.

"And if you are right about their aims, how does that fit in with your objectives?"

Again, Will was forcing me to think about things about which I was still vague. I said that to a certain extent my goals and theirs corresponded. In the process of freeing the captives and possibly apprehending the chief outlaws, we would have gone some way towards stabilizing the country. We might in the process have marshaled a fighting force that would support leaders like Laval and Robles and Javier. We might then be in a position to bring the murderers of Catherine and Richard Tipping to justice.

THE BLOOD-DIMMED TIDE IS LOOSED

"I agree," my uncle answered, "but I want to make something clear. To find out about the murders, to free the captives and apprehend those responsible for the kidnapping, I support you on that. When that is done, if you want to go farther in support of Robles and Laval, I have no advice for you either way."

I couldn't see involving myself in further action once the captives were free and those responsible in custody, unless there were some further promise of solving the murder.

Will continued. "By the way, it's a good thing you told me that your major was dealing with Colonel Marchand. I was mostly wasting my time with the others. This is what Marchand and I worked out. The Canadian military will not commit to further pursuit of those responsible for the kidnapping. The Minister of Defense, who has the spine of an ameba, has stated that pursuing guilty parties is the job of the Talcayan authorities, about whom he knows five degrees less than nothing. The Canadian military can do a couple of things without having to involve the Minister of Defense: first, provide security so that the Tipping murderers, if apprehended, can be held for extradition hearings and, if extradited, brought to Canada for trial; second, as a completely separate operation by the section of our armed services concerned with terrorism, we can provide limited support for resistance to a criminal takeover. Since the Canadian budget for this kind of operation is small, Colonel Marchand can see the wisdom of concentrating for the moment on a country the size of Talcayan, and perhaps learning something that would help our efforts elsewhere. When I say that they can do this without involving the Minister of Defense I don't mean they'll be going behind his back. He'll know about it, but he doesn't have to give the order to make it happen. He can blame someone else if anything goes wrong, fearless leader that he is."

I wondered what this would mean in terms of actual help.

"I'm getting to that," he said. "Here is what Colonel Marchand can offer. This is it. He's not open to further negotiations. He can provide a reconnaissance plane. It's a single prop Cessna, old but in good shape. We agreed that there was no use trying for one of the fancy ones even if there were a chance of getting it. What you need is just something that will give you an aerial view of the terrain. So that's as good as on

- 203 -

its way. It comes with a crew of two pilots and two photographers. He offered to throw in a helicopter. I told him that if they could spare a half dozen of those old crates that the Canadian forces have been using, we would just leave them out in the open with the keys in the ignition so Flores can steal them, and within a week some of his most daring men will have crashed and burned. The colonel was not amused. He did point out however that they are testing a new helicopter with a view to the possibility of buying more. This new model has the latest air-to-ground missiles, improved radar, the whole bit. He can send that to Talcayan with the excuse of testing it in combat conditions and giving the crew experience. He is also ready to provide two M2 Bradley IVFs. The people down there will probably mistake them for tanks, because they move on tracks rather than wheels. They're good machines. They too come with crew. Anything else?"

I asked whether he could get several sets of night vision goggles and maybe a few hand-held rocket launchers with something for them to launch. Will thought that should not be a problem. He continued.

"Marchand is being a tad stingy about troops that are not attached to some machine. He says he can justify only a dozen, given the official description of the mission in Talcayan. He can however give us a whole boxcar full of equipment. It's all crated, ready for shipment. They got some newer stuff so this was slated for storage in case of emergencies. It's perfectly reliable, he says. To an outsider it may be unclear how a dozen men are going to make use of hundreds of mortars, rifles, machine pistols and enough ammo to stop a fair sized army. So a delicate question arises. You said the other day that both Robles and Laval are ready for action. With their blessing and the promise of all these toys, do you think it would be possible to raise a fighting force capable of searching out and freeing the captives, and maybe also of apprehending Flores and his main henchmen?"

It was the crucial question. I thought I knew the answer but was uncomfortable uttering it. But losing a cause because I was afraid to speak my mind is not a legacy I would cherish, so I gulped and said that if they had confidence in an officer who could lead them to victory, I thought there would be an adequate number rally to the cause; but there was no such military leader in Talcayan.

The Blood-Dimmed Tide Is Loosed

"I want your honest answer now," Will said. "You realize that nothing but your best judgment has any place in this conversation. When we left the country six months ago, the two of us had a reputation; whether it was deserved or not on the basis of the limited evidence is another question. They thought you were indestructible and they had the impression that I could organize and lead a fighting force. Do you think we still have that reputation? If so, would people rally around? If the answer is yes, then I'll come."

It was the answer I wanted, but I was so relieved to hear it that I stammered before answering that I thought that our reputations probably endured, but the best people to consult on that would be Robles and Laval, and perhaps others that they would want to talk to. I would try to have an answer in a day or two.

So when I met Mayor Laval that evening I had something to discuss. His immediate response was that Colonel McGrath's reputation as a military genius still endured. Would this reputation rally a sufficient number of potential fighters to his side? It would bring quite a few, but Mayor Laval would give no estimate of numbers. I pointed out that the outlaws probably did not have a lot of trained fighters on their side, and that as far as I could see they had no leader to match Colonel McGrath. Laval agreed, but he thought that the ordinary citizens of Talcayan might be terrified of the enemy and be rendered passive as a result. He would talk to the major estancia owners tomorrow.

I didn't wait for my return to Amparo but called Señor Robles immediately. He was less circumspect than Laval. He was overjoyed at the prospect of Colonel McGrath coming to Talcayan accompanied by some effective weapons. Concerned lest his enthusiasm influence his judgment, I repeated that an objective assessment was essential. Would the presence of the colonel, a few Canadian troops, two aircraft, two IVFs and a pile of small arms be enough to recruit a significant number of men from south of the Rio del Rey?

Robles switched to a sober, considered tone. The Chavarria family was ready to fight to get back their son-in-law, Felipe Diaz, and their workers were ready to join them. About the Sangallo family and their employees, he wasn't sure. He would feel them out tomorrow. The Calvinos were timid, but it was a timidity borne mainly from fear of

- 205 -

loss of property and standing in the community. Robles believed that if others joined the fray and they had hopes of success, the Calvinos and many of their people would not be afraid to fight. Regarding his townspeople, the five policemen had been cowed by the murder of Aldomar, but they were not afraid of danger. Unless there were Flores spies among them, they could be counted on. Regarding the farmers who made a living on the plots along the river near Amparo, the mayor did not hold out high hopes. We might get several volunteers, but they would need a lot of training before they would be effective fighters. Mayor Robles would sound out the estancia owners tomorrow.

I could have used someone with Major Knobel's skills. I had to gather information from different sources, evaluate it, relate it to a task whose ramifications I hardly understood, and then pass it on with advice. Two days later I was in the mayoral office in Amparo. In spite of stressing our advantages in weapons and leadership, Robles had not received firm commitments from Señor Calvino or Señor Sangallo. The most he could count on was that they would not object if Colonel McGrath & Co. recruited from their employees. The Chavarrias were ready to march. The mayor hazarded a guess that he could count on between fifty and one hundred recruits from south of the Rio del Rey.

Señor Robles had also spoken to two other mayors. Presented with Robles' proposal, Guzman in Magdalena agreed to participate and to urge the participation of any able-bodied people who would listen to him. Robles remarked: "You understand, I trust Señor Guzman like a brother. I should perhaps add that my brother is not very trustworthy. Mayor Guzman probably thinks that if he sends some of his people to swell the ranks of an army it will give him more power. But we are not in a position to insist on people's purity of motives before we admit them to our ranks. I think we just accept their cooperation and keep an eye on them. Do you agree?"

I agreed.

"Now Mayor Rendon presents a different picture," Robles continued. "I think he feels vulnerable. Maybe he's just nervous about any army that is large enough that it will overshadow his own. Or possibly Señor Rendon is afraid of the extent to which his own police have been infiltrated by Flores. In any case, he sounded worried, and I don't know what we can count on him to do. I do know, however, that he is sufficiently scared of Flores as to want him defeated. He will probably come in with us if he sees that the tide is moving in our direction. But even if he throws in his lot with us, we can't be sure how many of his followers will stay with him."

My next session was with Mayor Laval. Most of the estancia owners in his area were anxious to get rid of Flores but were unwilling to commit to do it. Laval decided that what he needed was an owner who would take the initiative, and he turned, with some trepidation, to Señor Villalobos, who owned the most prosperous estancia in the area. Fiercely independent, he had never been persuaded to cooperate with anyone on anything that he did not himself control. Villalobos agreed heartily with Señor Laval that Flores was a blot on the landscape and should be removed. To counter the hints by Villalobos that he himself was the natural leader of a military force, Laval pointed out that a problem that had plagued similar efforts in the past had been jealousy among the different owners, and to avoid this happening again the anti-Flores people were bringing in a military leader of proven ability. Colonel McGrath would coordinate the efforts of the different groups, but was wise enough to leave the natural leaders in charge of immediate operations.

"Señor Villalobos agreed with me," Laval said. "At least he said he agreed with me. That is all we needed to get some action out of the other owners. Villalobos talked to two of them and they are willing to cooperate, although they wanted to continue to have a say regarding the conditions under which their people would serve. I think that others may follow.

"I also talked to Augusto Calderon in Avila. As my daughter explained to you some months ago, Calderon is weak. The most I would expect from him is that he will not oppose us and he will not prevent his people from joining us. But he is afraid of reprisals if he takes a public stand. There are followers of Flores in his city and they are not reluctant to make threats and actually to carry them out."

I reported the opinions of Mayors Laval and Robles to the colonel that evening and he took it as sufficient evidence of support to justify getting started. It was a shaky foundation, but if we didn't have enough recruits when the time came for action we would scrub the mission. The colonel's main concern was training the men quickly to work together and follow orders. It would also take them a while to learn enough about the weapons we would be giving them so that they could inflict more damage on the enemy than on themselves.

"We'll be conducting a hurry-up boot camp," he said. "And by the way, with the scaled down effort we won't have to wait to rent transport planes from the U.S. Air Force. We can load the people and equipment on to our own aircraft and head south."

CHAPTER TWENTY FIVE

The next morning I gathered four workers and we went out to the improvised landing strip to fill up a few potholes. We were still at work when we heard a buzz and in a few seconds a blue and white striped Cessna "bird dog" came into view, flew over the strip, dipped a wing and then headed west towards the mountains. It did a slow circle over the foothills, dropped down, climbed again, approached, landed and taxied up to were we were finishing our repairs. The pilot and three passengers climbed out and walked towards us smiling. It struck me that I had not seen much smiling recently, especially not in the mirror.

The pilot, a lanky balding figure whose insignia indicated the rank of warrant officer, led the way. "I'm Serge Demarais." He introduced the other three in English with a Quebecois accent. The other pilot, younger, shorter and equally lean, was Harold Pelletier, a Canadian native. One of the photographers, slight, blond, who looked about eighteen years old, was Jonathan Mackie. The fourth member, a diminutive woman, also blond, was introduced as Sarah Black. Pelletier deadpanned: "Sarah came along because these Cessnas are kinda cramped on long flights and she doesn't take up much room."

"The real reason I'm here," she countered, "is that some busybody complained that women in the Canadian armed services are being

- 209 -

coddled and not being sent on dangerous missions; so I'm balancing things by flying with Harold."

Since the four laborers with me spoke only Spanish, there was more bowing and smiling than articulation as I made introductions all around.

I would have liked to start flying right after lunch and at least get a look at what was going on in the upper end of the Valle Colorado, but the plane was low on fuel, so we had to wait for supplies. The best we could do until that happened was to go over a map of Talcayan and adjacent parts of Chile and Argentina. At about 3 P.M. a fuel truck rumbled across El Puente Ingles, where I met it and led it to the landing strip. Once Harold had filled the tank he, Jonathon and I climbed aboard and headed into the clear sky. After a few minutes to get a sense of the air currents and how the plane reacted at this altitude Harold turned to me: "Okay, where do we start."

We flew low over Amparo with El Puente Ingles to our right, then followed the Camino Leandro north to the entrance to the Valle Colorado. We climbed considerably higher and circled, with Jonathan taking pictures all the while. From that height we could see El Alcázar, the structure at the top of the valley where, we suspected, some of the kidnapped people were being held. It was larger than I had imagined, nestled between two rock cliffs where the sides of the valley came together. There was a more-or-less square courtyard and attached to the front of it another somewhat smaller courtyard. Several figures were moving in the area but from what we could see no construction was underway. There were structures built against the interior of the walls of the fortress, the whole looking capable of housing personnel and supplies for a small army. Mayor Flores and associates did not lack resources.

We then flew over the valley just to the north which I had traversed on foot some days earlier. We circled again, lower, above the Valle Colorado. I was interested in whether the outlaws had established any protected positions from which they could fire on intruders traveling up the newly built road. We could spot some people here and there, and there was enough unidentified stuff around them to support a presumption that they were there to protect the valley from intrusion, but my binoculars did not have high enough resolution to give a good image. Jonathan assured me that with his telescopic lenses his pictures would reveal more details.

I wanted a better look at the wooded area between the enclosure and the Valle Palencia to the north. Unfortunately for our purposes most of the trees were coihué evergreens, and they were thick enough to obscure much of the space. Here and there were clearings, and other spots contained only deciduous trees that were losing their leaves. Harold dropped down so that we were barely missing the tree tops. There were walking paths through the woods, and a couple of them appeared to reach the general vicinity of El Alcázar.

Coming out over the plains again, Harold asked whether I wanted a closer look at the Valle Colorado. When I nodded assent, he asked whether I thought that anyone would shoot at us if we come in low. I said that I honestly had no idea. Were we vulnerable to rifle fire? I presumed they wouldn't have any weapons other than rifles.

"Sure we're vulnerable to rifle fire, if the bullets happen to hit you or me or a fuel tank. But unless they are very good marksmen, we're pretty safe." Harold probably would use the same flat tone of voice to tell you the time of day or to announce the end of the world, and I didn't know whether to be reassured or terrified. We turned, came in low and thundered into the valley a few feet from the ground. We were flying at full throttle and with the engine noise bouncing off the hills on each side the little plane sounded like a B-29 bomber. As the trees sped by just off our wingtips I forced myself to keep my eyes open and look for gun emplacements. Jonathan, apparently used to this sort of thing, moved quickly from one side of the cabin to the other taking photographs. We arrived at the top of the valley, and Harold lifted the plane enough to clear El Alcázar by a few feet. By that time I had disciplined myself to keep my eyes open, and in spite of the blur I got a look at the place.

As we pulled up to a less chill-inducing height Harold announced: "That was exhilarating, but I don't think we'll do it again," and we turned for home.

Warrant Officer Demarais approached me after dinner and asked how the flight had gone that afternoon. I replied that our objective was to find out what we could about the area north of El Rio del Rey where we thought the captives might be held, and that we had gotten as close a view as was possible. It looked like a couple of the trails we spotted led to the fortress at the top of Valle Colorada, but the trees prevented any exact tracing of them.

"A close view," Demarais smiled. "That does not surprise me. Harold is not afraid to get close for a better look."

I didn't want to get Harold into trouble for what might have seemed to be hot-dogging, so I replied in a non-committal way that he was obviously a skilled pilot and had allowed us to find out as much as we could in the circumstances. Demarais however was not making casual conversation. "Maybe we have to strike a balance here," he suggested. "To get the information we need we can't stay out of sight. On the other hand, don't we have to stay as much as possible in the shadows so that the enemy doesn't learn any more about us than necessary?"

I agreed that ordinarily what he said would be true, but I wasn't so sure it applied to our particular situation. We wanted to get the locals to join with us in a battle against the outlaws. The main obstacle to that end was that they had been cowed by the violence that the enemy had already shown and which they threatened to continue. A major factor in our favor was that a number of the citizens of Talcayan had been impressed with the military leadership of Colonel McGrath and the fact that under his guidance a small number of them had been able to get rid of a long-time menace in San Martin. In this situation it might be a mistake for the Canadian contingent to slip into the country unnoticed. Maybe it would be helpful to let people see a Canadian pilot flying like a bat out of hell.

Demarias looked a bit skeptical. "You know more about the situation than I do," he granted. "I can tell you this, if you want someone to impress them, Harold is your man. I'm a competent pilot myself, and I've flown three times as many hours as he has, but he's better than I am. He was offered a position with the Snowbirds, but he said that if he was going to risk his life in the air he preferred that it be in a combat situation rather than in an air show."

The next day I got in touch with Colonel McGrath to coordinate preparations in Canada with the situation in Talcayan. The materials and personnel were ready to go. There was no question of the transport planes landing on our rough landing strip. Officials at the airfield at San Isidro, the largest in the country, were not anxious to let our materiel pass through. Their objections may have been political but the reason they gave was that theirs was a passenger facility and not designed for heavy cargo. That left the problem of transporting everything from Mendoza to where it was needed. There being no railroad into the southern part of the country, the alternative was to rent trucks. The colonel agreed that there was not much to be gained, and perhaps something to be lost, by trying to enter the country stealthily. The caravan would take the shortest route therefore, crossing the Rio San Isidro at the city of San Isidro and travelling south on Camino Leandro. Because the enemy, so far as we knew, didn't have advance warning of the arrival of a force from Canada, security along the route should be relatively simple.

Two days later Mayor Robles and I were in San Isidro arranging with border officials and local police to assure an uneventful passage of our personnel and equipment through that area. San Isidro, the capital and the largest city in the country, had more architectural pretensions than its sister cities, particularly the legislative building, the president's palace and several structures on the campus of the country's only university. It lacked the natural beauty of Magdalena and the distinctive atmosphere of either Marino or Amparo, but it was a pleasant enough place except for the political situation.

At about 12:30 P.M Mayor Robles and I were standing at the Talcayan end of the main bridge crossing the San Isidro River when the lead vehicles of our convoy hove into sight across the river. The convoy clattered the three or four hundred meters over the four-lane bridge and stopped at the barrier on our side where a swarm of customs and immigration officials strode with official mien to the vehicles, took papers from the drivers, cursorily examined each vehicle and waved them on. Once the last vehicle had cleared customs and immigration, Mayor Robles joined Colonel McGrath and a driver in the lead jeep, which sprouted a Canadian and a Talcayan flag, one on each front fender. This was followed by a second jeep carrying a rather stout officer with the insignia of a lieutenant, along with his driver. They eased onto the main street leading from the bridge through the center of the city.

- 213 -

After them came a flat-bed truck with the two Bradley Infantry Fighting Vehicles, a man standing in the turret of each behind a mean-looking gun. The next flatbed had a container the shape and size of a box-car, presumably holding the small arms that we had been promised. This was followed by two large fuel trucks, then two more trucks loaded with building supplies—bags of cement, nails, pre-fabricated doors and windows. Most of the lumber we could buy locally. At the back of the parade came an armored personnel carrier. As soon as the convoy was under way a helicopter materialized and followed noisily, a few hundred feet above the ground materiel.

Once the convoy was moving I ran along side it on the Harley-Davidson. There was no assembled crowd to watch our passage, but most of the people scattered on the sidewalks stopped to watch. The visible members of the entourage played the muted role that the colonel had no doubt outlined for them. They looked around with casual interest. If anyone waved at them or shouted, they waved back. Traffic officials had obligingly set the lights so that the cavalcade was able to move at a steady pace. I increased my speed until I got to the front, waved at the colonel as I passed and settled in at head of the procession. The Canadian contingent had arrived, business-like and without fanfare.

The organized, calm, purposeful activity of the next few days provided me with more satisfaction than I had experienced for some time. The colonel had advised and Lieutenant Winfield, who was in command of the Canadian forces, agreed that the base should be established in an open area near the makeshift airstrip south of El Puente Ingles. The Canadians, excluding Colonel McGrath and myself, numbered thirty one. That included the crews of the Cessna, the helicopter and the two IVFs, a couple of construction supervisors, three instructors on the handling of mortars and rocket launchers, and a few infantry personnel. Señor Robles had gathered about an equal number of workmen from the estancias, the town of Amparo and the farmers along the river. No one was exempted from labor except the senior officers and the Cessna crew. Work gangs were formed; tents sprouted up; barbed wire barriers appeared around the perimeter. The pleasant smell of newly sawed lumber spread through the camp as a barracks, headquarters,

THE BLOOD-DIMMED TIDE IS LOOSED

supply depot and mess hall took shape. A parade ground was leveled and cleared of rocks. The surrounding territory was scouted to identify spots where potential attackers could hide. Multiple pairs of soldiers and workmen took shifts on guard at night.

Within a week Lieutenant Winfield and Colonel McGrath were ready to start their experiment in compressed-track military training. The camp opened with a disappointing thirty five volunteers. Some of the workers that Mayor Robles had recruited stayed on to train, and Marino sent several members of their police force and a few others. Robles was anxious but not despondent. It all depended, he said, on whether Mayors Guzman and Laval were able to deliver the numbers of volunteers that they hoped, and whether recruiters we had sent into the Avila area had any success. By the end of the week there were seventy trainees in camp, the additions coming from the Magdalena and Marino areas, with three tardy recruits from the Sangallo estancia. Señor Villalobos had grandly declared that his men were already well trained, and he was putting them through a few exercises to make sure they were at their best. We had made no headway in Avila. Since we really didn't know the number of our enemies we couldn't say whether we had enough personnel to do the job, but McGrath and Winfield thought it was enough to justify continued training. More would come later.

CHAPTER TWENTY SIX

When a telephone line had been run into the camp I made belated contact with Señor Gallego. For the call to his office I resumed my identity as Ronald Bernard, agent for race horse owner Archibald Manley, and was quickly put through to the editor. I announced that I had received clearance from Mr. Manley to negotiate for the purchase of the three-year-old bay mare that we had discussed at our previous meeting. Señor Gallego, after commending my good judgment, stated that another offer had been made for this fine beast. He would contact the breeder who had made the offer, and if the latter didn't want to close the deal immediately Señor Gallego would get back to me.

Having given the editor the telephone number where I could be reached two hours later, I hung up. I hoped our eavesdroppers would not wonder why the editor found a business transaction so amusing.

On his call back on an outside line Gallego informed me that Maria, his spy in the Valdez police department, had determined that at the time of the call concerning the bodies of Catherine and Richard Tipping the dispatcher was a woman who was probably a Flores loyalist from whom we should expect no help. A check of the records indicated that on that morning only two officers had been sent on non-routine assignments. One was a young man who probably would not be sent

- 216 -

alone to initiate a likely murder investigation. The second officer was a certain Cesar Garza. I recalled Señora Rossi's statement that her husband had been looking for information about Officer Garza just before Antonio's disappearance.

"Maria doesn't know Officer Garza well," Señor Gallego explained. "He is a very nice man who is well-liked by nearly everyone on the force. She thinks he would probably cooperate on any effort to bring about justice."

I asked whether, by any chance, the editor knew anything about Veronica Contreras, a young lady about whom Antonio Rossi had been seeking information. He replied that he had never heard of her, but that was no problem. Valdez is not a large city. If she lives in Valdez, then he, Señor Gallego, must know someone who knows someone who knows her. He would make inquiries.

"Now stay close to your telephone," he concluded. "For the benefit of our listeners I will return to my office and we will continue our conversation about that splendid bay mare in which Archie Manley is so interested but certainly cannot afford."

Two days later Señor Gallego informed me that Veronica Contreras was a young woman who had been Emilio Flores's girl friend, but they had broken up acrimoniously several months earlier. Rossi had no doubt seen her as a possible source of damning information about her ex boy friend. Gallego's go-between had told Señorita Contreras that there was someone in Talcayan who was investigating a crime for which Emilio was a suspect, no mention being made of the Tipping murders. She was willing to meet with me.

"I understand that our Veronica is not the type of girl who contemplates entering a convent," the editor cautioned. "I wouldn't put it past her to make up things to punish Emilio. So I suggest you don't give her any details. Just find out what information she provides on her own and see if any of it adds up."

Two days later I was back in Valdez. The meeting with Veronica Contreras had been set up by the reliable Señora Mendez, a motherly type who did not seem to fit the profile of under-cover agent, although that pretty much described what she was doing for Señor Gallego. She dropped me off at a small cottage that Señorita Contreras had designated as the site of the rendezvous. When she asked whether I would be safe I took reqfuge in the neutral observation that things looked okay. I was greeted at the door by a large young man in a muscle shirt who led me without comment to a room at the back of the house. His display of biceps in a way was reassuring. A cougar ready to pounce doesn't flex its muscles to impress its prey with how tough it is. Of course this guy might not be nearly as smart as a cougar. Just to be safe, I didn't let him get behind me.

Señorita Contreras was short, very dark, and probably pretty if relieved of layers of industrial-strength mascara. She did not introduce herself or her companion. As soon as I was seated she asked, point blank, how much I was willing to pay for her information. After a moment to digest this frank opening gambit I replied that if I paid for her information it would be suspect if introduced in court. She replied that if I thought she was going to testify against Emilio Flores in court I must be out of my mind. I pointed out that if it ever came to a trial it would be after Flores, father and son, had been thrown out of power and placed behind bars. She countered that we were not going to be able to arrest every friend of Emilio Flores. I had to admit that she had a point, but I added that I could not pay for information that might be of no use to me, so first I would have to hear what she had to say. At this her associate growled at me in what I took to be his most threatening voice, "Just pay the lady," and he named an exorbitant figure.

I smiled at him and asked him to call a cab. That set him back, but only for a few seconds. He informed me that Veronica Contreras had not come to this meeting in order to be trifled with. I replied that I wasn't crazy about traveling from Amparo to be faced with a demand for a large amount of money for information that might be useless. I turned back to Veronica. "Here's what I suggest. Tell me what you know and I will pay you what I can afford, which is perhaps a twentieth of the amount your friend here is asking. Otherwise, we are wasting time."

She was silent for a few seconds, then cleared her throat as though about to get down to business. "I have evidence that Emilio Flores committed a serious crime several months ago."

"When and in what circumstances did you discover this evidence?"

- 218 -

"I was in Emilio's apartment. A police officer came to the door. His name is Julio Lara. He is a powerful man in the police department."

"Yes. I know about Officer Lara. What happened then?"

"Officer Lara came in and told Emilio to get rid of me. They stayed in the kitchen. I went to the bedroom, but I left the door ajar. I could hear most of what they were saying because they were talking loudly, especially Emilio. Lara said that Emilio was acting like a fool, doing whatever he wanted and expecting his father to protect him, leaving Officer Lara to clean up the mess. Emilio said that Lara was not in a position to give orders. He would do what his superiors told him to do. At that point Officer Lara's voice became quieter, but I think he said that the next time something happened he would leave Emilio to face the music alone."

"When did this conversation take place?" I asked.

"Quite a while ago. In the spring some time."

"When specifically last spring?"

"I don't know exactly. September or October. Why is it so important?"

"It's important because the conversation you heard might have been about any of several foolish things that Emilio has done. It doesn't connect Emilio to any specific crime unless you can tell me more exactly when this conversation took place."

"It connects Emilio to the crime that you are investigating, because Officer Lara mentioned you."

"What do you mean, he mentioned me?"

"He said that his work was getting dangerous. He said that he could have gotten shot by one of those damned Canadians. You're the only damned Canadian who has been involved with Officer Lara. He must have been talking about you."

Discovering somehow that I was Canadian and connecting me to the Canadian referred to by Officer Lara were the first signs of intelligent life that either of the two had exhibited since I entered the building. I spent several minutes trying to get more information but had trouble framing an inquiry that could elicit something useful without it being a leading question that would make what she said suspect. I placed about

- 219 -

a hundred dollars worth of Talcayan bills on the table, got up and left without letting Mr. Body Beautiful out of my sight.

The encounter with that pair had left me in a less than receptive mood for my next meeting, which was with Officer Garza. I was walking towards a corner where I could catch a bus when an automobile drove up beside me, the passenger door opened and Señora Mendez shouted at me to get in. Our understanding had been that I would make my own way after my meeting with Veronica Contreras. Señora Mendez stated rather matter-of-factly that she had not been in a hurry and thought my interview with the Contreras woman would probably not last long, so she had cruised around the neighborhood for a few minutes in case I needed a ride.

A day earlier I had sent a message to Officer Garza stating that I wanted to discuss a police matter in which he had been briefly involved and I believed that each of us possessed information that could interest the other. I told him that at two o-clock I would be at a certain restaurant in a private room reserved for small meetings. I had no objection to him bringing an associate with him to the meeting, provided it was someone he could trust completely. I had no idea whether he would show up.

Cesar Garza showed up. He was perhaps in his early fifties and spoke deliberately, as though measuring every word. His companion was a pleasant woman whom he introduced as his wife. "You said to bring someone whom I could trust," he explained.

Having described my interest in the Tipping murders and what I knew about it, I asked him whether he was willing to let me know about the circumstances of his early involvement in the case. He replied, very deliberately, that he sympathized with the loss of my cousin, that he thought that it was a good thing that I was trying to bring about a just and honest resolution of the case, but that it might be difficult and even dangerous. However, he would give me whatever information he could.

One morning in early September the dispatcher had informed him that someone had discovered two bodies in a grove of trees just outside of Valdez. Officer Garza, followed by an ambulance, had driven to an address near the edge of town where they picked up a lad of about fourteen who had discovered the bodies. The youth guided them to the site, where he stayed in the car while Officer Garza and the two ambulance attendants proceeded into the woods. They found two bodies, one of a naked woman and the other of a fully clothed man who had been shot in the head. There was very little blood on the scene. Also at the scene were a number of personal items including an almost empty woman's purse and some items of women's clothing. In the man's pocket was a wallet empty of contents except for a driver's license that led to quick identification. It looked as though the bodies had been thrown there in haste. The reminder of my gentle cousin's horrible last minutes provoked the same black feelings that I had felt when I had first heard of her death.

After Officer Garza had taken a number of photographs the ambulance attendants brought the bodies directly to the coroner's quarters in the basement of the police station and Officer Garza detoured to drop the lad off at his home. Back at the police station, Garza had conferred with the coroner's staff briefly and then proceeded to Capitan Langer's office to inform him of events and ask about the resources to be assigned to the investigation.

Langer had not been in his office, so Officer Garza returned to his own desk to write his report. He had finished the report and had gone on to routine matters when two well-dressed strangers entered the station and asked to speak to Langer. They were told that he was away but was expected back shortly. When the chief returned several minutes later he immediately invited the two visitors into his office. They left after twenty minutes and Officer Garza was on his way to confer with his superior when the latter stepped into the hallway and gestured for him to enter his office. He then instructed Officer Garza that the case was politically sensitive and he was assigning it to Officer Lara. No other explanation was given. Officer Garza had learned nothing further about the case. Several hours later Julio Lara had dropped by to pick up Officer Garza's report on the finding of the body. Lara had seemed to be unhappy about something and had instructed Garza not to discuss the case with anyone.

Officer Garza presumed that it was a case of rape, murder and robbery by someone whom the authorities wanted to protect. When I asked who he thought the culprit might be, Officer Garza said he had some suspicions about people close to Mayor Flores, but he was not willing to name them because when he was taken off the case and reflected for a while he began to suspect there were other interests at play. The origin of his suspicions was the appearance of the two strangers at the police station that morning. It was not often that strangers appeared at the station and were ushered directly into the office of the Chief of Police. If it had been Mayor Flores who wanted the case quashed a telephone call to the station would have been enough. Of course the two visitors may have come on some other matter all together. The more he thought about it however, the more convinced did Officer Garza become that their presence was not incidental to his removal from the investigation and its assignment to the man known as the fixer.

I asked Garza whether he had any idea about who the two visitors were. He shook his head. "There is little sharing of information in a station under the command of Capitan Langer. My guess is that they represented drug interests that for years have been at the edges of Talcayan business. Local operators suddenly start investing amounts of money beyond what could be expected from their businesses. A couple of times people have disappeared and the local police have made only perfunctory investigations. The two visitors wore expensively tailored suits that are uncommon in Valdez, and the elder of the two gave the impression of visiting the station as an authority, not a petitioner."

The mention of a drug connection was confusing, and I stated that probably neither my cousin nor her new husband had ever so much as smuggled a pack of cigarettes or an item of clothing across the Canada-U.S.A border. It was difficult to see how their deaths could be drug-related.

For the first time Officer Garza became animated and hurried to assure me that he in no way implicated the two victims in anything illegal. "Some of the drug lords are smart," he continued, "but they hire the stupidest people imaginable. Maybe it's because they want employees who won't think for themselves. What I meant to convey was not that the crime was drug-related but that the murderer or murderers were connected with drug interests. You realize, Señor Hannigan I am only giving an opinion. I could be mistaken. If you wish to find the guilty parties, you should know that it might be local thieves and rapists, but it could be someone else."

I had seen no evidence of drug production in the country and no possible sites had raised the suspicions of our reconnaissance crew. Garza explained that as far as he knew there were few illegal drugs produced in Talcayan. "The trade here thus far is mainly an import/ export business. The weakness of the central government means that customs officials are either careless or easily bribed. It is handy for suppliers to export their products into Talcayan awaiting distribution elsewhere."

Señora Garza had joined the conversation here and there, emphasizing or elaborating on things her husband had said. As we rose to leave she placed a hand on my forearm and said, "Cesar and a few other officers do what they can to provide honest policing in Valdez. You realize that it would be very dangerous for him if the officials learned that he has given you information."

I assured her that until Flores and Langer were safely out of the way the only use that would be made of her husband's information would be to guide my investigation, and I would be very careful not to do anything that could cast suspicion upon him.

On the way back to Amparo I reflected that, if solving crimes involves continually narrowing the number of suspects, I was not making much progress; and once again, nothing came to mind as an obvious next step. The only people who could answer my questions were those least likely to cooperate. One improbable but possible source of information was Julio Lara. He was angry about having to clean up messes created by others. Veronica Contreras had said so and Officer Costa and Officer Garza had both suggested it. Could Lara be so disaffected as, under certain circumstances, to help to bring the guilty to justice? Exactly what those circumstances might be I couldn't imagine.

Meanwhile the crew of the Cessna had continued to search for places that might be sites either for marshaling the Flores forces or for detaining the prisoners. Each evening the four crew members would add details to a map of Talcayan that they had drawn on a six by four foot plywood board. Numbers on the map referred the observer to books of photographs.

- 223 -

On Friday of the second week of training, with the numbers of trainees now over one hundred twenty, we gathered for the regular session that Lieutenant Winfield called our "intelligence review". The flying crew had discovered frustratingly little for all of their efforts, but they had decided that four sites merited closer study than could be done by aerial reconnaissance. One of these was the residence on an estancia a few miles southeast of Avila. What brought the house to their notice was that on several evenings a number of automobiles had converged on it. This was very weak evidence that the site should interest us, but when there are no promising clues you start looking at the long shots.

It had been easy to discover that this was the property of the Barca family, but about that family there seemed to be some mystery. As someone whose services could be spared, I was given the task of investigating the place. To help me I was assigned a new recruit from the area south of Avila who professed to know about the Barcas. Lieutenant Winfield had not had time yet to run the usual security checks—talk to the family and neighbors, etc., but he thought the lad seemed all right. They didn't have anyone else with any special qualifications to help me. Would I be willing to undertake the mission with the help of this young man?

His name was Jorge Marti. He was small and wiry and was probably in his mid-twenties. As we drove northward the next morning he handed me a note from Mayor Laval that had arrived the previous evening. The subject of the note was a Señor Quinones, the owner of a prosperous estancia that bordered on the Barca property. It was not clear where he stood in the present political situation, but he definitely would not sympathize with the kidnappers. However, he had a reputation for not getting involved in politics. Mayor Laval thought it might be a good idea if we started our investigation by visiting Señor Quinones to find out what he could tell us about the Barca family but also to ascertain whether he intended to remain strictly neutral in the current crisis.

In Avila Jorge guided me to inexpensive lodgings at a posada near the center of the city. The family that ran the modest establishment leased rooms by the month but kept a few extra rooms that they would rent for the night. That evening all they had free was one double-occupancy room. It was plainly furnished but clean and quite satisfactory for one unaccustomed to four-star accommodations. Before settling in we dropped by a store and bought Jorge appropriate clothes so he would not look out of place meeting a member of the local aristocracy.

CHAPTER TWENTY SEVEN

That evening I called Señor Quinones and introduced myself as an agent acting on behalf of Mayors Laval and Robles, who wished to rally the honest citizens of the region in response to the recent kidnappings. He agreed that the kidnapping was an outrage but added that it was important to avoid hasty action that could worsen the situation. I replied that it was in order to hear his opinions on such matters that the mayors had asked me to consult him. He agreed to meet with us but insisted that this did not mean he would join in the military action that, he heard, was being planned.

The next morning Jorge and I drove to the Quinones estancia. There were herds of fine, white-faced cattle in the several pastures we passed. Atypically for this region, much of the land was under cultivation. A stone mansion surrounded by carefully tended plots of shrubs and flowers stood at the edge of a number of buildings: five or six cottages, presumably inhabited by employees; a long, low unpainted wooden building apparently used to store and repair his machinery, a large barn and several silos.

We were greeted at the door by a housemaid who bowed us into an office-like room near the front door and left to inform Señor Quinones that his guests had arrived. After a minute we heard slow footsteps in the hallway, and a tall, impeccably dressed, elderly gentleman appeared

- 226 -

THE BLOOD-DIMMED TIDE IS LOOSED

at the doorway leaning on a gold-headed cane. After bidding us to be seated and lowering himself carefully on to a straight-backed wooden chair, Señor Quinones noted that when I had called the day before he had not paid particular attention to my name, but he now recognized it. "I understand that you played a part in that affair with Fraga a while back. You are a solder I believe."

I explained that I had served in the military for several years but was currently the safety and security officer in a mining company. Señor Quinones smiled. "Yet it seems to be your military accomplishments that have recommended you for your present task, Señor Hannigan."

I assured him that although the present situation might at some point involve military action, my main function at present was to gather information for the people who were responsible for planning. A responding nod suggested that my answer would have to do for now and we could move on.

I then informed the patriarch of the preparations under way to train a certain number of armed men to intervene to free the prisoners, stressing that the planners hoped to confront the criminals with sufficient power to encourage them to surrender the prisoners without bloodshed, something that had already happened in the release of the Canadian captives. Señor Quinones had several questions. How many people did we expect to recruit? How many people did we think our enemies could muster? I had to admit that any answer to those two questions would be guesswork, but added that the planners were keeping their options open. If we failed to recruit as many people as we needed and if the enemy had many more resources than we expected, then the operation would be terminated or postponed rather than engage in a bloody and perhaps fruitless battle.

After discussing the situation for a few minutes Señor Quinones, as I expected, remained cautious. If we were asking him to support the military effort, he would have to consider the question carefully. Because he was beyond the age that would allow him to participate in any physical way, it would be a question of sending men into danger that he himself did not share. He could contemplate providing financial help according to his modest resources, but only if he judged that

- 227 -

the chances of success were good. He could not forgive himself if he contributed to injury and death in a hopeless cause.

That sounded like the kind of careful response that was not likely to be modified by anything further that I could say, so I proceeded to the second question. We had been trying to locate the sites where the prisoners might be held or where there were concentrations of armed supporters of Flores. Not finding any likely clues, we were left to pursue unlikely ones. Did Señor Quinones know anything that would throw light on what appeared to be regular gatherings at the Barca estancia? Or did he know of anyone who could provide the information we needed?

Answering this question could verge on gossiping, something likely to embarrass someone of the gentility of our host, but I couldn't think of a more subtle line of inquiry that would get to the point. The old rancher's manner became more guarded, and he noted that he did not leave his home very often because he had difficulty getting around, and so he had little information about what was going on in the neighborhood. He would not know much that we had not already been told by trustworthy people like Mayor Laval. He had always found the Barca family to be honest and fair in their dealings, and he would be shocked if they were engaged in anything so disreputable as kidnapping.

I tried another approach and remarked that the land around the Quinones and Barca estancias seemed to be quite productive and the farmsteads impressive. I understood that the Quinones family had owned this estancia for a number of generations. Was the Barca family another of those historic families? Señor Quinones replied that the Barca family had resided in Talcayan for three generations. He remembered Alonzo Barca, the grandfather of the current owner, as a venerable patriarch who had emigrated with his wife and family from Uruguay where, it was said, he had been active in politics. His first purchase was a modest parcel of land but he had added to it steadily so that at his death he passed on to his son an estancia as fine as any in the country, with the stately stone mansion that we may have seen on our way.

Unfortunately Lorenzo Barca, the present owner, was incapacitated. However his wife, Leticia, who was from Brazil, had proved to be very

THE BLOOD-DIMMED TIDE IS LOOSED

competent. Under her direction the estancia had continued to prosper and she had also become involved in commercial operations in Avila. Señor Quinones understood that Leticia visited her rural property only occasionally, residing in Avila and spending much of her time attending to business there. The day-to-day running of the estancia was left to Pedro Santana, who had served the Barca family since his youth.

It would have been interesting to know exactly why Leticia had taken over the running of the family business, but for Señor Quinones to enlighten us on that point would come close to indulging in gossip, and this he was unlikely to do.

On the drive back to Avila Jorge asked in a subdued voice whether the Canadian army would let him keep the new clothes that I had purchased for him. I assured him that the clothes had been bought not with army money but with funds from Hannigan Industries, so there was no problem. The clothes were his. Back in the city we stopped at a store, he darted in and returned with several yards of wrapping paper. His purpose became clear once we got back to the room we shared. Jorge changed back into his everyday clothes and then laid his new suit out on the bed that he had claimed for himself, and carefully folded the clothing, wrapped it in the paper and placed it carefully in his suitcase. He explained that these clothes were better than anything he owned and he didn't want to get them dirty. Without having to buy clothes for himself this year, he could afford to get something nice for his wife. It appeared that our expedition had accomplished at least one useful thing.

Early the next morning Jorge and I dropped by the offices of *La Prensa*, Avila's main daily newspaper. They had no index that would direct us to items about Leticia or Lorenzo Barca, so we had to search back issues. Jorge was not enthusiastic about the task and offered instead to talk to some of his acquaintances in the city to find out what he could about the Barcas; but given my lack of language skill, he would be quicker than I to spot relevant newspaper items. He began with the current issues and worked backwards while I began with issues thirty two years earlier and worked forward.

We finished at about four o'clock that afternoon, with meager results. I uncovered a report of the wedding of Lorenzo Barca and

- 229 -

Leticia Tavares twenty seven years earlier, the bride being identified as an actress from Sao Paulo, the groom as a prosperous land owner, philanthropist and frequent guest at social events in Avila. I found no further references to the Barcas except for obituaries for Lorenzo's father and mother. Jorge discovered Leticia Barca's name in connection with several social events. There was also an announcement fourteen years earlier when, in the name of the family, she had purchased the Hotel Avilana and announced plans to establish a first class restaurant on the premises. He found a picture of her attending a movie premiere in Sao Pablo, the caption identifying her as someone with business interests in Brazil and Argentina. Jorge found no mention of Lorenzo Barca.

By half past four I was back at the posada writing a note to Señora Barca stating that, acting on behalf of the mayors of Amparo and Marino, I wished to speak with her on a matter that the two mayors believed would interest her. Jorge and I walked four blocks to the Hotel Avilana, where I told the clerk at the registration window that I wished to deliver a message personally to the office of Señora Branca but was unsure where that office was located. The young woman put aside what looked like a college text book and led us to a hallway, indicating that the fourth door on the left was the office of the owner.

The door to the outer office was open. The man at the desk looked more like a bodyguard than a receptionist. I told him that I wished to deliver a message to his employer, explaining that we would like to meet with her briefly. If the time for such a meeting could be arranged now, that would suit our purposes admirably.

The receptionist took the letter, looked at it for a few seconds, nodded, asked us to wait, knocked at a door and entered. After a minute the door opened and a slim woman of slightly over medium height stood there for a moment sizing us up with eyes half closed. Señora Barca was expertly made up, her hair dark with wisps of gray, her dress and single strand of pearls more suited to a social event than to work. Perhaps she was going directly from the office to a dinner party. Time had added some lines to Señora Barca's face, but she was still a striking-looking woman.

She shook hands with us rather formally and addressed me by name, so she had decided which of us was the possessor of the foreign name on the note. She inquired about the health of Mayor Laval and Mayor Robles, and when assured that they were well, continued: "If the matter you wish to discuss can be handled in a few minutes, I can accommodate you immediately. Will that be satisfactory?"

We repaired to her office, which was modern, utilitarian and several degrees less decorative than the lady herself. We sat around a small table and I launched directly into my spiel. She no doubt knew about the unfortunate kidnapping, etc. We recognized that the law abiding citizens of Talcayan would probably not know the whereabouts of the prisoners, but they might be aware of details that, when combined with information supplied by others, would tell us something. Señora Barca was highly respected in the community and Mayors Laval and Robles had indicated that she would be anxious to help. She knew many people and was aware of what was happening in Talcayan, especially in Avila. If she could inform us of anything unusual that had come to her attention it might prove helpful to our search.

I wondered whether my running on at such length in fractured Spanish might have annoyed Señora Barca, but she remained gracious. She replied that she was flattered that two men as eminent as Mayors Laval and Robles had mentioned her favorably. She was of course happy to cooperate if she could. However, she was not sure what kind of information might be relevant. Perhaps if I could tell her more about the situation she would know what to look for. What did we know already about who was involved in this crime? Did we have any suspicions? Did we have any sites under observation at this time? If we suspected the presence of the prisoners anywhere in the vicinity of Avila, she might be able to provide us with background information.

The lady had neatly directed the conversation to her own purposes. I could hardly object to her thorough questioning. As intelligent as she obviously was, she had apparently seen through my ploy and divined that she was under suspicion, and she probably enjoyed teaching a lesson to this brash foreigner who dared to match wits with her. Unless I were to throw in the towel all together, the only strategy seemed to be to play along, to supply information eagerly, to be happy to find an ally willing to help. I had to act, in other words, like an unsuspecting bumpkin. I was quite forthcoming about the resources at our disposal, especially the help from Canada. I was less informative about what we had found out or suspected, keeping as far as possible to generalities. There was no point in hiding the fact that El Alcázar was under consideration as the most likely site for at least some of the prisoners. Concerning three suspected individuals and two suspicious sites I was able to be quite specific, since they existed only in my imagination.

After a few minutes of this exchange I noted with alarm that we had taken up almost a half hour of the señora's time, more than we had anticipated. I thanked her for giving us her attention and assured her of our gratitude if she were to inform us of anything further that she might learn. I felt I had kept up my feckless pose rather well.

Back in our room I asked Jorge what he thought about Señora Barca. He replied that she was quite a grand lady, that she seemed to be very well disposed and she should prove to be a valuable ally. I asked him whether he had noticed anything peculiar about her questions. He looked a bit puzzled and shook his head.

"Did you notice what she wanted to know about?' I asked him. "She wasn't interested in the number of our recruits, what kind of training we were giving them and so on. When I gave her vague answers to those questions she didn't follow up and try to get details. She was interested in how much we knew about those things our enemies would not want us to know, our guesses about where the prisoners were being held, who we suspected, etc. She seemed much more interested in that kind of question. What does that suggest to you?"

Jorge was taken aback. "What are you driving at?"

"My point is this," I replied. "The kidnappers probably already know how many people we have recruited and what training we are giving them. Some of those people training at our camp are probably spies. But our enemies really want to know how much we have found out about them. So Señora Barca was curious about exactly those matters concerning which our enemies would be curious."

Jorge still looked puzzled. "I don't understand. If she is a friend, she would want to know the same things. I think you are being too suspicious."

"You may be right," I conceded. "After searching day after day for clues, maybe I'm trying to make a clue out of everything I hear."

Jorge muttered something about all this being too complicated for him and then indicated that he had been in touch with a close friend and his wife and was invited to their home for supper. He would like to use the rented car if I didn't need it that evening. I replied that I did need it, but Jorge should feel free to visit his friends and I would provide money for a taxi.

I went in to the bathroom to shower, and when I came out Jorge was gone. The ignition keys that I had dropped on the side table were also gone. I checked to make sure that I had not absent-mindedly put the keys back in my pockets, and a quick check of the room confirmed that they were gone. While I was fuming at Jorge about the keys a more unsettling thought struck me. I checked the compartment in my bag where I kept the Beretta when I was not carrying it on my person. That too was missing.

Jorge simply taking the car against my explicit instructions was puzzling. Jorge taking the gun had an easier explanation, and it was not a reassuring one. I had intended to make a meal out of some of the provisions we had brought with us, but I had lost my appetite. I couldn't imagine Jorge as a cold-blooded killer. More likely he was a naïve lad pulled out of his depths by misguided loyalty to those whom he thought of as friends. However, it looked like he was working with some very dangerous people, and by taking the gun he had neatly removed my main means of self-defense. He would surely realize that once I discovered both the car and the gun missing I would be on my guard, so if they (whoever "they" were) wanted to come after me it would probably happen soon, before I had time to disappear and rearm myself.

I had changed out of business suit to jeans, shirt and windbreaker. I put on a pair of sneakers, grabbed my wallet and threw the rest of my stuff back into my overnight bag. A peek through the window revealed eight or ten automobiles in the parking lot but no people. I hurried down the stairs, checked out of the posada, retrieved my passport and asked the woman at the desk to call a taxi and let them know I was in a hurry. I spent a nervous twenty minutes until a cab drew up to the door.

The driver introduced himself as Marco. How much would it cost to drive me to a location about twenty kilometers southeast from Avila and wait for about an hour before returning? He pondered for a half-minute and quoted a figure that would have made it his lucky day. I replied that if he cut his price in half we had a deal. He offered to take thirty percent off the price, though it would be a great sacrifice for himself and his wife and four children. I didn't want it written in my obituary that my enemies had caught up to me while I was haggling over cab fare, so I nodded and Marco, resigned to the hardship I was visiting on himself and his family, steered out of the lot and into traffic.

The drive south gave me time to begin second guessing myself. Was Leticia Barca behind Jorge's disappearance, or was Jorge working for someone else, and was this someone else being protective of Leticia? If Señora Barca's suspicions were aroused and if there were indeed prisoners being held at her estancia, then our enemies might be moving them at that moment. Should I have gotten in touch with Will and have him send Harold Pelletier in the Cessna to check out the place? It would be getting dark in less than an hour. I would probably get to the Barca estancia as quickly as Harold could, so continuing with my original plan seemed as good an idea as any. Of course Señora Barca might have nothing to do with any prisoners or with Jorge's behavior. I was wallowing in a swamp of conjecture.

What I was really looking for? Would a meeting taking place at the estancia prove anything? Did I want to keep the place under surveillance for several hours in case prisoners might be moved? How would I know if vehicles contained prisoners? If I asked Marco to follow any suspicious vehicles travelling in the direction of El Alcázar he might conclude, with some justification, that I had passed beyond mere eccentricity.

CHAPTER TWENTY EIGHT

Daylight was fading by the time we approached the Barca property. The buildings stood about a half kilometer from the highway on which we were travelling. A parked taxi near the turn-off to the residence would be easily seen by observers there, so I asked Marco to turn on to a side road, where we parked. I took my binoculars with me and made my way through several rows of trees to a vantage point from which I might survey the Barca farmyard.

Five vehicles were visible in the yard—two cars, two mini-vans and a pick-up truck. While I had the site under observation two more cars turned off the highway and joined the others in the yard. It looked like there was a meeting of some kind. In a few minutes it was dark and I stumbled back through the trees to the taxi. I wanted to get closer to the farmyard, perhaps get the license numbers of the vehicles and from that maybe to identify the owners. There was a chance that still more vehicles would join the group in the yard, but if I walked up the lane to the yard I should be able to find cover if that happened. I went back to the cab, wakened Marco from a brief snooze and asked him to get back on to the highway and park near entrance to the lane, turn off the headlights and be ready to vacate the area quickly if necessary.

I got out of the cab and walked towards the farmyard. I wasn't a quarter way there when the front door of the house opened, several people emerged and walked towards an automobile, and I prudently retreated. Before I had rejoined Marco several others left the house. The meeting was breaking up. Back in the cab, I asked Marco to drive slowly so I could get a look at the departing vehicles. The first two, a light colored sedan leading a dark colored minivan, came to the highway and turned left, away from us. Another car followed closely behind but turned in our direction. Another minivan was now headed down the driveway and it was time for us to turn on our headlights and get moving.

Marco maintained a reasonable speed and the driver behind us seemed content to stay a more-or-less constant distance behind us. I asked Marco to slow down, hoping that the vehicle behind us would pass us and give me a look at the license number. The car behind us slowed. We resumed speed. The other car resumed speed, and in that way we arrived at the edge of Avila. The driver must have been on to our little game. I was unarmed, and in any case had no right to put Marco in danger, so I didn't press the issue by having Marco stop and more-or-less force the car to pass us. It didn't follow us when we made the first turn within the city.

We drove by the posada I had vacated several hours earlier. As expected, Jorge had not returned the automobile. Marco then deposited me without incident at the Hotel San Mateo, which he recommended for someone in need of a night's sleep. I apologized if anything on the trip had made him feel uneasy or in danger. He remarked that he felt more threatened every day by Avila drivers. Like most cabbies I have met, he showed a salutary lack of curiosity about the behavior of his fares.

Before retiring I reported the stolen vehicle to the police. Awake early the next morning, I called Colonel McGrath to brief him on my adventures. Before we do anything, he suggested, let's wait and see if the police find Jorge and perhaps persuade him to provide some useful information. Should I remain in Avila to await further developments? Will would get back to me, but at the moment he thought that in view of my experience of the previous evening it might be prudent to put some distance between myself and that city. I hung up, packed my bag and lay down. I was awakened some time later with a knock on the door and the announcement that I had a call. It was the colonel, this time with specific instructions. Mayor Robles had been in touch with Mayor Calderon in Avila. If apprehended, Jorge would be held until Robles could question him. Calderon would not allow prisoners in his jurisdiction to be interrogated by foreigners. I should leave Avila by bus and someone would pick me up in Amparo and return me to the training site.

Several hours later in Amparo, while I was briefing Mayor Robles, a call came through from Avila that Jorge had been found driving our rental car, claiming that he was on his way to deliver it back to the posada. Señor Robles left in a hurry, and a driver and I proceeded at a more leisurely pace to the camp.

That evening Lieutenant Winfield, Warrant Officer Demarais and I gathered around a table in a bunkhouse fragrant with the smell of newly sawed wood to hear Mayor Robles' report, with Colonel McGrath translating. At his interrogation Jorge Marti had tried to present an innocent interpretation of his actions, but Robles had pointed out that he was in no mood to waste time. After infiltrating himself into our training camp under false pretences Jorge could hope for no mercy if he continued to ally himself with criminals. His only sane choice was to provide Mayor Robles with information. If he did so and it turned out to be reliable he would be faced only with the charge of theft of an automobile and not with the more serious crime of conspiracy in a kidnapping. Mayor Robles wanted information on two points. Where were the prisoners being held? What was Señora Barca's involvement in the affair?

Regarding the first question Jorge claimed to know only that the main body of the prisoners was being held in El Alcázar. Three prisoners had been held at the Barca estancia, but the plan was for them to be transferred to El Alcázar the previous night. As far as Señora Barca was concerned, all Jorge would say was that when he had informed the police in Valdez that Miguel Hannigan was suspicious of Señora Barca he had been told to inform her immediately. Jorge pretended to be shocked that Mayor Robles would suspect that there was any intent to harm Señor Hannigan. He was unclear about what other interpretation was to be put on the fact that he had taken my handgun. Should we believe anything that Jorge said? Mayor Robles merely raised his eyebrows. Jorge would remain in custody until appearing before a judge.

Two days later I returned with Mayor Robles to Avila to meet with Señora Barca and Augusto Calderon, the mayor of Avila. The señora had been informed that Mayor Robles had come into possession of information that could affect the welfare of the Barca family; the mayor and Michael Hannigan had been delegated to consult with Señora Barca in order to come to a better understanding of the significance of this information and, if possible, prevent serious harm to her and her family.

Mayor Calderon, a tall, athletic-looking man probably in his mid forties, greeted us outside of his office and informed us that Señora Barca had already arrived. Apparently she believed the mayor of Avila should be properly briefed before the meeting. When we entered the high-ceilinged office she was standing, looking out of one of the windows. She greeted Mayor Robles with great courtesy, offered her hand to me without comment and took her place on one of a circle of chairs. Calderon began with an unctuous preamble to the effect that he appreciated the expressed desire of Mayor Robles and his colleagues to avoid harm to the Barcas. He had the highest esteem for that family, whose members had been upstanding citizens of the district for several generations. He presumed that the information which was the occasion of this meeting was related to the issue with which Señor Robles and others were so concerned—the victims of the deplorable kidnapping that had taken place some weeks ago.

Señor Robles thanked him for helping to bring the parties together and by his presence assuring a fair hearing for all concerned. He thanked Leticia Barca for making time to deal with the issue promptly. He continued. "We have learned very recently that three of the kidnap victims were being held at the Barca estancia. These prisoners have recently been transported from the estancia to El Alcázar in the middle of the night. We do not know how many people at the estancia might have known about their presence. The transfer took place shortly after Miguel Hannigan had spoken with you, Señora Barca, soliciting your help in locating the prisoners. It seems likely that someone concluded from that meeting that you were under suspicion and the estancia could

THE BLOOD-DIMMED TIDE IS LOOSED

come under observation, thus necessitating a transfer of the prisoners. Yesterday, when two officers from Marino called at the Barca estancia to speak with Pedro Santana, your foreman, he was reported to be away for several days.

"All of these events could be used to direct suspicion towards you, Señora Barca. However, another person was at the meeting between you and Miguel Hannigan. That person was Jorge Marti, who has shown by his subsequent behavior that he is allied with the kidnappers. This provides a more plausible interpretation of events that suggests that you, Señora, need not have known what was going on."

At this point Señora Barca broke in, calmly and elegantly. "You have said, Mayor Robles, that this information need not imply my involvement in the lamentable business of the kidnapping; but you sent Señor Hannigan to talk to me. So at that point mustn't you have suspected me of something?"

"That is a legitimate question," Robles replied. "I should first clarify that Señor Hannigan is not under my authority. He has much experience in issues of security, and on such matters those of us who are working to free the prisoners are disposed to defer to his judgment. So it is not accurate to say that I sent him. But as to your question—when Miguel sought a meeting with you, the Barca estancia was already a place of interest to us, one of several sites that had exhibited considerable activity and therefore might be a place where prisoners were being held. You must understand that at this point we have only limited information. We are in a sense grasping at straws. Señor Hannigan's visit with you had a two-fold purpose—to solicit your help in the search for the prisoners and to get some sense of your attitude in this whole affair."

"Mayor Robles," she replied. "You claim to have information about the time of the transfer of the prisoners. Does this mean that the estancia was under surveillance in the middle of the night? You seem to have been doing considerably more than grasping at straws."

Robles smiled. "It is true that someone was observing the residence on the Barca estancia that night. You must understand that in Señor Hannigan's profession suspicion is a virtue. He noticed in his conversation with you that the subject concerning which you showed

- 239 -

most acute interest was the extent of our knowledge of the kidnappers. That would also be the thing that our enemies would most want to know. Besides, on the evening after his interview with you he found that his companion had made off with his gun. He could not help but conclude that there were forces at work against him, and it was natural for him to think that you might have been involved. As we have reviewed what we know, however, it is clear that there is a more likely interpretation of the events, one that, happily, clears you of complicity."

"Then what is the purpose of this meeting?" she asked sweetly, and Mayor Calderon made supportive noises.

"If we could be sure that we knew where all of the captives are being held," Robles replied, "this whole issue would fade away. Until we know their location there will be unrelenting pressure to find them. You cannot expect someone like Rodrigo Laval, whose daughter is a prisoner, to accept that we cannot find her. People will insist that the police follow every lead, and that will include questioning the employees of the Barca estancia. It is not realistic to think that in such an atmosphere your family can be kept out of the news.

"Once we know where the captives are being held, freeing them will become our focus. The fact that three of them were held temporarily on your property will be of little interest to anyone. It has occurred to us, Señora, that you may be in a good position to find out where most of the prisoners are being held. You will no doubt want to get to the bottom of the question of what has been happening at your estancia. Once you find out who has been responsible for those happenings, you may be able to prevail upon someone to give you whatever information they have about where the prisoners are being held. They must be informed that withholding evidence that could lead to the freeing of the prisoners would make them complicit in the crime of kidnapping. So we are here to ask you to use this opportunity to get the information we need as quickly as possible."

Señora Barca replied in the same low, controlled voice. "Mayor Robles, I wonder whether your information is accurate regarding prisoners being held at my estancia. It sounds highly unlikely, and I assure you that if there were people being held there I knew nothing about it. I appreciate the need to get the information you require and

THE BLOOD-DIMMED TIDE IS LOOSED

we shall indeed do everything we can to get it, but I do object to Señor Hannigan pretending to solicit my help when he was really investigating me as a suspect."

Robles remained calm. "Insofar as he may have been investigating you, Señor Hannigan was doing what honest investigators do, which includes protecting the innocent by establishing their innocence."

There was a pause. After a few seconds the mayor of Amparo continued. "I have found the families whose loved ones have been taken captive to be surprisingly patient. I have been told by Colonel McGrath, who is helping us with this investigation, that if this had happened in his native Canada people would be carrying placards in the streets accusing the government of not doing enough, and the police would be pulling in persons for questioning on the basis of even a hint of suspicion. Newspaper reporters would be hounding you on your way to your office, Mayor Calderon, asking why you have not done more. Families would be hiring detectives to search for the captives and those detectives would not be scrupulous of reputations."

There was more silence, broken after a few seconds by Leticia Barca's low voice. "You ask me to provide you with information that may be difficult to obtain."

"I recognize the difficulty," Mayor Robles replied. "If you need help in interrogating your employees, we can provide it. If in the end the information is not available, then we will have to deal with that when it happens and try to minimize the damage. Do you have any more questions or observations?"

The two seemed to be content to let matters rest, so Mayor Robles and I prepared to leave. Mayor Calderon was silent as we shook hands. Señora Barca smiled at Mayor Robles and assured him that she would be in touch with him shortly to let him know of her success or lack of success in seeking information from her employees. She then turned to me, and with a look somewhere between rueful and coquettish, remarked that she should have listened to her mother when she warned her not to trust handsome young men.

There seemed to be no gallant reply to this sally, so I took refuge in the formula: "It has been a pleasure." She had no doubt spent much of her life wrapping men around her little finger. Driven into a corner,

- 241 -

she might count it as at least a small victory if she could still cause a bothersome and not particularly handsome meddler to blush.

Two days later Mayor Robles received a call from Señora Barca, who reported that her foreman, Pedro Santana, should have returned the previous day but had not. Were he to remain missing the señora would have to suspect that he had been involved in improper and perhaps criminal activity and had fled when it appeared that he might be caught. The other employees at the estancia steadfastly maintained that they had not known about anything illegal. Several of them knew that three persons were being held against their will in a building on the property, but Pedro had explained that the Avila police had arrested these persons on suspicion of drug trafficking and asked that they be held incommunicado at the estancia. Were they to be detained in the jail in Avila, he said, their associates might try to free them, and because some of the police might themselves be involved in the illicit trade, that attempt could be successful.

Señor Robles had come to the training camp to report all this as we gathered for our usual evening strategy session. You had to admire the señora. Blame Santana and hide him so he couldn't be questioned or apprehended. But Robles had more to report.

"I was a trifle irritated at dear Leticia's cleverness, so I thanked her for her excellent work and added that we now had several more questions and would be sending police to the estancia to conduct a second round of interrogation. That stopped her for a moment, but only for a moment. She agreed that a second interrogation might be useful, but Mayor Calderon would need to be in charge of it, because the persons suspected of wrongdoing were in his jurisdiction.

"I countered that we had been acting under the mandate of President Gracida because the prisoners were from all over the country. We were confident that the president, having commissioned us with the task of freeing the prisoners, would want us to take all legitimate steps to that end. If Leticia insisted we would of course consult the president about who should question the employees of the Barca estancia. I added in a conciliatory tone that it was a shame that we had not received information about the whereabouts of the prisoners, because once that was established we could forget about this messy business of interrogations. That seemed to refresh Señora Barca's memory, because she replied that she had been just about to tell me that she had received what seemed to be reliable information on that point. One of the estancia employees had been present when the three prisoners were being conducted to the van in which they had been transported to El Alcázar. He had overheard the driver remark that they should have brought all the prisoners to El Alcázar in the first place. That suggested that the prisoners were all there or would soon be moved there."

Robles concluded: "So the upshot of this cat-and-mouse game is that we have Señora Barca's word that probably all of the prisoners are in El Alcázar. How much is that worth?"

The rest of us thought that it was not worth very much. On the other hand, probably most of the prisoners were at that stronghold, and we agreed that we should take action as soon as possible and not wait indefinitely for information that might never be forthcoming. Mayor Robles would look into the possibility of interrogating the employees of the Barca estancia without the owner's interference.

CHAPTER TWENTY NINE

Had my stay in Talcayan ended at that moment I could probably look back at it with something like equanimity. The downward spiral of events began with an impasse. We couldn't attack El Alcázar with rockets or mortars fired from a safe distance without endangering the prisoners, so it looked like we had to get troops into the fortress and engage the enemy at close quarters. We had neither the aircraft nor the trained personnel for a parachute attack. A ground approach up the Valle Colorado against fortified positions would be suicidal. Judging from photographs our reconnaissance people had taken, our enemies had fortified their gun emplacements in the valley and positioned them in such a way as to make it difficult for an enemy to attack them one at a time without coming under fire from other emplacements.

That left an approach from the opposite direction, across the mountainside through terrain unknown to us. For all we knew, the Flores people under cover of the coihué trees might have fortified this area as well, but it was unlikely that they had enough personnel to patrol that large area effectively. To discover what lay under the canopy of trees was beyond the technical ability of our intrepid photographers. Lieutenant Winfield had asked his military superiors to send us a plane with more sophisticated instruments to make a couple of runs over the area, but his request had been denied.

There seemed to be no alternative but to throw the main body of our imperfectly trained troops into an assault through this unexplored area, counting on our superiority in numbers and weaponry to prevail with minimal losses. I argued that before we took that risk I should slip into the area under cover of darkness and find out what I could about the defenses. The mission was not impossible. I would have an advantage over any enemy patrols because they probably would not have night vision equipment, or if they did it would be inferior to our state-of-the-art stuff. Our goggles allowed us not only to detect objects with a minimum of light but also to use lamps that cast a beam invisible to the naked eye but visible to one wearing the goggles. So when the forest was at its darkest one night Will drove me several miles up the Valle Palencia road. I got out of the jeep and headed to the left along a path into the forest that, our aerial photographs suggested, led to El Alcázar.

I had not mentioned to Will or the lieutenant that I suffer from a childish fear of the dark, a weakness that was not helping me at that moment. Once I was well on my way into the forest my jitters subsided a bit. Having the goggles gave me some sense of security, and busily threading my way among the trees and trying to maintain a sense of direction kept me from dwelling too much on the mysteries lurking in the darkness on either side of the path. Normally in combat situations I prefer a rifle, but in this case I carried a machine pistol. If it came to shooting I would probably be facing a number of the enemy at relatively close quarters and they could be invisible in the underbrush.

So with only a medium level of terror I edged along the path. It was a clear night, and whenever I came into an opening in the trees I would check with the stars to find out whether I was moving in the right direction. I was perhaps half way to El Alcázar, pausing every little while to listen, when I heard the first sound that might signal that there were other human beings nearby. At first it was just a rustling in the woods ahead of me and a bit to the right, a sound a little more substantial than that of a nocturnal bird or small animal. I stopped, scarcely breathing. The rustling stopped. I continued my forward

- 245 -

progress again for a minute or two. There was that suspicious sound again, another stop, and again silence; but before the silence there was something else very faint; or was it my imagination? Then there was something that certainly was not imaginary, a quiet but distinct thump, probably of something hitting the ground. My searchlight revealed nothing but the path and the trees on either side.

If the enemy was near, even a quick and silent retreat carried no guarantee of safety. Besides, I had argued that it was worthwhile to take what was admittedly a serious risk in order to lessen the danger for others. Was I to return to camp and announce that I had turned back because I thought I had run into a serious risk?

I remained motionless for a minute, less from strategic considerations than from indecision. I tip-toed forward a few more steps and suddenly there was a bright light behind me and a voice screamed at me to drop my gun immediately. I threw down the machine pistol and pulled off my night goggles so I would be not completely blinded if I turned towards the light. The same voice instructed me to place my hands behind my head, and another bright light, this time ahead of me on the path, let me know that I was surrounded.

The people behind those lights probably didn't much care whether I lived or died, so I obeyed. In a few seconds hands patted me down, relieved me of the Beretta in the holster at my side and cuffed my hands behind my back, and we headed along the trail towards El Alcázar. My captors, contrary to my confident statement to Will, wore night vision goggles much like mine. They maintained a quick pace while I stumbled in the dark over the branches and rocks on the path. The two men behind me, apparently in good spirits at having taken a prisoner, kept prodding me in the back with the muzzles of their guns. There were four more men ahead of me. None of them made any attempt to question me. Apparently their mission was to bring in the fish, leaving the gutting and filleting to their superiors.

The two behind me were chattering to each other, but their accents and rapid speech allowed me to make out only part of what they said. None of it was either informative or reassuring. Within a minute the older man who had been leading the procession dropped back and addressed the two behind me. He was small, and his elaborate officer's hat gave him a top-heavy look that would have suited him well for a role in a Gilbert and Sullivan operetta. There was nothing comical about his demeanor, however. As he chastised the two he waved his pistol for emphasis in a way that made me very uneasy. Apparently it made an impression on them too, because they were silent for the rest of our journey

I had never been incarcerated, but it was an eventuality for which we were all prepared somewhere in our basic training. Recalling remnants of those lessons, I tried to keep my mind active. I began, between stumbles, to list what I had learned. The first thing that came to mind was the voice of my old instructor, Herb Jansen, warning against fixating on escape. "Some officers like their men to spend their time in prison plotting to escape. They think that concentrating on this will keep you from becoming passive and therefore easily manipulated by your captors. But if you put all of your stock in wanting to get out you become obsessed. You build up false hopes. Your captors can use that to manipulate you. If you have nothing else on your mind but getting free, you have very little on your mind that you can use to remain your own man."

That I was still alive suggested that I would be added to the captives already in El Alcázar. Dieter and his crew had not been mistreated, but they were more-or-less hostages, and I was a militant, the enemy. Probably my captors would try to extract information out of me by whatever means they thought necessary. I had no idea how I would stand up to torture. On the other hand, I couldn't think of much that I knew that would be particularly valuable to the enemy, so my ignorance would be my best protection against betraying my colleagues.

If I survived, how long would I be a captive? What were the chances of Will and Winfield figuring out how to attack El Alcázar with the rag-tag army they had assembled and begun to train? They would know from my failure to return that the Flores people were not conceding the "back door" approach to us. If ordered to fight their way through that forest, McGrath's new recruits had no code of military conduct requiring them to do so, and the limited success of Will's recruiting effort was based to a considerable extent on the assurance that running a high risk was not part of the deal. So what alternatives were there for our would-be saviors? Would they negotiate? Did they have anything they could give to Flores in exchange for the prisoners? After a few minutes of taking stock I decided that, whereas passivity was no doubt a danger, pondering alternatives wasn't doing much for my morale either.

Presently we approached the west end of the fortress. The wall silhouetted against the night sky looked larger than it had seemed from the air, perhaps twenty feet high and thirty five yards wide, without a door or window. As we approached we began to climb over rocks that had apparently been placed there to provide a level base for the structure. We turned left at the wall, and then turning right we followed along the side of the fortress for about eighty yards. The flashlights of the guards revealed that the wall on this side was solid concrete with several windows higher up.

Rounding to the front of the building, we entered through a gate, a thick metal affair that looked like it might withstand any rockets that our troops had at their disposal. Inside the compound a few fixtures on the walls gave off enough light to reveal the general layout. Like the plan of Spanish missions in the American Southwest, the living quarters and other facilities were built against the inner side of the outer wall, leaving the center open.

Just inside the gate my guards stopped, the leader of my captors rapped on a door and a stout, balding man with a heavy black moustache and in the uniform of the Valdez police came out. He talked for a minute with the diminutive leader, took a sharp look at me, spoke in a more animated way with the other, and then turned to me and demanded my name. I replied that I was Mick Hannigan. He nodded with satisfaction and told me that it was a good thing I had told the truth, because he knew who I was and if I had lied he would have made things unpleasant for me. I don't know why he thought I might lie about my name.

He turned back to the men and, like a potentate patronizing his serfs, told them that they had done well and their work was finished for the evening once they threw me in with "the others". They marched me through a gate into another part of the compound. In the middle of the courtyard stood a ground-to-air rocket launcher that had not been there when Harold had buzzed the place. Apparently the proprietors didn't want to suffer that indignity again.

The guards stopped in front of a door and took off my handcuffs. Any hope that I might enjoy a humane incarceration comparable to that of Dieter and his associates was quickly shattered. As the door opened to the room in which I was to join the other prisoners I was hit by an overpowering stench of human feces and urine. I must have shrunk back for a moment, and one of the guards drove the butt of his gun into my back, I stumbled forward into the dark and the door slammed behind me.

There was a bit of light coming through two small, barred windows looking out on to the courtyard. I could make out forms, some stretched out on the floor, some seated propped against the walls. No one uttered a word and the only motions I could detect were a couple of heads turning towards me. I groped past several prone figures near the door, found a clear spot and sat down on the earthen floor. I was tired, but I didn't feel like lying down in that fetid place.

For the first few minutes, squatting with my hands under my chin and my elbows resting on my knees, I fought off nausea brought on by the stink. The sense of smell gradually adjusts to odors, so that was not a critical matter. What worried me more was that captors who subject their prisoners to these conditions are not likely to be considerate in other ways. I dozed fitfully for an hour or two. Eventually I gave in and lay on my side in a fetal position. In preparing for the mission I had put on a sweater over a coarse plaid shirt. I didn't need the extra layer of clothing to stay warm in that room, but it provided some measure of padding against the dirt floor.

I awoke to the sound of someone moving softly across the room. A man was making his way to a curtained-off corner of the room which, I concluded, was what served as a lavatory. A pre-dawn light revealed something of my surroundings. Several of the people sitting propped against the walls were awake, and they stared at me wordlessly and without much interest. Most of the people were still asleep, or at least motionless. The forearm I had been using as a pillow was numb and where it wasn't asleep it hurt. I was still drowsy, so I turned over and succeeded in dozing off again. Coming fully awake after a while, I heard voices whispering. I kept my eyes closed, not wanting to confront the

- 249 -

group until I got my bearings, and caught the words: "Are you sure?" and an answer, "Yes I'm sure, that's who it is."

I opened my eyes and found myself staring across the floor at a bearded young man with long, black hair. As he got up and walked towards me with a look of recognition I realized that it was the assistant editor from Valdez, Antonio Rossi. Normally when in trouble one welcomes a familiar face, but the confirmation that this courageous man and the others had already endured weeks in this foul place brought little comfort.

I struggled stiffly to my feet. My back was sore from where the guard had whacked me the night before and my body ached from the extended contact with the floor. As Antonio approached he didn't hold out a hand to be shaken. After we had exchanged greetings he explained that as much as possible the prisoners were minimizing physical contact with each other. Hygienic conditions were atrocious, and they were afraid they might spread infection by contact.

Antonio, like the rest of the prisoners, knew nothing about the events since their incarceration, so there was much to tell. He then explained a little about their conditions, discretely pointed out a few of his fellow prisoners, including Felipe Diaz, who like several others was still apparently asleep. I looked around to locate the third person whom I had heard was imprisoned. There were only three women in the room. Two were middle aged and somewhat stout. The third was a depressed-looking, gaunt younger woman, her dark hair bristling out from her head in all directions. She was staring across the room without seeming to focus on anything, and I realized with a shock that it was Señorita Laval. "Dolores is not in good shape," Antonio whispered, "We are worried about her."

By this time Felipe was awake and stretching, and as Antonio and I approached his eyes went wide in surprise. "Señor Hannigan!" he blurted, "How is it you are here?"

Rather than have me repeat my story to Felipe, he and Antonio called the group together, told them who I was and asked me explain what had been happening in Talcayan since their incarceration. Having made a preparatory run over the events with Antonio, I was able to refine the story into something close to coherence. The people naturally were most anxious to know about what was being done to secure their release. The part of my story that some of them found hard to take was that, having freed their countrymen without firing a shot, the Canadian authorities had then abandoned the other prisoners. The official explanation may have sounded reasonable in the House of Commons in Ottawa, but it was not convincing in El Alcázar. I had no more success in answering their questions about when they might expect to be freed. Throughout the conversation Dolores Laval stayed in her place, staring straight ahead and giving no indication that she was listening.

Afterwards the inmates except for Señorita Laval gathered around me, nodding and trying to smile instead of shaking hands, assuring me of their appreciation for my trying to help them. There were twenty one of us in all. According to the estimates of Mayor Robles, that coincided with the number of people known to have been taken prisoner.

There was a loud banging on the door. Everyone moved towards the opposite wall. Two armed men in battle dress came a couple of steps into the room, made sure that everyone was where they were supposed to be and made room for a third person, a woman also in uniform. She carried a plastic bag and a plastic container of water, both of which she placed on the floor, and the three walked out and slammed the door.

As one of the women of our number carried the bag around the room each person reached in and withdrew one bread roll. Felipe explained that this was their breakfast every day. At the bottom of the bag was a plastic cup, apparently intended for me. The others had secured similar cups from the meager packs spread around the floor next to the wall, and in a similarly orderly way the other matron filled each cup with water. Talk died down as people retired to their chosen spaces and munched on the bread. The rolls were a fair size, and since I don't usually eat a large breakfast it more or less satisfied my hunger. My sense of smell had been deadened to the extent that I was no longer nauseated.

I asked Antonio whether he thought it would help Señorita Laval if I talked to her and he thought that it wouldn't hurt. She was sitting alone, leaning against the wall. Her eyes followed me as I approached but she didn't greet me when I sat down beside her. I told her that I had spoken to her father several days earlier. Her parents were well, and her father was helping to recruit troops to bring about our escape. I asked how she felt and she remained silent. We sat side by side quietly for a minute, munching on our breakfast. Then, without turning towards me she said in English, "It is a bad thing that you have come."

I agreed with her that I had taken a risk that had done little good. "No," she answered, "I mean that now that you are here your uncle will not want to attack this place for fear of harming you."

"He will attack," I said, "but it will take some time to organize an attack that will not risk killing the prisoners."

"He should attack even if it kills us. Better to be dead than to be like this."

Her despair was like a millstone, but at least she apparently was sane and in contact with reality. Talking with her might not be a waste of time. I reassured her that Will and Lieutenant Winfield had been able to provide at least basic training to some of their troops and would be coming to our rescue soon.

She answered, still without looking at me: "You yourself don't know how they will do it, do you?"

"I'm not a strategist," I said. "Colonel McGrath and Lieutenant Winfield are the experts. I wouldn't know how to make a plan."

"But if your uncle had a plan you would not have tried to probe the defenses of this place."

"He doesn't have a plan yet," I countered. "He can't make a plan until he has the information he needs, but that won't take long."

We fell silent. After we had both finished our Spartan breakfast I reminded her that everyone in this room was anxious to help her, and she should rely on us to help her get through this ordeal; and there were thousands of people throughout the country who were just as ready to help, and many of them were in a position to do so.

She replied in the same listless voice, "I just need it to end," and fell silent.

There had been a brief flurry of talking after I gave my report, but now the prisoners had lapsed into silence. This is something to avoid if you want to keep up morale, so I spent the next hour talking to individuals, getting their stories and answering their questions. They were willing to talk, but mostly they just answered or asked questions,

- 252 -

offering almost nothing spontaneously. This was not a good sign, but for the moment it was not clear what we could do about it, and I made a mental note to discuss it with Antonio and Felipe.

My effort to keep people talking let me get to know my fellow inmates. One of the men, Señor Ruiz, was hardly able to walk. Apparently when he and his wife had been arrested he had resisted, and one of the men arresting them had shot him in the leg. The bullet had gone through the fleshy part of his right calf, missing the bone, but the wound had become infected. The pleas of the prisoners that he be released so that his wound could be treated were ignored, as were their requests that antibiotics be brought into the place. His wife was the woman who had distributed the rolls at our breakfast.

I asked her why she and her husband had been arrested. "We have always minded our own business," she said. "We have a vegetable farm near Amparo. The only reason that they could have for arresting us was that I am a friend of Señora Robles and of Señora San Pedro. Maybe they want to scare Mayor Robles."

Part way through the morning there was again a loud pounding on the door, and again I followed the other prisoners as they moved towards the opposite wall. The first time they had moved with a sort of routine indifference, but now they were silent and sullen. The door opened and four armed men in uniform entered. Two of them had their automatic weapons pointed at us, while the other two strode across the room, seized Dolores Laval by the arms and half walked, half dragged her across the floor and out of the door. The men holding automatic weapons smirked as though challenging anyone in the room to do anything about it.

I was standing near Antonio and asked him what was going on. He hesitated, as though too embarrassed to reply, and then muttered simply that they do this to her every day. I didn't bother to ask him what the "this" was, and it dawned on me why Dolores had withdrawn into herself. The prisoners in that room suffered in many ways, but surely one of the worst must have been their powerlessness to get help for Señor Ruiz or to do anything about the treatment of Dolores Laval.

After a few minutes there was another pounding at the door. This time the more active among my fellow-prisoners looked at each other questioningly as they made their way to towards the back wall. Three men entered with automatic weapons at the ready and one of them shouted out my last name. Such are the difficulties of many Latin Americans with Irish names that at first I wasn't sure what he was saying, but it became clear when he repeated it and my fellow prisoners looked at me. They marched me out of the room, the spokesman leading the way with the other two guards behind me. We crossed the courtyard and went through the gate between the two sections of the enclosure to an office near the front gate, the place where we had stopped the night before.

I should have been dreading the likely outcome of this event, but at the moment I was mainly relieved to be away from the squalor of our prison. There was a sign painted on the door in front of us: "Comandante Alonzo Langer", the name of the feared police chief of Valdez. They marched me through the door into an antechamber where a uniformed man behind a desk turned away from a small television set against the opposite wall and examined me with mild distaste. Apparently the presence of another bedraggled prisoner held little interest for him, because after a moment he turned back to the television. One of my guards rapped at an inner door, was admitted, came back out and ordered me to precede him into the office.

Seated at a desk was the officer who had questioned me briefly the night before. He waved me to a chair directly in front of his desk and my three escorts stood behind me. He remarked that he had been remiss in not introducing himself to me the night before. He was Alonzo Langer, the comandante of El Alcázar.

"We have had dealings before, Señor Hannigan," he said, "when I was the Chief of Police in Valdez. As you see, I have moved on to take a place in national affairs. Some months ago you responded to our hospitality by shooting and seriously injuring one of my officers. I am delighted to have this chance to treat you with the same kind of consideration that you showed to my officer."

I replied that perhaps his officer had misinformed him about the facts of the case. I was about to explain, but Langer interrupted me with a wave of the hand before I had finished the second sentence. "You

- 254 -

surprise me, Señor Hannigan, taking refuge in such excuses for your behavior."

Before he could continue I stated that one of his prisoners had an infected wound, and to deny him medical help was tantamount to murder. At the same time, some of his men were sexually abusing one of the women prisoners. I reminded him that both of these offenses were immoral and illegal and that he, as commanding officer, would be held accountable by the international community.

Langer opened his eyes wide in mock surprise. "Really! How shocking. I must report this to the international authorities. Have you seen any of them around recently?"

He then began to question me, mainly about the numbers, equipment and preparedness of the group that Colonel McGrath and Lieutenant Winfield were training. My answers were mostly accurate, since Flores would already know the answers to those questions from spies like Jorge Marti. I exaggerated the amount and sophistication of the weapons available to the recruits, supposing that the stronger we looked to Flores and company the less anxious they would be to attack us.

Tiring of getting answers that he probably already knew, Langer raised his voice: "You think because your company has millions of dollars you are going to defeat us? Let me tell you, behind us we don't have millions, we have billions of dollars. For every soldier your uncle can hire, we can pay for ten."

This confirmed my suspicions about why six months ago they could on short notice hire an international hit man, why they could afford sophisticated equipment, a refurbished fortress and a rocket launcher. I replied, "If you play with international drug lords, Señor Langer, remember that they don't have friends. They have enemies and they have lackeys who do what they are told. When all of this is over, whoever wins, you lose."

He nodded to the men standing behind me, and suddenly my head was rammed forward. I instinctively put out my hands on the desk to brace myself. No sooner had my hands hit the desk than I heard a sudden whack, and in the split second before the pain came I was aware that Langer had struck the index finger on my right hand with a hammer that he then held smilingly in front of him like a trophy. Blood oozed from the crushed end of my finger. As the pain shot up my arm I had to struggle to keep from screaming.

Langer looked at me with satisfaction and spoke with slow deliberation. "Señor Hannigan, I'm sure that as a renowned marksman you will not be bothered by something so minor as the loss of your trigger finger. Perhaps we can continue this conversation when I have more time."

He nodded towards the door and two of his henchmen grabbed me by the elbows. I shook them off for a second and with whatever self-command I had left I said to Langer, "Your drug friends can hire goons to shoot your enemies one by one in the dark, from hiding. Do they know how to engage an army?"

I was back in the prison room just a few minutes after I left it. Antonio Rossi and Felipe Diaz joined me as I squatted against the wall, trying to keep from moaning from the pain. In answer to their inquiries I displayed the finger that I had wrapped in my handkerchief to contain the blood. Felipe cursed under his breath but neither of them showed much surprise. It was the kind of thing that they had grown to expect.

CHAPTER THIRTY

The next few days were as close to a nightmare as I expect ever to experience. The routine was repeated each day. A few minutes after Dolores was dragged away the second detail would arrive to march me to the office of Comandante Langer. Each day I reminded him that there was a prisoner who would die if he got no medical attention and that that the rape of prisoners was something that would bring extremely harsh penalties when the inevitable happened and he was brought to justice. Each day he got his sadistic thrills with his hammer until every finger of my right hand was crushed. Each day I was marched back in the prison room, where I would try to keep from moaning.

When I would get myself more-or-less under control I would try to do what I could to help out. It was the only way to keep a shred of dignity. I tried to talk with those who seemed most depressed. To their repeated questions about when relief might come I could only say that it was certain that Colonel McGrath and the others were working as hard as they could, that there had to be a certain amount of preparation. There was no evidence that anything I said helped. Some of them asked about my injuries. Most of them were wrapped up in their private suffering. Felipe and Antonio were the only ones who had the strength to try to help others, except for Señora Ruiz, who constantly fussed

- 257 -

over her husband with reassurances that masked what must have been a terrible foreboding. The sight of them quietly reciting the rosary was about the only encouraging thing I remember from those endless days.

For me the pain was constant. After several days without sleep I began to doze at odd times during the day. At nights I couldn't get even that relief. Gradually I sank into a state in which everything seemed to be happening in a dream, where I seemed to be a passive observer trying desperately to wake up. I dragged myself on my rounds of talking with others, not fully conscious of what I was doing, clinging to the belief that had been drilled into me somewhere that, whatever happens, there is some good you can do, and if you don't do it you lose the last vestige of control of your life.

On the fourth day, when the little finger on my right hand was still intact, we heard gunfire and explosions, the sound coming apparently from the west—the opposite end of the fortress from the front gate. When it continued sporadically for a few minutes Señora Ruiz came to me. "Is it your friends?" she asked. "Are they coming to rescue us?"

I was able to reassure her with some confidence that it was almost certain that the sounds were coming from a confrontation between our captors and our would-be liberators. "When will they be here, Señor Hannigan? My husband cannot last much longer." But to this I could only say that it would be soon, but probably not today. She looked uncertain, was about to say something else, but turned away and went back to her husband.

After about an hour the gunfire and explosions stopped. I was supposed to be the expert, and a few gathered around me and asked what this meant. Had my uncle's soldiers been thrown back? What would happen? The most I could say was that the troops trying to liberate us would not be in continual contact with the enemy. Much of the time they would be moving forward quietly, taking up new positions, consolidating the territory they had gained. That was a possible explanation. It was certainly not the only one, and my listeners must have known it.

That night at about ten o'clock there was an earsplitting explosion in the courtyard. We could feel the impact on our wall and the acrid fumes of explosives filled the room. The screens that covered our two windows were torn by the blast, but none of us was injured. The smoke cleared gradually, and by pushing our faces against the bars of the windows we could look eastward and see that the missile launcher had been reduced to a tangle of twisted metal. If our group had possessed the energy there might have been cheers. As it was, they stared hopefully, expectantly; but nothing else happened and gradually they settled down and slept.

The next day for the first time the guards did not arrive to drag Dolores Laval away. This further sign of change slightly encouraged our sad group, but they were uneasy. If an attack was imminent, would our captors decide to use us as hostages and begin to send out bodily parts to show that they were serious? Or would they send out whole bodies?

Señorita Laval had a reprieve, but at the regular time the three guards arrived to march me to my daily session with the comandante, who warned me not to get too excited about the explosion the previous night. He didn't need the missile launcher to hold off an attack. When the ragtag bunch that the colonel had gathered together got a taste of real fighting they would decide that they had better things to do than to stop bullets; and now that fighting had started, Colonel McGrath would discover that his enemies were not only the garrison in El Alcázar. He would be attacked on his flanks and annihilated. Langer's words were more plausible than I wanted to admit.

He then smashed the remaining sound finger on my right hand and dismissed me with the remark that tomorrow we would start on my left hand. On the way back to the prison room I warned my guards that time was running out for them to save themselves. Just let us prisoners out of the room and help us over the wall and we would see that they were treated generously by the soldiers who would almost certainly overrun the fortress within a day or two, if not within hours. They responded by prodding me with unusual ferocity with their rifles; but their bravado was missing. The psychological impact of that pile of twisted metal in the courtyard was perhaps as important as any strategic effect.

That afternoon we heard more sounds of gunfire, and even louder explosions, this time seeming to come from the east, beyond the front gate of El Alcázar. Felipe and Antonio were exultant. The battle was continuing. The explosions continued for several hours this time, but at nightfall silence fell. My fellow prisoners again looked at me for an explanation. The most I could offer was the assurance once again that battles do not consist only of gunfire and explosions.

That evening my fingers began to feel numb, and that frightened me. In my addled state I remembered stories about people freezing to death who, before they lost consciousness, began to feel warm. Maybe something parallel to that was happening to me. Then, for the first time since Langer had begun his handiwork, I actually fell asleep.

I was awakened in the middle of the night by Antonio, who whispered urgently that there was someone on the roof of our prison who wanted to talk to me. I may have been only half awake, or maybe I was a state of mind in which I couldn't tell the real from the imaginary, but this announcement struck me a so bizarre that it should be ignored. Antonio shook my shoulder again and repeated the message. This time I struggled to my feet, felt a wave of nausea and crouched back down on the ground. I waited for a minute to recover, but Antonio was urgent. I got to my feet again, Antonio kept hold of my arm and steered me to the window. There was a microphone hanging by a wire through the window. I fumbled with it, so Antonio took it, told the person on the other end that Mick Hannigan was here and held the mike in front of my face. I think I said something like "What is it?" A vaguely familiar voice asked whether this was Mick Hannigan. I replied that it was, but that I was groggy and could he just talk to Antonio, and I would listen.

The speaker then explained that he had rappelled down a cliff to our roof. Was there was any chance of us being able to escape through the window and get into the courtyard? In the middle of Antonio's explanation that the bars were set in concrete, the nausea overcame me and I stumbled towards the make-shift lavatory. There I kept retching well after every morsel in my stomach must have been brought up. When I finally emerged the crowd around the window had dispersed. Antonio began to explain something to me. One of the women came up with some water and suggested that I drink it so that I would not become dehydrated, and I was able to drink down the full glass of water without ill effects. I asked Antonio to delay his explanation until I could clear my head. I fell back to sleep and my companions apparently decided that whatever I needed to know could wait until I was in better shape.

When I awoke again a faint light had begun to filter into the room. I was aware of mosquitoes and remembered that the screens had been torn by the explosion when the missile launcher had been destroyed. Felipe was sitting propped against the wall next to me. As soon as he noticed I was awake he began talking in a low voice. Our visitor had said that the Talcayan troops were approaching the fortress and hoped to be at the west wall of El Alcázar sometime the next morning. They were prepared to climb the wall and use machine guns to keep the enemy pinned at the east end of the compound while we escaped. The messenger lowered several packets which Antonio and Felipe pulled in through the window. The first contained a machine pistol and four hand guns with a small pile of ammunition. The second contained plastic explosives and a detonator to blow the door of the room off of its hinges. We should expect our liberators to arrive about mid morning. They would first hit the open area in front of us with smoke bombs. When we heard something like a train whistle we were to blast off the door and make our way to the southwest corner of the compound, where there would be troops waiting to help us get up on the roof of the shed next to the wall and then over the wall to freedom.

Antonio had pointed out that at mid morning there was a good chance that Dolores Laval and I would not be in the room, and an escape at that time might leave us hostages. The mysterious figure on the roof mused about that for a minute and then said that the rescue would be attempted around 7 A.M. The main force attacking the fortress would not get to the wall by that time, but a few of the Canadian soldiers would be brought in part way, lowered from the helicopter and hope to make their way to the wall without running into resistance. Once we were outside of the enclosure it would be a matter of making a run for it, with the hope that Langer's men would be too busy defending themselves to bother about a few escapees. I glanced at my watch. It was already 6 A.M.

Antonio had told the anonymous messenger that one prisoner was in bad shape and would need to be carried. The rest of us were able to make our own way, with the possible exception of myself. The weapons had been distributed the previous night. When I asked who had taken possession of the machine pistol Felipe nodded towards Dolores Laval.

"None of us men have ever fired such a weapon," he said. "Dolores says that she has. She also says that she will be quite happy to use it."

Felipe asked me whether I was able to handle a gun. Although the pain had returned to my fingers, my head was clear and my nausea gone, so unless others of our number were accurate shots, I should probably take charge of one of the pistols. Felipe walked over to the wall and pulled one out of his pile of bedding and handed it to me. He pointed to my injured fingers with a questioning look and I explained that I was left handed.

The weapons and plastic explosive were hidden in the bed clothes spread around the room. Four of our five mattresses had been pulled over into two corners of the room to serve as shields when it came time to blow the door off its hinges. For several hours either Felipe or Antonio had kept watch in case our captors discovered how close our liberators were and decided to use us as hostages or do something worse. "I don't know what we would have done if we saw guards coming," Antonio said. "We could fire at the ones that appeared first, but we couldn't hold off a full scale attack. They would simply blast us into oblivion with grenades or whatever explosives they have."

We waited as the sky gradually lightened. Several times we spotted movement at the other end of the yard but began to breathe again when no one came towards our prison. The minutes crept towards seven o'clock. Then it was seven o'clock and there was no sound. People stirred restlessly. Five minutes after. Ten minutes after. Silence; and then it came, the sound of a train whistle loud enough to shake the room. Almost immediately there were popping sounds and the far end of the yard began to fill with smoke. While the rest of us crowded behind the mattresses, Felipe and Antonio pushed the explosive into several spaces around the door, strung out a wire and attached it to a switch, which was in turn wired to a small battery. The blast was deafening, and as the smoke cleared we saw that the door was hanging precariously by one hinge, leaving enough room for a person to pass through. With a precision that spoke well of Felipe's organizing ability, Dolores Laval and I stepped out of the room with weapons pointing towards the smoke-filled end of the compound, four men picked up Andres Ruiz on a stretcher made out of a couple of blankets and hurried along the wall

THE BLOOD-DIMMED TIDE IS LOOSED

to the southwest corner, the rest of the prisoners following closely. The other three of our men with weapons left their posts at the windows, joined Dolores and myself, and we backed towards the same corner. Miraculously, no one emerged from the smoke to challenge us.

Thus far the operation had been run with the efficiency of a caper from television's *The A Team*, but when we got to the southwest corner of the compound there were no rescuers in sight. Felipe Diaz and I laid aside our guns and with the help of a couple of others hoisted the four stretcher bearers on to the roof, conscious that we were completely exposed if any of Langer's troops should emerge from the smoke. Then, carefully, we raised the patient as far above our heads as we could. Somehow the men above caught hold of him and pulled him on to the roof. Dolores had a death grip on her machine pistol and was staring towards the smoke-filled space at the opposite end of the compound as though daring anyone to appear. I told her that her weapon would be more effective if she were positioned on top of the roof. Without changing expression she silently walked over and allowed herself to be hoisted onto the flat roof, where she immediately rolled on to her stomach and aimed the weapon again at the east end of the courtyard. In a minute we had all scrambled on to the roof. Still there was no action from our captors, but neither was there any sign of our rescuers.

We could not have been mistaken in thinking that the whistle was the planned signal. It had been accompanied by the cascade of smoke bombs that had covered our escape. The others were looking at me to do something. I looked over the edge and saw nothing but the same kind of smoke that blanketed the courtyard we had just left. I ducked back and without being able to think of anything else to do I shouted in English, "Are you Canadians down there?" There was a moment of silence and a voice answered, "One Canadian, coming up."

Antonio whispered, "I think it's the same guy we talked to last night."

After some banging and clattering the tip of a ladder appeared over the edge of the roof, followed in a few seconds by the handsome face of Captain Albert Tamayo. He took in the scene, spotted me and drawled, "Being just a tad fussy, are we, insisting on being rescued by Canadians?"

His eyes rested for a second on Señor Ruiz. He disappeared, reappeared, shoved a stretcher on to the roof and climbed after it, followed by three others in military uniforms. Without wasting time on greetings he looked down at the courtyard, then along the roof, and shouted in Spanish to those of us with firearms: "Keep your guns trained in case our friends down there get curious." The four soldiers moved Señor Ruiz on to the stretcher, buckled the straps to keep him in place, and within a minute had lowered him to the ground. Señora Ruiz, not waiting for instructions, climbed down the ladder. I was the last to leave the roof, and by the time I got to the ground there was a medic injecting Señor Ruiz with a needle, presumably with antibiotics.

Señora Ruiz was looking on with a beatific expression. She rushed over, thanked me and gave me a hug that crushed the breath out of me. I replied that I was not one of the rescuers, but she insisted, "It was you who brought them here." When you have seen your husband brought back from the brink, strict accuracy may not be your main concern.

Captain Tamayo was barking out instructions in Spanish and as I looked around I couldn't see anyone else in a Canadian military uniform. Observing my puzzlement, Tamayo explained that there had been no need for troops to be helicoptered in. The main force had advanced more quickly than expected.

"But how the devil did you people get on that roof so fast?" he asked. They had sounded the whistle as soon as they reached the wall. Then someone had aimed badly and the first smoke bomb had hit the wall in front of them; that accounted for the delay in getting the ladders in place and their men in position. They were still digging around to get a solid base for the ladder when they heard my shout.

"And exactly how do you happen to be here?" I asked as we set off behind the four stretcher bearers. "Aren't you supposed to be back in Dundurn rescuing our fighting men from the local bars?"

"It's a bit complicated," he explained. "Lieutenant Winfield asked for Major Knobel to help with military intelligence. The major however seems to have made himself indispensible in his new position. Someone must have remembered that I had all of two weeks of experience of intelligence work here while assisting Knobel. The long and the short of it is—they cared enough to send the very best and here I am. Actually

Winfield is happy to have me. You see, I outranked him when I arrived. It wouldn't do to have a lieutenant giving orders to a captain; so it's now Captain Winfield."

Our parade was led by eight soldiers, followed by the four stretcher bearers carrying Señor Ruiz, then his wife and the other middle-aged woman who had shared our captivity, and then a half dozen more people with guns, including Dolores Laval, who maintained her grip on the machine pistol. Then came the rest of the released prisoners except for Felipe and Antonio, who with Captain Tamayo, six other soldiers and myself constituted the rear guard.

While we moved along as briskly as the stretcher bearers could manage, Tamayo explained what had been happening. The explosions and gunfire we heard two days ago came from a probe led by Colonel McGrath along the path of my ill-fated foray into the forest. One part of his little army spent a day pushing through the bushes as though getting ready to attack El Alcázar from the west. They made little progress but they made lots of noise. A bull dozer began to clear a path through the bushes but hardly made a dent in the stand of trees next to the Palencia road. Meanwhile another portion of the colonel's new recruits, joined by the Canadians, took up positions high up on the slopes on either side of the Valle Colorado.

The next day our men on the slopes of the Valle Colorado began to lob shells down towards the gun emplacements that Langer had established closer to the road that ran along the bottom of the valley. Langer's men had reason to regret having conceded the higher ground to the enemy. Our men higher up couldn't see the gun emplacements, but they had a general idea of where they were. This was not a major problem, since their purpose was not to kill as many men as possible but to give the impression that Colonel McGrath had abandoned the attack from the west and was preparing for an advance up the Valle Colorado. Our troops to the west gave up their noise making and began to slip eastward quietly through the woods on foot and met little resistance.

Captain Tamayo had been detached from the Canadian company and joined the group led by Señor Villalobos, which spearheaded the advance from the west through the forest towards El Alcázar. "They're a tough bunch," Tamayo remarked. "I think the main reason the colonel wanted me with them was to argue them out of shooting anything that moved."

"If you don't mind my saying so, Mick," the captain said, "You look like hell. I'm surprised that you're able to keep up with us."

I explained that I had not had a lot of sleep until the previous night, and showed him my mangled fingers. He took a look at them, hustled up to the medic who was walking beside the stretcher and returned with an envelope with a dozen pain killers. "Take a couple of these, he said. "Only a couple. More than that and your whole system could shut down. We'll get you on that flight with Señor Ruiz."

When we reached the road in the Valle Palencia there was a welcome party waiting, along with our helicopter and several trucks and cars. The thirty or so people standing around cheered as we emerged from the forest. Mayor Laval greeted his daughter like one brought back from the dead, and the two of them came over and thanked me. With the accumulation of unmerited thanks, I figured that to balance the books I would have to be accused of something really heinous within the next few days.

"We have to get this girl back home and let her get some rest," Señor Laval said. "I don't know what happens next, but before you leave you must visit us."

It was still a bit chilly and Dolores, who had left behind the jacket that she had worn in captivity, was shivering in spite of the fact that her father had given her his coat. She stared at the ground, then looked up at me for a second and murmured, "God bless you, Miguel. I wish . . . ." She paused for a moment, then repeated, "God bless you," turned with her father and walked to a waiting automobile and they drove off.

By this time the crew had loaded Señor Ruiz on to the helicopter. I climbed in after him, along with Señora Ruiz and the medic. The pain killers had begun to take effect, and we had scarcely gotten of the ground when I fell asleep. The ordeal was over.

CHAPTER THIRTY ONE

The hospital in Magdalena had all of the facilities needed to take care of Señor Ruiz. We landed in an open space nearby where an ambulance was waiting. The medic thought that to avoid permanent effects from Langer's sadism I should see a bone surgeon, and for that I needed to go to Mendoza. The helicopter flew me to the training camp south of El Puente Ingles, and before joining Harold Pelletier in the little Cessna I told one of the soldiers to get word to Colonel McGrath that I had fairly convincing evidence that Flores and his gang were being financed by drug lords.

Harold at the controls of the Cessna explained that he would be doing only a few routine loops and dives on the way to Mendoza. I began to feel that to merit all of this attention I needed to develop some really serious ailment. It might be embarrassing to arrive in Mendoza by plane from a foreign country, be rushed to the hospital and then have it revealed that all the fuss was about a few broken fingers.

To my relief, the surgeon at Magdalena took it seriously. They froze my hand, and blessedly free of pain I immediately fell asleep in the operating room. When it was over the surgeon told me that four fingers should be "as good as new" in several months. My thumb, however, had been shattered and he couldn't put it together in a way that would allow the joint to function. "You might try some place up north," he said, "But I'm not sure that they can do much more. If you can tolerate going through life with a stiff thumb, then you shouldn't need any more surgery. I've clipped off your finger nails where they got separated from the base, but they'll grow back."

He prescribed pain killers, with special ones to let me sleep. "Frankly, I don't know how long the pain will last. I've operated on other injuries like this but I've never done the follow-up care. If you have to take pain killers for more than two weeks, see a doctor about changing the prescription. Otherwise your body could react badly when you quite taking these things."

Back at the training camp I attempted to get back into action the next day. On my first attempt I found myself dizzy and weak within an hour. Captain Winfield informed me that my attempt to go to work was not the smartest thing I had ever done. I had put off calling my mother and my Uncle Hugh, and having been grounded by the captain I had lots of time to figure out how to tell my story without being imprudently generous with the more sordid facts. As it turned out, the captain's authoritative intervention was not needed to keep me idle. The next day I experienced stomach cramps along with dizziness. Apparently in my run-down condition I had fallen prey to some sort of virus and it was several days before I could get back to work.

Some days later Captain Winfield called a strategy session. Mayors Laval and Robles joined the usual military planning group with Captain Tamayo as translator. Colonel McGrath reported on the mopping up operations at El Alcázar. The Flores people at the gun stations in the Valle Colorado apparently had begun to feel exposed and quietly slipped back into the fortress, which made things simpler for our side. For some days after our rescue Colonel McGrath had kept the place surrounded to prevent any break-out. A group had attempted to escape in the direction being patrolled by Villalobos' men, who commanded them to halt. Two did. Three made a run for it and were shot. Two died immediately. The third, Comandante Langer himself, was injured and taken into custody.

The next day the eighty five men who held El Alcázar surrendered and were now back in the fortress as prisoners in more humane conditions than they had provided for us. The best prepared of our

THE BLOOD-DIMMED TIDE IS LOOSED

troops were stationed there in case of a rescue attempt by Flores. The rest were back at the training camp, where they were joined by a considerable number of new recruits encouraged by the apparently easy victory of the government forces at El Alcázar. Villalobos had led his men back to his estancia.

Captain Winfield then reviewed the mandate of the Canadian forces in Talcayan. They had been sent to work with and train local troops to prevent the takeover of the country by outlaws. We had learned that drug lords were most probably backing Flores. While focusing closely on freeing the prisoners, we had learned little about the size and quality of the total fighting force commanded by Flores. Here the Captain asked Colonel McGrath to present his assessment of where we stood.

"We have put about ninety of Flores' gang out of action," the colonel replied. "We simply don't know how many more there are. Some of them are members of the police forces in San Isidro and Magdalena. There are a several dozen in the Valdez region supposedly policing that area and an unknown number lying low waiting for instructions. My guess is that, if Flores intends to engage in open battle he probably has a commitment from his backers to provide help from outside of the country."

I recalled that in one of my sessions with Langer he had boasted that if Colonel McGrath tried to rescue us, his troops would be attacked not only by forces within the fortress but by others from outside. It had not happened. Colonel McGrath noted that he had been watching for that eventuality and had kept Serge Demarais and Henry Pelletier in the air constantly to identify any suspicious movements of personnel. Maybe our display of firepower in the approach to El Alcázar had helped to discourage outside troops from entering the fray.

The plan was for President Gracida to resign soon. Mayors Rendon, Calderon, Guzman, Laval and Robles had agreed to throw their support behind Pablo Javier, and he should be sworn in as president in a couple of weeks. It had been something of a coup to get Rendon and Guzman on board, but apparently they recognized that the best and perhaps only chance of thwarting Flores was to support Professor Javier's election to the presidency.

- 269 -

"If all goes according to plan," Captain Winfield explained, "with the recent increase in the number of recruits we have a good chance to have a trained army in place within several months. In the meantime, this partially trained army has to be ready to intervene to keep Flores from grabbing power. He isn't going to go away after the inauguration of a new president. It may take months to clear out all of the conspirators he has gathered together. That leaves us with a financial problem. Only the Canadian troops draw their pay from the Canadian government. The mayors of Marino and Amparo have been paying the wages of the others, with a little help from Magdalena and Avila. They can't afford to do that for long, especially with the added expense of providing for the new prisoners. Once Javier becomes president and has time to get the finances of the country organized, the army becomes the responsibility of the national government. We don't have enough funds to tide us over until that happens."

The captain deferred to Colonel McGrath for a further explanation of where we stood financially. "We've followed up on the supposition that Flores is supported by drug money. We have tried to convince some outside parties to help us prevent a takeover of the country by drug lords. Talking to international agencies of any kind has gotten us nowhere. They need more evidence and then they need to consult others about whether the evidence is sufficient, and then someone has to evaluate how we plan to use the money and someone else has to check our accounting system.

"At the same time, others of us have been trying to convince the U.S. and Canadian governments that money spent to prevent a drug takeover of a country is cheaper than paying an army of agents to guard hundreds of airports and thousands of miles of shoreline and border. They agree in principle, which of course doesn't tell us whether they intend to do anything. The Prime Minister, as usual, is preparing for the next election and he will do whatever the editorials indicate is the wise thing to do. That means that he is guided by people who are paid to entertain the public, not to ponder affairs of state. The situation with the Americans is a little more hopeful. Their war against drugs is so complicated that no one person seems to have a grasp of the details of what's going on, and if you can convince an official high up in the chain of command that you have a good case he or she can slip you a million or two without anyone being able to object until the next audit. They've given us enough money to tide us over for a week, maybe ten days. After that, if we don't have firm evidence of a threatened drug takeover we're broke.

"So our main job has been to get evidence of drug interests, and that means tracing the money. I got the president of Hannigan Industries to put Mick's assistant, Alex Brosky on that trail. He and four computer whizzes whom he has hired temporarily have been assembling a mountain of data, a lot of it from bank statements and drug enforcement agencies. He has also been in touch with people operating in the shadows who sell you information if you are willing to pay enough. I suspect that Brosky doesn't lie awake at night worrying about how these people get their data. If they can save him the time and trouble of breaking into data banks himself, he's happy to use Hugh Hannigan's money to pay them off. For all I know, they may even gather some of the information legitimately.

"Anyway, Brosky and his crew are running all of this junk through their machines to detect any suspicious movements, like a lot of money leaving a bank known to be used by a Columbian dealer and a similar amount showing up in a bank that we suspect our friend Flores patronizes here in Talcayan. It's way more complicated than that, but you get the idea. Brosky has actually had the humility to bring in Mick's cousin, Toby Hannigan, to help, and Toby has several of the mathematics gurus at the University of Waterloo working on how to break down the data in order to figure out what is significant. The university guys can only work part time while they're teaching, and they haven't gotten anything definite yet, but they're just getting started. Now we just keep our fingers crossed."

"One last item," Colonel McGrath added. "With all the fireworks we used to impress the garrison at El Alcázar, we're short of ammo. So I have been back in touch with Colonel Marchand, and he has diverted another consignment of ammunition to us to arrive any day now."

For the time being there was enough work to keep us busy. Winfield and McGrath were responsible for continuing the training of the troops. The reconnaissance crew continued surveillance for signs of any troop concentration and Captain Tamayo with an aide was assigned to question the new prisoners in El Alcázar. I would join them for the questioning of some of the prisoners, including Alonzo Langer, to look for leads towards solving the Tipping murders.

As the meeting broke up, Señor Laval pulled me aside and stated that he would like to join me for the interrogation of Comandante Langer, and the next day the two of us visited the former Chief of Police of Valdez in a hospital ward in Magdalena. He was hooked up to an intravenous line, had a cast on one leg where a bullet had damaged the femur and a large bandage over the right side of his chest. The attending physician explained that he was receiving medication to control the pain but was fully conscious. Mayor Laval and I took chairs on each side of the bed while a guard leaned against the wall in front of the patient.

The mayor began by asking Langer whether he was satisfied with the medical treatment he was receiving, and received no answer. Laval continued: "I have visited Señor Ruiz, who is recovering from the wound in his leg, now that he has received antibiotics to fight the infection. You may recall refusing to help Señor Ruiz. My daughter is not so fortunate. It is not easy for a woman to recover her peace of mind after being raped repeatedly. Señor Hannigan, would you show Captain Langer your right hand. Señor Hannigan will probably never recover the use of his thumb. Even with pain killers he has trouble getting to sleep.

"Now, Comandante Langer, we have to do something with you. I might add that we are running short of resources, and the expense of keeping you here in the hospital is considerable. It seems that the people who were your prisoners in El Alcázar should be heard when we decide about your future. Can you give Señor Hannigan here any reason to recommend a merciful treatment?"

The captain stirred a bit but remained silent. Mayor Laval waited a while before continuing. "Do you have any message I can take back to Señor Ruiz and his wife, some reason why they should recommend mercy for you?"

Further silence. After another long pause, "Comandante, do you have anything you would want to say to my daughter, and to my wife, and perhaps to me, some reason why we would want you to be treated mercifully?"

When the captain remained silent, the mayor turned to me. "Señor Hannigan, what would you recommend we do with Comandante Langer?"

"The merciful thing," I said, "would be a quick trial and execution. Quite apart from his time at El Alcázar, Alonzo Langer has been guilty of a number of offences that deserve severe punishment. Joining the effort of Mayor Flores to bring down the government of Talcayan by force is only one of his crimes. The less merciful thing would be to do nothing. Just quit treating the comandante. Leave him in a cell with enough food and drink to keep him alive, and let nature take its course. He did that to Señor Ruiz, an innocent man. How could he object to it as a punishment for himself?"

There was another long silence, broken finally by the mayor. "I must say that what Señor Hannigan suggests does not seem too harsh a punishment for someone who has allowed the repeated rape of my daughter. However, we are in need of some information, and for that information we are willing to be lenient, even to the extent of recommending that you be treated until reaching full health and then stand trial. Explain this to him, Miguel"

I explained what we already knew about what happened after the discovery of the bodies of the Tippings: Officer Garza's initial investigation, Langer's two visitors, the transfer of the case to Officer Lara, Lara's instruction to Officer Costa, etc. I concluded: "What we need to know from you, Comandante Langer, is who was being protected."

The captain replied that he didn't know what I was talking about. Even if there were visitors to his office six months ago, how could he be expected to recall details after all this time? I replied that if someone sufficiently powerful to give him orders about handling a criminal procedure visited him, his survival would depend on being able to remember that event. Langer then claimed that the visit of the two strangers had no reference to any criminal investigation. After several minutes of this I observed to Mayor Laval we were wasting our time. Langer should get the punishment he deserved.

The mayor turned back to him. "Don't think, Comandante, that you have nothing to lose. If you cooperate with us you will get a fair trial. If convicted, you will get a sentence that may be shortened by some years because of your cooperation. You will be incarcerated in a prison where living conditions are not too bad. You may even be freed from prison quite soon if your friends take power in this country. But if you don't cooperate with us, very soon you will be experiencing excruciating pain as infection eats away at your body. You will be looking for ways to kill yourself, but you will be afraid to die. You will look back at this moment and curse yourself for having made the wrong decision."

When Langer replied he whined like a complaining child. He could not be expected to give information that he did not possess. Mayor Laval responded: "I am going to ask you some questions now. If you keep saying you don't know, then Señor Hannigan and I will leave this room and you will face some terrible days. Now, who were the two strangers who visited you early in the month of last September?"

Langer seemed almost to sob. "I don't know their names."

"I find it very unlikely," the mayor said, "that two important people should visit you and not give you their names, or that you, a senior police officer, should be so absent minded as to forget the names. If you give another answer like that we will have to conclude that you have chosen not to be honest with us. The next question: who did those two visitors represent, that they should have so much authority over a Chief of Police?"

Langer shifted his gaze a half dozen times, as though looking for a way out. Finally he muttered that the two represented financial interests. What kind of financial interests? Well, they helped to finance Mayor Flores' projects. Mayor Laval pointed out that this did not answer his question. What kind of financial interests did they represent? Hardly above a whisper, Langer stated that they represented a drug cartel. Why would people representing a drug cartel want to quash this particular murder investigation? Again Langer, in the tone of a child protesting the unfairness of his treatment, responded that he didn't know.

The mayor kept up the pressure. "You are not being helpful, Comandante Langer. You seem to know very little about something that was very important to your department. What do you know about who committed the murder? Are you going to tell us that you don't know anything about that?"

THE BLOOD-DIMMED TIDE IS LOOSED

"We never investigated the murder." There was desperation in Langer's voice. "We were instructed not to investigate it."

"But someone in your department may have found out something. Do you think that Officer Lara would have learned the identity of the murderer?"

"I don't know. He might have. But he had no business trying to find out. He was instructed to leave things alone, to record it as an insoluble crime."

"Comandante Langer, I have not decided yet whether I will recommend mercy or ask that you be given the most severe punishment. If Señor Hannigan wants you to get the worst punishment I will probably agree with him. I have another question. If you tell me you do not know who under your command at El Alcázar would dare to rape a prisoner I will conclude that you have chosen to face the kind of punishment Señor Hanigan has suggested. So, who raped my daughter? Quickly now, just answer that question."

Again Langer looked around the room as though trying to find a way out. Finally he whispered, "Leonel Reyes . . . and Marco Fernandez."

Mayor Laval warned Langer that if he had given false information then any reason for mercy would have vanished. Langer muttered that he was telling the truth. I remarked that, if he didn't know the names of the two strangers who visited him on September 3, he must surely know something about the drug lords who were financing Mayor Flores. When he claimed not to know a single name I asked him rather impatiently whether he knew anything about them that would enable us to identify them. He was obviously scared and seemed to be genuinely searching his memory for some clue.

Finally he said, rather tentatively, "They produce their drugs in Colombia. Most of their drugs go to the United States. They want a base for distribution in Talcayan because the American and Colombian officials are always discovering the path taken by the drugs from Colombia to the north. They also want to start producing drugs in Talcayan. The two threatened that if I didn't do what they asked they would inform someone called De Castro. I don't think De Castro is the leader. I think he is an enforcer. Now I have told you all I know."

This time I believed him, more or less.

- 275 -

CHAPTER THIRTY TWO

The next day I travelled to El Alcázar, where Captain Tamayo and an aide had begun to question the inmates. I gave the captain the names of Leonel Reyes and Marco Fernandez, the two who, according to Langer, had abused Dolores Laval. He checked a list and reported that the Villalobos troops had killed those two attempting to escape from the surrounded fortress. Perhaps Langer had thrown the blame on two people whom he knew to be dead; or maybe the two were in fact guilty and ready to risk death rather than face the consequences. It could be investigated later if Dolores Laval ever reached a stage when she could endure talking about her ordeal.

Most of Langer's garrison at El Alcázar had been recruited from the area of Valdez. Captain Tamayo and his aide had identified five who might have been in a position to know something about the Tipping murders, but under questioning only one offered any information. He was a broad-shouldered, shaggy individual named Ricardo Castillo who as a member of the Valdez police force had been an assistant to his hero, Julio Lara. According to Ricardo, there was tension between Lara and Langer. Flores had put Langer in charge because he judged correctly that Langer was the more easily controlled of the two. Lara was opposed to Flores' campaign to become president. The mayor was already making plenty of money with the flow of drugs into and out of

- 276 -

Talcayan but was seduced by the thought of entering into the big time, presiding over a country that would become a profitable haven for drug interests.

Ricardo had been in an office with Lara at the police station the previous September and learned about the Tipping murders. Having been ordered to leave the case unsolved, Lara went about the task grumpily, but his professional curiosity had been aroused. He found a slip of paper in a pocket of Richard Tipping's jacket with three columns of numbers. At the top of one column were the letters CAN, of the second column the letters US and of the third column the letters ARG. Lara concluded that he probably had in his hand a list of serial numbers of large bills in the currency of Canada, United States and Argentina.

No money was found on the bodies. Guessing that the couple would not have spent all the money represented by those numbers, Lara sent word to the banks in Valdez to look out for anyone presenting American, Canadian and Argentine money to be exchanged for local currency. He intended to widen the inquiry if nothing showed up locally, but the next day the manager of a bank in Valdez informed Lara that a number of bills of the three countries had been exchanged for Talcayan currency that morning. Examination showed that the numbers on those bills corresponded with numbers on the paper that Lara had recovered from the coat of Richard Tipping. The name of the person who brought in the foreign currency was Luis Cerna.

This information had infuriated Officer Lara even more. Cerna was, as Ricardo described him, a nobody who was trying to be a somebody. A local agent for drug interests, he had quarreled several times with Officer Lara. Cerna thought that because of his powerful backers he could do what he liked and ignore the police. That Lara should now be ordered to cover up a crime committed by this person whom he despised was enough to rid the officer of any lingering allegiance to Langer.

Lara was convinced that Flores' attempt to take power was bound to fail because a first-world nation had become involved, and this had happened because of Cerna's stupid crime. Lara had declared to Ricardo before the latter had departed for El Alcázar, "You can't tell me that Canada sends a colonel with McGrath's ability to a tiny third-world country to train a bunch of raw recruits. They're playing with us. If Flores and his drug people come out into the open, they won't be facing a bunch of untrained local boys. They'll face air power that will shoot them to pieces and leave the local boys to clean up the mess."

Oh to be as powerful as our enemies think we are.

At long last I had the name of a likely suspect for the murder. Ricardo might possibly have been getting even with an enemy named Luis Cerna; but he hadn't been forewarned of my interview with him, and as soon as I brought up the question of the Tipping murder he had spilled out his rather complicated but coherent story without hesitation, so it sounded like the truth. I passed Cerna's name on to Captain Tamayo in case he was among the prisoners.

By the time I returned to camp the colonel had left for Avila to stiffen the spine of the reluctant Mayor Calderon. Two days later I was whiling away my time on guard duty at the front gate practicing loading a rifle with only one good hand when a jeep approached from the north churning up clouds of dust. It had the markings of the Canadian armed services and as it came closer I was able to make out the figure of Colonel McGrath sitting up very straight in the passenger's seat.

The vehicle screeched to a stop at the gate, and taking my cue from the speed of the approach I hustled over to the colonel, who told me to jump into the back of the jeep, and we headed for the barracks. On the way he asked me whether I could handle a rifle. I replied that I couldn't get shots off as quickly as I could with the full use of both hands, and certainly it took my longer to reload. My accuracy, however, was close to what it had been before Langer's handiwork on my fingers.

"Would you be comfortable going into a situation where you may have to be the sharpshooter people think you are?"

I replied that I could probably get the job done as well as anyone he was likely to find on short notice. Following his instructions, I stuffed my gear, including my painkillers, into my duffel bag. Within five minutes we were back on our way with the colonel driving and myself holding on tightly in the passenger seat.

As he steered around potholes and the jeep bounced like a jack rabbit, the colonel explained that events had begun to spin out of control. Flores had infiltrated a number of his men into San Isidro in the preceding days, and this morning, with the help of his allies within the San Isidro police force, they had taken control of the national military camp in the city. This consisted of an armory and a barracks within a walled parade ground along the San Isidro River, a couple of kilometers from the center of the city. Forces loyal, at least for the moment, to President Gracida held the government buildings and president's palace in the middle of the downtown district. The colonel had left in place most of our men guarding El Alcázar in case Flores should try to retake that stronghold and free his men held prisoner there. Mateo Villalobos had been asked to move with his men directly to San Isidro. Not only were they one of the most effective fighting units available, but their imperious leader would not appreciate being kept on the sidelines. Even as Will and I careened northward Captains Winfield and Tamayo were organizing the movement to San Isidro of almost the whole contingent at the training camp, along with weapons and ammunition.

"This thing may be decided in the next several days," McGrath said. "There's one good thing about that. Paying the troops for an indefinite period will not be my worry. But there's something that concerns me more than our financial problems. Flores is not a complete fool. Up to now, in an open fight we can beat him, mainly because we have better weapons. But he's apparently moving towards a public battle. Why would he think he can win now? Time is on his side. All he has to do is wait. We'll go home. The troops we've been training will disband if the money runs out. Why gamble everything now?"

I suggested that maybe he was having trouble with his own men. After all, giving up the Canadian prisoners without a fight and then losing El Alcázar couldn't have been good for their morale. To keep them with him he might need some sort of victory. My uncle shrugged. "Possibly. But if he has drug money behind him, he can pay his troops. As long as they lie low they don't run much risk. I can't see them running away from a regular pay cheque unless they're really scared, and I'm not sure they're that scared."

I wasn't so sure. Suppose Javier became president with a lot of popular support. Then all the government had to do was to pick off Flores's men one by one, beginning with Flores himself. If Javier went after him, Flores would have to go into hiding or come out into the open and fight. I could see why he might gamble and come out fighting now, and he would have more weapons having taken over the armory.

McGrath paused for a minute before answering. "It's possible, I grant you. But that armory used to be under the control of Rendon, and he assures me that there are no sophisticated modern weapons there that would shift the balance decisively towards Flores. What I am afraid of is that Flores is going to get a whole new level of support from the drug people. What would happen if they got him a couple of state-of-the-art fighter planes armed with rockets and with some mercenaries to fly and maintain them? How would you feel about a couple of those coming out of the sky at you?"

The colonel continued after a minute. "We've a few ground-to-air missiles that our Canadians know how to handle. We'll make sure they're in place wherever we gather in force. It's chancy, though. A modern fighter coming at you with missiles of its own will very likely get the best of an exchange with anything we have on the ground. We'll see. Maybe it won't be planes. Maybe they've something else up their sleeves. . . . But don't spread any of this around. I've talked to Winfield and Demarais and Tamayo about it, but no one else. Well, one other. This guy Villalobos is no fool. He called me with the same question I asked you. Why has Flores come out into the open? Villalobos wasn't ready to cut and run, mind you, but he's as worried as I am."

"A couple of other things," Will continued. "There are several people doing some emergency recruiting to reinforce our so-called army, but I don't put much stock in that for the short run. Anyone they recruit will be untrained and unorganized. Also, we've got some mechanics working on that Leopard tank in Amparo that we confiscated from Fraga. The motor was messed up by the foam we used on it. The tank would be a big help to us and we have ammunition that can be used by a Leopard I. But it's not ready yet, and I don't know how many days it will be before it is ready. I should have put people to work on it the day I arrived. I didn't think of it until a few days ago."

Our immediate job was to pick up Professor Javier in Magdalena and bring him safely to San Isidro. Mayor Rendon had informed Colonel McGrath that Rendon couldn't count on the support of the majority of his own police force in San Isidro unless three people appeared in that city: Professor Javier, Colonel McGrath and myself. Mayor Rendon was insistent. His people had to see those three if they were going to stand up to Flores.

I remarked on the incongruity of my name being mentioned along with those of the future president and the military commander. The colonel chuckled; I wasn't sure whether it was because he found the situation incongruous or he was just enjoying the ride. I had to grant that bouncing along the road was much like something what you would pay good money for in the midway at the Calgary Stampede.

"You may find it hard to believe," he said, "but for some people in this country you have become a kind of myth. They need a hero and you're handy. So for a few days you're going to have to be John Wayne."

The colonel continued. "The people around Professor Javier assure me that they've kept his location secret for his own safety. They thought that any of his enemies looking for him would be watching Marino and Amparo, so they figured they'd outsmart Flores by housing the professor with a friend of his in Magdalena. Turns out now that there may have been a leak somewhere, and there have been reports of suspicious characters making inquiries about him in Magdalena.

"So far there have been no approaches to the house where he's staying. Guzman has put two officers whom he trusts inside the house. The mayor doesn't want to send any more police there. It would mean revealing Dr. Javier's location to more people, and he doesn't know whom he can trust; and any sizable force located in one place might be spotted by our enemies. So you and I have to get Javier out of there and into San Isidro as quickly and quietly as possible; and we won't know how close the bad guys might be while we perform that operation."

The fastest way to get the professor to the capital would have been to fly him there in the Cessna or the helicopter. However, the airport in San Isidro, while not officially in the hands of Flores, was not secure for our side, and it was almost certainly under surveillance by our enemies. The helicopter, as luck would have it, was currently hundreds of miles away carrying Mayor Laval back from his thus-far-unsuccessful attempt to get support from Argentina against Flores' attempted coup.

- 281 -

We took the less scenic route to Magdalena, but even so the majesty of the Andes around the city was enough to make you wonder why, with the whole world to enjoy, we work so hard to mess things up. We stopped at a station where the chief of police was in on the secret of Professor Javier's location. As we walked into the building we were greeted by a severe-looking woman seated behind a large desk with a name plate that informed us that the occupant was one L. Martinez. When Will explained that we were here to confer with the Chief of Police she gave a pro forma look at a book on her desk and informed us that we did not have an appointment. Her tone of voice suggested that she was handing down an edict from which there was no appeal. The colonel explained that, even though no appointment had been recorded, Chief Venza was expecting us. She countered that Chief Venza did not see anyone without an appointment. While this exchange was going on I wandered over to a door with the chief's name on it and rapped sharply, much to the annoyance of L. Martinez.

A loud voice shouted "Enter," and I obeyed. A harried-looking officer, his thinning hair in disarray, looked up at me from behind a desk at the opposite end of the room. He looked startled for a moment, as though he had been expecting someone else—presumably the receptionist and guardian of his privacy. Then he got to his feet and inquired, "Oh . . . Colonel McGrath, is it? No, you must be . . . uh . . . ."

By this time Will was standing beside me. Chief Venza shook our hands and explained that he was very glad to see us, and that being responsible for the security of Professor Javier was a great honor but it had put a strain on his already burdened staff.

It took only a couple of minutes to get the address of the house where Javier was staying, inform the two officers on guard there that we were coming and arrange to switch our jeep, which was too conspicuous for our purpose, for a Honda Accord. I was anxious to get moving, but the colonel made two telephone calls, one back to camp to see what progress Winfield and company were making in preparing for the move northward, another to San Isidro to check on any developments there that might influence our choice of route into the city and to the president's mansion, to which we were to deliver Professor Javier. Both calls dragged on because people wanted further instructions from the colonel concerning one thing or another. It was probably twenty minutes after our arrival when we finally left in the Honda.

We passed a few blocks of old apartment buildings three or four stories high, then climbed higher to where the separate residences were set back from the street. We turned into the driveway of one of the grandest of these. The lot of about one acre was surrounded by a whitewashed stone fence a couple of feet high topped by iron railings that went up another five feet. Inside the fence were carefully trimmed hedges and flower beds still in bloom.

We had scarcely reached the front door when it was opened by an officer, followed by a slim, white-haired, distinguished-looking figure who came down the steps with a cane and holding on to the officer's arm for balance. So we were going to all this trouble in order to entrust the welfare of the country to someone who needed help to walk down a few steps. Once he was settled in the back seat of the Honda we accelerated down the driveway, braked as we came to the street, turned and were on our way.

Our troubles began shortly after we got on the road. Will, who was driving well within the speed limit to avoid attracting attention, looked in the rear view mirror and growled, "Uh oh, we've got company. There's a light-colored Opel been following us for the last while. I'm quite sure that same car was behind us for a few blocks after we left the police station, and then it disappeared. I've accelerated and slowed down, and it stays the same distance back."

I turned in time to see the Opel begin to gain on us. Before Will could react it had gotten close and a hand holding a gun reached out of the passenger window and fired. The shot was wide. We were on a broad avenue and the traffic was light in the mid-afternoon. Will accelerated and began to weave back and forth, but a Honda was not going to win a race with an Opel. I think at that point I came as close as I have ever come to what people refer to as going berserk. The thought of them hunting down the professor made me think of an attack by a mad dog. I shouted at Will to turn left at the next corner, let me off and then get out of there and don't stop.

The Honda skidded as he braked and turned. Before the car had stopped I had my rifle in hand and was out on the street and screaming at him again to get out of there and keep going. Seconds later the Opel swerved around the corner in pursuit. As it braked for the turn I managed to shoot out both of the front tires; the Opel jumped the curb and hit a brick wall. I found myself smashing a side window with the butt of my rifle and shouting at the two occupants to get out and get on the ground. They were in the process of doing so when another car roared up, screeched to a stop and a police siren indicated that a third vehicle was getting close. The odds that these were friendly police officers who happened to be close at hand were not good. Recovering a certain amount of sanity, I kept the rifle trained on the cars and backed away until I was maybe seventy yards up the street.

I came to a corner and looked in the direction that I presumed Will had taken to get out of the city. The Honda was not in sight, so he must have made another turn. If I went down that road the second car would easily overtake me, so I continued to back away up the street. The car whose tires I had shot out was still blocking the way, but a couple of men, one with a rifle, had gotten out of the second vehicle. I leveled a couple of shots close enough to send them scrambling for cover, then turned and dashed the few yards to where the street ended at an eight foot concrete wall that offered no visible footholds.

I found myself engaging in a move I had never practiced or performed. I threw my rifle over the wall, leaped up and grabbed the top of the wall, then like a pole vaulter I swung my feet up in the air and my body followed up and over the fence. I landed on the other side without injury, surprised at my success. I grabbed my rifle and ran across a clearing towards the forest that began not far away. I was at the edge of the city where it begins to climb the mountain.

CHAPTER THIRTY THREE

Farther up the incline the trees and shrubs were sufficiently dense to hide me. I was about half way there when several men appeared, looking over the top of the wall. I ducked down behind some shrubs but it was too late. One of the men pointed towards me and shouted something. I fired a couple of shots in that direction to give them something to think about, then ran a zigzag course towards the edge of the forest. Even had I been bloody-minded enough to engage in a battle, I didn't have the ammunition to sustain it.

In that terrain my chances of escape were pretty good. I had probably recovered enough physical conditioning to allow me to outdistance most pursuers in a race up the slope. If one or two of my pursuers happened to be in good enough shape to gain on me, I liked my chances in a rifle exchange. Within a minute or two I was far enough away that I couldn't see them, which meant, I hoped, that they couldn't see me.

I slowed my pace in preparation for what could be a lengthy chase. The main threat was that they might follow some easy path through the woods while I hopped from rock to rock and stumbled over roots; or if they had police dogs at their disposal they could trail me at their leisure, but bringing in dogs would take some time. Of course they might have already realized the insanity of chasing me when their real purpose was to prevent Professor Javier from reaching San Isidro. It dawned on me, when it was too late to do anything about it, that before disappearing I should have engaged them for a few minutes in an exchange of gunfire to give Will and the professor a little more time to get away.

Climbing that slope was warm going so I took off my jacket and tied it around my waist. I continued upwards at a gradually slowing pace and within a short time was far above the city. Eventually I emerged from the trees and was faced with a steeper incline that discouraged further progress in that direction. If I went to the left the topography would force me to angle back towards the city and a possible encounter with the enemy. I turned to the right where the terrain would allow me to continue climbing gradually while heading north by northwest.

I followed a crooked course in that general direction, trying to pick open spaces with fewer obstacles. In my anxiety to keep an eye out for pursuers I had paid little attention to the time. I was sweating from the heavy uphill climb and getting thirsty. It would be nice to come across a clear mountain stream but so far there had been no sign of water of any description. My crushed fingers began to hurt, and I swallowed the two pills I had with me, without the benefit of anything with which to wash them down. Sundown would come in a couple of hours on the plain, somewhat earlier up there. It was time to head back to civilization. It was a clear day and I judged from the position of the sun that going straight down the mountain would take me more-or-less due east. I had no idea of whether that was also the quickest way back to civilization, but it was as good a guess as any.

I worked my way downwards for a while and for the first time in my wanderings that afternoon I came across a trail, running more or less north and south. It couldn't be called a road. Two people could walk side-by-side on it, and the clearing was wide enough for someone to follow it on a horse or donkey without brushing against branches, but it would hardly allow a vehicle, even a donkey-drawn cart, to pass. It was the first connection I had made with anything human on the mountainside and I debated whether I should follow it. But to go north or south at that point would surely leave me alone on the mountain at nightfall unless I came across a human habitation, and that seemed unlikely.

THE BLOOD-DIMMED TIDE IS LOOSED

I continued my downward progress and after a while the sun disappeared behind the mountain, and although there was still plenty of light to travel by I was getting anxious. Then up ahead there appeared to be a clearing in the trees. My feelings soared at the thought that I had come to the edge of the forest faster than I expected. Perhaps I had not climbed as far upwards as it seemed. Or maybe at this point the plain extended further to the west than it did at Magdalena. It was a cruel illusion. Another minute brought me to the top of a steep rock cliff hundreds of feet high. In other circumstances it would have been a scene to savor. In the far, misty distance I could see the plains still in the sunlight, but below me stretching out towards those plains lay mile after mile of forest. The cliff stretched off to the right and to the left as far as one could see. Even the thought of trying to climb down gave me vertigo.

I had gotten myself lost in the mountains. To call it a rookie mistake would be insulting to rookies. I couldn't recall John Wayne ever having missed a showdown because he had gotten lost on the way.

Daylight was fading and to wander in the dark would be a waste of effort. The prospect of sleeping out of doors without warm clothing in what promised to be a chilly night would in normal circumstances have been unpleasant enough, but by this time my thirst had driven other considerations into the background. After a few minutes of mentally beating myself up for my stupidity I hiked back towards the trail that I had discovered. By the time I got there it was getting dark and it was time to gather up leaves and grass into which I could eventually burrow and endure the night. At least the locals had said that there were no dangerous predators in the area.

If tiredness were the only requirement for sleep I would have been unconscious within minutes, but as I tried to get settle down I discovered that to the discomfort of thirst was added an increasing pain in the fingers of my right hand. My painkillers were now with the rest of my gear, presumably in San Isidro if Colonel McGrath and Professor Javier had managed to get that far. Then there were the bugs, real or imagined, crawling down my neck or making their way up my shirt and pausing to regroup before marching across my face.

- 287 -

After several hours I finally got to sleep and was awakened I
don't know how much later by a feeling of dampness. A light rain was
falling; it must have been coming down for some time because the pile
of vegetation that I had used as a bed was soaked through, as were
my clothes. I thought of trying to catch some water to slake my thirst
but there was nothing in sight in which to catch it. In any case, the
rain at this point was little more than a heavy mist. There was now
enough light to allow one to find one's way through the trees. My watch
registered slightly after 6 A.M.

By that time my thirst had turned into a general feeling of dizziness
and weakness. I couldn't remember what we had been told about how
long one can last without water. I had depleted my bodily supply of
water with my exertions of the previous afternoon, so I would probably
not last as long as the book gave as an average survival time.

I had endured several dangerous "peace keeping" experiences; and
my brief time in Talcayan had put me more in harm's way than had all
my time in the army; but it occurred to me that until that moment I
had thought about death mainly tactically. You're in danger—what's
the best way to stay alive? Don't think about dying or you'll freeze up;
think about what you need to do. But that morning there was not much
to consider tactically and I began to think about dying. After a few
minutes it became almost comforting. At least it would mean the end
of my present misery. I was going to have to depend on the mercy of
God, but I hoped that I was not being a complete hypocrite when I asked
for mercy. Dying in the mountains because of a stupid mistake was an
inglorious way to go, but at the moment that didn't seem to make much
difference. What did bother me was the thought of my mother's grief
brought on by my stupid mistake.

There was no point in standing in the rain. Some exertion would
keep me from shivering and work some of the stiffness out of my joints.
I might even come across a stream. To the north loomed a mountain
with a sheer rock face. To go that way meant to gamble that before
I got to that mountain there would be some access to the east, and I
didn't like the odds. I began to plod southwards, hoping to more-or-less
retrace the path I had taken the day before, if I lasted that long. I took to
shaking moisture from evergreen needles into my hand in tiny amounts

and licking it up. Whether or not those miniscule amounts would be of any use to keep me alive, they did little to assuage my thirst.

Within a few minutes the rain had stopped all together, and soon after that the sky began to clear to the east and the sun came out. My clothes were drying, except for my shoes and socks. Wherever there was a break in the forest that allowed me to look any distance, all that could be seen were miles of forest without a habitation in sight.

I had covered a mile or two at a snail's pace when I noticed something that seemed to be moving farther up the mountain, some hundreds of feet higher than my trail. I stopped to take a closer look. If it had been moving, it had stopped. At first I couldn't make out whether it was man or beast or an inanimate configuration that had just seemed to move. Eventually there was movement and I was able to discern two human figures. They stopped again, appearing to have paused on a ledge well above me. I tried to attract their attention by shouting, but the first sound out of my parched throat would not have alerted a listener fifty yards off, and this pair might have been a half kilometer away. Then I fired off a couple of rifle shots, but from what I could see this had not drawn their attention, or they had heard but were not anxious to meet a trigger-happy stranger. Then the two began to move to the north, and were soon out of sight.

I plunged into the forest, heading upward and to the north of where I had seen the two. They seemed to be following a trail more or less parallel to the one I was on, and if I could get to that trail I just might intercept or catch up with them. Within a minute I was out of breath, my dizziness increased and, try as I might, my progress was so slow that the strangers would be far away before I got up to their level.

Without much hope, but with no better alternative, I continued to push upwards. Several times I came across what looked like paths but within a few yards they became overgrown with weeds or brambles and showed no sign of recent use. A little further on there was something that looked more like a beaten trail. It wasn't very promising, but I didn't feel like climbing upwards any longer, so I followed the trail to the north, where the two strangers were headed. At some points the path seemed to disappear and it was a matter of hopping from rock to fallen tree to gnarled root until something like a path appeared again. I plodded on, becoming increasingly convinced that I would never catch up to those two strangers.

Then, wonder of wonders, I came over a rise and there about two hundred yards ahead of me were two figures. They were walking away from me, apparently unaware of my presence. Sensing that approaching strangers with a rifle might not be the best way to establish trust, I stashed the weapon next to a magnificent evergreen, threw away the holster that was carrying my Beretta, stuck the gun in my belt, pulled out my shirt from under my belt in the hopes of concealing the weapon, and got back on the trail. I didn't try to repeat my unsuccessful attempt at shouting, and with what must have been the last bit of energy in me I broke into a shambling trot. I must have made some noise because in a minute or so the two turned around and looked at me. I waved and stumbled as quickly as I could towards them.

One of the figures was close to a caricature of the mountain man—long hair, beard, battered hat, rifle in hand—the type that, if he appeared in a scary movie, would be the monster who preyed on innocent strangers. Next to him was a younger version, beardless but similarly clothed and armed. The two exhibited neither friendliness nor hostility as I approached. I explained that I was lost and had had nothing to drink for about a day. Could they give me some water or show me where I could find some, and then tell me the shortest way to get to where I could find transportation to San Isidro? The older man looked at me curiously but apparently without suspicion. Or for all I knew, he was sizing me up as easy prey. At first I had trouble understanding him, but eventually I figured out that he had no water with him but there was a cabin down the road where they kept their food and drink when they hunted in this area. I asked whether I had their permission to enter the cabin to get a drink. He explained that they hadn't seen any game on their way up here, and had just as good a chance of finding some if they walked back towards the cabin rather than continue where they were going.

As we walked the two would from time to time exchange brief remarks in an impenetrable accent. After a few minutes the lad led the way off the trail along an even narrower path where we had to walk single file and deflect tree branches from either side. I followed the youth and the older man followed me. They may not have appeared suspicious but they weren't taking chances.

We came to a small clearing around a tiny log cabin with a galvanized metal roof. The youth unlatched the door and led the way into the rough interior. The one window let in enough light to reveal a camp stove and a table. Without speaking the lad scooped up a cupful of water from a pail on the table and handed it to me. The finest product of Chateau Rothschild could not have tasted better.

"You must also be hungry?" By now the elder was taking account of my trouble understanding him and was speaking slowly and distinctly.

I agreed that I hadn't eaten since before noon the day before, and with hours of walking ahead of me I could use some food. The lad rummaged in one of the bags on the table, pulled out a long, narrow loaf of bread, cut off a generous chunk and handed it to me with a jar of honey and then refilled my cup. They were silent while I ate. When I had downed three more cups of water and stood up the man asked, "Enough?" I assured him that I was now ready to resume my journey, if he would tell me the quickest way to get to a travelled road. He explained that I should stay on the path where we had met, follow it more than a kilometer to the north and turn right where it crossed a graded road. I had better try to catch a ride on that road, because I would still be about thirty kilometers from the highway. At the intersection of the road and the highway I would find a place where the bus to San Isidro stopped to pick up passengers. He had no idea when the bus might run.

I explained that I had left a good rifle up on the path near where we had met, beside a giant evergreen. I told him he could keep the weapon as payment for his kindness towards me. At this point he looked at me so sharply that I was afraid that I had made a major blunder. He took a couple of steps over to the window and looked out for a few seconds and then turned back to me.

"You are going to San Isidro?"

I agreed that I was.

"Then you will need your rifle."

I explained that if I needed a rifle when I got there I could easily get one.

"And Professor Javier, he is in San Isidro?"

I said that I hoped he was. The man reached out a large, calloused hand. "I am Clemente Torres. This is my son, Francisco."

I replied that I was Miguel Hannigan. We shook hands, they wished me God speed and I was on my way.

I had neglected an elementary rule by failing to wring out my socks before hitting the trail that morning. My feet, already chafed from my exertions of the previous day, were now rubbed raw at both heels. Along with that, the drink of water didn't immediately remove the effects of dehydration; nor did it help that the pain starting in my fingers had moved up my right arm to the shoulder. But I was on my way with some hope of getting where I was supposed to be.

The trail began to wind upwards, and within a few minutes I had crossed over a ridge and was looking down into a deep valley. Across the valley loomed a towering mass of rock. I had better find that promised road soon or I would be as lost as ever. Following the trail downwards, half way to the floor of the valley I finally reached the road and began to walk slowly along the shoulder, hoping that an outstretched thumb meant the same in Talcayan as in North America. In the first twenty minutes a dilapidated mini-van and a sedan in similar condition rattled past on their way down the valley without slowing down. Eventually a pick-up truck hove noisily into view and ground to a stop. In the passenger seat was a comfortable looking, middle aged matron. Next to her the driver, a reasonable facsimile of the bearded mountain man I had just left, waved to me to get into the back of the truck. Given the length of time I had been without benefit of soap and water, it was probably just as well that I not share a confined space with anyone.

One hears stories, perhaps fictitious, of children who have put their wet pets in clothes dryers. After that drive down the valley I have some idea of what those pets might experience. At first I thought that the driver might be drunk, but in fact we were travelling no more than thirty miles an hour and the swerving back and forth was the only way to stay on the winding road and avoid the worst of the potholes. The sides of the back of the truck were scarcely a foot high, so standing up was not an option. To sit down, however, was to risk serious injury to the tailbone. Eventually I jammed myself into a corner, crouched on my haunches and reflected that Wile E. Coyote in pursuit of the roadrunner had enjoyed better days that this.

After a wild, swaying forty minutes the truck slowed and stopped at the point where our mountain road met the Camino Leandro. I climbed out stiffly, the driver waved and turned south towards El Puente Ingles and I crossed the road to what looked like the site of a garage sale. A neat little cottage stood off a ways from the highway. Closer by was a rectangular area enclosed by a chain link fence. Inside the fence were about twenty tables of different shapes and sizes on which various articles were laid out for sale. A short conversation with the proprietors, a middle-aged husband and wife, established that the San Isidro bus indeed stopped there whenever there were passengers to be picked up, but I had missed the morning run and the evening bus would not arrive until after six.

There were no edibles or potables for sale but I was directed to a pump located back near the cottage. I rummaged through the wares scattered on the tables and found a loud, red and yellow shirt that could replace the one I was wearing, which was badly in need of laundering. I also picked up a cup, a metal wash basin and a towel, paid for them and headed towards the pump. Having satisfied my thirst and performed such ablutions as modesty allowed, I had set about rinsing out my sweaty shirt and socks when the husband, who seemed to wear a perpetual smile, approached with a box of detergent, which I accepted and proceeded to wash the shirt and socks properly and lay them out on a wooden fence to dry in the sun. A few minutes later his wife, as cheerful looking as her husband, offered me a plate of beans and rice and a mug of coffee. Maybe they felt guilty because I had paid the listed price for my few purchases without haggling; or maybe they were just kind people; or probably both.

CHAPTER THIRTY FOUR

I spent the afternoon alternately dozing in the breeze with my back against a tree or joining a few others who wandered among the tables loaded with merchandize. It would have been a good opportunity to rest after the rigors of the last few hours had I access to some pain killers. By the time the bus arrived I had added to my purchases a wide-brimmed straw hat that didn't rise to the level of elegance of the sombreros one sees in Mexico, but it would ward off sunstroke and maybe even help me blend into the local scenery; and because arriving at lodgings without luggage could arouse suspicion I added a slightly frayed but serviceable backpack to my purchases.

I have had some acquaintance with antique vehicles in the Third World, so it was a pleasant surprise when at dusk a modern looking bus pulled up and stopped. I shook hands with and thanked the wife and husband, who were closing down their market, then picked up my backpack which now contained my Beretta along with several items of clothing. The few seats not occupied by passengers were filled with packages and luggage, but the driver hoisted a couple of items on to the overhead rack and cleared a place. The bus stopped every few miles along the highway and occasionally wandered off to villages some distance from the main road. The routine was repeated each time: stop in front of a store or eating place, a puffing sound as the

- 294 -

bus door opened, noisy greetings for those who got off the bus, hugs and subdued goodbyes for those getting ready to board, the door of the luggage compartment being slammed shut, the vehicle lurching back into motion, maneuvering through dark streets and eventually getting back on the main highway.

So I was finally on my way to some kind of showdown in San Isidro, with no idea of what to expect. I didn't even know whether Colonel McGrath and Professor Javier had reached that city safely. I had been intent on getting to San Isidro, but now I began to ask myself why I was going. Did I have a real choice? During the previous hours on the mountain I had focused on survival. When Will asked me to go along and help the professor get to San Isidro, I agreed without hesitation. Come to think of it, maybe the last real choice I had made about this whole Talcayan adventure was when Will and I decided to intervene against Fraga over six months ago. Yes, I could have refused to return to Talcayan, or I could have left after the Canadians were freed and let the citizens of Talcayan deal with the mess created by Flores; but was there any real chance I would do that? Was this the point that Mayor Laval had argued when we first met him? When you meet force with force you feel that you have to win, and then the enemy determines what you do. As the bus moved and stopped and started in the night, I felt like a pawn in a game that someone else was playing. It was probably the most depressed I had felt since leaving the army more than five years earlier.

At one of the stops I noticed a *farmacia* sign and the shop was still open. I begged the driver to give me a minute, hurried into the store, paid for a bottle of the strongest pain killers that the clerk would recommend and bolted back on to the bus. The instructions said that an adult dosage consisted of two pills, to be repeated if needed at six hour intervals. I swallowed four.

After a time the pain in my hand eased and I dropped off to sleep. I woke up thinking for some reason about a highlight, really the only highlight, of my teen-age baseball career, so I must have been dreaming about it. Being left-handed disqualified me for the so-called skill positions in the infield, and I was not much of a hitter, so I spent much of my youthful baseball career on the bench, occasionally called on as a pinch runner or defensive replacement at first base or the outfield. In the second last game I played, our under-eighteen team was pitted against a very good outfit from Burlington, Ontario. They had beaten us soundly in the first game of a best-of-three series for the national championship. Our starting pitcher in the second game was Walt Gessner, a burly, affable side-armer who kept both opponents and teammates on edge with his frequent wildness, but that afternoon he was in a groove. Unfortunately the fellow throwing for Burlington was just as good. We were behind one to nothing with two out in the top of the seventh when our number six hitter was grazed by a pitch and became our first base runner since the third inning. Our shortstop, scheduled to bat next, had struck out twice without fouling off a pitch. The coach waved to me. "Hannigan, get in there and see if you can at least get your bat on the ball. Give them a chance to make a mistake."

I strode to the plate with all the confidence I could muster. The opposing pitcher had tended to start off each hitter with a fastball, as low as he could throw it and still have it called a strike. True to form, his first pitch was a fastball over the plate just below the knees. I swung and connected, somewhat to my own surprise, and the line drive headed into the gap between center and right field. The base runner ahead of me took off like a scared jack rabbit, didn't slow down rounding third and scored easily, while I loped into second, assuming my best casual, all-in-a-day's-work demeanor. Gessner was up next and he managed to drive the ball through the middle of the infield, and at the crack of the bat I took off like a heavier-footed jackrabbit and beat the throw home by a couple of feet. Gessner, noted more for the speed of his fastball than for his speed afoot, was thrown out at second base, but it didn't matter. He atoned for his base running gaffe by mowing down the remaining Burlington hitters and we had all the scoring we needed.

I'm not sure what, if anything, my unconscious was trying to tell me with this memory—maybe just that every once in a while things go right. If it was trying to cheer me up it failed. I felt an aching nostalgia for that time now lost forever, something as different from the present as one could imagine.

It was ten o'clock when we reached the outskirts of San Isidro and began to move through the dark, quiet, almost deserted streets, through the dilapidated cottages of the only slum that I had encountered in Talcayan, then through a neighborhood of four or five story brick apartment blocks with lights peeping out through a few of the curtained windows. The bus terminal lay across a wide plaza from the *casa municipal*. A short distance down one of the streets leading away from the plaza was La Posada Margarita, which the bus driver assured me was "quite genteel, and not very expensive". It appeared to be a mansion that had been elegant in its time. Through the front door with its leaded glass one entered a wide hallway with dark wood paneling. Behind the desk at the foot of the winding staircase a youth with carefully styled hair looked at me with what I took to be distaste. Given my appearance I didn't much blame him. I signed my name and he took my passport and directed me to a third floor room that, judging from its size, must have served originally as servants' quarters; but it was clean and had a comfortable bed.

I showered and pondered putting on the only clean item in my back pack, my recently hand-laundered khaki shirt, but decided that until I knew more about the local situation anything that might identify me as a combatant was not in my interest. I returned to the first floor and asked the clerk whether there were any eating places open at this hour in the neighborhood. He shook his head.

"Any place where I could find food?"

"No, sir. The groceries close at seven."

"I've just arrived," I said, "And I haven't heard any news today. What's happening in the city?"

The young man was wary. "Not much new today."

"And Mayor Rendon? Is he in the city?" I needed to get some idea of what was going on, but I wasn't going about it very expertly.

"I don't know, I suppose so."

"And Mayor Flores? He's in town?"

"Yes. He's in town. Excuse me, but I don't get involved in politics."

"I'm not much interested in politics myself," I said. "But I want to know whether it's safe to go out on the streets. Are the regular police keeping order? Has there been any violence? I heard a couple of days ago that there was a threat of violence."

Now he sounded suspicious. "If you want to be safe on the streets and you heard there was going to be trouble in San Isidro, why did you come here?"

"I've been offered a job here," I replied. The statement was technically correct. "I'm not a rich man, and when there is a job opportunity, I take it."

He seemed to be reassured and became more forthcoming. Flores had taken over the military base and was basically in control of the city. Many of the San Isidro police force had gone over to Flores. Yes, my informant had heard that Professor Javier had supporters and was going to arrive in San Isidro soon, but there had been no sign of him. No, my informant had not heard of a Colonel McGrath and certainly had not heard of any such person having come into the city. He had heard of some soldiers entering the city to support Professor Javier, but he knew of no one who had seen them. Everyone said that tomorrow morning President Gracida would resign and the senators would elect Mayor Flores as president because his police and army were powerful and the senators were afraid to oppose him. My informant stopped at this last remark, perhaps aware that he had strayed across the line into political commentary.

I asked for my passport back, explaining that I wanted to take a short walk and would need to identify myself if I were accosted by a policeman. He handed it over and raised his eyebrows, thinking perhaps that anyone fool enough to venture abroad at that hour deserved whatever he got. I wasn't crazy about the idea myself, but I didn't want to go to bed if Will was waiting and maybe depending on me.

I saw no one as I crossed the plaza and entered an avenue running westward. On the left side of the avenue there were blocks of apartment buildings several stories high. On the right was the bank of the San Isidro River. Presumably there were points along here where during the day one could enjoy a view of the valley, because the river bank at this point was perhaps a hundred feet above the river; but at this time of night all that was visible across the street was a bicycle path and, beyond that, rows of trees looming out of the darkness. At one point a

THE BLOOD-DIMMED TIDE IS LOOSED

couple of youths cycled by, but otherwise the place was deserted. A mile or so from my starting point the avenue turned slightly away from the river and there, the first building on the right, was an impressive stone structure surrounded by a high iron fence and lit up with floodlights. It was the presidential mansion, which I had seen on my previous visit to the city. I approached the guardhouse, told one of the men that I had a message for Colonel McGrath, and offered him the folded paper on which I had written that I was in the city and could be reached at La Posada Margarita. The guard waved me away. "There's no Colonel McGrath here."

It was a long shot. Even if Professor Javier had made contact with the president, that need not mean that the colonel was here or would be known to the guards. On the other hand, the fact that the guards had indicated no interest might mean that they were not in the pay of Flores. Of course if they were in the pay of that thug then I hadn't improved my situation by mentioning the colonel's name.

The National Assembly Building was another fifteen minute walk further, and it was as deserted as the avenue. I walked around the building and the plaza in front of it and came upon no sign of life. On my way back to my lodgings the guards at the presidential residence paid no attention to me. Whatever might be going on behind closed doors, this part of the city was dark, quiet and seemingly calm. I was alone and felt like a loose bolt that had fallen off a truck and lay in the gutter.

I awoke the next morning shortly after five. The youth behind the desk near the front door had been replaced by a dark, sharp-featured woman of perhaps forty years of age. A name plate on the desk indicated that she was Adriana San Felipe. When I gave my name she closed the drawer where she evidently was prepared to retrieve my passport, put up a finger to indicate I should wait just a second, and disappeared into a room across the hall. She returned promptly, handed me the passport and said quietly: "The police were here in the middle of the night to check passports. Before you arrived yesterday evening a couple of men came by, friends of yours I believe. They said that if you should happen to stay here over night it would not be good if the wrong people should learn about that fact."

- 299 -

I wanted to call our training camp to see if anyone there might know where I could contact Colonel McGrath, and I asked Adriana San Felipe if I could use the telephone. She answered that it was quite possible that the telephone in the posada was tapped. Then she gestured to the passport in my hand. "Perhaps the information you need is there."

A note stuck inside the cover of the passport indicated that there were friends of mine to be found at 64 Isabella. A map on the wall indicated that Calle Isabella was only a ten minute walk away. There was a small restaurant just off the plaza on one of the side streets, and anxious as I was to join my friends, my stomach had just about run out of patience, so I splurged on a couple of omelets and other edibles that I presume were bad for me and washed them down with multiple cups of coffee. Thus fortified I strode out to meet the day feeling almost human.

CHAPTER THIRTY FIVE

There were a few people on Calle Isabella at that early hour, most of them walking purposefully as though going about their daily business. The three or four loiterers made me a bit nervous, but there wasn't much I could do about it. I came to a massive, four-story stone building that extended several hundred feet along the street, stopped at an entrance marked "64" and was looking for a bell or buzzer when one of two heavy doors opened part way and a soldier in a Canadian uniform bade me enter. I remembered him from the training camp.

Without wasting time on greetings, he led the way through a vaulted passage into a courtyard packed with soldiers and scattered pieces of equipment and shouted, "Colonel, Mick Hannigan is here." In a few seconds the colonel made his way through the crowd and greeted me with a "Thank God". In answer to his solicitude about my welfare I stated that I was well and all I needed to get to work were a weapon and my pain killers. Will explained that, assuming that if I was able to get to San Isidro it would be by bus, he had sent a couple of men down to the terminal to watch for me. However, they had noticed that they were under surveillance by several other persons. Will's two men had decided that rather than attract further unwelcome attention

- 301 -

they would leave messages for me at the five hotels or posadas in the neighborhood of the bus terminal.

"We're in a bit of a rush here," the colonel continued. "We leave in a few minutes for the National Assembly Building. Soldiers have a favorite prayer: 'Please Lord, make my enemies stupid.' This time it's been answered. Flores decided to consolidate his position by occupying the barracks and fortified parade ground and he has gathered the main body of his forces there. Two nights ago we brought most of our tiny army into town quietly and hid them as best we could throughout the city. The barracks and grounds that Flores occupies run along the San Isidro River. In the middle of last night we moved most of our troops and equipment and set up not too far away from each of the three gates to the parade grounds. We trucked in some concrete barriers and sand bags so we have some protection. At the same time a gunner in our helicopter shot holes in several boats that Flores had docked along the river front. The consignment of ammunition arrived yesterday from Canada by way of Mendoza, and that's out there too.

"If he wants to move his army out of the barracks to take over government buildings this morning he has to overrun our position, which he must realize he's not likely to do. We don't have many men there, and most of them are inexperienced, but they will be shooting from behind barriers. Captain Winfield and the Canadians with a few of our recent recruits are facing the west gate. In front of the east gate we have Villalobos and his men and a few others, and one of our IVFs. The main body of those we have been training and the other IVF are in front of the central gate, along with those of Rendon's police who have not deserted and can be spared from duties elsewhere. Here in this courtyard we have fifty of our greenest recruits. This is one of our many weak spots. These fellows have to defend the National Assembly Building this morning. If Flores has hidden away a reserve force somewhere close, then we're in trouble. We simply don't have enough men, and certainly not enough experienced men, to repel a serious attack.

"Well, here's the plan. At eight o'clock President Gracida will announce his resignation. Flores has been pressuring him to do so, presuming that when Gracida accedes to his demands the way is clear

THE BLOOD-DIMMED TIDE IS LOOSED

for Flores to take over. Until two this morning I don't think he had any idea we had an organized force in the city. Rendon's people are in charge of security inside the National Assembly Building. We have four guards whom the mayor trusts inside the senate chamber and two more outside the main door. If there's an effort by pro-Flores people already in the building to storm the senate chamber we'll need someone to help the two guards at the door. I scouted the place yesterday. I'll tell you when we get there where I want you stationed. Now get a rifle. We'll be leaving shortly."

The events of the morning proceeded like a well-rehearsed pageant. The fifty soldiers in the courtyard piled into two army trucks. Four of us led the way in an open jeep, the colonel and I standing in the back, Felipe Diaz in uniform seated with the driver in front. There was little immediate risk. As far as we knew, Flores and his men had no indication of what was going on, and it was hard to imagine that one of his followers would happen to be on our route and risk death by attacking us. Our bravado in standing up was mainly for the benefit of our troops, although the few people we passed on the way seemed to sense that something important was happening and they looked on with some interest.

Once arrived at the square, our troops formed up in two lines and marched smartly across the square towards a reviewing stand set up before the glass-fronted National Assembly building. Soldiers at the rear of the lines dropped off at intervals to form a guard of ten men on each side of the walk. The remaining thirty men marched to their assigned places at the back and on each side of the building. On cue, the senators began to arrive, leave their automobiles and make their way between the two rows of troops to the building. Will, Felipe and I had remained where the automobiles were unloading their passengers, and Will whispered that the senators who could be trusted had been told what was going on. Those in the Flores camp had expected to come to confirm his election and were showing understandable confusion. A few whose loyalties were unknown had been told only that President Gracida was resigning and they were to be at the National Assembly Building at eight o'clock to elect his successor.

- 303 -

With the electors duly ushered into the Assembly Building, a limousine drove up and President Gracida debarked. He was a tall, ruggedly handsome, relatively young man. This must have been a painful ordeal for him. In a situation requiring less ruthlessness and guile he might have been a successful president. Two senior senators had remained behind to welcome him. Will, Felipe and I walked ahead of them to the reviewing stand. When we reached it, President Gracida approached the microphone and addressed the soldiers and a small group of onlookers briefly, graciously conveying the thanks of the nation to the soldiers for making possible the continuation of democracy in Talcayan. No sooner had he quit speaking than another limousine drew up. Professor Javier emerged, still with his cane but walking confidently between another two senior senators to the reviewing stand where he was welcomed in a few words by President Gracida, and the two of them entered the building together. The choreography was proceeding as planned.

Passing through the front door of the National Assembly Building we entered a sunny, three-story atrium that ran the width of the structure. Will motioned to a stairs at one end and directed me to the uppermost landing, from which I could command pretty much the whole space. After I had taken up my position the two guards at the door of the senate chamber looked up, grinned and saluted. If I made those two guards feel a bit more secure, then there was a morsel of validity in Mayor Rendon's insistence on my appearing in San Isidro.

Apparently events unfolded with equal order and decorum in the senate chamber. The outgoing president made a short speech tendering his resignation, expressing his thanks to those who had helped and supported him in office and offering his prayers for the honorable man who would take up the burden of government. The chair of the senate then read the rules governing election of the president. Senators in alphabetical order stood and stated the name of the person for whom they wished to vote. The results: Pablo Javier, sixty one votes; Miguel Flores, forty one votes; sundry other candidates, seven votes; absent, six members. Will emerged from the chamber following the last senators to leave and muttered as we made our way towards a meeting room on the second floor, "That was the easy part. In the next day or two we find out whether we have been play acting or saving the country."

In the meeting room the new president took his place at the head of a conference table. Around the table were seated all of the mayors except Flores, several prominent senators who were expected to take a leading role in the new regime, and two younger men and a woman who would serve as special assistants to the new president. The session began with Will's report on the military situation. He stressed that we should not put too much stock in the smooth process that morning. It was made possible by a blunder by Flores when he allowed his main force to be hemmed in at an important time. But before that, Flores may have made a smarter decision in dictating the time of battle. The colonel had been wondering why Flores was willing to provoke an open fight in spite of the fact that the government forces had better weapons. However, the mayor of Valdez no doubt recognized that the government had not yet recruited enough troops and had not had time to train them properly. For all we knew he might have as many or even twice as many armed men in the city as did the national forces, and his troops would probably be mostly mercenaries and experienced veterans whereas most of ours were insufficiently trained and completely unseasoned.

"Unless something unexpected happens," Will cautioned, "in the short term Flores probably has an advantage. We don't know how many soldiers he has outside of the military camp/parade ground where we have him hemmed in, but there are some. Our little reconnaissance plane has been busy and it in combination with our helicopter have discouraged the movement of larger collections of Flores forces towards the capital and within the city, but inevitably a considerable number will get through. We have had to commit most of our resources to one spot to keep Flores confined. That means we have few resources to counter any incursion by the enemy elsewhere. So they can attack or harass us at times of their choosing, and maybe cut off our supply lines. Also, by this time they must surely have figured out that they have been hurt by our reconnaissance plane and helicopter. I suspect that right now they have an order in with their drug lord friends to send in a couple of aircraft to blow us out of the sky.

"Meanwhile, our effort to recruit more fighters is going slowly. Yesterday morning our recruiters reported that they had gathered a group of maybe seventy people, some on horseback, some on foot, a hundred kilometers to the south. We sent some trucks and buses to get them into the city as quickly as we could. When the buses got to them a few hours ago the numbers had gone up, and that has slowed down their progress because they wanted to keep together and they couldn't all get on board the vehicles. We hope they get into the city by tomorrow morning. But few of these are trained. Also, over the next several days we face the real possibility of defections from our troops in San Isidro. These men may already recognize that their tactical position is not good. It should not surprise us if some of them decide that this is not their fight."

The colonel paused for a moment, and then continued. "I've given you the bad news. There is some good news. Thus far we have much better intelligence than the enemy has. So long as our little plane is allowed to roam at will, we will probably keep that advantage. Actually, I'm not sure that Flores recognizes the importance of intelligence. It helps that by and large the population is on our side, or at worst neutral, so not many people are going to tell our enemies anything and quite a few of them are willing to keep us informed. Our other advantage is that, for the time being at least, we likely have considerably more firepower than Flores has. Any time they come out into the open to attack us we can probably destroy them. As long as our helicopter can operate in the open, some of our fire power is mobile. It can hit almost any target with rockets. Are there questions?"

Colonel McGrath could be overpowering, even intimidating. That isn't always easy to take, but it comes in handy when you have to deliver a bleak message and still give the impression that you are in command of the situation.

Mayor Guzman spoke up immediately. "If we have superior weapons, then do you plan to attack Flores before he gets reinforcements from outside of the city?"

Will explained that our superior fire power gave us a great advantage if they came out into the open and attacked us. We didn't have the heavy artillery or bombs that would destroy their defenses.

If we attacked the walled parade ground today we could use up all our ammunition and perhaps not dislodge them.

"So what are we going to do?" Guzman asked.

Will replied that what we would do depended on what the enemy did. "Our advantage in the present situation is that we don't have to attack, but Flores eventually must either attack us or surrender. If he attacks he must come out into the open and then he loses. That's the situation unless Mayor Flores gets substantial outside help. If his friends show up in such numbers and with the kind of weapons that might overwhelm us, we will make a tactical retreat, possibly even moving some of our troops into the mountains and put up only token resistance until we get outside help. Even the best planned retreat can involve serious losses."

President Javier then officially confirmed Colonel McGrath as the temporary commander of the national army. It might sound unorthodox to make a foreigner the commander-in-chief, he granted, but our soldiers do not believe that any of their own people could lead them to victory. If the colonel were not in command, few men would be willing to fight. "And," the president added, "I am not one of that few. If the colonel were not with us I would not have been elected, and even if I were elected it would have been an empty charade."

President Javier asked whether it would discourage defections if he visited our troops to show them that the president is with them. Will agreed that it would be an excellent move for the president to make, but there would be no desertions during the day. Perhaps the president might come in the evening and put some heart into the men before they settled down for the night watch.

From there the discussion went on to other matters. President Javier was concerned that Flores had gotten so many votes in spite of the fact that none of the other mayors had supported him. It showed either that many of the senators were scared or they had been paid off by the mayor of Valdez. Some may even have believed that he had the power and resources to bring order and security to Talcayan.

Will and I left the meeting at that point and drove to the east end of the city to the level piece of land that was the present focus of operations. For the last part of the trip we got into an armored personnel carrier.

The driver explained that Flores probably didn't have anything that he could fire at us that would be likely to hit a moving target, so we should buckle up but be ready to unbuckle just in case a shell fell close enough to topple the carrier. He then took off like a drag racer and sped us into the shelter of our encampment facing the central gate.

The south wall of the parade grounds facing us was almost a quarter mile long. The largest gate was approximately at its centre. There was another gate in the west end of the enclosed area and a third at the east end. We referred to them as gates, but they were really heavy metal doors. We had come to a stop behind our IVF (M2 Bradley Infantry Fighting Vehicle), which stood with its guns ready to fire point blank across approximately two hundred yards at the central gate. Sandbags were piled around the front of it. Stretching for fifty yards on each side was a combination of concrete slabs and sandbags and behind these were soldiers armed with rifles, grenade launchers, mortars, rocket launchers and whatever else they could get their hands on from the supply that had arrived the previous day. A similar, smaller blockade faced each of the other two gates.

Why hadn't Flores blown our people to bits as they were getting all of this stuff in place? Will explained that at two A.M. they had put on a sound and light show. The first vehicles that slipped into the area had carried sound equipment and very bright lights. When in position they turned on the amplifiers to full volume and started flashing a couple of dozen lights for about two seconds at a time, moving them between flashes so that marksmen would not get a fix on them. Behind this wall of noise and light the heavier equipment moved in. The enemy fired off round after round without hitting anything. Even when they began sending up flares, their marksmen seemed to be sufficiently dazzled by the intermittent flashes that they were missing their targets. Besides, for most of the time our troops were either in relatively rapid movement or hiding behind cover. So the equipment had been put in place by four o'clock. Then the sound and lights were turned off and our troops either rested or began filling sandbags and digging shallow trenches. Aware that in time they might have to hold off an attack from the other side, they had begun this morning to put up sandbags on either side of the shallow trenches.

"Even if we hadn't put on that show," Will said, "I think there was only one way that Flores could hope to stop us from setting up our equipment. That was to order his men out into the open and try to overrun us. That would have taken a while to organize, and I suspect that most of his people would not be anxious to expose themselves to our IVFs and other gadgets."

I took my place with the soldiers, alternating between keeping watch for any action by the enemy and digging the trench and filling bags with dirt and piling them up as a shield against direct enemy fire. The armored vehicle in which we arrived sped away and after a while returned at equal speed with our noonday meal. The food reflected Colonel McGrath's belief that soldiers will usually tolerate danger, poor pay and rigorous conditions for at least a little while without serious grumbling if they are well fed. Will drifted over to where I sat munching on a roll and sat down.

"Just between you and me," he said in English, "I hate this situation. There's too damn much that we don't know. What kind of ammunition do they have behind that wall? Are there people getting ready to attack us from behind? How many of our boys are going to slink away when the sun goes down? How long before some drug lord sends them some high tech help? From here on we don't control the fight. We wait for them to act and hope they make a mistake. That's a helluva shaky strategy, but it's the only one we've got. Maybe they'll decide they can't dislodge us and they'll want to bargain rather than be starved out—but I don't think so. Maybe they'll underestimate us and try a frontal attack from their position behind that wall. First they'd have to try to soften us up with a bombardment, but I think we can do more damage of that kind than they can, especially because of our air-to-ground rockets from the helicopter. Anyone ever tells you that the uncertainty of battle is exhilarating—he's insane."

During the morning there had been a good deal of chatter and even some laughter among my fellow diggers. After lunch things were quiet. I hoped that it was just because they were missing their siestas, not because they were starting to get cold feet as the time for confrontation neared. I took comfort from the thought of Flores and his men watching us quietly expanding our defenses while they, apparently, were doing

- 309 -

nothing. Of course they may have been waiting for reinforcements to arrive and give them an easy victory. Will was right. There was too much that we didn't know; but digging the trench and filling the sandbags at least gave our men something better to do than to wait and bite their nails.

CHAPTER THIRTY SIX

An hour later I was taking my turn at the surveillance part of our routine when there was a shout, "Man approaching from the gate." A figure was coming towards us and waving a white flag. I trained the scope of my rifle on him to get a better look. It was a young man, hardly more than a boy, dressed in military garb. About half way between the gate and our position he broke into a run. Will shouted to our men to be alert but in no circumstances to fire in any direction. But a shot was fired, not from our side but from behind the young man, and he pitched forward.

There were several stretchers stacked a few yards away and I grabbed one, scrambled over our sand bag fortification and ran towards the fallen figure. Within a few strides I realized there was someone else running almost beside me. Then there was a second shot, this one hitting the dirt just to one side of us. I dived to the ground and shouted to my companion to do likewise. There was a hush for an instant and then it was broken by the colonel shouting orders that I couldn't quite make out.

Within seconds all hell broke loose, volley after volley of rifle fire, rockets shooting over our heads, then explosions of mortars up ahead. All of the firing seemed to be coming from our side. Actually, if the training of our men for the last few weeks had been successful my companion and I were not in acute danger, but it's hard to relax when explosives whistle over your head and you know they've been launched by men fighting their first battle.

After perhaps a minute the firing suddenly ceased. Will bellowed over the megaphone: "Stretcher bearers, either return to base or proceed to pick up the injured man." I looked over at my companion, who was dressed in the light green, loose fitting trousers and shirt that identified him as a non-combatant. He was unscathed, so I got up with the stretcher and ran the few yards that separated us from the injured man, who was conscious but bleeding from a wound in the back. We placed him as gently as we could on the stretcher, walked quickly back to our post and handed the stretcher with the injured man over the pile of sandbags to waiting hands. I clambered back over the barrier and more-or-less collapsed. My companion, apparently made of sterner stuff, accompanied the stretcher at a brisk walk as it was carried back to where we had set up a makeshift medical unit. The colonel watched him go and just shook his head.

The central gate two hundred yards in front of us was in shambles. Both doors had been blown off their hinges. The two pillars that held up the doors had been partially destroyed. The few windows in the wall in front of us were smashed and clouds of smoke and dust rose from within the enclosure.

Will was at my shoulder. "Interesting little diversion that. What would you say happened here?"

When I didn't have anything to say, Will continued. "My guess is that the lad with the white flag was trying to pull a fast one. He was deserting. I doubt that Flores is in any mood to bargain at this point, and if he were he would let us know that a negotiator was on the way, and the negotiator wouldn't be a lad in his teens. Thank God for the presence of mind of you two. We couldn't let him bleed to death in front of our eyes."

I asked him whether he thought that this turn of events would hurt us. Will pondered a moment. "On balance, I think it could help. Yeah, we can't afford to keep blasting away at a brick wall or we'll be run out of ammunition; but we had to do something about them not honoring your attempt to rescue a wounded man. So they know we want to play by the rules and we'll be a mite testy about violations. They already know we have lots of fire power, but it doesn't hurt to demonstrate it. I doubt that they'll be anxious to engage us in an exchange of fire until they get some outside help. That may buy us some breathing room."

Will got our sound system cranked up to full volume and announced to the Flores people that if they had injured men and didn't have adequate medical care they could send them out to us and they would be attended to. The people who brought them out would be allowed to return to their base. As he put down the microphone he explained, "It's the humanitarian thing to do, and it tells any waverers over there that, if their leader hasn't provided proper medical support and we have, maybe they're on the wrong side."

There was no response to the colonel's offer. The smoke had scarcely cleared when the now-familiar armored personnel carrier sped into sight and drew up next to our troops facing the west gate. From where I was digging I couldn't get much of a look, but word came down the line that it was *El Presidente*. He didn't stay there long, perhaps realizing that the Canadians would not be inspired to greater efforts by being reminded that they were fighting Talcayan's battle, and the local recruits who had been integrated rather completely with the Canadians, even if they wanted to steal away during the night, might not find it easy to do so.

The armored vehicle sped away from the west gate, circled and approached our position partially sheltered by our primitive fortifications. The president emerged with his cane and in the same gray suit in which he had taken the oath of office a few hours earlier. With Colonel McGrath at his side he tramped along the uneven ground next to the trench, shaking hands with the diggers and those keeping watch. His presence and demeanor must have been a powerful reminder to our raw recruits that they were part of something historic. We just might get through this mess.

It was getting dark when the president had finished his review of the Villalobos brigade in front of the east gate and left in the personnel carrier. Will called me aside and gave me an update. The young man whom we had rescued that afternoon had not revealed much about his own intentions, but he was grateful that we had saved his life and he provided some information that Will thought was probably reliable. Flores had on his payroll a soldier of fortune known simply as Volmer, of unspecified national origin and with no known loyalties or principles. When Volmer rented out the services of his band of mercenaries he didn't consider only the money but also the chance of success, having no intention of dying for a losing cause merely to enrich his heirs. He and his crew were not with Flores in the barracks, no doubt because he was too canny to get caught in a situation that limited his mobility and his options. Now Flores was depending on him to spearhead an attack on our camp, but first Volmer had to assemble and organize a considerable number of men who had remained scattered around the country because they hadn't been deemed necessary for the kind of swift operation that Flores had envisioned.

The colonel added more discouraging news. In the last twenty four hours the new recruits who were coming north to San Isidro seemed to have slowed down. Will had expected them in the city by dawn tomorrow at the latest, but now the word was that they would be lucky to get here any time tomorrow. Equally disheartening, apparently the tank was not yet operational and was still being repaired in Amparo.

"It's curious," Will said. "Until today I talked to either Dolores Laval or a man named Diego Sanchez. Today neither of them has called. The reports have been given by some guy named Augusto Mayo. Just in case there's something fishy going on I asked him, both times we talked, to put me in touch with Laval or Sanchez. He said he would search for them and have them call. Neither has called and I can't get through to either of them. I've sent a couple of our men in a jeep to try and contact them and make sure our information is accurate, but we probably won't hear from them tonight. One more damned thing we don't know."

Most of the land around the barracks and our camp was flat with sightlines of a quarter to a half mile in each direction. The exception was the area around the position held by Villalobos. Behind him was a small ravine, deep enough that he was able to keep the horses on which most of his men had arrived out of the line of fire of the enemy behind the wall. But on the other side of this depression was a considerable hill with a flat top. That would be the likely staging area for any force assembled to attack us. As long as anyone up there stayed away from the brow of the hill they were out of sight of our guns. To keep the space clear of the enemy would take more troops than we could spare.

In their last reconnaissance of the parade ground Harold Pelletier and his photographer had detected a shift of men and equipment within the enclosure to the east end. Flores presumably realized that the east gate was our weak point, and that if Volmer could assemble a force on the hill to attack Villalobos from one side and Flores' forces behind the wall hit them from the other, he could break out through the east gate and inflict severe losses on us and perhaps demolish our whole force.

I asked Will whether he had plans in case that scenario began to be played out. He grunted that there was not much we could do, but his "not much" was quite a lot. He would divert some of his men watching the central gate to reinforce Villalobos. Half of our mortars were being set to fire on the hill. Two of the three "mad pelicans" would leave Captain Winfield's company at the west gate and take up a position from which they could quickly swing into action in case of an attack on Villalobos from the hill. "Mad pelicans" was what we had taken to calling vehicles that consisted of a heavy machine gun mounted on a chassis with four solid rubber tires and some armor to protect the motor, the driver and the gunner. The advantage of the weapon was its mobility. Being able to bring heavy machine guns into action at a particular point on short notice could be decisive in a limited skirmish.

Will continued. Once an attack had started or seemed imminent he might move our IVF from our position facing the central gate to join the Villalobos troops and attack either the forces descending from the hill or those coming out of the east gate. Every mortar we had would be aimed either at the hill or the east end of the enclosure. Meanwhile, Winfield had on hand a couple of rockets large enough to blast the west gate off its hinges, and his troops would move forward as quickly as possible while the enemy was getting its bearings after the blast. Winfield would try to get through the gate and bring machine guns and rockets to bear on whatever they could see, and give the Flores forces at the east gate something else to think about. The helicopter, whose main job thus far had been to stand by and be ready to protect our ammunition supply, would move to attack the hill, unless there were signs that the enemy was also preparing to bring pressure to bear on our supply depot.

"And," he added, "we'll pray a lot, because every single move we make could fail; and we need every one of them to succeed. One more thing. I always save the easy parts for you. Villalobos has had the unexpected humility to admit that he needs some more marksmen to make sure the people behind that wall keep their heads down. Flores will want to attack Villalobos directly. If they just exchange mortar fire with us we can probably match them two to one or better, and maybe with more accuracy. I told Villalobos that we had a sniper or two to spare, so if you agree, I'll send you and a couple of others over to join him."

So in the gathering dusk three of us approached the encampment in front of the east gate, satisfied the sentry that we were the reinforcements whom they had been told to expect and had our first face-to-face encounter with Villalobos, who was living up to his reputation as a man to be reckoned with. He was younger than I had expected, perhaps in his early forties, over six feet tall, bearded, gruff and peremptory in manner. He greeted us briefly and took a look at my bandaged fingers. "You can handle a rifle with a hand like that?"

I assured him that I was left handed and had figured out how to use a rifle without putting pressure on the fingers of my right hand. He then pointed to two spots behind us where his men had build up piles of dirt to give their marksmen a slightly higher vantage point. Between the two mounds he had positioned the second IVF. But, Villalobos pointed out, his snipers were still lower than the top of the wall facing them. His fear was that prior to an all-out attack Flores would have machine gunners pop up behind that wall and fire down on the Villalobos forces. The IVF was crucially important if Villalobos was to repulse an attack, and so it had been protected with sandbags. Men shooting from the top of the wall, however, could fire over the sandbags and take out the IVF or at least cripple its crew.

Villalobos then led me over to a contraption that was something like a cherry picker, the kind of machine that city workers use to trim the high branches of trees and electricians use to work with overhead wires. "My idea," he went on, "is to have a couple of people get in the bucket at the end of the arm of that machine, raise themselves high enough to spot anyone that appears over that wall before they come into the view of our snipers or the IVF. Don't go too high or you come within the line of fire of the Flores people on the ground behind that wall."

The ravine behind us dictated that the trench and the sand-bag barrier here were much closer to the wall than was the case in front of the west and central gates. We were maybe seventy yards from the gate. There were no windows within range of our position, so if the enemy wanted to fire at us it would be from the top of the wall or through the east gate, which was of course closed at the moment. Villalobos continued. "The IVF and our snipers will fire at anything that pokes up above the wall. But from that bucket a marksman could spot any movement a second earlier. It could make a big difference. What do you think?"

My unexpressed thought was that with marksmen in four or five cherry pickers to cover the expanse of wall, it was a good idea. For two men in one cherry picker, it was the kind of adventure you probably wouldn't boast about to your grandchildren, because there was a very good chance you would not be around to talk to your grandchildren about anything. The snipers up in that bucket would be the target of choice for Flores' men preparing to attack. Once fighting began one might enjoy a brief moment during which one could keep the enemy ducking, but eventually they would have five or six shooters appear at different points along the wall and fire at the snipers in the bucket at the same time.

On the other hand, it might be the only available way to protect the men we had asked to join us in the fight, so I agreed. Villalobos sent the two men who had accompanied me up to the mounds behind us. He then introduced me to Juan, a young lad who would join me for the night watch. Villalobos explained that when it looked like an attack was imminent Juan would be replaced by a more experienced marksman. I got into the bucket and fiddled with the controls until I had a feel for how to maneuver up, down and crossways. As an afterthought I removed the scope from my rifle. In answer to a quizzical look from

Villalobos I explained that aiming with the scope would take longer than with the usual sights, and in that situation it was speed that counted.

There was not likely to be much action unless or until Volmer had assembled a force on the hill behind us, and at the time of the evening meal our scout up there had reported no sign of action. Juan and I began to take two-hour shifts aloft, with the person off duty trying to rest. Surprisingly perhaps, I actually slept for a while.

As I was getting ready to begin another shift aloft a report came in from our spies on the hill. Apparently at least a few of Volmer's men had arrived, slipping in silently on foot. Villalobos ordered our observers to retreat off the hill. A few minutes later from my perch in high I detected movement near our camp in front of the central gate, and from the noise my guess was that the colonel had already ordered the two mad pelicans to take up positions closer to the hill. For the next while we kept getting more messages—more build up of hostile forces on the hill, no evidence yet of mechanized armament, but a steadily growing number, impossible to estimate, of foot soldiers. In view of the number of small rockets and other weapons that can be carried by men on foot, their lack of mechanized weaponry was a limited blessing.

By four o'clock the build-up on the hill had continued, and now we could hear motors up there, and observers closer to the action reported that a couple of armored personnel carriers had arrived. A tall, tense young man with thick glasses appeared at the base of our cherry picker and waved me down. He introduced himself as Carlos Villalobos. "Yeah," he said. "I'm his son. I'm not a bad marksman. Father wants two men up in the bucket from now on."

So I spent the rest of the night in the contraption talking with Carlos to keep the two of us from dozing off. Every minute or two I would shift our position a bit. It probably wouldn't save us if those behind that wall were really anxious to pick us off, but there was no point in making things easy for them. The night dragged on. As light began to show on the eastern horizon we concluded that Flores preferred to attack by daylight. He had to dislodge us from behind our sand bag barriers, and for this he might prefer visibility.

The sun rose on an almost cloudless autumn day. Several hundred yards to the east along the river a stand of trees appeared in the morning haze. I thought of what must be one of the most familiar quatrains in American poetry.

> The woods are lovely, dark and deep,
> But I have promises to keep,
> And miles to go before I sleep,
> And miles to go before I sleep.

Yes, the woods were lovely, dark and deep, and they beckoned seductively; but what had become of my promises, or at least assurances, to the folks back home that I would not take serious risks? As to the miles to go before I slept, it was a nice thought, but there was an excellent chance that my long sleep would begin before I had traveled fifty yards.

Shortly after daybreak Villalobos senior approached, signed to me to descend to the ground, waved his son out of the bucket and got in himself, explaining that he wanted a minute with Miguel Hannigan. Once we were back to the upper level he explained the situation as he and Colonel McGrath had assessed it a few minutes earlier. Volmer had gathered a crowd on top of the hill, many more than we had expected. There might be five hundred men. There might be a thousand. There were so many that to find space some of them had taken positions down the far side of the hill. Meanwhile, over twenty of Colonel McGrath's men had deserted during the night. The colonel still didn't have definite word about the number or whereabouts of the reinforcements that Dolores Laval and Diego Sanchez were accompanying from the south. If Volmer came at us from the hill and Flores attacked from the barracks we could inflict heavy losses, but if they were willing to sustain those losses there was a good chance that they would overrun us.

In the opinion of the colonel, the situation was grave but not hopeless. If Villalobos wished to withdraw, then the señor could retreat with his men and the colonel would cover their retreat if they were fired on. Señor Villalobos had then asked what McGrath intended to do if Villalobos pulled out. The colonel would retreat with his own men, and Winfield would hold his position in order to cover the colonel's

- 319 -

retreat. Then Winfield would withdraw. "It's up to you," McGrath had told Villalobos. "If you choose to stay and fight, we will stay."

"My men and I are staying," Villalobos told me. "But in fairness you should know the situation."

We dropped to ground level and Señor Villalobos hurried back to his command post, his son took his place and we went aloft again, feeling especially exposed because, while we had to keep our eyes on the wall in front of us, the first enemy assault would very likely come from the hill behind us.

CHAPTER THIRTY SEVEN

Hardly had we settled in to continue our watch when there was a faint rumbling in the distance. As it got nearer one could distinguish, first the sound of motors and the grinding of gears, but then, unmistakably, the sound of human voices. It was coming from the south, behind our company facing the central gate. I dared not take my eyes off the top of the wall for more than a second or two at a time, and reminded Carlos to be equally vigilant. Then a jeep appeared more than a half kilometer away, where a road led into the field where we were encamped. It was moving slowly, then a tank appeared behind it, and that was followed two columns of men on horses, and bringing up the rear a less orderly crowd of people on foot.

Judgment Day, I thought. Here were Flores' reinforcements moving into position to cut off our line of retreat. Our allies were not due for hours, and they didn't have the tank in operation. I asked Carlos to keep an eye on my section of the wall as well as his own, and picked up the scope that lay on the floor of the bucket. A jeep sped south from Will's station opposite the central gate towards the cavalcade, followed by an orderly column of maybe fifty troops moving on the double. As the two vehicles met, my scope revealed something that gave me a jolt. One of two figures standing in the back of the jeep leading the parade was a woman. She was too far away to make out her features, but there

- 321 -

was no mistaking that mane of dark, tied-back hair. Another former prisoner of El Alcázar had arrived.

It was stretching my luck to leave all the surveillance to young Villalobos so I went back to what I was supposed to be doing. The rest of the proceedings I followed with a quick glance every minute or so. The tank turned and began lumbering towards the hill and then stopped while the column of men that had come on the double formed up on each flank. Two men climbed out of the tank and several of the new arrivals got into it. The riders dismounted, left their horses in the care of some of the people who had arrived on foot and formed a second line of foot soldiers. Of the rest of the new arrivals, some formed a much more numerous third row of infantry behind the tank while the others made their way towards Will's position in front of the central gate. While this maneuvering was going on a truck arrived with ammunition for the tank's guns. Then the tank began to move again slowly and the three lines of infantry followed. They had scarcely begun their advance when we heard explosions at the top of the hill. It was mortar fire originating from Will's troops facing the main gate. The first few salvos seemed to overshoot the target but they soon began to find the range and land on the top of the hill.

I would have expected the two mad pelicans to have accompanied the tank, but instead they moved quickly to the side of the hill nearest us. By this time Mateo Villalobos and maybe thirty men had mounted their horses, and formed up behind the mad pelicans and made their way up the hill, approaching from the north while the tank and accompanying crowd moved in noisily from the west.

Just as the mad pelicans reached the brow of the hill the first shots erupted from the top of the wall in front of us. Carlos was keeping watch over everything to the right of the gate and I was responsible for everything to the left. It was clear from the start that the enemy was aware of our perch and they began by opening fire on our bucket; and apparently they had already realized the wisdom of firing at us from a number of positions at once.

What saved us, for the moment at least, was that they were not perfectly synchronized in their first attempt. A figure popped up behind the wall slightly to Carlos's side of the gate, but I saw him first and I was able at least to wing him after his first burst of fire went over our heads. Immediately two and then three figures appeared on my section of the wall. My second shot at the nearest target was accurate, but by that time I realized that the jolt from bursts from Carlos' Uzi was throwing off my aim. I hit the down button and we dropped to ground level. A couple of the enemy stood up a little higher to keep us in view, a move that cost them dearly when they came into the line of fire of our snipers on the mounds behind us.

I shouted to Carlos that having the two of us in the bucket at once was not working, and reluctantly he stepped out and ran to join the men behind the barricade. I snapped a full clip into my rifle and went back up. When the bucket reached the higher level there was only one gunner in sight. For a couple of seconds we fired point bank at each other. I had an advantage in that I was using a rifle while crouched behind the steel sides of the bucket, while he, standing up to fire his machine gun, presented a larger target. His first burst was slightly off, and before he could adjust my second shot had found its mark.

By this time a second sniper had joined the exchange, and several bullets ricocheted off the lower part of the bucket. In the split second in which I had to make a decision I realized that he could adjust his next volley a few inches higher before I could draw a bead on him, so I ducked, hit the down button again and plunged to ground level. The sniper made the same mistake his buddy had done seconds before, stood up a little too high to keep me within sight as I dropped. The sound of gunfire and explosions coming from the hill behind us was deafening, but I didn't dare to take my eyes off of the wall in front of us.

Once on the ground I became aware that that some snipers on the wall had turned their attention to our marksmen on the two mounds. So back up I went, cursing this as the stupidest damned way of fighting a battle that I could imagine. This time I had the advantage that the enemy were focused somewhere else and it took them a moment to shift their attention to me. I hit one gunner on a second shot, and then, emboldened, I fired at a more distant figure. By this time several marksmen were shifting their attention towards me and I continued my imitation of a yoyo.

The chances of surviving this game for five more minutes were somewhere between slim and nil. Some of our men on the ground had begun to fire rockets at the top of the wall. I suppose they just needed to do something; and it might make the snipers on the wall a bit nervous and less accurate. Our helicopter maneuvered into position, quite low and off the other end of the compound and fired a rocket that hit something in the middle of the enclosure and there was a terrific explosion. A second rocket struck just behind the wall we were facing. As the helicopter veered away to join the battle on the hill I went aloft again. This time the snipers behind the wall had ceased to coordinate their efforts, and for a minute I was able to take them on one at a time without having to keep ducking. That improved my odds of survival, but it was still not an experience I am anxious to repeat.

There was another explosion from the other end of the enclosure, then machine gun fire in the distance. Winfield had joined the fight. Within a few seconds the east gate opened prematurely and a number of Flores's troops charged through. Presumably they were supposed to make this charge after the snipers had decimated our company; but Flores or someone else behind the wall must have panicked at the number of things that were happening at once and given the fateful order.

The soldiers charging towards us were firing machine guns and several carried grenade launchers. Before they could do any damage they were simply mowed down by our men shooting from behind their sandbag barriers. The line of men rushing out of the gate wavered and stopped and our men began to fire through the gate. After a minute of mayhem someone managed to close the gate, and the last of our rounds splattered harmlessly against it. During this brief and brutal exchange only two figures appeared above the wall, and both ducked back down when I fired at them. The enemy was showing little sign of organized activity; but one of the points they drilled into us in training is that battles ebb and flow. You haven't won just because the first encounter has gone your way.

Someone behind me had commandeered a megaphone and shouted to the people behind the wall that we would cease firing long enough for them to come out and pick up their wounded. They could either bring

- 324 -

them back to their side, or if they lacked facilities they could carry them to our side and we would transport them to our medical station. This time the humanitarian announcement was not ignored. After a half minute two men emerged from the gate, which was now slightly ajar, ran to the fallen soldier closest to us and more or less dragged him over to our side. As our men lifted the wounded man over the sandbags the two who had dragged him there scrambled over the embankment and announced that they were surrendering.

No sooner had the first party arrived than a second pair dashed through the gate, and then a third. There was screaming, a few shots fired from the gate at the men fleeing towards us, and the gate that had stood slightly ajar closed again. There was a pause and then the gate opened again, two men emerged waving a large white sheet, followed by a swarm of others without weapons and with hands held high. Some of them stopped to pick up their injured fellows along the way. Several were carrying wounded men from behind the gate. One pair reached our barricade bearing a dead body. It was the mortal remains of Miguel Flores, mayor of Valdez and aspirant to the presidency of Talcayan. He had been shot in the back. I had never seen the mayor of Valdez and had imagined him as a swarthy, unkempt, scowling ogre. The body in front of me looked more like an artist's conception of a heroic General Wolfe fallen on the Plains of Abraham.

As we were trying to organize the milling crowd of prisoners and our own men into some kind of order, Villalobos led his cavalry back down the hill at a relaxed canter. "They don't need us up there," he announced. "There are too damned many there already."

As we pieced together the story of the battle on the hill afterwards, it became clear why Will McGrath had told President Javier and colleagues that future strategy would depend on what the enemy did. Apparently Volmer had just finished arranging his troops for an attack on Villalobos when the tank, horsemen and accompanying throng appeared at the edge of the field and then turned to approach the hill. Volmer's troops were rushing into new positions to meet this threat when the mortar fire started. Our helicopter, after firing the two rockets at the Flores forces within the compound, directed its remaining firepower at targets on the hill before veering off to rearm. At that moment the mad pelicans and Villalobos' horsemen surprised Volmer's harassed troops from the side, and no sooner had the latter begun to shift to meet the attack from the north than the tank crested the hill from the west followed by what must have looked like a sea of infantry. Most of Volmer's men on the hill either surrendered or turned and ran. Those who stayed and fought were hopelessly outgunned.

Those in flight might have escaped with relatively low casualties if Volmer's troops on the far side of the hill had held their ground and covered the retreat. They had not been blindsided and they could have fought from their pre-established positions and inflicted heavy looses on any of our people who tried to pursue the fleeing men; but many of the people on the far side of the hill, seeing the devastation in front of them, turned and ran. Some escaped. Some were killed or wounded in flight. Most surrendered, including Volmer, who insisted that he was a prisoner of war, subject to the Geneva Conventions, to be released at the cessation of hostilities. The claim provoked some profane laughter in his captors, who apparently failed to appreciate the finer points of international law.

Villalobos was now organizing the able-bodied prisoners into a single line ready to proceed to a space that had been designated as a holding area. I approached him to say that I wished to join the guards accompanying the prisoners and then rejoin Colonel McGrath's company. He nodded, remarked that he was sure that I had conducted myself well during the skirmish, and turned his attention quickly to more pressing issues. He was not taken in by any Hannigan-as-hero mystique.

As we headed towards the holding area a line of prisoners under guard was emerging through the central gate. Apparently more people had surrendered to Captain Winfield than had taken their chances with Villalobos.

When you put the numbers coming out of the parade ground together with the mob of prisoners being marched down the hill, along with the dead, the wounded and those who had fled, it was a good bet that, even after our crowd of friends had arrived, the combatants under the command of Flores and Volmer still outnumbered us.

THE BLOOD-DIMMED TIDE IS LOOSED

In the middle of mopping-up there was a loud whipping sound to the east and a moment later three helicopters whirled into view. They were flying low so we didn't see them until they were almost upon us, like three huge, ungainly dragonflies, the middle one a little lower and in the lead. I was standing next to Will when they appeared, and it was the only time in those two days that I saw him ruffled. He muttered, "Now what the hell is this?" and the two of us watched the three aircraft fly over us, dipping from side to side to catch a better view. They were past us in a matter of seconds. An officer ran up and asked Will whether the men should fire at the helicopters if they made another pass. The colonel made a downward wave of his hand, then said after a moment, "Make sure that the men handling the ground-to-air launchers are in position, but don't fire unless those birds look like they are moving into a position to fire on us. Don't provoke them. I think they're getting used to the idea that they got here just a little too late."

The three copters turned, made a wide circle around us, then rose and returned in the direction from which they came. The tension drained out of Will and he turned to me, rubbing his neck. "What do you think about that?" he muttered. "Flores' friends have gotten their hands on three AH-1 Cobras. They're not exactly the latest thing, but the U.S. army still uses them. They could have ganged up on our helicopter, then taken out our tank and the two IVFs in maybe a minute, blown half of us to bits with their rockets and used the survivors for target practice."

Will mopped his face with his sleeve. "Think about it, those copters may have saved us. I couldn't figure out why Flores and Volmer didn't attack once they had us outnumbered. Now it makes sense. They expected those choppers to shred us before Volmer attacked from the hill. They knew that otherwise with our arsenal we could hurt them badly before they could overrun us. Think about the timing when you say your prayers tonight."

There were a hundred things that had to be done at once. Miraculously, only two of our men had been killed—one of Villalobos' snipers and one of the motley crew that had followed the tank up the hill. Those bodies had been brought back and placed close to the medical station. Unfortunately many more of our men were wounded. Prisoners under guard were going through the area behind the wall and carrying out the dead and the wounded. Many of the men whom Will and his group had been training in recent weeks were doing the same for the hill. Others had been detailed to help the medics deal with the growing numbers at the first aid station. Prisoners were being searched and settled into something looking like order in another area ringed by guards. President Javier had arrived and was at the center of a little group, with messengers running to and fro, especially between that group and the command post that Will had set up and where he was conferring with Captain Winfield and several others and occasionally sending one of us underlings to carry messages or get information.

In the middle of the hubbub a figure approached from the Javier group. As he got closer I recognized Antonio Rossi, the intrepid assistant editor from Valdez whom I hadn't seen since our release from the hellhole of El Alcázar. He was a bit out of breath, and informed us that President Javier once more expressed his profound thanks for our performance, and that the president's priority at the moment was to move swiftly to assure order in all the cities of Talcayan and to assure that order be established by forces loyal to the central government. Of special concern was Valdez. Flores had left his son Emilio as acting mayor of that city. President Javier hoped that by quickly displacing Emilio we might avoid any sustained resistance in Valdez by supporters of the deceased mayor, a resistance that could easily spread to other parts of the country where Flores had made friends.

Antonio had been sent to convey the request that the colonel free up some personnel to travel to Valdez and replace the authorities whom Flores had appointed. This was the most reasonable of requests but one not easily met. Will had a limited number of people to accomplish a large number of tasks. Villalobos, after a perfunctory obeisance to President Javier, had vacated the premises, presumably to return home with his hired hands and resume ranching. The crowd that had arrived that morning consisted mainly of unknown personnel, and their disorganization made them as much of a liability as an asset in the mopping up operations. Then there was the question of how many people would be needed to occupy Valdez, and neither Antonio nor Will would hazard a guess—anywhere from twenty to a hundred, not an especially helpful suggestion.

- 328 -

The Blood-Dimmed Tide Is Loosed

Will looked around. "Where is Dolores Laval? She might know something about those people who followed her here. There must be a few who could help in Valdez. Or maybe get some of them to help with the wounded here and free up a few of our troops to go to Valdez."

While we were waiting for someone to find Dolores I asked Will how the reinforcements had managed to arrive so far ahead of time, and in possession of the Leopard tank.

"Now that's a story," he replied. "Early yesterday this person who claimed his name is Augusto Mayo arrived at the place where most of the new recruits had camped overnight and announced to Diego Sanchez and Dolores Laval that I had sent him to take care of communications. The two of them were happy enough to have one less thing to worry about. So our friend Augusto did his best to misinform us concerning the whereabouts and number of our friends approaching the city. His tactic would have been disastrously effective if we had withdrawn because we thought that all was lost. This Mayo character has not shown his face this morning."

Antonio was holding a warrant issued by President Javier for the arrest of Emilio Flores for the murder of Aldomar San Pedro and another for the arrest of Julio Lara for unlawful detainment of Colonel McGrath. Will turned to me. "Much as I might enjoy serving that warrant, you better attend to it, Mick, if you think you can do it with one hand."

Meanwhile several vans drove up and began to distribute food, first to the wounded who were able to eat, then to the medical corps, then to our troops and the prisoners. The quality was not up to the standard of our previous meals, but some of us, including myself, hadn't eaten since the night before, so we weren't about to complain. They must have cleaned out most of the *abarroterias* and *restaurantes* of San Isidro.

Not long after we had eaten a couple of dozen people approached, led by Antonio and Dolores. The woman looked eminently presentable in a combat uniform in spite of the harrying time she must have had not only in the last several hours but probably in the preceding days. When she and Will had exchanged greetings and congratulations she walked over to me, shook my hand and remarked that from what she had heard I seemed to have retained my aversion to safety.

- 329 -

After we had exchanged just a few words she turned her attention back to Will and explained that she knew that a number of the riders in her group were brave and were also good marksmen but she had no idea how well they might perform in taking control of a city and policing it. She pointed out two women and three men in the group around her. They were from Marino and she knew them and thought they would be helpful in a variety of ways. The rest of the people who had walked over with her were anxious to help with the wounded if they were needed, and that might free up some of our trained personnel to go to Marino.

She explained that she had been interrupted in briefing President Javier and should be getting back. She glanced quickly in my direction and I said, rather more hesitantly than I intended, that I was supposed to go with Rossi and company to Valdez to arrest Emilio Flores. Would she be here when we got back, probably in the evening? Or if she planned to return to Marino, could I drop by and see her there? She replied, "I'll be here." That could have meant "You can count on it" but then again it could have meant "If I must I suppose I must."

CHAPTER THIRTY EIGHT

We set out for Valdez with Rossi driving an almost new Mercedes, compliments of the deceased mayor of Valdez. In what was getting to be a habit, I was in the passenger seat with a rifle next to me. In the back seat were the two women whom Dolores Laval had recommended, apparently the competent types who can be found trying to lessen the chaos in offices around the world. Behind us, in a makeshift personnel carrier, were twenty four soldiers whom Will had been able to release from the mopping up operations. I looked at my watch as we left the last houses of San Isidro behind. It was just past noon. Half a lifetime seemed to have passed since dawn.

Our first objective was to arrest Emilio Flores. If taking control of the city turned out to be beyond the capabilities of our detachment, we would try to occupy city hall and the police station and await reinforcements. I was curious as to why Antonio, who was in charge of the mission, had excluded anyone from Valdez except himself. He explained that he didn't want people settling old scores, and it would be easier for combatants from Valdez to return to peaceful civilian life if they had not been trying to kill each other.

Talk lagged after a half hour and I was left alone with my thoughts. We were on our way to arrest the man who had murdered Aldomar. We

- 331 -

might be able to confirm the identity of at least one suspected murderer of the Tippings. I had left the name of Luis Cerna with the people in charge of the prisoners, with the request that if found he be handed over to authorities to face the charge of murder. The arrest of Emilio Flores and Officer Lara might be dangerous, but after my time on the cherry picker anything that took place on solid ground would look easy. We seemed, finally, to be winding up our business in Talcayan. I was happy to be going home and resuming peaceful existence, relieved at our victory, but uneasy at its human cost and wondering whether anything lasting would come of it. Six months ago I had for the first time killed a man and it had nauseated me. I didn't know how many men I had killed today.

We arrived at Valdez and Antonio parked next to the offices of the newspaper of which he was the assistant editor and ducked into the building. He was back in a minute and explained that his editor, Cezar Gallego, had confirmed that Emilio Flores was still the acting mayor of the city and Officer Lara was the chief of police. Our first stop should be the headquarters of the latter. Put the head of the police out of action and the mayor might lose his power base.

We were scarcely on our way again when Rossi spotted a couple of toughs emerging from a small grocery, one of them carrying something like a policeman's billy club, the other sorting through a wad of money. Rossi braked, double parked, jumped out and talked briefly to the driver of the troop carrier. A few seconds later a dozen troops hit the concrete running. The two thugs caught sight of them and took off. Several of more robust of the pursuers seemed to be straining to take the lead, like hounds fighting to be the first in at the kill. The sight should have inspired the quarry to establish new personal bests in the sixty meter getaway dash, but the miscreants apparently needed more work on this important skill. They were quickly subdued and Rossi spoke briefly to our men. As he resumed his place behind the wheel he explained that gangs had been terrorizing local merchants and this was the kind of thing that would have to be hit hard if law and order were to be restored.

We drove another few blocks and came to a wide section of the street, angle-parked in front of an eating place and the troop carrier

THE BLOOD-DIMMED TIDE IS LOOSED

pulled in beside us. Rossi explained that he and the two women would drive to the police headquarters to find out, as discretely as possible, the location of Chief Lara. The police station was only a few blocks away. The rest of us could find sustenance in the cafeteria.

As we filed in to pick up some food I was happy to see Albert Tamayo among the group. We weren't hungry after the late breakfast on the battlefield, so the captain and I each got a mug of coffee and a roll and settled down at a small table. "That was some exhibition of field generalship," Tamayo exclaimed. "I was with Captain Winfield before that crowd arrived this morning. The colonel had told us that all his mortars were trained on the hill and on the east end of the enclosure. He was about to begin the bombardment, and we were supposed to attack through the west gate if the mortars didn't keep Volmer from attacking Villalobos from the hill. Whether that strategy would have saved us, we'll never know. That crowd appeared on the field and it took the colonel about a minute to decide to go by the book and follow up the bombardment with tank and infantry. The poor buggers didn't know what hit them." He paused for a moment. "But I do fault the colonel for having his nephew ride in luxury while we grunts have to bounce our backsides on the planks of a troop carrier."

We had scarcely finished our coffee when Rossi was back, looked around, spotted us and came over to our table. The officer at the desk at headquarters had told the two women that Chief Lara had been away most of the morning and had called in to say that he was having lunch with the mayor. The officer didn't know where. The two women could wait for the chief, but it was not known when he might be back. Meanwhile, Officer Galvez was in charge. Would they like to confer with him? The two thanked him and explained that they had a couple of errands to run but they would be back later.

Antonio thought he knew where Emilio would be having the noon meal. We decided to try to arrest Flores and Lara first and then move quickly to take over the police station. So four of us, Rossi, Tamayo, another soldier and I set off for the eating place where Antonio expected to find the two. I had questioned whether Rossi, who was needed to direct this whole operation, should really be going on this mission, but he pointed out that, having excluded other residents of Valdez from

- 333 -

our group, he was probably the only one among us who could identify Emilio. So Tamayo and I drained the dregs of our coffee and followed Rossi and our fourth man out to the Mercedes.

The restaurant where the acting mayor was likely to be dining was far enough away that I began to fret about whether we would get there on time, a problem exacerbated by Rossi's preoccupation with the gangs who were shaking down the merchants of Valdez. This time he spotted three men, identifiable by the headbands and cargo pants that were a sort of uniform, entering a small hardware store. Without taking time to reflect he pulled over and instructed us to follow him, explaining that "This will only take a minute."

He, Tamayo and I entered the shop, where the three were talking to a scared proprietor. Antonio informed them that we were officers of the law empowered by the new government of Talcayan, and would the three of them please empty their pockets. A big brute who appeared to be their leader stared at him as a wolf might look at a lamb that had suddenly stepped in front of it and bared its teeth. He asked Antonio why he supposed they would obey him. Antonio replied that he himself did not believe in violence. He paused for a second and then nodded towards Tamayo and me and continued, "We have specialists for that sort of thing."

I was standing next to the big fellow and he threw what was meant to be a surprise punch at my head. I ducked, stomped on his foot as hard as I could manage on short notice, and then punched him in the nose as he doubled over. This last move was not well-considered. Reverting to reflexes learned in my boxing days I led with my right, and the impact of my fist with his face jammed the tips of my doubled-up fingers back against my palm. It was a case of the punishment hurting me more than it hurt him. I stifled a scream however, regained a certain amount of composure and looked up to see what was transpiring with the others in our cozy group. The two other hoodlums had their hands half-way up, Tamayo was pointing his handgun at them and remarked laconically: "Actually I don't believe in violence either. It's just Mick there." He nodded towards me. "He's unhappy unless he gets to punch at least one person every day."

We hastily cuffed the three, left our fourth man to stand guard until help could be summoned from our troops at the cafeteria, and hastened back to our automobile. Before Rossi could start the car Tamayo suggested that arresting Flores and Lara without bloodshed, perhaps involving our own blood, was going to be tricky, and before going any farther we should plot out what our approach would be. He added that Miguel Hannigan was perhaps the best trained of the three to handle this kind of situation. For a moment Antonio seemed to be thrown off stride by what could appear to be a challenge to his authority, but he quickly righted himself and agreed. How did I think we should proceed?

I had him describe the layout of the eating establishment where we expected to find our quarry. It was an almost square room with a counter in the corner next to the entrance. When Flores dined there he usually had a table in the corner farthest from the entrance. At this time of day the noon crowd would be thinning. Rossi had no idea whether, now that Lara was police chief, they might have brought along a bodyguard or two.

I suggested that if we found Flores there, Tamayo and Rossi should take up separate positions from which one or other would have a good view of each person in the room, and I would approach Flores and Lara. Rossi asked whether that procedure was prudent. They were hardened and capable men who did not stop at killing, and especially we must watch out for Lara. Maybe we should go back for more reinforcements. Tamayo said softly, "We are running out of time. I think Señor Hannigan can handle it."

We drove quickly and without further conversation to the restaurant. It was a building standing by itself surrounded by parking space and a lawn. The structure was old-style, orange colored adobe with blue window shutters. There was no one at any of the outdoor tables. We parked and walked along the side of the building that contained the kitchen, if we could judge by the sounds and smells emanating through the windows. We stopped in an anteroom to let our eyes adjust to the dim interior light. Then I heard myself say "Let's go" and we stepped into the dining area.

It took Antonio a few seconds to adjust to the still dimmer light, and then he said to me quietly: "The table in the far corner. That's Emilio facing us. The one in the uniform is Lara. I don't recognize the woman who has her back to us."

Emilio was dressed in a crisp shirt and a business suit, appropriate for an acting mayor. He was dark, good looking in a baby-faced sort of way, not what one expected of a murderer and contrasting with the rugged features of Julio Lara sitting next to him. Here was another answer to Will's prayer, "Lord, make my enemies stupid." If Flores and Lara had any safety concerns they had planned their position badly. The female guest blocked the way if Flores wanted to shoot at me surreptitiously under the table. I was approaching Lara from his right side so any motion he made towards a gun was going to be visible, unless he was left-handed. Of course he just might be left-handed. We have to make our way in an imperfect world.

Emilio caught sight of me as soon as I moved in his direction. He said something to Lara, who turned in my direction and the two eyed me as I approached. I stopped just behind the woman and explained that I had with me a warrant, signed by the president of Talcayan, for the arrest of Emilio Flores for the murder of Aldomar San Pedro and another warrant for the arrest of Julio Lara for illegal detainment with intent to harm Colonel McGrath. Would they please bring their hands into view slowly and place them, palms down, on the table.

Flores looked at me contemptuously as I recited my lines and turned rather sharply towards Lara when I included his name. He turned back to me and sneered that he had merely defended himself against an attempt by Aldomar San Pedro to arrest him illegally on the basis of the spurious authority of the mayor of Amparo. I replied that he would have a chance to challenge the charges in a court of law.

"So you think that you will be more successful than Aldomar in arresting me, because you are hiding behind a woman's skirts? Or are we supposed to be in awe of you because you are the great marksman 'Annigan? How are your fingers, by the way?"

I raised my right hand with its bandaged fingers and moved it back and forth a couple of times. When the two shifted their gaze to my left hand it was holding the Beretta that I had pulled from under my belt.

I explained that Captain Langer had mistakenly supposed that I was right handed. "Now," I said, "I have told you to place your palms down on the table. I don't care much whether you do or not. If you don't I will simply shoot each of you through the head. Are you ready to meet God face to face? The way you've been living, I don't like your chances. And forever is a long, long time. Now you make that choice. Hands on the table or you take that last trip."

Emilio seemed stunned. Lara's jaw muscles bunched up. Slowly hands came into sight and their palms placed flat on the table. We went through the standard routine while I disarmed them and cuffed their hands behind their backs. Their female companion, a middle aged, white haired woman, seemed too shocked even to speak. I told her that she was free to leave, and we would provide transportation for her to return home, but she did not respond.

Our fear that some patrons of the restaurant might come to the aid of Flores and Lara was unfounded. Most of them looked on in a bemused way, except for an elderly couple who seemed to be getting a certain satisfaction from the scene and waved at us in what I took to be a sign of approval as we moved towards the exit. As Captain Tamayo reached the door he touched the peak of his cap with the tip of the barrel of his pistol in a sort of salute, apologized for the interruption and assured the diners that it was unlikely that we would be bothering them again.

As we walked the prisoners to the automobile Flores suddenly turned and cursed at Tamayo, who had touched his shoulder to guide him into the back seat. "You—, he snarled. "You come here and meddle in our affairs. You think you've won because you survived today. Well let me tell you. Miguel Flores has more powerful friends than you have, and he's not going to lose this fight. And when our time comes we'll go after you wherever you are, you—."

So Emilio did not realize that his father was dead. It was not enough to win sympathy for the killer of Aldomar, but maybe then I saw him as a human being, however despicable.

Eventually we got the prisoners into the back seat. The woman seated between them remained silent. From the conversation it became apparent that she was Emilio's mother. Once back at the cafeteria where we had left our detachment I took her aside and with as much tact and sympathy as I could I let her know that her husband had been killed in the fighting that morning in San Isidro. I expected that this, on top of the arrest of her son for murder, might drive her half out of her mind. Instead she just looked even more sad. It may have been the dreadful news that she had been expecting. I asked her whether she had friends that we should call. She just shook her head and asked quietly whether someone could drive her home.

Rossi diverted one of our men to that task while the rest of us piled into the troop carrier. Before we started Antonio asked me whether, in view of the success of the arrest, I would like to direct the takeover of the police station. I replied that my specialty was restaurant and bar room brawls, and that I had very little idea of how one would go about taking over a police station. As someone familiar with the situation he was in a better position than I to take the lead.

Within several minutes we reached the station, a relatively new, one story, brick building that was in better repair than many of its counterparts in North America. The dirt parking lot was ringed with flower beds. We parked in front of the main entrance. Our two prisoners stayed in the carrier, six of our men and the two women remained in the parking lot and the rest of us filed through the front door.

We were the only people in the foyer except for a balding, middle-aged, anxious looking man behind the desk. His name, according to the sign on the desk, was Viator Sandor. He hung up the telephone as we entered. Presumably he had been consulting someone farther back in the building about this small army of invaders he had seen approaching. Eighteen men in uniform carrying side arms can make even a fairly large space seem crowded. Rossi introduced himself politely to Officer Sandor and explained that we had been sent by President Javier to help assure that good order would prevail in the city in the coming days. The president was anxious that lawless elements should not take advantage of the change in government to create problems for local law enforcement agencies. Rossi concluded, "We would like to confer with Officer Galvez, if you please."

"I think that this is something that needs to be handled by Chief Lara," Sandor replied in a manner that suggested that he was following

THE BLOOD-DIMMED TIDE IS LOOSED

a prepared script. "Unfortunately, Chief Lara is out, but he will no doubt be back before long."

"In fact Chief Lara is back already," Rossi said. "He's in that vehicle you see in front of the door. Chief Lara is no longer in charge. That is why we must see Officer Galvez."

This threw Officer Sandor into a still more acute state of confusion. He picked up the telephone, spoke briefly in a whisper, then hung up, got up and explained that he would have to go back and confer with Officer Galvez. Rossi volunteered to accompany him in order to save Officer Galvez the trouble of coming out to the foyer. He motioned to Tamayo, another man and myself and the four of us followed a nervous Officer Sandor down a hallway to a closed door on the right. Sandor knocked timidly and failed to get a response. Rossi stepped up and rapped less timidly, and this brought forth some profanity from within and a shout that he was not to be disturbed. Rossi opened the door and walked in without hesitation. My choice would have been to review my options before entering the lair of a hostile and well-armed man.

I ducked in quickly beside Rossi with Beretta in hand, but the precaution was not needed. Galvez was standing next to a window and turned as we entered. The voice may have been belligerent but it was alarm that registered on the heavy browed face. He demanded to know the meaning of this intrusion. Rossi repeated the explanation he had given Officer Sandor, ending with the statement that the government of President Javier had removed Mayor Emilio Flores and Chief Lara from office, and until new elections could be held senior police officers would continue to receive their pay but would be at least temporarily relieved of duties. They might be reinstated by a newly elected mayor.

"And why should I agree to this illegal takeover?" Galvez snorted.

"It is fully legal," Rossi replied. "The president has the authority to issue warrants for the arrest of persons accused of serious crimes and suspend them from office and to appoint temporary replacements. Furthermore, there are twenty five soldiers of the national army here to enforce this presidential order."

"Twenty five!" Galvez sneered. "I have twice that many on my force.

- 339 -

"And I will have as many men as I need to enforce the president's order," Rossi said. "We have come with a small unit in an effort to resolve this peaceably; but if we have trouble we can have two hundred troops here tomorrow. If you co-operate most of your police officers will be able to carry on. If you make trouble and lead them in resisting the national army, they will all lose their jobs and maybe their lives, and you yourself will be a prisoner, if you are lucky."

"There is no need for you to replace me," Galvez said, a little less fiercely. "I know how to police this city better than some damn outsider."

"Would you say, Officer Galvez, that you have control of the city?"

"Of course I do. Look for yourself."

"In short time we have been here we have arrested two groups that were collecting money by threatening local merchants. Do you support these groups, Officer Galvez? Are they working for you?"

"The police have nothing to do with such people," he exploded.

"Then, my dear fellow," Antonio answered quietly. "It looks like you don't have control of the city. Now, hand over your gun and your identification as an officer of the law and leave the building. Any attempt by you to exercise authority in this city prior to your possible reappointment to the police force will be regarded as a criminal act."

Galvez continued to glare at Rossi for a few seconds, then slowly and carefully withdrew his pistol from its holster with just thumb and forefinger and placed it on the desk. He pulled open a drawer, withdrew a wallet and took out a plastic card, threw it on the desk and slowly walked out of the room.

CHAPTER THIRTY NINE

Captain Tamayo and I left a few minutes later with our two prisoners in the back seat of the Mercedes. Rossi and the man he had brought as his interim police chief were busy. One of the women who had come with us had contacted Officer Cesar Garza and asked him to return to headquarters as soon as convenient to help reorganize the Valdez Police Department. While waiting for Officer Garza she was working with Officer Sandor to establish a roster of all the members on the force and then summon them to drop by the station as soon as they could. The other woman was going through the list of prisoners, consulting with Rossi and Sandor, making telephone calls and setting in motion the mechanism for freeing those whose only crime had been opposition to the Flores regime.

Once back in San Isidro, we stopped off at the scene of the morning's fighting. Plenty of signs of battle remained: the wreckage of much of the wall enclosing the barracks and parade ground, the trenches and sand bags, wrappers and scraps from the meals, and the large tent that had housed our first aid operation. Had we been in a more macabre frame of mind we might have climbed to the top of the hill where most of the dying had taken place. A few workers were cleaning up the debris and several lads scavenged through the parade ground, maybe hoping to collect casings for sale as scrap metal. One of the workers told us that

- 341 -

the bosses had gone a couple of hours ago. President Javier would probably visit his office before retiring for the day, but our interest was in the whereabouts of the military "bosses" and concerning this our informant was vague. We tested the suspension of the Mercedes by bumping over the parade ground to warn the scavengers that there might be unexploded shells, so they would be well advised to let others clean up the mess.

Before leaving for Valdez we had neglected to get directions about where to deliver the prisoners. The receptionist at city hall informed us that General McGrath and the Chief of Police were at the police headquarters less than a mile away. I had passed the place on the bus two nights ago, an aging, two-story, gray stone fortress of a building that had earlier housed government offices. The only provision for parking was a space for five vehicles at the front, and because these were all occupied we parked on a side street and walked our prisoners around to the front door.

The officer at the desk was expecting us. We had no sooner appeared than he spoke a few words on the telephone and a minute later two policemen appeared and escorted the prisoners back into the bowels of the building. Then a well-dressed, graying gentleman with a thin moustache appeared, identified himself as Pablo Lopez and explained that he was a lawyer and was helping to sort out possible charges against the leaders of the conspiracy. He led us back into a rabbit warren of rooms to an office that was his temporary accommodation while he worked with the national administration. Albert filled out a form giving, in such detail as was possible within two pages, a description of the arrest of Flores and Lara, the names of others who had participated in the operation and what either of the prisoners had said at the time. In view of the rich vocabulary displayed by Emilio on the occasion, the captain thought it appropriate to paraphrase.

Having recorded our contact information in case we were needed to give testimony later, the lawyer then explained that Colonel McGrath was expecting us in the conference room that had been placed at his disposal for a couple of days. A minute later we were describing to the colonel what had transpired in Valdez and assuring him that Antonio Rossi was displaying considerable aptitude for organization and a

- 342 -

reasonable sense of what had to be done. At this point Captain Tamayo left to join the other Canadians who were preparing for repatriation, taking with him our sincere thanks and the promise to keep in touch.

When the captain had gone I reminded Colonel McGrath about the need to question Officer Lara concerning the Tipping murders. I could supply background information, but the colonel or someone else more practiced than I in interrogation should do the questioning. I began to brief Will and after a couple of minutes he interrupted me, left the room and returned in a minute with Pablo Lopez. "Now," he said, "Start from the beginning. We need a lawyer if we are going to do this properly." I told them what I had found out on my visits to Valdez in the previous weeks, they discussed strategy for a few minutes and then summoned Officer Lara. Will did not believe in putting things off for another day.

From his manner on entering the room, Lara might have been a prosecuting attorney, not the prisoner. We had hardly settled in our chairs when he noted that he had not been part of any of the civil unrest that had led to the battle this morning. He was a policeman and if there were objections to his police actions they should be investigated by civil, not military authorities. Will replied that President Javier had declared a state of martial law, and Will was the present head of the army, which was acting as the national police force for as long as martial law was in force. Furthermore, Will pointed out, the main purpose of this meeting was to inform Officer Lara of his legal situation. If, having heard the facts, Officer Lara chose not to cooperate further with authorities, that was his prerogative. Will then asked the lawyer to outline Lara's legal situation.

"I will recite the facts in chronological order," Lopez began briskly. "I am not going to take the time to tell you how we discovered these facts. That will be revealed in testimony at your trial. You may challenge the veracity of my recital, but again, that is a matter for your trial, when your lawyer will have at his disposal a variety of legal artifices to cast doubt on testimony. To save time, I ask you to leave all such challenges until you have the services of a lawyer."

Lopez then outlined what we knew about the murder of the Tippings and of Officer Lara's involvement in the investigation, or non-investigation, which followed. Lara made as if to interrupt, but

Lopez held up an admonitory hand and continued, mentioning the false report that Lara had requested Officer Costa to sign. At this point Officer Lara broke in, insisting that none of this so-called evidence would hold up in court.

The lawyer calmly replied that in his opinion the facts as he had presented them would hold up in court, and that any doubt about it would be resolved in due time. He then went on to describe Lara's commendable investigation to discover the identity of the person who was, in all probability, the murderer or at least one of the murderers of the Tippings, and added that Lara had been arrested because of another matter—his forceful detainment of Colonel McGrath with apparently malicious intent.

Lopez continued: "I will now, Officer Lara, give my legal opinion of your situation. You will no doubt get at least one legal opinion from counsel before your trial, but I think it may be helpful to you to get an honest legal opinion at this early point in the investigation. First, you could be charged with obstructing justice by your conduct of the investigation of the Tipping murders. You could plead that you were following orders. There is a chance, but not a very good chance, that a judge or jury will be sympathetic to that plea. You might challenge the veracity of the testimony against you. It will then be simply a matter of whom the judge and/or jury choose to believe.

"Second, you are charged with unlawful arrest with intent to harm Colonel McGrath. Your only defense would be to challenge the veracity of the two prime witnesses, who are seated with you in this room, who, incidentally, reported the event to others shortly after it occurred. Any attempt to cast doubt on their testimony would have to show why these two gentlemen had begun the fabrication over six months ago. With that, I have completed my summary of what I judge to be you legal position. I believe that Colonel McGrath has something of further interest to you."

The colonel took up the recital. "Officer Lara, there may be further charges brought against you on other counts. Such charges would be made after I have completed my brief service as commander of the national army and so would not concern me. Miguel Hannigan and I were sent here originally by the father of Catherine Tipping to find out the circumstances of her murder and the murder of her husband. This remains our principal interest. There is one legal point in your situation on which I wish to elaborate. You as a police officer know the identity of a prime suspect for a murder. Although you are at the moment suspended, you are still a police officer and as such retain the obligation to make known that identity to the responsible authorities. In this case, I am one of the responsible authorities, so the information can be properly given to me and your responsibilities in the case would be fulfilled at that point.

"Michael Hannigan and I, you must recognize, are the two witnesses whose testimony would be essential to any prosecution of you on the charge of unlawful arrest with intent to harm. If you correctly identify the prime suspect for the murders of Catherine and Richard Tipping, we would be happy to return to North America and not take part in any legal proceedings against you on that count.

"I recognize that there may be considerations that would make you unwilling to reveal the identity of the suspect. You may wish to protect Mayor Flores and Captain Langer or the interests which they represent. You should know that Mayor Flores was killed in the battle this morning. Captain Langer was injured while attempting to escape from El Alcázar and is now recuperating in hospital. He faces very serious charges for his recent conduct. Perhaps you are a friend of the principal suspect and wish to protect him. You must balance all this against the fact that you face incarceration for an indefinite period until you fulfill your legal duty to make known the identity of this prime suspect."

Officer Lara had maintained a cool, dismissive manner until that point, but at the mention of him protecting the suspect he clenched his teeth momentarily and then burst out, "Why would I protect him? I hope you fry the little bastard."

Will remained unruffled. "Just the name, Officer Lara."

That officer, probably aware that he had already as much as confirmed the lawyer's account of the situation, uttered two words in a more subdued voice: "Luis Cerna."

"Thank you, Officer Lara. And where might we find this Luis Cerna?"

"I have no idea of where he is. I can tell you this, if the little ＿＿ knew there was a battle coming, he'll be as far away from it as he can get."

"Thank you, Officer Lara." And the session ended.

When Lara was escorted away and the lawyer had left, Will looked at me rather sharply and remarked that he understood that I had arranged a certain assignation to take place on my return to San Isidro. I replied that I had indeed arranged to meet someone, but the term "assignation" made it sound like I was messing around with someone's wife. Will responded that, happily, the woman in question was, to his knowledge, not married.

He continued. "This young lady betrayed some agitation when informed that your assignment was to arrest the redoubtable Julio Lara on his home turf. She has taken some pains to make herself presentable after her travels and the day's battle. You yourself might want to freshen up. There's your kit over in the corner, and there are facilities down the hall to your left."

Showered and shaven, I ventured to the foyer of the building where "the woman in question" was reported to be waiting. She was wearing a simple, expensive-looking, red dress with a wide belt that showed off a waist that seemed even slimmer after her El Alcázar misadventure. She grinned at my ill-concealed admiration, and striking a modeling pose that amused a couple of by-standers, remarked in English, "You probably did not know that I owned a dress, did you?"

I was speechless for a few seconds and then conceded that the dress did remarkable things for her, or perhaps it was she who did remarkable things for the dress.

"You realize, Miguel, with that kind of flattery you are encouraging my worst vice, or one of my worst vices, which is snobbery about clothes." She paused. "This is my favorite time of day—the sun at that angle makes things look better. We can stroll over to the park down the street."

She asked me about how things had gone in Valdez, and when that subject was quickly exhausted she said she hoped that maybe now I could take a holiday from risking my life; or was I addicted to it?

- 346 -

THE BLOOD-DIMMED TIDE IS LOOSED

"Actually," I replied, "when I'm home the most dangerous thing I do is eat my own cooking on days my mother is away. But you. You look wonderful. Does this mean you are getting over that horrible experience? . . . making some progress anyway?"

Dolores paused a few seconds. "The first several days at home . . . I acted like a sick patient. Not that I stayed in bed . . . but I did almost nothing except to help Mama a little with housework. I guess I thought that time would heal me. Then one day I think Mama got tired of me just moping around. She said that in her opinion what happened to many rape victims was that they make things worse by allowing the rapist to dominate them for a long time after the attack. If you are preoccupied by revenge or feeling sorry for yourself you let that person continue to control your life. So I must try to direct my thoughts and my actions in the direction that I choose. I obeyed her advice. It has helped.

"I think even my going out to recruit men to help Colonel McGrath was part of the cure. I told people that they must take responsibility for their country; and I was really starting to take responsibility for myself. I am not over it. It is hard to foresee a time when I will be completely over it. But I am better."

"I'll be leaving in a day or so," I said, "and first I have to talk to you."

"Yes, I am glad of that."

I stumbled on. "I . . . um . . . if we lived closer together I could start pestering you for dates . . . and maybe you could get to know me better . . . we really haven't spent much time together . . . and . . . I'm sorry I'm making such a hash of this . . ."

She turned to me and grinned. "Miguel, do you realize how flattering this is? Here you are, this guy who goes out and arrests the scariest man in Talcayan as though it was like buying groceries, and now you sound like a schoolboy who has not done his homework. Hmm. Let me interpret your meaning. You, the party of the first part, after a limited acquaintance, find me, the party of the second part, sufficiently interesting to merit further attention. The party of the first part now wishes to know whether the party of the second part is interested in continuing the relationship. Does that more or less sum up the matter?"

- 347 -

"Precisely," I said. "But you lawyers are so sentimental."

"So I must decide," she continued. "On the one hand, I can look forward to a lonely old age, embittered by the thought of what might have been. On the other hand, maybe get to know this guy who is kind of good looking . . . and he . . . ."

Her voice broke and she reached out and hugged me. After a minute she let go and began to dab ineffectually at my shoulder with a tiny handkerchief. Then she looked up as she wiped her eyes. "I guess a simple yes would have been sufficient?"

"Sufficient, yes," I replied, "but I like your way of putting it."

"But Miguel, I was so worried. I thought that you probably liked me . . . but knowing what you know about me, maybe you would think that your life would be much simpler if you forgot about me."

"Don't worry about that," I said. "I've discovered a couple of positive things about you, you know. First of all, when you're dressed up you really do improve the scenery."

"You said a couple of things. What is the other?"

"I also have to admit that you are very good at coming to the help of your friends. You'd be surprised at how hard it is to find a woman who will show up when needed with a Leopard tank and a small army."

"I will be sure to keep that tank close by just in case. Or perhaps we should try to change your habit of needing to be rescued?"

"Oh, and there's one other thing," I said. "You kind of like me, and I have always admired that quality in a beautiful woman. . . . But to be serious for a moment, there is one thing you need to know. It's that I have come to the conclusion . . . that I couldn't live in Talcayan. I'm sorry . . ."

"Because of your mother?"

"Well, the possibility of leaving my mother half a world away is a big factor. But there's something else. Two nights ago on the way to San Isidro I fell back into a depression that I hadn't felt since leaving the army. And I'm sure it was the fighting. Since coming here I've been swept from one thing to another. And if I stay, I'm afraid that it will continue. But worse than that, this afternoon . . . when we were arresting Flores and Lara, I wanted Flores to draw his gun so I could shoot him. I wanted to kill him. I hated him that much. I mocked him about being sent to

THE BLOOD-DIMMED TIDE IS LOOSED

hell, about not being ready to meet his Maker . . . and how ready was I
to meet my Maker if one of them had managed to put a bullet through
me?"

"But Miguel . . . he had killed your friend Aldomar; and Julio Lara
was probably going to kill your uncle before you stopped him. You
cannot be expected to like them."

"Well . . . the Lord didn't say to hate only those who offend you.
If you want to kill someone that seems to qualify as hatred. Dolores,
I'm afraid that if I stay here I'll just keep getting dragged into the
violence."

She said quietly, "And you think I would not leave this country with
you, Miguel."

"I thought maybe you would. But after this morning . . . You're not
just Dolores Laval any more. You're a national heroine. Can you leave
all that? Should you?"

She motioned to a bench and we sat.

"Let me tell you about this national heroine. Over a week ago I left
Marino and went many places. I was angry. You and Colonel McGrath
were risking your lives for us and we were doing so little. Miguel, for a
week I was like a mad woman. I found out things about myself I never
knew. I talked in public squares and in restaurants and wherever there
were people. I shouted, I scolded, I was more eloquent than I ever
thought I could be. At first people listened but almost no one made a
move to help. Then four or five days ago a few started to meet with me
after I talked. Two days ago, when news spread that there was a . . . a
crisis, a showdown you say . . . it was coming in San Isidro, they began
to come not one at a time but in groups. I was no longer recruiting
for a training camp. I was leading a crusade to come to the aid of our
defenders in San Isidro.

"For the last few days I have been . . . intoxicated. Then this
morning we gathered outside of the bus station. They put on extra
buses and trucks from Magdalena and Marino and Amparo to bring the
people here. I looked around to see who would lead this crowd that I
had gathered. There was no one else. There was only I. So I stood on the
back of that jeep with old Diego Sanchez. He and his wife are friends of
my parents; and we rode through the streets. When we came onto the

- 349 -

field I awoke from my week of madness. I said to myself, 'Dolores, you foolish woman, you are trying to prove that you can be as brave as that man, and you will probably get yourself killed.' I thought, it is Miguel's business to be brave. It is not my business. I promised myself that if I survived I would never, ever, let myself get into a situation like that again. I was afraid that I would die and there would be all those things we had never said to each other. I did not even know whether there was anything you had to say to me."

Dolores' voice had begun to break, she leaned against me and we sat in silence for several minutes. Then she took her arm off of my shoulder, sniffled a little and remarked that usually she wasn't such a crybaby. After a few second she asked: "Miguel, when did you start caring for me—I mean caring about me seriously?"

I had to think about it. "Well, one question is—when did I admit to myself that I was thinking about you seriously. That was in El Alcázar. I realized that there was nothing more important to me than getting you out of there, and the awful thing was that there was nothing I could do."

"El Alcázar." She shuddered. "I was sure that nobody who saw me there could ever love me."

I continued. "But I must have been seriously interested in you long before that. Remember when we drove to Mendoza, when we arrived and you got out of the car and left with that confident walk of yours? I felt, what right have you, Dolores Laval, to walk away from me without even turning back to wave? I thought it was just my male vanity, but since then I know it was more than that. I didn't like that you could leave without at least turning back and waving. Kind of stupid, eh?"

Dolores squeezed my shoulder. "Miguel, do you know what I was thinking when I was walking away from you? I would have liked to turn back and wave and let you know I was not walking out of your life, but I was also thinking, 'Dolores, you goose, you have met a soldier who is tough as rawhide but he is nice to you and the second time you see him you tell him all your deepest secrets that you have not even told your father.' I was sure that you must think that I was desperate and I was clinging to you. If I turned back and waved, you would think that for sure.

"After a few days I thought, he is just a soldier. We have had only one conversation. So I was half-reconciled to not seeing you again; but at the same time I liked that you might return to Talcayan. Then I became a prisoner. You know that a prisoner only wants to get out. Maybe men think about how to break out. I am afraid that this woman mostly thought about being rescued. And when I thought of that I always had the image of you coming to rescue me. But I said to myself, I am acting like a fourteen-year-old girl, dreaming about a hero riding to her rescue.

"Then you actually came. But of course you had been trying to rescue everyone, but you had come, and that was the important thing. But I hated you seeing me like that. Then I saw that in spite of your injuries you still went around helping people, while I had withdrawn into a shell. When I got out I thought of you all the time; but I was cautious. You had never said how you felt about me. Why would you? We hardly knew each other. And I thought maybe my obsession with you was the thought that if I married you no one would ever dare to do that to me again. Maybe that is still part of my obsession—a little part."

We got up and walked and wandered through various subjects. It struck me that then was a good time to get all the sensitive subjects out on the table, so I asked her what, if we married and had children, she would think about the raising the children in the Catholic faith.

"Of course they should be raised Catholic," she said. "Even if I married a pagan I could not ignore Catholicism. You know, I am really Catholic most of the time, even though I have enough hesitations that I do not receive communion. But I go to Mass every Sunday with Mama and Papa. All day long, at my work, with my family, I am a Catholic. It is only when I'm alone, lying in bed trying to get to sleep I get wondering about things, and then I wonder whether I am a Catholic."

She paused for a second. "Maybe the problem is that I am sleeping too much by myself?" She turned away, put her hand on her hip, looked back over her shoulder and winked. Almost immediately an alarmed look crossed her face and she blurted out: "Miguel, I hope you do not think I meant . . . whatever, . . . I should be more careful about what I joke about."

I started to giggle, and after a few seconds Dolores joined in. A man and woman passing on the other side of the street looked over to see what the fuss was about, so we sobered up for a moment. The attempt to stifle our laughter set us off again. I laughed at Dolores, and I laughed because I didn't hate Emilio Flores and Luis Cerna any more. I laughed because the sun had gone down on that terrible day and because it would rise again tomorrow.

CHAPTER FORTY

Several months later Uncle Hugh wandered into my office, settled into a chair and asked me whether I thought that I could visit Talcayan sometime soon and manage, just this once, to come back on time and without serious injury. I replied that if he insisted I would give it a shot. He had probably guessed that I was getting ready to ask him to give me a week or two off to make the journey on my own.

"I've been talking to Dieter," he continued. "He tells me that before the bandits grabbed him and his crew he had done most of what he intended to do. Now he thinks they should finish the job. I've been in touch with Perth Industries and they'd be happy about any further exploration. Things seem to have settled down in Talcayan. Have you heard anything different?"

I replied that from what I had heard President Javier was firmly in control with broad support, the national army under the tutelage of Captain Winfield was gradually becoming an effective force and there was no sign of outside interference in national affairs. Some interim funding for the government had become available because Toby Hannigan and his crew had helped locate a stash of illegal drug money which the authorities had then confiscated. Because Talcayan had suffered a good deal from those who had amassed the funds, the authorities had seen

- 353 -

fit to direct several hundred million of the ill-gotten dollars to President Javier's government. The only negative news had nothing to do with the business climate. No one had been able to find Luis Cerna. He had apparently fled the country.

Hugh continued. "I've pretty much decided to send a crew back there. If you're caught up on your work here, I'd like you to go with them. It's only a few days you'd be away, and you're the only person we have who knows his way around the country. You can handle Spanish and you know the main people we need to contact. So what do you think?"

I agreed to start preparing right away. Hugh told me to work it out with Dieter and report in a day or two. As he was going out the door he turned. "Your mother assures me that it'll be cheaper sending you down there than to keep paying the long-distance telephone bills."

So it was that a couple of weeks later Dieter Helfrich, myself and five other employees of Hannigan Industries were in the airport terminal in Mendoza waiting for our baggage. I was standing a little apart from the others when an elegantly dressed woman approached purposefully, threw her arms around me and greeted me with a certain enthusiasm. When I had been released and caught my breath I inquired whether I should conclude from the greeting that she was happy to see me.

"I guess I was a tiny bit exuberant," she confessed. "But Miguel, I hate that you have been thousands of kilometers away for three months now."

I replied that I had been bothered by similar concerns, but I thought that if we put our heads together we should be able to work out some solution. In some more appropriate setting . . . maybe a candle-light dinner.

"With champagne!" she said. "Ooo . . . promise you will ply me with champagne!"

We walked over and I introduced Dolores to the rest of our crew as the agent who had made arrangements for us. The expected verbal equivalent of an elbow in the ribs came from an unexpected source. Dieter shook Dolores' hand, bowed in his usual courtly way and remarked that Mr. Hannigan was to be congratulated on his taste in business associates. Outside of the terminal there was a seven passenger van and a truck to convey the two large boxes of tools and instruments we had brought with us. We took the shorter route to Talcayan, entering at San Isidro where we picked up whatever supplies we could get locally and proceeded south to Amparo where we stopped overnight. Our arrival, Mayor Robles declared, was the culmination of his efforts as mayor, and now he looked forward to retiring from office to return to his neglected retail business.

Within a couple of days, when the grunt work at the assay site was finished, I journeyed to Marino to fulfill the promise of a candlelight dinner and to give the Lavals a chance to check out a prospective son-in-law. Mama Laval was closer in appearance to Leticia Barca than to the motherly type I had expected, and she had an intense, no-nonsense manner. It was just as well that Dolores had filled her head with exaggerated assessments of my worth. She welcomed me but was a bit reserved at first. The next day she took me aside for a heart-to-heart talk.

She began rather formally. "Miguel, I hope that you will always feel welcome in our home even if we are different from what you are used to. This first visit may be hard for you because you must feel that my husband and I have been judging you. For myself, I believe what Dolores says, that you are a good man. I can see that Dolores is very happy and that makes me happy. Most important, I think that you, Miguel, are one of the few people who realize how good a person Dolores is, and that is why I think you will be a good husband for her."

Rodrigo Laval rendered his official verdict a day later. I had voiced my intention to rejoin my co-workers and the mayor insisted that the local bus would be uncomfortable but he himself needed to drive as far as Amparo in any case and we could travel together. After we had nicely settled into the trip he eased into the conversation that was, I suspected, the real motive for his offer of transportation.

"When Dolores told us that she intended to marry you," he began, "I was not surprised. She has spoken about you often, especially after she got out of El Alcázar. I confess to you that at first I had two concerns. First, I worried that what attracted her to you was that after her ordeal she wanted a man who could protect her, and your reputation recommended you for that role. To be protected by a man is a legitimate desire for a woman, but it is not a sufficient basis for a marriage, especially for a woman like Dolores who does not like to depend on others. My other concern was your reputation. Understand me—it is a good reputation; but in this country you are a hero, a formidable fighter with reckless courage. I believe that the reputation is merited. But does that make you a desirable husband for my daughter?

"However, I have talked with Dolores about this. She tells me that you joke that when you are home in Canada the most dangerous thing you do is to eat your own cooking. So I believe that you are not engaged in dangerous work. There are people who are courageous and who do not have to prove it by looking for danger, and I believe that you are such a person. I still believe that one of the reasons Dolores is attracted to you is because you are strong. But it is not just because you are a formidable soldier. You are a strong person; and Dolores needs a strong husband, because although she has overcome much in her life and has emerged from it healthy and independent, I think there are still times when she will turn to you because she cannot carry all of her burdens by herself. And you are someone she can count on, more than anyone else she has met. That is not a bad basis, at least a partial basis, for a marriage."

It does bring you back to earth with a jolt when your intention is to impress people and then you discover that the real problem is how you are going to live up to their exaggerated opinion of you.

Some time later, with winter approaching and the trees already bare, Dolores came through customs and into the reception area of Edmonton International Airport wearing a stylish gray wool coal over a dark blue dress. She grinned and waved as she got sight of me and then hesitated slightly when she saw the woman of regal bearing standing next to me. She was given little time to hesitate however. My mother could hardly wait for the introductions to end and impulsively hugged Dolores as though she were a long lost daughter. I don't know whether Mom had been thinking of what she would say to her future daughter-in-law, but what she did was to step back, look at Dolores and blurt out with unaccustomed spontaneity, "Michael was not exaggerating. You are . . . beautiful."

During her visit Dolores stayed with Uncle Hugh and Aunt Phyllis and was subjected to a round of social events that constituted a crash course on Hannigan relatives, friends and family customs. She and Mom would set off in the morning, ostensibly to tour the city, and return, walking companionably up the front walk, with arms full of bags and parcels indicating that they had thoroughly toured Marks & Spenser. Some days when I got back from work I would hear their muffled voices in the kitchen, punctuated by bursts of laughter. Dolores insisted that she was receiving extensive instruction on the care and maintenance of male Hannigans, though a single sentence to the effect that "He'll eat almost anything but liver and Brussels sprouts, and keep him away from French fries" would more or less cover that subject.

One day Aunt Phyllis called me before I left for work. "Mick, dear Dolores finally has an evening free, so I thought she might have a nice quiet dinner with us this evening. Can you come?"

Some hostesses bring in a cook for special occasions. Aunt Phyllis, on the other hand, gives the cook the evening off and presides over the kitchen herself when she wants the dinner to be special; so it was a good sign when I arrived and found her at work there. Ellen and Cyril, the other guests, had already arrived. Uncle Hugh was in good form, energized by the fact that there was now a new prime minister and cabinet to be scrutinized with jaundiced eye. It mattered little that the party now in power was the one to which Hugh contributed regularly and which was forever trying to recruit him to run for parliament. At election time Hugh was as partisan as any party hack, but between elections he distributed acerbic criticism with generous impartiality. Someone whose name I have forgotten said about a notable curmudgeon that he chastised his enemies conscientiously while neglecting not the daily admonition of his friends. The quote pretty much sums up Uncle Hugh's approach to political commentary.

For the previous couple of days something seemed to have been bothering Dolores, so after dinner on our way to the Citadel Theatre I asked her about it. She fidgeted quite uncharacteristically and hesitated, obviously not comfortable with the question.

"Miguel," she began, "I have been uncertain whether to talk to you about this or not. You may think that it is silly. And remember—I do not for a moment doubt that you love me and you would never ever do anything underhanded. But since you ask, I think it is better for us to talk about it than for me just to worry."

The ominous introduction set me wondering what egregious mistake I had made this time. Dolores hummed and hawed some more before continuing.

"It . . . I know it sounds silly . . . it is your cousin Ellen." Then her words tumbled out as though she needed to forestall any misunderstanding that her introduction might have provoked. "I know you and Ellen are close. You enjoy each other's company. You . . . you sparkle when you are together. Tell me if I am being silly . . . but here you are, two attractive people and you are only now approaching marriage. Sometimes I wonder whether, maybe unconsciously, you compare women to Ellen and find them lacking? It would be easy to do. And Ellen may be comparing men to you.

"I know that you love me and that makes me very happy. But . . . if in spite of that, you really do compare women to Ellen, I cannot compete. She is more beautiful than I am. She is more intelligent, wittier . . . more charming. And maybe I am getting paranoid, but when Ellen and I are in a room I see people looking at one of us and then at the other and I imagine they are comparing us, as though they think I am taking her place."

This is not the kind of question that men like to hear, and so I did what any reasonable man would do. I obfuscated. I remarked that people could hardly avoid comparing the two most beautiful women in a room. Dolores was silent and if there was any change in her expression it was that she looked disappointed, so I hurried on.

"I'm sorry, Dolores. That was an attempt at a joke and it came out sounding like I was making light of your question. It's true though. When you and Ellen are together, it's going to occur to men to compare two beautiful women, and a lot of women will try to decide which one of you has the better taste in clothes. But would you like to know the first thing Ellen said to me about you?"

Dolores made a wry face. "Am I going to like this?"

"You should," I said. "Remember the night after you arrived? We were at Uncle Hugh's just like tonight and it was the first time Ellen met you. As I was leaving she walked by and raised her eyebrows and whispered 'Spectacular!'"

"Really? Are you sure she was saying it about me?"

"Of course she was saying it about you. I wouldn't risk giving you a swelled head by telling you this if it wasn't true. But back to your question. I want to answer it as truthfully as possible and that takes a little thinking.

"It's true that Ellen and I are close. We enjoy each other's company. When I talk to her I try to keep up with her repartee. I play the solid, big brother and she falls back into the role of impish little sister. If we hadn't been cousins, I suppose it's possible that we might have fallen in love. But . . . what Ellen brings out in me are things I already know about myself. But the second time you and I met—that drive to Mendoza—when you told me about yourself, that brought out something new in me."

"You mean you felt sorry for me?" Dolores asked. "That surely would not be new . . . or anything."

"No, no. Why would I have felt sorry for someone like you? I don't know how to say it . . . Here you were, a strong, mature woman, and you let me into your life, you laid your thoughts and your secrets out there for me to see. I was scared. Nobody had trusted me with themselves that way, and I didn't know how I should handle it. But to have you trust me like that—me, just an ex soldier, not much education, kind of a roughneck. I was able to see you, I don't know, see into your mind maybe.

"It began on that drive to Mendoza, but that was just the start. Maybe you have had the experience—I do sometimes—when something strikes you and lifts you out of ordinary, everyday life. Maybe it's a piece of music or something that looks really beautiful. I've even had that experience in an airplane looking down on the clouds. But it only lasts a short while. I go back and try to recapture it, and it's not there any more. But you . . . when I come back to you, you are still there and you always lift me above everyday life.

"You've seen Ellen. She's found someone who does something like that for her. Before she met Cyril it was hard to imagine her as a mother. But see her now with those two girls who are going to be her step-daughters in a couple of weeks. They adore her. It's just one of the things that Cyril has inspired in her."

Dolores shifted around so her back was against the side door, in flagrant violation of Alberta's seat belt laws, and looked at me speculatively for a few seconds. "You know, Miguel Hannigan, with a little effort I could get to like you."

I replied that I was hoping for some modest development in that direction. She kept looking at me for a few seconds and continued. "And do not look so smug. You know that when you get out from behind that steering wheel you will be in danger of being attacked by a love-starved female."

EPILOGUE

We are now well into our seventh year of married life. During Marriage Preparation one of the speakers remarked that many young people think success in marriage is all about marrying the right person, as though it were a sort of lottery. The speaker said in some cases this could be true in a negative sense. Once in a while you run into a union that seems doomed from the start. For the most part however, the speaker maintained, it's not a matter of being lucky and marrying the right person. If you know each other well and are in love, then if you are willing to work at the relationship you will have a good marriage. If you will not work hard at it, the marriage will fail. Luck has little to do with it.

Dolores and I have taken to heart the message about hard work. It's just that she makes it look easy, while I come along blundering through a dozen false starts before finally getting it close to right.

Many have commented on the powerful experience of becoming a parent. I wonder at the strange arrangement by which ordinary people are entrusted with the task of bringing human beings into this world; and I am in awe of the woman who enters into this role as though it were the most natural thing in the world, which I suppose it is.

Dolores escapes the Edmonton winter for a month or so each year, fleeing to Talcayan, accompanied now by children who practice their

Spanish and are spoiled by their grandparents. I accompany them for part of the visit and at the same time keep an eye on the safety of the flourishing mines that the Hannigan and Perth companies manage jointly in that country. Back home we have fallen into a typical Hannigan pattern according to which the males attempt, with occasional success, to don old clothes and escape to the wilds, or at least to the back yard, while the women of the clan conspire to get them to fulfill "social obligations" invented by the women. When asked occasionally whether she has a hankering to go back to the practice of law Dolores replies that she may do so when she gets tired of little people.

Every marriage has its difficulties, but Dolores has learned to cope with my occasional moodiness, and I have learned that, whereas noticing and commenting on mistakes is a virtue in a Director of Security, it is not a virtue in a husband and father. Perhaps our most severe trial was when our first child was born with spina bifida, a defect in fetal development of the spinal cord. In some countries these children are left to die. Little Daniel went through a series of operations beginning soon after birth and is now, thank God, a healthy five-and-a-half-year-old whose only abnormality, as far as we can see, is that he considers it a great treat when he is allowed to accompany his father and his great uncle Hugh to greet the autumn sunrise from the vantage point of a cold, wet duck-blind in northern Alberta.

Daniel is a serious lad. One day last winter when I was lacing up his skates getting ready for a few turns around the pond in Hawrelak Park he remarked, "You and Mama must like us kids, eh?" I said that of course we liked them, but wondered why he had brought up the subject just then. He replied, "Because you play with us." I explained that this was just something that parents do; but when they have good kids, like his Mama and I have, spending time with them is easy. More recently on the road to Elk Island Park when we had finished a rendition of *Danny Boy* our own Daniel asked how come we sing when we drive.

"Why, don't you like singing?" his mother asked.

"I like it. But Charlie's Mom and Dad don't sing when I ride with them. And Aunt Ellen and Uncle Cyril don't sing either."

"I'll let you in on a secret, Daniel," Dolores answered. "When you're older and you want some girl to like you, just take her for a drive in your car and get her to sing along with you. She'll fall for you, every time." In the rear view mirror I could see Daniel's skeptical expression as he looked from one to another of us, suspecting that his mother was pulling his leg. "A secret, eh?" he finally replied. "You guys sure have a lot of secrets."

Dolores leaned back and ruffled his hair. "You better believe it, Kiddo. We've got enough secrets to make your head spin."

Daniel ducked away from his mother's hand and grinned. Maybe the grin was because of contentment at his mother's gesture, but I suspect it was because once again he had held his own in the conversation.

Our second child, raven-haired, dark eyed Alicia, will probably go through several identities on her way to womanhood, but right now it's easiest to think of her as the mud girl. Drop that child in the middle of the Sahara a hundred miles from the nearest oasis and she'll come back from her initial exploration of the site with mud up to her knees. When this phenomenon began to appear some months ago and her mother asked her why she splashed around in mud puddles, Alicia denied the allegation. Putting my keen investigative powers to work, I observed that the mud was always in the front of her trousers and concentrated at the knees. Further observation confirmed that our daughter is curious about tiny animals. With a wisdom shared by only a few adults she has learned that nature is best observed when undisturbed. She can outstare any toad she has ever met and is fascinated by ants and wooly bear caterpillars going about their daily chores. A lot of tiny animals are to be found in marshy areas and at the edges of puddles and pools, and because they have to be observed at close range it is necessary to get down on one's knees. Hence mud.

This has led to a controversy in our family regarding proper attire, eldest daughter apparently believing that a pair of play trousers with mud up to the knees is just comfortably broken in, mother convinced that to send said daughter out to play thus clothed is to invite neighborly disapproval of the mother and pity for the child. This particular mother however does not want to be cited in a future autobiography of a renowned lepidopterist as having suppressed her daughter's scientific bent, so she has acquiesced in a *modus vivendi*. Alicia has become precociously capable of changing into and out of play clothes without maternal help and has taken to hiding the offending trousers in the back of a closet, where they remain deliberately undetected until they are miraculously produced on Monday morning to placate a parent in resolute pursuit of objects launderable.

Our third child is Kaitlin. It is serendipitous I suppose that the child with the Celtic name is the only one to show any sign of Celtic coloring. They say that a child learns an immense amount in the first months of life, and pretty Kaitlin has learned in her first fifteen months that she can get away with a lot if she laughs. Spilt milk? Just chuckle. Tumbler falls off the table and breaks? Open your eyes real wide and then start laughing. Dolores has remarked that if we don't nip this in the bud we may be enablers in the development of a consummate con artist, but I figure we don't have to worry. In due time fair Kaitlin will graduate to the rigors of Grandma Hannigan's school of culinary arts, where careless cookie dough squishers are cut no slack and even the cutest giggle will merit nothing more than a slightly raised grandmotherly eyebrow.

From time to time immersion in my domestic good fortune fails to keep at bay those memories of Talcayan that I would sooner leave behind. It's not the gory events that haunt me most. It's two contradictory images. One is of Aldomar the last time I saw him, walking away to resume the task of keeping Amparo safe, and my vague feeling of letting him down. The second is the memory of the bus ride through the night to San Isidro and the feeling that I was being carried along by a current into violence beyond my control.

Fasten only on the first memory and I feel an obligation to protect the innocent by force if necessary. Dwell only on the second memory and I hear the accusation that if you resort to violence you are the problem, not the solution. But I can't escape from either of those memories. Quite a few years ago we were discussing this problem at one of the informal seminars conducted by my army buddy, Diz. One of the guys quoted from Shakespeare's *Hamlet*: "Whether 'tis nobler in the mind to suffer the slings and arrows of outrageous fortune, or to take up arms against a sea of troubles, and by opposing end them?"

THE BLOOD-DIMMED TIDE IS LOOSED

Diz was not impressed. Hamlet, he insisted, was naïve if he thought that by taking up arms against a sea of troubles you would end them. You might end or ameliorate some of them, but you'd be sure to produce more troubles, probably troubles just as bad or worse. In any case, our problem as soldiers was rather different from Hamlet's. He didn't have the guts to do his duty and kill the usurper of the Danish throne. After all, he couldn't appeal to the Supreme Court or to the United Nations for justice. We soldiers, on the other hand, are more likely to take up arms as a matter of course.

Several years ago Canadian Brigadier General Romeo Dallaire returned from the horrors of the civil strife in Rwanda a broken man. The ferocity of the murderous vendettas and the unwillingness of world powers to listen to the general's pleas for help convinced him that in Rwanda he had looked into the very face of evil. Compared to the carnage in Rwanda, our trouble in Talcayan would not merit the attention of the Prince of Darkness himself, but was perhaps in the care of some second-level demon, perhaps one who had messed up by letting something good happen on his last assignment. But if evil has a face, I suspect that it is smirking most of the time because he, or she, or it, has been operating for a very long time and we humans have still not figured it out.

We bring children into a world where there is massive evil beyond our control. I have heard people say that they cannot bear to do so. Their position is understandable if you look only at the evil, just as hatred is understandable if you look only at the evil of your enemy. Hatred devours the strong and drives them to destroy life; despair can crush the weak and keep them from allowing new life to enter this world. Hatred and despair combine to destroy peoples and nations. Could such evil grow and grow until there is no sheltered island left?

People in North America usually don't think about such a possibility. They seem to think that the ethical world will follow some sort of balance like that which we find in the physical world. There are temperature highs and lows, dry spells and wet spells, but all within limits. Individuals and even limited populations may suffer from the extremes, but most of us (until recent concerns about global warming at least) don't expect to be severely inconvenienced. Conditions will

- 365 -

go on more or less as they have. So, it seems, most people seem to think that you get good people and bad people, good regimes and bad regimes, but within limits. Some individuals and even whole countries will suffer greatly from evil people, but the threat passes and we return to normal.

But is this sort of balance, now challenged by some in the physical world, in any way guaranteed in the world of human behavior and character? Could it not happen that evil might grow and spread so far that our whole human world, not just parts of it, would become a nightmare? Might we not reach a point at which there would be no hope for a rebound that would bring us back to normality? That is what some people in Europe thought was happening in the 1930s with the rise of totalitarianism; and today we have a worldwide slaughter of innocents that governments dare not ban.

If the near-complete fading of the light should come to pass it already has a name. It has been called the coming of the Antichrist. But if there is such an event it will not be the final coming. I believe that truth as it is proclaimed in the measured prose in which an age-old Church frames even its most urgent truths. I have seen it in the fierce love with which his mother watched over our deformed infant son.

CPSIA information can be obtained at www.ICGtesting.com
Printed in the USA
LVOW080800110512

281247LV00001B/10/P